THOSE
LANCASTERS

OTHER BOOKS BY ANNE CAMERON

Fiction
Aftermath
Selkie
The Whole Fam Damily
A Whole Brass Band
Escape to Beulah
Deejay & Betty
Kick the Can
Bright's Crossing
Women, Kids & Huckleberry Wine
South of an Unnamed Creek
Stubby Amberchuk and the Holy Grail

Traditional Tales
Tales of the Cairds
Dzelarhons

Poetry
The Annie Poems
Earth Witch

Stories for Children
T'aal: The One Who Takes Bad Children (with Sue Pielle)
The Gumboot Geese
Raven Goes Berrypicking
Raven and Snipe
Spider Woman
Lazy Boy
Orca's Song
Raven Returns the Water
How the Loon Lost Her Voice
How Raven Freed the Moon

Stories on Cassette
Loon and Raven Tales

THOSE LANCASTERS

ANNE CAMERON

HARBOUR PUBLISHING

Harbour Publishing
P.O. Box 219
Madeira Park, BC
Canada V0N 2H0

THE CANADA COUNCIL | LE CONSEIL DES ARTS
FOR THE ARTS | DU CANADA
SINCE 1957 | DEPUIS 1957

We acknowledge the financial support of the Government of Canada through the Book Publishing Industry Development Program for our publishing activities. We further acknowledge the support of the Canada Council for the Arts and the Province of British Columbia through the British Columbia Arts Council for our publishing program.

Printed in Canada.

Cover design and illustration by Warren Clark.

Canadian Cataloguing in Publication Data

Cameron, Anne, 1938–
  Those Lancasters

ISBN 1-55017-227-1

I. Title.
PS8555.A5187T56 2000   C813'.54   C00-910769-X
PR9199.3.C275T56 2000

For my kids: Alex, Marianne, Erin and Pepe

For my grandchildren: Terry, Sheldon, Jen and Andy

For my cousins who have made my life richer and *much* more fun

And for Eleanor: Whatever your little heart desires, kiddo.

PREFACE

I have lived for almost two decades with a woman who is, without a doubt, the most colourful speaker I've ever met. Eleanor uses words and phrases in ways that would thrill any writer: she plays games with words; she invents and creates incredibly descriptive and often hilariously funny phrases and sentences, even paragraphs. She ought to be a writer. She is, however, one of the most hyperactive people you will ever meet, and a writer has to be able to *sit* for hours at a time, focussing on the story, the characters and scores of other things which will keep you in one place, staring at the glowing screen until long after your back has called it quits and turned itself to toast. Both physically and emotionally, probably even genetically, Eleanor simply cannot sit still long enough to write what deserves to be shared. And so, she lives with a word thief. The funniest lines, the best descriptions, are sure to have come from my roommate, my Sweetie. Any clunkers, mistakes, or terms objectionable are undoubtedly mine.

I am a very lucky person. My Uncle Tom, who might well be the funniest man ever to walk the face of the earth, has been a warm and loving constant in my life; my cousins are great; I have a sister who is probably just about ready to amaze the rest of the world the way she has amazed me most of her life; and a publisher—Howard White, Mary Schendlinger and the rest of the staff at Harbour—who understands what it is I'm trying to do and gives me plenty of room to try to do it.

Those Lancasters are in no way at all representative of me, my sibs, my cousins, or any other members of my family, either biological or extended. Having said that, please allow me also to say the coast is covered with people like them.

CHAPTER ONE

Tom and Jessie were digging a cave in the side of the slag heap, about halfway up, more toward the big maple tree than to the middle. Dorrit and Little Wilma had the near-new wagon and were busily moving the growing heap of trickle-down and discard from beneath the future hide-out, taking it to what sometimes got called the driveway and dumping it in the potholes and temporarily dry mud puddles. Dorrit jumped up and down on the loose fill, doing what he could to flatten it. When he heard the sound of the engine, he looked toward the highway, then grinned widely and began waving. Little Wilma didn't notice, and of course the other kids were so busy with what they were doing they wouldn't have heard the Last Trump.

Colleen drove her little pop can over what really ought to be a lawn but never would be, and parked near the back steps. Her car was so low slung she didn't dare attempt the supposed driveway: she was almost guaranteed to get hung up, at the least, or puncture her oil pan, or worse.

"Hey, you kids," she called, her voice mostly pleasant, "if you haven't got something in there to shore up the roof the whole shootin' match is going to come down on you." They froze, even the ones busy with the wagon and potholes, as if stillness brought invisibility. At this point Colleen had two choices: she could get stern and order them out, possibly kicking off a real tantrum, or she could avoid the whining and complaining and use chicanery and bribery.

"I've got a brand new pack of gum," she said, as if to the trees and the sky, "not even opened yet."

The stillness broke. The ones with the wagon got there first, but the two cave-dwellers weren't far behind, and all of them grinning. She opened the pack, and they reached politely, their hands like black paws from the coal dust and shale.

"Anybody home?" she asked, already knowing the answer. They shook their heads, stuffing gum into their mouths, dropping the wrappers. Colleen stared at the kids, then down at the wrappers, and finally, one by one, they reached down, picked up their trash and stood holding it, chewing noisily. She held out her hand, and again one by one, they dropped their crumpled wrappers; she nodded and Dorrit sighed contentedly. Dorrit was always on the verge of fear—the slightest sign someone was less than totally happy always stiffened him up, and if anyone said so much as one disapproving word, he would start to shake. Well, why not? It might be an exaggerated reaction, but the circumstances that had given rise to it were pretty exaggerated too. Not "pretty" exaggerated. "Ugly" exaggerated would be more like it.

"What did you get for lunch?" Colleen asked. They looked away, unable to meet her eyes, and then Jessie shrugged.

"Okay, make you a deal; you clear away that little heap of trickle-down and fill some of those potholes with it, and while you're doing that I'll get some supper for us. And if you do a good job, and *if* you remember to scrub your hands and faces before you come to the table . . . well, with enough flarching, coaxing and flattery I might be prevailed upon to take a drive down to the creek. *After* the dishes are done and the kitchen cleared, of course."

They moved, fast as snakes, grinning widely and chewing damply. Colleen made sure she didn't shake her head or sigh: the little monsters would take it as an insult, or even worse, pity. And then there'd be hell to pay.

Her room was small, really only half a room, with some old Goodwill drapes strung from a length of clothesline as a divider to give her some small measure of privacy. Darlene had the other half of the room, and if you didn't mark and stand ready to defend the boundaries, the next thing you knew Darlene would be halfway up your nose. Which in itself was bad enough, but you never knew who she was apt to bring home with her after her shift was finished.

She changed, checking her work drag, hanging it carefully in her curtained-off closet. She was hoping to get her own place soon, one she knew she wasn't sharing with anyone, not ever, so she wouldn't have to dream of solid doors and sturdy locks. It was the thing about boundaries again. Darlene didn't even ask permission to borrow clothes: she just waltzed in, took what she wanted, and somehow forgot to bring it back. If you needed it, wanted it, or missed it, you had to go to her side of the room and dig through the heap of stuff on the floor to retrieve your belongings. And of course you also won the chance to do the washing or, if you were really covered in luck, pay the dry cleaning bill. Well, when she got her own place, there'd be an end to all of that!

She couldn't find anything in the fridge that looked as if anyone had intended it for supper for the kids. Obviously, nobody had collected eggs either. She went down into the basement, and with the help of a flashlight that surprisingly and blessedly had charged batteries in it, she got two quarts of jarred venison and went back upstairs. If there were batteries in the flashlight—working ones—it meant one of the boys either intended to go out pit-lamping or had already gone.

She put the deer meat on to warm up and scrubbed enough spuds to make a big potful, then put them on to cook and headed out to the weed-strewn garden to see what, if anything, could be salvaged. She got enough green beans for herself and the kids, but the only peas on the vines were little ones. She supposed that's where the kids had found some food for themselves. Jesus, you'd think if people were going to go to so much sweaty effort to get kids, they'd be prepared to do something once the little mutts had arrived!

She put the beans on to cook and found an unopened can of cream of mushroom soup, which she added to the meat. Mixed with the juices it made a fine gravy. While the beans cooked, she set the table, and when the spuds were ready, she drained them and started mashing them. As if they had heard her, the kids came in the back door and trooped to the big fibreglass sink near the washing machine in the backroom. By the time they came out—so clean she couldn't have found reason to criticize if she'd wanted to, which she didn't—supper was ready.

One thing about getting sucked into cooking for this bunch, you came away from the table feeling like Madame Benoit. Their table manners were enough to give you grey hair if you allowed yourself to care, although Colleen had at least won the part about not eating with your mouth open and not making too much noise.

"You're sure a good cooker," Little Wilma said, so busy pushing food into her mouth it was a miracle any words managed to find their way out past the forkloads.

"Thank you."

"What's this green stuff in the spuds?" Tom asked, frowning suspiciously.

"Basil."

"What's that?"

"One of the herbs."

"Herb who?" He was teasing, and they both knew it. "And what's old Herb got to do with my supper?"

"Basil's a herb."

"If he's a Herb why are you callin' him Basil?"

"Because he's the green stuff in the spuds."

"Basil Green is in the spuds? Well, then, where's Herb?"

"Don't talk so dumb!" Jessie snapped. "You guys do that same stupid thing all the time. What do you think, you're those guys off TV? Those two fools who do that thing about who's on first?"

"That's right," Colleen answered.

"No, he's on second, what's on first," Tom cackled.

"You make me sick." Jessie glared and looked so much like the old woman—her grandmother—Colleen nearly laughed.

"If you're sick, I'll eat your supper for you," Dorrit dared.

"Eat your own, I don't need help from you."

"Stop bickering or I'll get a headache and won't be able to drive you to the creek."

For a while there was just the clink of cutlery as the kids packed away enough food to make a person wonder why they didn't burst.

"Is there more?"

"Plenty. Help yourself. *But . . .*"

"Eat what you take!" they chorused.

Dorrit took seconds and got it packed in place, but made no move for thirds; he sat, eyes glazed, sipping his milk and smiling. Sometimes Dorry almost seemed either gassed or heading for another planet. Colleen wondered about his blood sugar levels: sometimes he fell asleep after a big meal, several times he had packed away his food, then put his head on the table and just dozed off, his forehead damp with sweat, as if eating was hard work. Little Willy went for thirds, but only took a bit, but Jess and Tom seemed intent on packing away enough food to fill both legs.

Colleen took her cigarettes to the back steps and sat, feeling tired and angry and concerned, feeling frustrated and almost, but not quite, put-upon and resentful. Just another evening, the same as most others. She was halfway through her smoke when she heard the rattle of dishes and cutlery, the nag nag of Tom's voice, the surly "up yours" reply from Jess. Before anyone hit anyone else Colleen went back inside and said the usual warning about staying home, not going to the creek, nothing better to do than fight you can do it here, no sense wasting gas to take you somewhere else so you can act like gomers. The bitching stopped, the cleanup proceeded, and Colleen pretended she didn't notice that the table didn't get scrubbed but was given only a lick 'n' a promise.

The big rock at the creek was warm, and Colleen lay belly down on it, her eyes shut, her hair drying quickly. The sun was still hot, and the yipping and yelping of the kids pierced the evening air, bright red flashes against the soft blue drone of bumblebees busy at the blackberry blossoms. The sharp scolding curses of a kingfisher sounded, and when Dorrit answered, the insulted bird moved downstream. The first skeeter hawks were out, calling to each other, criss-crossing the sky, busily catching mosquitoes, blackflies and anything else that caught their sharp searching gazes.

Colleen squirmed, but the crick in her back wouldn't go away, so she rolled over, but that didn't help, the crick tightened. She sat up, folded her towel and put it between her back and the outcropping they all called the backrest. The crick eased, but she knew she wouldn't nap sitting up, she never could. Still, it was relaxing to lean her head back and stare up at the hawks trolling the air. She smiled, remembering her brother's family-famous ditty, "Lovely to look at, they seem so nice, but pick one up and you'll be covered in lice." She missed Al, but she knew he'd be home soon, and the world wouldn't stop spinning before then.

"Don't you *dare*!" Jessie warned angrily. Colleen opened her eyes. Tom was trying hard to look innocent, but his face gave him away entirely; he looked guiltier than if he'd never bothered trying to seem harmless.

"Who, me? What?"

"You even think of dunking me, Tom Lancaster, and they'll have to phone the undertaker and make arrangements for your funeral."

"What did I do?"

"Tom, you behave yourself or you can start walking home right now," Colleen warned.

"I didn't *do* anything."

"Well, then don't."

"He was gonna try to dunk me. I know him," Jessie raged.

"Put a sock in it, Jess, okay? Tom, you know strife and contention give me a headache."

"But I didn't do nothing."

"Didn't do nothing means did do something," Jessie barked, still angry, and no more liable to be distracted from her focus than a pit bull with a juicy bone. "You were getting ready to try to dunk me. And don't bother lyin' about it, Tommy, because if you think you're man enough to push me around, then at least be man enough to admit it."

"I'm not going to try to dunk you, Jessie," Tom reassured her. "I promise I will not come over there and put my hand on your head and shove it under, okay? I absolutely promise."

Jessie didn't really believe him—but after all, he had promised, so she turned her back to show her scorn, then started stroking back and forth across the creek. Jessie wanted to learn to do a proper crawl, and she just about had it down pat. Colleen could see Jess's lips moving as she counted *one*, her right arm coming out of the water and reaching forward as her face turned into the water, *two*, the right hand went into the water, *three*, the left arm stroked forward as the face emerged and turned sideways, *four*, she took a breath of air, *one*, the right arm came out, the face turned into the water. Jessie would keep it up until it all became one smooth movement, and she would never be one of those energy wasting dumb-looking swimmers who moved their heads with every awkward stroke.

Colleen smiled and leaned her head back against the rock. No sooner were her eyes turned from the pool than the shriek sounded and was cut off. She jerked upright. Jessie was under water; Tom had her by one ankle, his other hand pushing down on her shoulder. He was laughing, and god, he did look gorgeous, he'd be a heart-breaker before long. If he lived!

Colleen didn't say a word. She just ran to the end of the rock and dove for the deepest part of the pool. Dorrit was yelling at Tom to stop, Little Wilma was shrilling about promises and how only scum broke them, and Tom was hollering gotcha, gotcha and didn't hear the splash when Colleen hit the water. He wasn't aware of a thing until Colleen's hands grabbed his ankles and yarded, taking him off balance, dumping him into the water. He let go of Jessie who came up spluttering and obviously frightened.

Colleen put her feet on Tom, holding him down on the gravel bottom. Had it ended there, Tom would have thought it all fun, would have been convinced they were all playing, even Colleen. But Jessie was past anger, past fury and into something else, something so totally Lancaster the others understood and stepped back, out of her way.

She went under water, grabbed Tom around the throat and began throttling him. Colleen grabbed her, but Jessie didn't care. Colleen tried to pry Jessie's fingers off, but all that did was make Jess so angry she bit Tom on the shoulder and wouldn't let go.

Colleen had to drag them both out of the water and onto the rocky bank, then struggle with Jessie to keep her from using a rock to pound in Tom's head. Jessie kicked Tom in the belly, scratched his face and chest, bit him again and finally, between Colleen's pulling and Tom's frantic tossing and bucking, her grip broke and he was free.

"You dirty rotten bastard!" Jessie yelled.

"Jesus, Jessie, you can't take a joke for shit." He was frightened, and small wonder.

"Joke, my ass, Tom! You aren't funny, okay? You're a fuckin' jerk is what you are and from now on you keep your stinking nose-picking ass-scratching hands *off* me!"

"Jeez, Jess . . ."

"Tom, keep your hands to yourself."

"I was just *playin'*," he insisted, looking for an ally where none could be found. The other kids just stared at him, shaking their heads. Jessie continued to rage, and Colleen went back to the rock, warning them she could feel a headache coming on, and if it hit they'd all be back home with nothing to do but dig in the slag.

🏃

By the time they got home, the kids were tired and more than willing to hang their towels and wet swimsuits on the sagging clothesline, then take themselves off to bed. Colleen had a cup of tea, watched a bit of TV, found it totally boring and went to bed herself. She didn't hear Darlene come in, but the rhythmic squeak of the noisy springs roused her. Obviously, someone had come home with Darlene. And obviously, the squeaking and soft laughter was going to continue for a while. Colleen got out of bed, shaking her head, and went to the kitchen. She heated a frying pan, put in some of the leftover spuds and some venison in gravy, and when it was bubbling, poured it into a bowl and took it and a cup of tea to watch television. She'd have far rather been asleep, but if that was impossible, well, almost anything was better than lying in bed feeling angry.

The big chair was lumpy and she had to sit in it just so or she'd get stabbed in the back by a broken spring, but she was used to it and knew where the valleys were and how to get comfortable enough to actually snooze. One sleepy moment a young woman on TV was coming out of a city apartment building, unaware she was being stalked by a maniac, and the next moment—or so it seemed—two women in a lovely big old Caddy were driving wildly down an open highway, and then Darlene was rattling the frying pan, slapping it down on the burner. "Is this all that's left over?" she asked.

"And you're quite welcome, too," Colleen yawned. "It always gives me such pleasure to have my efforts appreciated."

"How come we're out of eggs?"

"I guess you didn't pick them up, eh?"

"Jesus, do I have to do everything around here?"

"Why not? Nobody else does."

"Did you make supper for those kids?"

"Are you asking me if I made supper for my nieces and nephews? Are you asking if I made supper for Maude's kids, Norm's kid and your kid? If that's what you're asking, the answer is yes, yes, yes and yes, and the question is: Where in hell are Maude, Norm and Wilma, and why didn't you feed the kids before you left?"

"I don't know where Maude is, but Norm and Wilma have a job outta town for the next week and a half or so."

"And might I ask who was left in charge of Little Wilma while all this is going on?"

"They never said, they just grabbed some stuff and took off."

"The kid is only six! You don't just hidey-ho off down the road and leave a six-year-old to look after herself."

"Well, she didn't look after herself, did she? There were other kids here. You made supper. What's stuck in your craw?"

"What's stuck in . . ." Colleen stopped speaking and stared at the hunk standing in the kitchen doorway just about as naked as when he emerged from his mother's body. She looked away hurriedly, his image fresh in her memory.

"Excuse me, ma'am," he said politely. "Should have known Slick there wasn't talking to herself. Be right back."

"No need." Colleen reached for the tea towel, tossed it in his direction, waited a moment, then moved toward the doorway. Tea towel held strategically in front of him, the hunk moved aside.

Colleen averted her eyes and went to her room, climbed into bed and fell asleep, wondering how Darlene found so many great-looking one-night stands. Oh, sometimes she came in with losers; after all, nobody bats a thousand. But most of her temporary friends were okay-looking and a surprising number of them were real catches. Of course, none of them stayed long—a couple of nights to feed the old snake, and then off over the horizon, usually at Darlene's suggestion. She was very open about her reasons: Dar figured that after a few days or nights you ran out of jokes and teasing and somehow started to talk about what really mattered. The next thing you knew, you were *involved*. "And damn if I'm trying that one again!"

In the morning the kitchen looked as if neither Colleen nor the kids had even bothered to clean it. Surely to god two people hadn't been able to make that kind of mess! The place was so depressing—with dirty plates and egg yolk hardened on the tines of the forks, with chutney jars left uncovered so the flies had been able to go in, get stuck and drown in mustardy sauce—that Colleen didn't even try to make coffee. She just got herself dressed for work, did her hair and left. She could put on her face in the washroom at the Save-Your-Life.

She couldn't remember the name of the woman who was working the counter, but she knew they'd been in school at the same time. Not together, but at the same time. The woman obviously recognized Colleen, and just as obviously preferred to pretend she didn't. That was fine with Colleen: she didn't have to pretend she recalled any previous connection.

She ordered scrambled eggs, white toast and a double coffee to start. She smoked a cigarette and sipped gratefully, paying no attention to anyone else in the place. Probably, they'd all reminded each other she was "one of those Lancasters," and were, even now, dredging up some old weekend wonder of a war story. She could ignore them, ignore the glances, even manage to ignore the old tales, but she couldn't fully ignore how she felt. The gossip didn't hurt anymore, it didn't even sting, but it did rub. This bunch had nothing more to do than regale each other with minorly scandalous behaviours from years past. And they are what is called the voting public? They have the destiny of the nation in their sweaty grasps?

The eggs tasted flat, but she ate them. You don't get free-range dark-yolked tasty eggs if you're buying battery-produced commercial ones at the supermarket. At least the kitchen here was clean, more than could be said of the one back at the place. No wonder the kids resented doing dishes and cleanup.

She finished her meal and ordered another coffee, single this time, and before it came she went to the washroom to put on her disguise. It didn't take long, she used very little by way of makeup, and what she did use was so skilfully applied it seemed it wasn't even there. She paid her bill and headed for work.

The morning passed quickly. The office was blessedly quiet.

Although she had been offered head office several times, nobody had been insistent about Colleen moving. She knew about the Peter Principle, how you got promoted to your first level of incompetency. She was good at what she did, researching and putting together employee benefit packages for a large Vancouver insurance firm, and being where she was probably had a lot to do with her success: she knew the clients, knew their backgrounds, knew things only a local would know, and even if they sniped at and about those Lancasters, they preferred dealing with one of their own rather than with some member of the parachute club who had been dropped in here for training. Funny how that worked.

The others drifted in from lunch and headed for their desks. Colleen was already busy, on the phone with the newly assigned head honcho at the mill. She had her facts and figures in place, she'd done her research. She'd been noodling at this one for several weeks—putting in unpaid overtime, coming in early, leaving a bit late, shaving the length of her lunch breaks. He was an asshole, of course. You don't get that high up by being anything else but. Still, he was listening, and she knew from his questions and responses he had the file she'd sent in front of him, and was going through it with her, line by line.

She couldn't believe it when he said if she could get to his office in half an hour, he'd have some time to talk about things in person.

She kept her voice businesslike, kept her choice of words professional and ladylike, and made sure nobody else in the office saw her sudden jolt of excitement.

She was so casual and easygoing when she left the office, a person would think she really was just stepping out for a half hour or so for a doctor's appointment. Inside she wasn't casual, she wasn't easygoing, and she almost wished she could go to the doctor and get herself some anti-anxiety pills.

She saw the mill boss, her stomach in aching knots the whole time, and when she left his office she thought she'd actually vomit. But she had the signed papers in her briefcase. Jesus aitch, thank you.

Colleen held it together while she got into her car and drove away from the mill, she held it together halfway back to the office, then it all hit her and she pulled off the highway and just let herself shake. Her hands were so busy trembling and flapping she couldn't manage to light her cigarette, and she'd have committed an obscenity for a few good lungfuls of calming warm smoke.

The traffic rushed past, and if anyone noticed the little black car pulled off the road and parked on the verge, they'd have probably thought she was a tourist getting an eyeful of the view of the valley, the town and the ocean beyond. She wanted to put her head on the steering wheel and bawl. After a while she calmed down enough to light the cigarette, satisfy her addiction and even drive back to the office.

Her boss Stan answered her knock with an impatient "What is it?" and when she went inside his throne room, she knew he was a bit ticked off, and she knew why, too. Brenda was in there with him, flustered and none too pleased. But her clothes weren't in disarray, her hair wasn't mussed and she still had her lipstick on, so things hadn't progressed too far.

"Got something for you," she said calmly and put the file on his desk with the signed contracts on top. Then she just stood and waited, looking as calm as jello in a bowl while he frowned and unknowingly did that oh-my-god-what-a-pain-in-the-ass thing with his mouth. The guy might think he was the hotshot of all time, but he'd lose his shirt in a poker game.

At least he had the sense to open the file folder and look at, then actually read the contracts. Obviously, he didn't believe his eyes because he started reading her facts, figures, statistics and proposal, too. Finally, it sank in, and he looked up at her with an expression on his face she couldn't quite read, almost as if his initial pique at the interruption had been intensified into something close to jealous dislike.

"Is this for real?"

"Yes, boss," she answered, without smiling. "It's for real, all right."

"Christ in heaven."

"My sentiments exactly. Do you want to phone head office or would you rather I do it?"

She knew he wanted time to think up some way to give the news to head office so they'd think he was involved in the sell, even somehow due a large measure of the credit or even the bulk of the glory. And she knew he knew she wasn't going to give him that time.

"You do it," he said curtly, closing the file folder and handing it to her. "It's your baby," he said grudgingly. "You should phone in the birth announcement."

She nodded, took the file folder, smiled, and left the office door open when she went back to her desk. He sat at his desk and watched her as she picked up the phone and started dialling. If his eyes had been lasers, she'd have holes burned all the way through her.

That resentment fell away as she listened to the excitement and glee that came out of the phone. The old fart's executive secretary practically jumped right through the line to dance on Colleen's desk.

"Are you serious?"

"I am. Oh, you bet your beautiful bippy I am." And some of what she was feeling leaked through; she could hear the satisfaction in her own voice. "I'll have everything to you by courier in—oh, god, I don't know. Probably it can get there on the five-ish plane, but they likely won't catch you before the office closes so it should be there first thing in the morning."

"Don't bust your gut; if you say it's true, I believe you. Anyway, the old man won't be back for at least two hours, maybe not at all today, so there's no rush as long as it's here in the morning. He's going to drown in his own cappuccino."

"I might drown in mine! Do you know what this means to me?"

"Yeah. Just exactly what it would mean to me. Do you realize that for as long as this remains in effect you probably don't have to worry about making any other sales? Your percentage on this will be like an inherited annuity! Right up until some bright thing from some other company outbids you, of course."

"I'm going home early."

"How's Stanley-the-Steamer doing with it?"

"I think he's very close to hating my guts."

"What a jerk."

Colleen left the office with the signed contracts and went to the courier office to fill out the envelope and see it safely into the canvas pouch. She was in time and even got to watch as the pouch was put in a huge canvas sack with a load of other deliveries and was rushed to the float plane in the harbour. She was so excited she sat in her car and watched until the plane took off, water spraying from the pontoons, and only when it was in the air and headed through the skies toward the city did she breathe easily.

On the way home she stopped at the supermarket and bought five bags of groceries. She wanted to babble her good news to the checkout woman, but didn't. She wanted to yell and holler and cheer and caper and cavort and give everyone in town reason to think she was drunk as a skunk, but she didn't. She saved it all, letting it build.

There was no sign of Darlene at the house and no sign of a casserole or any effort or attempt to provide anything at all for the kids' supper. But the kitchen was clean, the fridge had been cleaned out and washed inside, and someone had not only picked up the eggs they'd washed them and put them in a big bowl in the clean refrigerator. Had Mary Magdalene come for a visit?

Her brother Singe wandered in by way of the back door and grinned at her. "Hey, you." He had the big skinning knife in one hand and his arms were gore-smeared to the elbow. "You know where the cheesecloth is?"

"I don't even know if we have any. You know where there's bodies to bring in grocery bags?"

"Hey, you kids!" he roared. They came running. When Singe called, they responded promptly. "Bring the groceries in from your auntie's car. And don't slam the damn door off its hinges." And without any sort of break or breath he continued saying to Colleen, "Guess if I can't find it I'll use an old wore-out sheet."

"What you got?"

"Government mutton." He grinned again. "And something or other that's as woolly as hell."

"Singe, you bugger, you didn't!" She didn't want to laugh but could feel it growing.

"Damn right I did. I warned the fool, Colly, I did, you know I did. Spoke to 'im on the street, and all's I got for that was a mouthful of sass. Phoned 'im twice and got hot tongue and cold shoulder, went over to discuss it and as good as got turfed off the place, so if the fool wants to play silly bugger, I'll show 'im how an expert does it."

"This'll be the first place they come looking."

"They can look all's they want. For all's I care they can kiss my dick."

Their old man had heard someone call someone else what he thought was Singeon. Probably it was some lime-juicer referring to St. John, but to the old man what he heard was Singeon and the newborn boy got the name. Singeon Lancaster. The next one was a boy, too, and the old man hadn't heard the name he tagged onto the poor mite: he'd seen it written but had no idea how to pronounce it, so instead of Juan it became Jewen. Good job he hadn't gone all the way and added the rest of the explorer's name—de Fuca. Well, no use complaining, at least he'd gone for Albert instead of Camus. Colleen was pretty sure Al would bless his luck all his life for that one. The girls got named by the old woman: Doreen, Darlene, Brady and Colleen.

Doreen was in Ontario, with the Air Force. She seldom phoned, never wrote except for a brief message on the Christmas card that came every year with a decent cheque in it, and Colleen couldn't even begin to imagine what her sister's life would be like. Brady, now, her life was easily imaginable, all too easily if the truth be known. Brady was an exotic dancer, which wasn't the same as a stripper and didn't necessarily mean she was a hooker, but somehow did mean that some of her best friends were, and you wondered if others wore their damn guns to bed.

The kids brought in the groceries and started putting them away. Colleen grabbed what she needed for supper and sent Dorrit out to the garden to gather salad greens. With Dorrit there were more than just greens, there would be orange nasturtium flowers, blue comfrey flowers, maybe even a yellow or reddish day-lily flower or two as well. She had no idea where he'd picked up some of his notions, but he did put together a fine salad.

She ducked into her bedroom to change her clothes and felt the same old dull anger when she saw her bed bedecked with things Darlene hadn't borrowed. That could only mean she'd been in here a while, picking and choosing, poking and trying on, probably going through drawers and even looking for jewellery—a ring, a bracelet, something that wasn't hers—that would, as she put it, spruce her up, because Colleen's clothes were all so conservative. Colleen was so angry she felt like crying. She got out of her drag and into her jeans and tee-shirt, then went back to the kitchen to pull supper together.

She sizzled the ground beef, chopped into the pan two medium-sized onions and several stalks of celery, added oregano, basil, thyme, a little shot of vinegar, another shot of ketchup, and then a jar of four-cheese spaghetti sauce. The kids grinned; they loved her spaghetti meals.

By the time the salad was rinsed the kids were finished putting away groceries, so she got Little Wilma busy with the salad spinner, Tom setting the table, Jessie mixing up frozen juice, and Dorrit in the bathroom washing his hands and face.

"Tommy, don't dawdle, okay? And you should have washed up before touching the plates."

"You never told me."

"I didn't tell you to swipe any of the grapes, either, but you did."

"I'll wash," he said hurriedly, hoping to get her off the subject.

"He's a pig," Jessie said casually. "Eats like one, looks like a dirty one, acts like a swine and is pigheaded."

"And you're perfect, right?"

Totally by good luck rather than good management, everything came together at the same time, and supper went off without a hitch. Singe was scrubbed and in clean clothes, his hair slicked down with water. With him at the table the BS from Tom evaporated.

"This is good, Colly," Singe said softly. "You're something else again, believe me."

"You working right now, Singe?"

"Naw, we're shut down. Not fire season yet, but . . . pogey time. Unemployment enjoyment. They never said why, they just said bye-bye."

"Could I hire you?"

"You? Hire me? Sure, what do you want, gonna make me stand against the wall so you can throw horse buns at me?"

"Can you build an addition to the house? Not a big one, but . . ." She felt her eyes flood with tears. "It's that or I'm moving into an apartment in town. I can't handle much more of this . . . disrespect from Dar."

Jessie said calmly, "I told her not to rummage in your stuff. Then when she still did, I told her to tidy up after herself, but she asked me when had god retired and put me in charge, and then she slapped my face, so . . ."

"She didn't slap you hard, for cryin' in the night," Tom defended. "It was just a tap."

"Not up to her to tap me. Nobody's supposed to tap me but my mom 'n' dad."

"I'll bloody tap you if you don't stop bickering," Singe said, his voice still soft and quiet. The nattering stopped immediately.

"Could you?" Colleen asked.

"Not a whole helluva lot of sense in putting an addition to this old wreck of a place." Singe spoke slowly, already thinking and planning. "Already the damn roof line goes in every direction except a good one, and the joint wanders around like a lost beach crab, sideways half the time. Be a real pain in the ass to try to fit something else on without having to rip into the roof, and if a person didn't do that,

25

well, you'd wind up with a damn low ceiling. Be easier to put togeth-er something free-standing." He stopped talking and packed away food, mopping at the sauce with a slice of sourdough bread. "Yeah, that's what a body should do." He nodded, licked his lips and smiled. "Could get 'er halfways done in the time it would take to rip into the roof for an addition. Put 'er on a cement pad. Yeah, I could do 'er. What you got in mind?"

"I want at least a nice bedroom of my own. With a closet. And a solid door. And a goddamned padlock on it!"

"You let me think about it for a day or two, okay?" And again his shy smile was turned on her. "Could you pass me the seconds, please?"

"Tom, pay attention. Your uncle needs the spaghetti and the sauce."

"Well, then, pass it to him, why don't you," Tom snapped. And just like that he was off his chair, his feet not touching the floor, held by Singe's hand under his chin.

"Excuse us, please." Singe nodded and headed for the back door, still easily holding Tommy off the floor.

Dorrit hopped off his chair, went around the table, got the bowl of spaghetti and moved it within reach of Singe's chair. Jessie moved the bowl of sauce, then the salad bowl, and they all waited, silent and worried, until Singe and Tommy walked back into the kitchen again. Tommy's face was white, his eyes wide, and when he sat back in his chair, his attitude was miles away and still running.

"I'm sorry I lipped at you, Auntie." He didn't look as if he'd been walloped or shellacked, but the fear of god rode on his shoulder.

"Thank you," Colleen said.

"Would you like some more?" Singeon offered, and Tom shook his head. "Beg your pardon?"

"No, thank you, Uncle."

"Well, I'm having more. Anyone else?"

"Please." Dorrit grabbed his plate and moved to stand beside Singe.

"Is there dessert?" Jessie asked.

"Did you see any?"

"Not in my bag of stuff."

"There was donuts in my bag," Little Wilma piped. "A big box."

"So who do you think paid for all this stuff," Singe demanded. The kids just stared at him. "Wasn't none of your moms, nor none of your dads either. Every scrap that's gone into your bellies here tonight was paid for by your auntie. So if I hear any bullshit between now and this time next year, you can be sure I'm going to make it my business. She don't have to *do* for any of you. Christ knows there's enough others do nothing for you's."

The kids were quiet only for a few minutes, then the meal continued, the laughter growing when the donuts came to the table. The kids teased Singe he'd be out of luck because he had a great big plate of thirds, and he pretended to gobble quickly, as if worried. But Colleen noticed it was Tommy who made sure two donuts wound up on a small plate near Singe, and Singe nodded and said, "Thank you, Tom, I appreciate it." And the last of the wary stiffness eased from the brat's shoulders.

"I'll wash dishes," Jessie offered. "Who's getting eggs?"

Singeon made some coffee, and he and Colleen sat on the back porch while the kids whipped around, doing chores and pretending they were having a wonderful time.

"So where the fuck is Maude, anyway?" Singe asked.

"I haven't seen Maude for probably a week," Colleen answered. "I hardly even remember what the slob looks like."

"Jeez, if she don't smarten up before Al gets out he'll have her ass in a jar for her."

"Well, she might smarten up when he gets back, but she isn't going to before he gets here. Someone should fold her up and put her in a damn crab trap."

"The people other people get hooked up with, eh?"

"Maybe I'll take these horrors to the creek for a swim. Get them out of your way while you do what you need to do."

"Sounds like a fine idea. Amazes me I didn't have it myself."

On the trip to the creek Colleen shrugged off her bitter anger over Darlene's invasion of her space, and by the time they got to the big

27

rock the bum feelings were gone and all her excitement and glee was at the surface again.

She watched the kids race for the water, and when they were in, and splashing, she suddenly started hollering "Yes, *yes!*"

"*Yes,*" Little Wilma screeched, not knowing what the fun was about but always willing to join in.

"*Yaaaaaaasssss,*" Dorrit hollered, trying to outdo Little Wil.

The kingfisher chittered and nagged, then headed downstream to the big arbutus that leaned over the white water. He sat at the top of the tree and raged about intruders, noise and the interruption to his fishing. Upstream from him the trespassers were yelling and shouting, splashing and screeching, even capering on the big rock and trying to drown each other out with noise. Even the big one had gone crazy: she was diving off the rock, grabbing kids and tossing them to splash in the deeper part of the pool.

When they got home, Singeon was gone and there wasn't a sign of his butchering activity. Even better, he'd collapsed the huge hole the kids had dug into the slag heap, and best of all, they didn't notice so they didn't complain. They just put their swim stuff on the line, then lurched off to bed, half asleep before they got to their rooms.

🐦

In the morning, the kitchen was spic-and-span tidy, dishes washed and on the drainboard, dried by god. The water was measured and in the coffee maker, so all Colleen had to do was flick the switch and wait for the rich scent to fill the house. She didn't get dressed right away, but put some granola with yogurt on top in a bowl and went out onto the porch to wait for her morning transfusion to finish dripping. She was sitting in the chair feeling fully covered and still cool in her old washed-almost-white, once-blue cotton pyjamas when the hunk walked out with two mugs of coffee on a cookie sheet with the sugar bowl and a cardboard container of cream. Suddenly Colleen felt indecently exposed.

"You make a damn fine spaghetti," he told her. "We warmed 'er up and finished 'er off when we got home last night. By way of thank you . . ." He handed her the dark blue mug and lifted the empty bowl from her fingers.

"Thank you," she managed.

"You figure there'll be coffee in heaven?" he asked, sniffing the steam coming from his mug.

"Won't matter if there is. I probably won't get there anyway." Colleen felt herself relax, suddenly and unexpectedly.

"That bother you?"

"Oh, hell no." She sipped, smiled appreciatively. "I'd be too lonely up there to enjoy any part of it. Every member of my family and any friend I ever had are going to the other place so I might as well go with them and have company."

When she got to work, the others had heard about the huge score she'd made, and each made a point to come over to say congratulations. Some of them obviously meant it; others behaved in such a way she wondered if they were hoping some of the good luck would rub off on them. Stanley used the back door, so he didn't have to run the gauntlet of eyes nor pass anywhere near Colleen's desk. She hoped he had developed an ulcer. A big one.

Brenda came in the front door and smiled her wide plastic smile as if she were best buds with each and every one of them. And everyone, including Colleen, nodded and found their own big phoneys to wear as if they liked any part of her. It made everything easier. After all she was wiffing the boss, and who needed the aggravation.

They were all at their desks, settling in to work, when Rose's Roses arrived with an arrangement of living plants that made all conversation stop.

"Colleen?" the delivery woman called. "Is there a Colleen here?"

"I'm Colleen." She stood up, feeling totally flustered.

"Here you go."

The woman wore jeans, sneakers and a short-sleeved, loose-fitting cotton shirt with a big rose stencilled on the back. She moved carefully, set the arrangement on Colleen's desk, stood back, studied it, then moved it to what she considered a better place. "Someone loves you," she grinned. "That's the most impressive one I've delivered, and I've been with Rose's for three years."

"My god," Colleen breathed.

"So, see, what you do is you put your water here, in the elf's head. Keep him full, okay? There's little tube-things go from him down to each of the pots. As long as you keep him full, they'll get the water they need . . . and they won't drip, okay? You can get extras of this at the store." She put a small packet near Colleen. "That's plant food. The elf gets one every two weeks, okay? Now when the plants start to get too big for the arrangement, you call us no extra charge, and we come and you can either get a bigger stand or we can take the arrangement apart, repot the plants in bigger containers, and you can either keep them here or take them home. Or, still no charge, you can just trade 'er in for a different one, same size as this is now."

"Thank you."

"And there's a card."

The card was signed "From Head Office" and beneath that, "Love, Bev." It took a moment for Colleen to figure out Bev was the Executive Secretary. Isn't that a crock, and how many times had they talked with each other? Strange, the things we pay attention to and the things we ignore. Strange, too, the way we relate to each other.

The office calmed down again, and Colleen went back to work. If she could sell a package to the mill, known to be not only the biggest employer in town but the toughest nut to crack, then she was sure she could sell specially tailored packages to some of the others as well. And she would do it exactly the same way she'd hooked the mill manager. She'd research like a mad fiend, tailor the presentation precisely, make the individualized attention obvious from the very first glance. The book, the book, the near-sanctified book was after all a general guideline, not the eleventh commandment.

When she got home, supper was made and the hunk was supervising the setting of the table.

"I hope you like roast beast." He smiled as easy as if he'd been born under this roof and raised in this kitchen.

"Love it. Dare we ask what kind of beast?"

"Singe said it was manna from heaven. I rubbed it with some powdered mustard; it helps cut the fat and that smooths out the taste. Someone check them biscuits, okay? How's that gravy coming? If there's any lumps let me know and I'll sieve 'em out before we serve it up."

"If there's time, I'd like to change." She felt shy in her own house.

"Plenty of time if you move fast as stink."

She went to her room, changed, hung her drag neatly in place, and wondered about things like strangers cooking supper, and what it meant, and why some others, who weren't strangers, could swan through a kitchen and not so much as rinse a cup. Was there some kind of celestial script, and were people born to take certain roles, play certain parts, with no growth or change in the characters, no room for anyone to improvise?

There wasn't a scrap left by the time they'd all stuffed themselves. Even the gravy was long gone. Colleen figured since she hadn't done any cooking she'd do the cleanup, but when she started the kids protested, a chorus of "No, no, Auntie, you take it easy, you've been working all day, here, take a fresh cuppa out to the porch and relax before you drive us to the creek."

"Oh, and when was that decided?" she said, laughing. They all worked overtime at trying to appear angelic, even the hunk.

She was sitting with her tea, feeling spoiled and pampered and very very lucky when the cop car turned off the road and lurched up the pot-holey, once-and-maybe-even-future driveway. Colleen sighed. What the hell now?

The cop was new to town but his eyes weren't: they looked as if he'd seen every dirty, mean, ugly and despicable thing the human mind could imagine. Probably a burnout from the city, sent to a smaller place to off-load some stress. She wasn't sure which was worse: the recovering burnouts or the snotnoses fresh from Wainwright, still impressed with their spurs and bullets.

"Is this where . . ." He checked his notepad. "Singeon Lancaster lives?"

"Yes."

"May I speak with him, please?"

"He's not here."

"Do you know where he is?"

"No."

"Do you have any idea when he'll be back?"

"No."

His neck pinkened, his hard eyes narrowed, and she supposed he had expected something more friendly. Well, you don't get friendly with someone wearing the togs of the Queen's Cowboys.

"Mind if I have a look around?"

"You got a search warrant?"

"Do I need one?"

"If you're going to look around you sure do."

"You going to keep me standing out here or you going to invite me into the house."

"Here's fine."

"You always this hard-nosed?"

"I'm not hard-nosed. I'm sitting out here having a nice cup of tea after supper. You always so shirty?"

"You think this is shirty just push me too far."

"Now why would I want to do that?"

"Does Singeon Lancaster own a gun?"

"Do you?"

"Is the gun registered?"

"I'm sure you can check all that out on your computer."

"Do you happen to know where he was yesterday?"

"I don't even know where he is today."

The cop looked at her long and hard, and shook his head as if greatly disappointed. "Do you know a . . ." Again he checked his notebook. "Robert Martin?"

"Lives down the road."

"Are you aware Mr. Martin's sheep have disappeared?"

"What do you mean disappeared?"

"Gone."

"All of them?"

"He has reported, let me see, six ewes and a ram missing."

"Probably wandering loose in the bush. They can usually be found just about anywhere except the Martin place. I don't think he's got a fence worthy of the name."

"Have you seen any sheep?"

"No. And that's odd." She smiled as if she and the cop were the best friends this side of China. "Because usually you can find the stinking shite-bedrizzled messes trying to get into my garden."

"They're over here often?"

"Martin must be sick and tired of hearing my voice on the phone telling him to get over here and take the stinking things home with him. Sheep are really very filthy animals. They've got willnots."

"Willnots?" He bit, and bit hard.

"Balls and clumps of shit that stick to the fur around their ass ends and will *not* come off! They probably died of flystrike. That's when the flies get under the willnots, lay their eggs, the eggs hatch and the maggots eat the sheep from the back end forward."

The cop stared at her, and no matter how well trained he was, his face betrayed him, and she knew he was as good as seeing what happened beneath the foul, stinking wool.

"What time did you say you were expecting Singeon home?"

"I didn't."

"You aren't worried about him?"

"He's a grown man, why would I worry? I'm not his mother."

"What is your relationship with him, if I might ask."

"What difference would that make?"

"Will you have him call me when he gets back?"

"I'll leave a note about it and if I see him I'll tell him."

"I really do wish you'd be more cooperative, miss."

"Really? What do you want me to do, find the sheep? Bobby Martin phoned you, not me. By the way, if you're going down to his place would you mention to him that he's cut three trees on our side of the property line and if it happens again I'm taking him to court. He's also"—she didn't sound like anyone who knew what it was she was dropping in the cop's lap—"been cutting on crown land but I don't suppose I can do much about that. At least the ones he stole from us were maples. If he'd'a taken any fir, like he took off the crown land, I'd have called you guys. But maple, well, there's lots of that and all's it's good for is firewood. But maybe you could drop him a hint, okay?"

"Does he do this often? Cut your wood or go onto crown land to cut."

"Well, cutting down trees and bucking them up into firewood rounds is work, and Bobby Martin, he doesn't like to do any more of that than he has to, so it's not as if it's an everyday occurrence. But he doesn't seem to understand about property lines, that's for sure."

The cop left and she snickered to herself. So there, Bobby Martin, you total dinkhead.

"What's the cop want?" the hunk asked from the doorway.

"Looking for Singeon again."

"What's Singeon done?"

"More than they'll ever catch him for, that's for sure."

The kids had a wonderful time, even better than usual, because Colleen drove them up to the lake. There was a buckshee thrown-together diving raft they could swim to, and a nice grassy place for her to sit with her back against a tree so she could read comfortably while they cavorted. Colleen didn't go in swimming so she didn't get cooled off or chilled, and consequently she didn't notice the passage of time and the kids didn't tell her. Dark was coming on fast by the time they got home. The hunk was gone, Singe wasn't home, the place was unnaturally quiet, and the kids so tired Colleen hung up the towels and swimsuits so they could go straight to bed.

She didn't sleep well, although she didn't truly awaken at any time. She heard Darlene come in with someone, probably the hunk, and when she got past that disturbance and got back to sleep, she was half-roused again by someone else, several someone elses in fact, arriving. She almost made herself get out of bed to go raise supreme hell, but she couldn't swim up out of the warm fuzzy hole.

In the morning the place looked as if the entire Mongol Horde had hit and held practice manoeuvres. She took one look, sighed, and went to the bathroom to pee, wash her face, brush her teeth and spit repeatedly. She had to practically use a map to find something she wanted to wear to work; obviously she was going to have to go into Darlene's den and excavate enough of the mess to find her own clothes. Bitch!

She took a walk instead of lunch and almost stopped traffic when she saw the display in the store window at the office supply store. She'd never thought of things like suitcases and travel trunks as being part of office supplies, but there it was: blue-painted metal, probably tin or something, with pretend-brass corners and hasp. Standing on end, the top of it open sideways like a door, and this wasn't one of the ones where you just folded stuff and put it in. This had coat hangers on a metal bar, so you could This Side Up it and send your suits and stuff off without getting them to their destination so crumpled it cost an arm and a leg to get them pressed. Oh yeah. Oh, yeah yeah *yeah*!

She went to pick it up after work, drove home with it taking up most of the space in the pop can. Even empty she had all she could do to get it to the foot of the steps, and on her own she would probably never have been able to wrestle it into the house. But Singe was there, and he just picked it up as if it didn't weigh any more than a brown bag lunch.

"Where do you want it, Colly?"

"In my cubicle." She was so excited she could have walked on air. He nodded, and followed her through the still messy kitchen.

She lifted everything out of her closet space and put it on her bed. Singe had to do some fancy wriggling to get the blue wonder into the space, and then it stuck out a few inches, but it was in, and on end, and she could get the hasp unlocked easily and open the lid.

"It'll do for now," Singe agreed.

While Colleen put her clothes in their new home, Singe sprawled on the edge of the bed, his boots carefully over the end.

"Cops were here," she said. He nodded, and that was the end of that.

"Dar's going to have a shitfit," he warned.

"Yeah," she said, nodding, and that was the end of that, too. "Want to go for pizza?"

"Sounds good."

"Where are the kids?"

"Maude showed up, I guess. Maybe Jewen, too. Took them to the beach."

"Hope someone thinks to feed them."

"I'll clean myself up so's you aren't ashamed of me." He grinned and rolled easily off the bed, walking on his hands for no reason other than to make her laugh.

It didn't take long to get her clothes in the travel trunk; most of her clothes were on Dar's floor anyway. While Singe showered and changed, Colleen barged past the faded drapes and started her archaeological dig. She separated everything into what had to go to the dry cleaners and what she could wash herself, and when she and Singe headed for her car he was carrying the cleaning. They stopped at the 18-hour and dropped it off, then went to the pizza house for a Loaded Downer. They were just finishing the last pieces when the cop walked in, looked around, and saw them.

"Hello, ma'am," he said politely. But he was looking hard at Singeon.

"Hello, yourself." She didn't introduce them.

"Did your brother show up?" the cop asked pointedly.

"And I gave him your message." She smiled.

He hesitated, almost turned away, and asked instead, "Are you Singeon Lancaster?"

"That's me," Singe agreed.

"I wonder if I could have a few words with you."

"Pull up a chair," Singe invited. "Like a coffee? Join us for dessert?"

"No thank you." The cop sat, pulled out his little notebook. It was like a tired rerun of his questioning of Colleen and it netted him just about as much.

"Too bad about the sheep being missing," Singe said with no sign of a smile at all. "But, you know, if people don't put up good fences or have enough feed to keep animals at home, well, they'll take a hike. You know, of course, the bush is full of black bears? Well, it is. More damn bears out there than anyone would believe. And they've all got to eat, right? And if your stock is just swanning around in the toolies, well, guess what bears like to eat? Old Bob, now, he doesn't even do a good enough job of looking after his hens to keep them at home. They're over to our place half the time." He smiled then. "Hell, one night I went out to close ours up and there must'a been a dozen of old Bob's busy at the feeder alongside ours. I didn't bother phoning." He winked at the cop." I figured the next day'd be plenty of time to do that, and I'd be ahead some eggs to pay for the feed."

"Are your relations with Mr. Martin cordial?" The cop gave every indication of believing Singe was being open and up-front.

"No. Bob 'n' me, we got no use for each other." Singe looked at the last bit of pizza crust, then looked back up, as if shy, or embarrassed. "Few years back me 'n' Bob kinda tangled. He had him a woman living with him and, well, she and I started seeing each other from time to time and then, well, she packed her stuff and moved out and he blames me because I drove the truck. Things were nasty for quite a while. Old Bob got himself some of those, like, index cards or something." Singe measured off a rectangle with his hands. "Put 'em up all over the place: in the pubs, in the bars, even put 'em in the men's can at the movie house, and they all said the same thing, words might'a been different, but there's lots of ways to call a man a thief, I guess."

"He called you a thief?"

"Said I stole his woman. As if you could steal someone who didn't want to be stole."

"What did you do about it?"

"Nothing. Right up until he jumped up and tried to take a bite outta me at the Wheatsheaf one night." Singe lifted his hair and showed the scar above his left ear. "Gave me one helluva whack with a full bottle of Carling Red Cap. Near dropped me to the floor."

"Did you press charges?"

"No, no need to bother you guys about a little thing like that. Just got 'er stitched up at the hospital."

"And that's all you did about it?" Obviously, the cop wasn't about to swallow that much of the line.

"Well, no, I mean I whipped his ass before I drove to the hospital. He hates my guts. But that was a long time ago, and I can only hope to god he hasn't been bothering *you* about it."

"No, no, nothing like that. I'm just looking for his sheep."

"Jesus, I guess he thinks I swiped them the way he thinks I swiped his woman."

And there it was, lying out in the open.

"Well, did you?" The cop grinned.

"I don't fuck sheep." Singe grinned, too. "Can't speak for old Bob, now, but . . ."

"Do you eat sheep?"

"I like a good lamb chop, that's for sure. Why, you want to come check my freezer, look for a heap of mutton or something?"

"Could I?"

"You get you a warrant and you sure can so."

"Maybe I'll do that."

The cop left, and after a few moments so did Singe and Colleen. They were halfway home before they spoke.

"You think he'll get a warrant?" Colleen asked.

"I don't think he will, but you never know with them."

🦅

Colleen had her laundry washed and on the line before Jewen's pickup arrived with all four kids bouncing in the bed as if it wasn't against the law to rattle them around without seat belts like that. The kids jumped down and raced to the house. Jewen got out and waved, then moved forward, arms spread, to give Colleen a hug. Maude sat for several seconds as if she expected the Duke of Windsor to show up and open the door for her, then, with a look that said she was just astounded at other people's bad manners, she got out and sashayed her way toward the front steps.

"Ah, Jewen." Colleen kissed his cheek. "You look like the cat drug you in from under the porch."

"I been better," he admitted.

She could smell the fruity composting smell of cheap plonk, and not only from his mouth, his breath. He smelled as if the stuff was leaking out of his very pores. When he smiled his teeth were stained, pitted with small cavities there was still time for a dentist to fix, to clean and fill. Jewen's teeth had been the envy of half the town at one time; not a buck nor a snaggle in them, and his hair had fallen thick and golden to his shoulders. Now he was, if not exactly going bald, at least working on a very high forehead. "You're as skinny as a bicycle," she scolded. "You should take better care of yourself, eat more often, take vitamins."

"Win the lottery," he teased, "invest it wisely, live a sober, godly and righteous life and die of boredom before I'm forty."

Maude interrupted. "Of course, nobody around here has enough good manners to say so much as 'Hello, Maude, nice to see you'." She was working on a hangover; it ought to hit at about the time she crawled out of bed tomorrow morning.

"Hello, Maude, it's nice to see you," Colleen answered, her tone deliberately casual. "Did you have a nice trip?"

"Wasn't no trip and wasn't so nice," Maude snapped, heaving herself up the steps, her hair freshly dyed, so close to the colour of ox-blood shoe polish it was a joke. Not a dozen years ago Maude had been gorgeous; nobody would have called her plump because she was too ripe, too bosomy, too hippy, but too wasp-waisted for such a word. Plump people don't have waists; plump people's breasts just sort of swell like one loaf of bread, they don't have distinctive cleavage and a slight jiggle and bounce guaranteed to make any male capable of a woodie get one immediately. Even after Tommy and Jessie were born Maude had kept her figure. Al used to say the town council could save a fortune with Maude: instead of paying to have a stoplight installed, they could hire Maude to just stand there and direct traffic. No electricity bills to pay, no new bulbs to buy, and traffic stopped effectively. In all directions at once.

But Maude was like a house plant that bloomed briefly and then went to seed. Frown lines had cut deep between her eyebrows, her mouth was always on the verge of hard disapproval, and too much booze and weed had cost her the waist she'd been so proud of. Now she was plump, and past that, to a kind of rotund shapelessness. She was like one of the Pillsbury dough-folk gone bad after too many years in a pool hall.

Her slide had begun before Al went away, but once he was gone it picked up impetus and became a headlong nose-dive into low-rent tacky motel queen. She was wearing a sleeveless tee-shirt with a deep

V-neckline, tight-fitting bright green shorts and some kind of cheap slip-on sandals with a huge plastic flower or something on the strap across her toes. That and wrists full of bangles, all cheap, and more rings than a phone, everything from the diamond Al had given her to a plastic jobbie that looked to be out of a box of CrackerJacks. Caught in the pinch between her breasts was a package of cigarettes and a cheap throwaway lighter. And the less blessed need pockets!

The kids were cooking eggs. It was hard to tell if they were supposed to be fried or scrambled but the biggest black frying pan was full of something yellowish with white stripes and clumps. Colleen looked at the stove, then at the table, and left them to it. She went to the back add-on to do her washing.

The washing machine was less than a year old, the biggest model made, supposed to be commercial quality. Norm had shown up with it one Sunday afternoon. He backed his truck to the door, then he and three bozos not seen before nor since had off-loaded it and set it in place. By noon the next day it was installed and not one question about its origins or price had ever been asked. There were no instruction booklets and no warranty papers, just the machine.

Colleen didn't want to have to pretend anything, and with Maude in the kitchen packing away eggs, Jewen already vanished somewhere (god knows where), Singe in the living room with the TV tuned to a boxing match—she could hear the noise of it clear at the other end of the house—there was really nowhere to go without having to pretend to be interested in conversation. So she knocked the collection of jackets, tractor hats and general mess off the wooden chair and sat there, watching out the open back door as the western sky streaked with twilight and the first of the mouse-sized bats began to flutter, harvesting mosquitoes. "Good crop this year, Battinella," she muttered. Just watching them made her arms itch and her scalp creep. Bugs!

After a while she got off the chair and went to find something to read. She would have preferred to open her briefcase and go over the research material, but that would be like inviting the entire assemblage out to see what she was doing. You could count on it, one of the immutable laws of the universe: the more important the task, the more unhelpful the interruptions.

She got the dog-eared copy of *Lonesome Dove*, her cigarettes and lighter, and a cup of tea and went back to her chair near the washing machine. She hadn't seen any sign of an ashtray, so she used the lid of a jar. She opened the pocket book near the middle, riffled pages until she got to the place where Blue Duck kidnapped the pathetic blond and Gus went off like one of the Round Table knights to bring her back. The beautiful thing about *Lonesome Dove* was once you'd read it from front to back you could dip in just about any old where and get sucked into the magic. She'd even seen Jessie reading it, and god knows anything that held a kid's attention for much longer than seventeen seconds ought to be government subsidized.

She read until it was time to take out the first load and put in the second. Then she hung her underwear, bras, shirts, blouses and socks on the line; they'd be ready to haul in and put in the freezer when she got up, and she could take them out and iron what needed it when she got home from work. If she just left them on the line, Darlene would pick through them when she got out of bed, and there'd be the whole thing to go through all over again.

By the time she went to bed her jeans were washed and on the line, the kids were in the living room with the TV, Jewen was still off wherever it was he'd gone, Singe had left the house, probably to go either to his woman's place or out pit-lamping again, and Maude was heavily into a quart of shine. It was shine and her thirst for it had started her on her silly doings, and it was the silly doings why Al had gone away. His leaving greased the downward slide and everyone knew it, most of all Maude, and so that made her feel so guilty and defensive she drank even more of the vile stuff. Well, Al would be home soon, and maybe that would put Maude back on the right track. You never know. Damn near anything is possible in life.

🏃

The clothes were off the line, rolled into bundles and stored inside a plastic garbage bag in the freezer. Colleen was breakfasted, washed, brushed, face on, and dressed for work, having one last coffee and cigarette on the front porch, when the first hint of a vertically rising balloon got out of bed and wandered into the kitchen, hair rumpled, dressing gown more open than shut.

"Who'n hell made all the mess in here?" Darlene grumbled. "Where are the clean coffee cups? And why are all those kids sleepin' in their clothes on the floor in the living room with that damn TV still playing?"

"And good morning to you, too," Colleen answered. "You'll probably have to wash yourself a cup, I know I had to."

"And you couldn't do three or four of them while you were doing yours?"

"I didn't need three or four of them, I only needed this one. Why didn't you clean up when you got in last night?"

"I didn't want to wake up the whole damn house is why."

"Right. And turning off the TV might have done that."

"What's with you, your PMS out of control or something?"

"Ah, yes, PMS, that's what I get one or two days a month that allows me to behave the way you do all the time."

A tall, broad-shouldered guy with hair past his shoulders and two gold studs in one ear came onto the porch with two mugs of coffee, one of which he handed to Darlene. He was barefoot and wearing faded jeans that showed just about every crease, swelling and hair follicle. "Mornin'," he drawled, and kissed Darlene on the neck. "Didn't know what you took in yours so I made it same as mine: bit of cream, touch of sugar."

"Just dip your finger in it, darlin'," Darlene flirted. "You're sweet enough to fix 'er up just right."

"I'm Greg," he said, smiling at Colleen.

"How nice for you." She smiled back, got up, took her mug to the sink, rinsed it and picked up her briefcase.

"What did you do with the laundry?" Darlene asked.

"It's in the freezer," Colleen answered. "I'll iron when I get home."

"In the freezer? Jesus christ! That's about the weirdest damn thing I've ever heard of anyone doing. I guess you rolled it all up so by now it's wrinkly and damp and, of course, it'll be colder 'n a polar bear's arse."

"See you."

"Jeez." Darlene shook her head as if tested beyond all powers of endurance. "I was gonna wear the pink shirt, too."

When Colleen came home from work the balloon was well up. Her bedclothes were on the floor, her mattress tipped off the frame, and the blue steamer trunk was half out of the cubicle, the hasp scratched and dented, but still shut tight. Darlene was still at home, and she looked as if she was just waiting for the chance to explode.

"You're a selfish bitch, you know that?"

"Really. Thank you for sharing."

"That's a goddamn cheap trick, that tin thing. It's insulting is what it is."

"So how did my mattress wind up dumped?"

"I was looking for the key!"

"Did it ever occur to you if I wanted you to have a key to *my* trunk I would have given you one? There's nothing of yours in it. Just *my* stuff."

"'My stuff my stuff my stuff', that's all anyone's heard from you since you were about five years old, 'mine, mine, gimme mine'. Anyone else around here'll share anything they've got, but not you!"

"Nobody around here has much of anything I'd want to share, thank you." Colleen moved to flip the mattress back onto the frame and Darlene took a swing at her. It missed, and so did the second one.

"Oh well," Colleen glared, "after all, it's the thought that counts, right?"

"You," Darlene hissed, "you and your fancy job in that fancy office with all those fancy townies. You and your steady paycheque and your good wages and enough money to buy decent clothes. You make me sick."

"No, I make you jealous. You're the one quit school in the middle of grade ten, you're the one didn't bother to get any kind of real training, you're the one said you were here for a good time not a long time, you're the one who made all the choices that put you where you are today. You didn't ask me before you jumped into the soup, don't ask me now that you find it isn't what you thought it would be."

"One day you're going to get what you deserve."

"Jesus christ, I hope it's soon!" Colleen laughed freely. "I mean I don't deserve to wind up being the only one making supper most of the time, or the one looking after other people's kids or the one whose clothes get used, filthied and left in a heap on the floor, and who else ever pays the cleaning bill or does the laundry and how come all you do is piss your life away and expect me to clean up for you and buy vitamin pills for the kid you had, seemingly all by yourself. I hope I *do* get what I deserve because I deserve a helluva lot more than what I've been getting around here, and I deserve something better than to buy tons of groceries for other people to eat and then not clean up after themselves!"

"Fuck you, Colleen," Darlene said clearly, and she walked out of the house wearing Colleen's jeans, the pink shirt she'd obviously ironed, and a pair of Colleen's clean white cotton socks. At least she had on her own sneakers and her own jewellery, although some of the makeup probably had been taken without permission.

Colleen got supper on the go and cleaned up the mess in the kitchen, scrubbed the spilled egg, spilled ketchup and spilled juice off the kitchen table, and, when the wood was dry, she took the time to quickly spread a coat of floor wax on it. The table had started off in life as a door and it sat on the sturdy chrome legs of what had been the old woman's kitchen table until Al and Bob Martin got into a go-round and smashed the top. They needed a table, and needed one fast, so Singe removed the legs, straightened the bent one, and took the door off the hinges of the upstairs bedroom. A few strategically placed bolts and there it was, and what had been intended to be temporary had become a fixture.

Colleen had to use the coiled wire scrubber to get the plates properly clean, and the two compost buckets were so full she couldn't help but dribble some of it on the floor when she took the buckets up to the hens. They were supposed to be in the hen yard, but of course they weren't, they were scratching at a punky log just inside the treeline behind the coop. She opened the gate to their pen and emptied the buckets, then went into the coop to check the hanging feeders. No wonder they were scrabbling for termites: there wasn't a grain of food in the bin.

She filled their feeder with laying pellets, checked the water supply, then went back outside, wiped her shoes carefully on a clump of quack grass and closed the gate. Some of the hens had already gone into the coop after the pellets, others were busy at the compost. She opened the coop door, looked in again, counted, then closed it and counted the hens in the pen. There seemed to be just about twice as many as usual. She couldn't recall them having any barred Rocks but there seemed to be at least a dozen of them, really big ones, too. Maybe they weren't barred Rocks, maybe they just looked like them.

She rinsed the compost pails and took them back to the house, finished tidying the kitchen, then drained the spuds, made herself a big salad, and cut three slices of the mammoth meat loaf. The rest she left for the kids to warm up when they got home from wherever they were.

She ate supper on the back porch, loving the quiet, imagining herself some sort of sponge, soaking up solitude instead of water. If it took so much constant tidying and cleaning to keep the kitchen from being a health hazard, what in god's name did the bedrooms look like?

She had her ironing done and either folded neatly or hanging in her blue tin trunk before the rest of them came thundering back. She made sure Jewen sat down and ate some supper and tried hard to ignore Maude's constant nagging at the kids. You'd think a mother could do more for her kids than just plunk herself down at the table and smoke cigarettes until the kids heated up some supper and handed it to her.

The kids took their plates to the living room, turned on the TV and pretended they couldn't hear Maude yelling for someone to refill her plate. Finally, she yarded herself up off the chair and went to the stove to get more for herself. Then she bitched because all the warmed-up spuds were gone and she had to get some cold ones from the big pot and put them on to heat. Scowling, she left the frying pan and went to get a glass. Then she had to go into the pantry to find a jug of shine. By the time she got back to the kitchen with her jug, the kids had raided the frying pan and taken all but the last slice of meat loaf.

"Got no goddamn manners at all you buggers," Maude screeched, scraping the last spuds from the frying pan and spearing the last slice for herself.

"Did you get enough to eat, Jewen?" Colleen asked softly.

"I'm going to have to shove it down to finish what's on my plate. I don't eat much," he added unnecessarily.

"I want to borrow your car," Maude said suddenly.

"I'm sure you do but you aren't going to. You're already half packed, and I don't need my car racked up, because I need it for work."

"Cheap slut."

"Not cheap," said Colleen, laughing.

"And not a slut." Jewen's voice was hard-edged, his eyes slitted. "You watch your fuckin' mouth, Maude."

"Whole damn family's crabby," Maude told the sugar bowl. "Well, I want to go out for a while, and the pickup's gone."

"Singe has it," Jewen answered. "It's his, after all."

"Well, then, where's the damn hearse?"

"Not in my pocket." Colleen yawned. "Hey," she called, "if you kids want me to do the dishes, you bring them here; otherwise *you're* going to wind up pearl diving."

They moved immediately. Colleen filled the sink, washed the dishes and left them on the drainboard for god to dry. Jewen went to the living room and stretched out on the floor, a cushion from the couch under his head. The kids sprawled beside and even on him, watching his choice of programme because they knew he wasn't going to watch theirs, and if they changed channels he'd turn off the TV and they'd be s.o.l.

🐦

Colleen wakened early, puzzled by the unfamiliar rumble. She hurried out of bed and ran to the kitchen, looked out the window over the sink. She gave a short harsh laugh, shook her head and turned on the coffee maker. The rumble eased, became some loud coughing, smoke or exhaust belched from an upright pipe-looking thing, and the earth mover jerked, then was silent. Singeon got down off the seat and moved toward the house.

He didn't come directly inside, he went around to the front. Colleen heard voices, then the front screen door banged open, and Singe and the hunk came in with two big cardboard boxes each.

"Just leave 'em near the door here," Singe told the stud, "and I'll put 'em away in the pantry later on. Hi, Colly, is that coffee I smell?"

"It is so." She moved to him and cuddled against his chest, enjoying the warm scent of him. "What are you doing out and around this early in the morning? Pee the bed again?"

"Lucy sent over the canning." He tapped his big boot against a corner of a box. "She put some fish in there, too; sort of a trade, you might say."

"God, she's good to us."

"She's a good-hearted woman," Singe agreed. He looked toward the living room and sucked his teeth. "Don't those rug rats ever sleep in their beds? And what the hell is Jewen doing on the floor?"

"Looks to me like he's sleeping."

"I am like hell," Jewen mumbled. "Too fuckin' much noise around here for a guy to die, let alone sleep."

They sat at the table with coffee and toast, and the kids slept on as if drugged.

"Lucy's brother's coming over after a bit," Singeon said, spreading peanut butter thickly. "He's gonna help figure out the best place for your shack. He says you have to watch where the light comes from and goes to, and you have to get yourself set at the right angle for the winds or you wind up with a dark, drafty, gloomy place. He's got this riggin's kind of like a compass that he can figure with."

"More like a cross between a compass and a light metre," the hunk said.

"Do you have a name?" Colleen blurted.

"Sure I do. It's Tony."

When Colleen left for work, Tony the hunk and Singe were drinking coffee and staring at the earth mover as if their eyeballs could inspire the rusty beast to do all the work for them. The kids were still asleep, Jewen was having breakfast, Maude seemed to have dropped off the face of the earth, and Darlene was still curled up in bed with Greg. Colleen was glad she wouldn't be there when Tony tumbled to the fact someone else was where he so recently had been. She hoped they didn't put each other in hospital.

On her way home she passed two firewood trucks heading away from the place. She didn't know the names of the drivers, but recognized them as relatives of Lucy's. They waved and honked. She replied, and slowed for the turn from the road to the tangle of grass that could have been a lawn if any of them cared enough to cut the grass, water the grass, fertilize the grass, fuss over the grass, level the area, reseed the bald patches and generally fixate and obsess.

She got out of her car staring, amazed. The clump of alders was gone, not even the stumps remained. They were piled off to one side, well clear of everything, and where they had been the ground was levelled. Down where the second-growth fir grew, a log truck was parked and a loader was carefully stacking logs. Jewen was there, too, in his caulk boots, his wide suspenders holding up the specially padded safety jeans that protected him from accidental slashes with the chainsaw. He had his hard hat pushed back and a plug of snoose under his bottom lip, while beside him his cherished Stihl waited. He was grinning widely at something the loader operator said and looked so much like his old self Colleen could have wept.

She moved to where Singe was signing papers of some kind, which he then passed to a guy in clean but well-worn jeans and a tight-fitting dark blue tee-shirt. The guy signed, he and Singe shook hands, then both of them grinned, satisfied.

"My heavens," she managed when she had picked her way across the cleared dirt and was standing beside Singeon, "you certainly move fast."

"Speedy Singe, that's what they call me," he agreed. "Except the women, they have another name for me." He winked, as good as daring her to respond.

"I've heard that one, too," she said gravely, "but you aren't to worry, darlin', because we've found a doctor who can fix it for you."

"So we're on our way." Singe hugged her one-armed. "Bryson's mill is trading us the dimensional and plywood we need in return for three loads of that second-growth. They wanted the first-growth, of course, but I told them not a chance, we need them for seed trees. We can get the flooring and window frames the same way, door frames, too, probably."

"You're a genius."

"Nah, I'm just a tinker, like all the ancestors."

Their old man would have slapped him for that. He had convinced himself they were directly descended from the House of Lancaster, with strong ties to nobility. How many times had he held forth about power and the abuse of power and how the laws of inheritance could be manipulated. He even had a story, probably one he made up himself, about the rightful heir being falsely accused of a crime, and how he had to flee in the night to save his neck, and when he returned twenty years later he found his sister's husband had taken everything, even the name Lancaster. Rather than dig up old bones and break his sister's heart all over again, he just went back to the docks and booked return passage. Of course, the old woman had another version of the story, one that involved a pick-pocket who struck it rich, then wisely decided to leave the old country on a colonist ship because the police were hot on her tail for several other crimes. She used the name because it was embroidered on the soft leather purse she'd lifted. Every time the old man told his version, the old woman offered hers, and the old man would sit glaring at her, as if any of it mattered.

Colleen changed her clothes, went out into the garden and picked a good feed of green beans, and dug another pile of fresh new spuds. Some of them were too small to make even a bite, but she took them anyway. Someone had taken a roast from the freezer and put it to thaw, but then been too busy to remember to put it in the oven, and if she put it in now it would be midnight before they sat down to dinner. She scrubbed the spuds and put them on to cook, got the beans ready, emptied a package of frozen corn into a pot, then used the wickedly sharp knife to cut the roast into steaks. She sprinkled every one of them with garlic powder and dabbed Szechuan sauce on them, then went out back to fire up the propane barbecue.

She cooked two steaks each, and everyone ate as if it had been a week since they last saw food. Jewen just packed it away; the day's work had taken him out the other side of his toot. He'd be fine now, until next time. The doctors wanted him on special medication and he wouldn't hear tell of it, so short of locking him up and shoving suppositories up the old fundament, there was nothing anyone could do except wait for him to bottom out so completely he became as worried and desperate as the rest of them were for him.

They ate in the living room, watching the evening news, the men sitting in their grey wool sock feet, their caulk boots at the back door. Even Tony the stud was wearing work socks; he must have borrowed them from Singe, or maybe even Jewen.

They weren't really paying a lot of attention to the TV news; it came from one of the city stations and the way it presented things you'd think the city was the only place in the entire province. Besides, the station had some kind of policy about a soft news item for every hard one, so you only heard about a few of the major crimes and then you had to sit through these feel-good bullshitty things like the baby woodpecker living in the bell tower of the Anglican cathedral or the woman whose pug dog had won top honours at a show in Coeur d'Alene. There would be some camouflaged advertising like the guy who came on to let you know all about the great deals in the travel agent industry, complete with little clips of people lying on tropical beaches or hiking wide smooth paths in the Alps.

"Jesus christ!" Jewen exclaimed. "Look at the fuckin' loot!"

They looked, and then they stared. The voice-over was telling about a drug bust and how they hadn't really caught any suspects, but their investigation had led them to a warehouse in the industrial district, and when they went inside they found a state-of-the-art production line for making methamphetamines and for turning cocaine into crack. They also found, neatly stacked in a broom closet, bundles and more bundles of money.

"Oh my god," Colleen exclaimed. "Why would they just leave it lying around like that?"

"How do you walk into a bank with a million three hundred fifty thousand dollars and say, 'Oh, by the way, I'd like to make a cash deposit'?" Tony laughed. "They'd have cops crawlin' all over you. Nobody uses money anymore, it's all plastic."

"Whack of loot like that you could open your own damn bank," Jewen sighed. "Now what happens to it? Cops keep it, I suppose. Or the feds take it. What a waste. Give me some of it and see how much fun I have."

A spokesperson for the cops came on and talked about the drug trade in the city and the constant efforts the police were making to try to stop it. She seemed to think the cops were winning the war, but the reporter, when it was her turn, was of the opinion even a big bust like the one in the report was a mere inconvenience to the drug lords. She said the police admitted they had been led to the haul by an anonymous telephone tip and—her face and voice became even more serious, too serious, an example of truly poor acting—the word on the street was a rival mob had been responsible and a drug war was imminent.

"She should use some of that damn money to go to acting school," Singe laughed. "The word on the street, my foot; that little dolly wouldn't last two minutes on the street. Someone would put her between two slices of bread and eat her for a sandwich."

The men drank beer and watched the rest of the news, but Colleen really wasn't interested in sports or weather, so she took the plates and cutlery to the kitchen and did the dishes. There were plenty of cooked spuds in the big stainless steel pot and plenty of vegetables to warm up, and she was sure the kids could find a way to cook the steaks she'd set aside for them. She put everything away, cleaned up, then went out and looked over at where her own place was going to go. That would be nice. More than nice. And nobody, except maybe Singe or Jewen, was going inside it once it was finished. She'd have her own hydro and metre, she'd maybe even have a phone, and nobody was using it, especially not for long distance, and what's more she wouldn't let anybody know her number, either.

They hadn't had a phone in over two years. Colleen had grown sick and tired of paying off the long-distance charges racked up by Darlene and Maude, and had just not paid the bill anymore. Singe almost did, but she took him aside and explained about how Darlene and Maude promised and promised and never delivered, and she showed him some of the calls, half an hour to Langley, an hour and fifteen minutes to Duncan. Singe agreed with her and didn't pay the bill, so the day came when it didn't work, not out, not in. Maude had screeched and yelled a bit but shut up when Singe said the whole thing could be ironed out if she just went into town and paid her bill. She shut up then, and Darlene, for a change, had sense enough not to even go there.

She'd have a security system of some kind, maybe deadbolts or something, and when she was at work the place would be locked tight. She could read without her book going missing between chapter six and chapter seven and then, when it resurfaced, be as good as wrecked. One time someone, she never did find out who, swiped her book and when she next saw it, the swollen mess was still wet; it had obviously been dropped in the bathtub.

The guys came out of the living room, put on their work boots and headed outside again. She followed, but there wasn't much she could do to help, so she went to the garden to pull some weeds. Tony got on the earth mover and, after a brief conversation with Singe, headed for the slag heap. He filled his bucket, took the slag to the driveway and dumped it, spreading it with the tipped bucket.

The old man's grandpa got the place for next to nothing because of the slag heaps and the rabbit warren of mine shafts and tunnels running god alone knows where beneath the surface. Of course, at the time, people said he was crazier than a bedbug: what if one of the tunnels collapsed and the house sank into the hole, what then, and what if someone got into the tunnels and got bad gas or lost and couldn't be found. None of it had happened, probably never would, and now, of course, entire subdivisions in town were built on less stable ground and nobody was having fits about that.

The original place was only five acres, but over the years other bits had been bought up and now they had more than two hundred acres of bush with more damn slag heaps than they'd been able to count. There was always some bright bunny wanting to buy a chunk for a trailer court or a subdivision or a motel or something but nobody was interested in selling. The taxes were starting to be a pain, though, and you could guarantee she and Singe would be the only ones picking up that tab. Well, maybe Jewen if he happened to be in good shape at the time the bill came.

She made sure there was plenty of hot water for the guys to bath or shower, and got herself out of their way before they came in. She even baked two rhubarb pies and left them out where they could find them; they'd be sure to be peckish by the time they got finished playing Tonka with the big toys.

She didn't hear the kids come in, she didn't hear Maude and Wotzisname come in, she didn't even hear Darlene and Greg. She was sound asleep and stayed that way until nearly ten in the morning.

Weekends were the reward as far as she was concerned. She could lie in bed and yawn or she could get up and wander around with coffee in a mug. Sometimes she got up and got dressed, then drove off for an entire day without voices and other people's cheeky faces. But, of course, she was just about the only one who had the kind of schedule that paid attention to weekends, and what wakened her at ten was the snarl of Jewen's chainsaw. She tried to ignore it, but couldn't. She was just getting out of bed when the heartwood screeched, then the tree fell and the house shook.

Darlene was even less enchanted with the industrious notions of the ones busy with saws, loaders and earth movers. She came out of bed less than fifteen minutes later, and the steam was coming from her ears. By then, Colleen was dressed and had a fresh pot of coffee, which she had taken outside, with mugs and fixin's, for the workies. Jewen had two trees down by then and Tony the stud was learning about bucking off the branches and tops. The driveway was more or less smoothed out, the relocated slag glittering in the morning light, and a good six inches of the stuff was spread where the shack was due to go.

"You guys got no damn consideration at all!" Darlene yelled. "I didn't even get off shift until past two last night, and here it is barely ten-thirty and all hell's bust loose!"

"Good mornin' darlin'." Singe smiled. He finished rolling his cigarette and scratched a match with his thumbnail.

"Don't bloody bother with 'good mornin' darlin'!' You, all of you, got your nerve, I'll tell you. Cuttin' down trees without askin' other people how they feel about it, cartin' 'em off without so much as a by-your-leave, roarsy roarsy with the noisiest damn front-end loader I ever heard and what for? So's little missy gooder'n all can have her a house! *She* don't own this whole entire place, you know!

It ain't up to *her* to decide to cut down good fir trees. You never made no move to build *me* no damn house!"

"You never said you wanted one," Singe said mildly. "I ain't no mind reader. If you want one, just say so and we'll get started on 'er when this is finished."

"What are *you* grinning at, you big ape?"

"Me?" Tony smiled gently. "I'm just enjoying this fine morning is all I'm doing. Sun shining, breeze blowing soft and gentle, the smell of fresh-cut fir like perfume in the air, and us with a nice pot of coffee and the hope of some fresh biscuits before long."

"You want biscuits, you make 'em yourself, I sure as hell ain't going to."

"Oh, I figured that much." Tony's smile widened. "I haven't any reason to suspect you even know how to cook, much less bake. But what you do do, you do real good, pretty lady."

"You're as crazy as the rest'a them," she replied, but most of her steam was vented.

Greg came out of the house with his hair combed and still damp, his tee-shirt tucked into his jeans. He smiled at everyone and poured two mugs of coffee from the pot, handed one to Darlene who sipped it, no cream no sugar, then shuddered.

"Christ, baby," she managed.

But Greg was staring at Tony as if challenging him. Tony just smiled and sipped his own coffee. Greg kept eyeballing, proddy as a banty rooster; he did everything except puff out his chest, lower his wings and parade. Darlene smiled and moved to the fixings to doctor her coffee. Colleen supposed she'd be prideful for days if the two guys got into it over her.

Singe watched the interplay, then looked at Jewen and winked. Jewen laughed, and Tony looked over at him, then shrugged.

"Well," he put his half full mug on the picnic table. "I guess I'm not getting anything done standing here doing nothing." And he turned away.

Singe and Jewen put down their mugs and moved back to work; Colleen picked up the empty mugs and the cookie sheet with the fixin's on it and went into the kitchen to get started on the biscuits. Maybe she'd do some cinnamon buns, too, the kids always liked them. And what in hell had Greg been trying to kick off, anyway? A blind man could see he wouldn't stand a chance in a go-round with the hunk, who looked as if all he had to do was reach out and squeeze Greg's curly little head. All that over someone he barely even knew and hadn't yet had time to begin to feel for very deeply. Too strange.

Colleen not only made enough biscuits to feed an orphanage, she made a big pot of eggs scrambled with onion, garlic, chopped sweet red peppers and a touch of curry. Of course, Darlene bitched about the curry, but Singeon loved eggs that way and only got them when Colleen made them for him because Lucy went into hives and red welts if she was anywhere near curry powder.

The kids were stuffing themselves on eggs and cinnamon buns when the guys came in to wash up and take their places at the table. Greg stayed on the front porch, separating himself from the family, obviously very aware he was a stranger. But not Tony: he bellied up to the meal with the others, laughing and joking, as if he'd been born in the back bedroom. Well, why not, he was working with them. That changed his status completely.

"Tommy, take a plate of eggs and a couple of buttered biscuits out to chummy on the front porch, please," Colleen suggested.

"Why me?" Tommy whined.

"Because your Auntie Darlene's got her hands full with her own plate, and if you don't do it you won't get anything else to eat," Singe said quietly.

"But I haven't finished . . ."

"And you won't if you don't get your lazy little arse up off the chair and do something for the auntie who put all this food together for you."

Tommy got off the chair mere seconds before Jewen swung a backhand that, had it connected, would have sent the kid to the floor. As it was, the slap hit him on the hip and lurched him sideways.

"I'm tired of your fuckin' lip." Jewen sounded as if he was saying hello to the local priest. "Do what you were asked to do and then after breakfast you 'n' me's having us a talk."

Tommy scurried to his task, and was back in seconds, but he seemed to have lost the edge off his appetite. The other kids were very quiet, especially after Dorrit asked where Auntie Maude was and nobody answered.

When Jewen had finished breakfast he rose, tapped Tommy on the shoulder, and they both left the kitchen. Jewen put on his work boots, and Tommy stood, looking as if he was waiting for the blindfold and last cigarette.

"We'll do the dishes," Jessie uttered.

"Why, thank you, lover." Singeon smiled. "And when you've got them done and the kitchen tidied, you can have some lessons on how to handle the earth mover, right, Tony?"

"For sure, need all the help I can get," Tony agreed, reaching for another cinnamon bun. "Ma'am," he smiled at Colleen, "I want you to know I have never, not in my whole entire life, had such good cinnamon buns. I appreciate the effort you made and the time you took."

"Why, thank you." Colleen practically gaped.

She helped the kids with the kitchen and took the compost up to the hens. When she had emptied it, she rinsed the bucket at the rusty tap on the side of the coop and went in to pick up eggs. She counted them as she picked them from the laying boxes. Either someone had forgotten to pick them up for a day or two or there was something new in the laying pellets.

Tommy had a chainsaw in his hand, and it was going, but once Colleen had swallowed her heart again, she realized the kid was being very carefully supervised by Jewen. The other kids stood watching, envious, as Tommy cut off the top of a tree and started stripping off the branches.

"If any of you want to come to the supermarket with me," she offered, "you get yourselves washed up and into some clean clothes."

She took the pickup because with three kids in the pop can there wouldn't be enough room for groceries to make the trip worthwhile. She stopped at the Dairy Queen for cones for them, stopped at the feed store for laying pellets for the hens, and stopped at the day-old for a whack of bread. The kids pestered her so much she bought a big box of donuts, too. The box said bananas, but when she checked the packages tumbled in it, they were all donuts, some of them cream filled. She couldn't understand why more people didn't go there; you could get more perfectly good food for ten dollars than you'd get for fifty in the supermarket.

She left more than fifty dollars in the supermarket, though. She bought the ultra giant-sized cereals and detergents; she got all her pasta and rice at the bulk bins; she had her discount coupons all ready; she bought generic brands; and still she left two hundred plus at the checkout. She stopped at the beer store on the way home; if they were going to be working today they'd need something, and it promised to be just about as hot as the outer hobs of hell. She also got four plastic bags of ice cubes because there was no way the little trays in the freezer were going to be able to keep up to the temperature.

Lucy's cousins—or uncles, or brothers or whatever—were busy at the alder clump. They had two firewood trucks in place and what looked like the Royal Winnipeg Ballet at work. She supposed they'd all done this often enough they knew exactly what and where, how and why, and could do it in their sleep. Two guys, stripped to the waist and sweating heavily, were busy with sledge hammers and wood wedges, breaking the rounds into halves, then quarters. Another fellow was working with a splitting maul, chopping the quarters into regular sizes, and the rest of them were slinging the pieces into the backs of the trucks. All they needed was an orchestra to put it all to music.

Colleen went to the back of the pickup and got two bags of groceries and headed for the front door with them, knowing the kids would have sense enough to bring in the rest. The kitchen was still reasonably neat, and while the kids put away the packages and boxes, Colleen started turning some of the loaves of day-old into sandwiches. She got two quarts of the salmon Lucy had sent over, chopped green onion into it, added some mayo and mixed. Then she started dealing out bread slices like a riverboat gambler laying cards.

Dorrit got the soft margarine and spread the bread, Little Wilma pulled over a chair so she could get up on it and start spooning salmon mix onto the slices, and Jessie finished the last of the grocery stocking.

Colleen got a water bucket, poured half a bag of ice cubes in it, then ripped open a case of beer and stuck the bottles in the ice. Some more cubes, some more beer, some more cubes, and now it weighed so much she'd have to get someone to help her carry it to the back door. "I did this whole thing bass ackwards," she confessed. "Talk about not using your head to save your back."

Jessie tried to help but they just got in each other's way and almost dumped the whole thing. Colleen shrugged, she didn't think she'd have trouble finding muscles to move it. She stacked sandwiches in a brown supermarket bag and got that ready, then mixed up a big jug of frozen juice for the kids. "Shall we see how long it takes to make all this vanish? It'll be like a magic act on TV."

And it was. They no more than stepped out the back door than the guys surged at them, wide grins on their faces. Singe slowed when one of the kids spoke, then he nodded and went into the house, coming out with the big bucket of beer.

Tommy looked just about ready to fall out of his sneakers. She would be willing to bet he felt as if his knuckles were ready to drag in the slag. Jewen had been working him the way the old man had worked everyone.

"Here, sweetheart." She handed Tom a big glass of cold juice. "Don't guzzle it, you'll get stomach cramps. And here's a sammy-sammich. You sit here in the shade."

"Thank you, Auntie." He looked at her, his eyes brimming suddenly, and to save him the embarrassment, she leaned forward, held his head in her hands and kissed the tears from his eyes.

"You're a good boy, Tom," she said clearly. "Your dad will be proud."

Tom as good as dropped boneless to the back step, sipping his juice, holding the sandwich as if he had forgotten about it. Colleen remembered that deep-boned tiredness and wished Jewen would lay off a bit, give the kid some slack. On the other hand, Tom certainly had been overdue for it. She couldn't remember any of them acting as if life owed them everything. She couldn't remember feeling or thinking that all she had to do was swan around being whoever she thought she'd be for the day and everything would just fall in place for her. The old man had put each of them to work, hard work, as soon as they were big enough, and his idea of big enough was fierce.

By the time the old fart had offed himself, Colleen had little hard lumps—pre-calluses—on her palms from using a hoe, and she had already chopped open her leg with the firewood axe. So how had Tommy grown up to be lippy and lazy, unwilling to see what needed doing and even more unwilling to do what was pointed out to him? Well, so far today Jewen had made it clear to the kid just how much hard work a person had to do to qualify for a glass of juice and a sandwich, let alone well-cooked meals with seconds and thirds. Maybe the old man had been onto something.

Just beyond the back steps, still in the shade of the overhanging roof, was a big green plastic garbage can, and in it, half a dozen salmon. She smiled, and one of Lucy's relatives nodded. Tommy was leaning back against the side of the house, his eyelids fluttering. Jewen leaned over, took the empty glass and set it aside, took the sandwich before it dropped, then pulled the boy sideways, to lean against him. The old man never would have done something that soft; he'd have razzed the kid about not being as tough as he'd thought he was. The change in position partially roused Tom; he tried to straighten and couldn't. He managed to murmur, "Uncle," and Jewen just patted the boy's leg, then gently rubbed his knee. Tom's eyes closed again, and Jewen continued eating, as if nothing much had happened.

Over where her house was to go the retainer forms were in place, and someone had made a half-dozen spreaders, alder saplings to which had been nailed a plank.

"Seaside Cement's coming this afternoon," Singe said quietly. "They said ha' past two, give or take. Maybe you could have the tads at the creek at that time, don't want to incorporate one of them into the concrete."

She was going to ask about Tommy—if he would be allowed to go—but she made herself bite her tongue. Either Jewen would relent or he wouldn't, and nothing she could say or do would make anything any better, or easier for the boy; in fact, she could only make things worse.

She took a couple of the fish into the house knowing someone would bring in the rest for her. By the time she had the heads off and the guts in the basin, the clean garbage can was near to hand. "Thank you," she said to whoever had brought it in.

"You're welcome." It was the voice of Tony the hunk. "Those were really good sandwiches. Best fish I've had, ever."

"Singeon's woman Lucy canned it up. She's wonderful. She puts a squeeze of lemon juice in with it, not enough to identify or even really notice, but it sure does waken up the taste buds."

They brought in the bucket of ice cubes and the remaining half-dozen beer. She put the beer in the fridge, drained the meltwater from the cubes and put them, bucket and all, in the freezer for later. She might have to whack at them with the hatchet to break up the lumps, but hopefully not.

The kids took the heads, tails and guts up to the hens, and when they came back, the fish were filleted and the backbones and ribs ready to take up, too.

"Be careful, the air will be full of wasps by now," she cautioned.

"Tommy's sleepin' on the back step," Little Wilma confided.

"Don't step on him, then."

"He's still sittin' up."

"Uncle Singe ate Tommy's sammich," Dorrit tattled.

"We'll make another one for Tommy, don't worry."

She put the salmon fillets in the big bread bowl to marinate, scrubbed the fish smell from her hands, and cleaned the sink thoroughly. She didn't want fish-tinged spuds for supper.

By one-thirty the huge pot of rice was cooked and cooling, the two big pots of spuds were cooked, and four dozen bread buns were on the rise. Tommy was awake, full of sandwich and juice, and back with the work crew, dragging branches and tops to the burn piles.

"You kids hurry up, and I'll take you for a quick dip," Colleen said. They scattered like baby quail. She went to the back door and waved at Singe; he nodded and said something to Jewen, who turned and said something to Tom. Tom looked at Jewen and then nodded. He didn't race for the house; he made sure he put the awkward branch on the pile before quitting the crew.

When they got back from the creek, Tommy looked as if he might survive his first day of real work, and the other kids were starting to flag. Colleen had four more cases of beer to put on ice. The cement was poured and levelled, Tony spraying it with the hose.

"Why's he doin' that?" Dorrit asked. "I thought it was s'posed ta dry."

"It will," said Colleen. She was thinking of Tommy; he seemed different, but maybe she only hoped he was. "If it dries too fast, though, it'll crack and go all crumbly. They'll leave the hose trickling on it until nighttime, maybe even tomorrow."

"How'll it dry?"

"From the bottom up. Towels on the line, please." Colleen really didn't understand the whole setting of cement thing herself, and she was sure Dorrit was just more confused than ever.

There wasn't much more could be done until the pad was ready, so the men concentrated on the burn piles while Colleen made supper. The spuds were wrapped in foil with plenty of butter and green onion and put on the rack above the barbecue grill to heat. The rice she fried with plenty of pod peas and green onion, chive and chopped peppers, and the buns came out of the oven at exactly the right time. "Someone go tell them to wash up and get their plates." She didn't set the table, just piled plates and cutlery for them to serve themselves while she concentrated on the fish.

When the dishes were done, the kitchen tidied, and everyone was sitting on the porch, with beer for the adults and pop for the kids, Colleen realized she was tired and her legs ached.

"The front yard looks great," she said, laughing softly, "but don't you think it would be easier if we just planted it to grass and got a ride-on mower?"

They grinned and sipped beer, looking at the evidence of their hard work. The ground was cleared of debris, the burn piles neatly lined up to wait for the rains of fall. Nobody would dare light them up in the summer: the entire district would turn to ash. Most of the slag heap was spread out, mixed with the sawdust and chips; the dust had settled and the smell of fresh-cut wood came to them on the cooling evening air.

"I'm going to bed, Auntie," Tommy announced, yawning. "I think I'm falling asleep sitting here."

"See you in the morning, Tommy."

"Sleep good, Tom."

"Thank you, Uncle Singe."

"Day off tomorrow," Jewen said. "Maybe go do a bit of fishin'. Wanna come?"

"Me?" asked Tom. "Love to, Uncle!"

"I'll give you a shake. If you wake up, fine, if you don't, that's fine, too."

Colleen awoke in the big old relic of a chair on the porch. Someone had put a crocheted afghan over her; someone else had lit the citronella candle to keep the mosquitoes at bay. She blew out the candle, then took the afghan with her when she went into the house. She didn't bother undressing and getting into bed, she just kicked off her sneaks, lay on top of her covers, afghan over her shoulders and bare arms, and plunged deep into sleep again.

CHAPTER TWO

The Net Loft was so crowded the fire marshall would have had a fit, if the fire marshall had been able to get through the door. The crush made it hard to clear tables, serve drinks, carry trays, and impossible to avoid the slaps on the rump and the strokes along her thighs. One of these days, when Darlene had won the big lottery, she'd come to work and do a final shift, and wouldn't it be different! Every smart pup who tried to get fresh would get, instead, a damn good crack to the jaw, and those who got lippy about it would find the tray none too delicately inserted between their uppers and lowers. She could even imagine the sound it would make: ker-chunk. Talk now, you mouthy worm. The dentists in town would think they'd struck the mother lode: all these yahoos lined up Monday morning to get the trays removed and teeth fixed.

There was one real cute guy she wouldn't redecorate, though. Curly blond hair, you don't see that very often, and one of those grins that wind up on the very verge of being too wide but isn't. Nice teeth, nice arms, well built without looking as if he spent big chunks of his life reefing on pulleys or working up a sweat in the fitness room at the complex.

But, of course, he was with someone. Well, what was it they said? The good ones were either taken or gay or both. She didn't want any skidder-trail Suzie-the-floozie clawing at her eyes, it just wasn't worth the hassle. Nice shoulders and back, though.

But Tony, well, wasn't he a horse of a different garage. Most of them sauntered off down the pike as soon as they got the hint of another tomcat spraying in their corner. Did he? No, not so's you'd notice. Just found another corner and tucked his tight little buns into it.

And this other one, Greg, well, they don't make many like that, and no lie. She knew absolutely nothing about him except his first name, the intimate details of his body, and the fact he invariably wore a condom. Not many guys would do that, you'd think they were made of stainless steel and immune to every virus and germ.

She'd asked him what he did for work, and he just grinned at her and said, "I'm in stocks and bonds."

"A stockbroker?" She didn't believe him.

"No, not a stockbroker." His grin didn't waver. "I just keep an eye on things for myself."

And what did that tell you about a person? Like saying you were a mechanic but never went near cars, or something. Oh, I'm a vet, but I'm allergic to all animals. Still, he always had money. Never huge amounts of it, but enough to pay his own way. Well, why not? She had to pay her way in life, god knows.

And Dorrit's way, too. Well, you couldn't play bingo without every now and again losing more than you won. Except, with Dorrit, she hadn't really lost, not once she got over the shock and the basic unfairness of biology. All those guys out there with semi-permanent stiffers, and if ever any one of them got pregnant there'd be glee in the streets and probably a couple of million dollars plus a lifetime supply of aftershave lotion. And though she'd narrowed it down to three possible candidates, the kid didn't look like any of them, and she sure as hell wasn't paying for a paternity test, even if she could track 'em all down and convince 'em to cooperate. She could have done what she'd already done a couple of times and gone to the clinic and had the problem solved, but when she realized she was late, and why, when it was time to make the appointment, she found herself incapable. She knew why, too.

There'd been this debate on the radio, the pro and con of abortion, and one of the ones talking had said, instead of the word "abortion," "evacuate the uterus." She'd howled with laughter at the time. The word "evacuate" had brought fantasy images of scenes from the TV news, of people in rowboats and canoes making their way down deeply flooded streets, past supermarkets where things bobbed in the aisles, waist-deep with water, past hardware stores and pizza parlours to where entire families sat up on roofs with the family cat or dog or both, waiting for rescue. She'd thought of helicopters hovering and rope ladders being lowered, thought of the scenes where people raced from their homes, counting the number of kids, and, all present, good, now into the car, quick-quick like a bunny, then race off down the road, past fire crews with soot-blackened faces, the kids staring wide-eyed and horrified out the back windows, their mouths turned to little round o's of terror as the brush fires torched their home, turned the bedroom and their toys into cinders. The thought of all that going on in her uterus had her laughing like a loon. She imagined a guy with a bullhorn hollering turn left at the cervix, then down and out.

It was funny right up until she reached for the phone to call the clinic. And the image of the kids staring out the back window of the station wagon—eyes wide with terror, mouths turned into O's of helpless fear—froze her hand. She told herself she was a goddamn fool; she told herself she was falling into the same kind of sentimental trap as the people who wore little pink plastic feet; she told herself a whack of things including how impossible it was to think she could single parent on minimum wages. But she didn't make the call. And now, there was Dorrit—should have called him Bingo— living proof that maybe the female sea horse got a fair shake, what with the male doing the care and guarding of the brood, but for the rest of creation, the scales were unjustly tipped.

The soles of her feet burned, the muscles up her legs were tight and threatening to knot, and her left arm, from carrying trays, felt as if it weighed more than the rest of her did. But the two-bit band was playing "Let Me Call You Sweetheart," and the bozos were groaning and complaining but finishing their drinks and lurching off toward the open door. Dear god, let me wake up tomorrow a fully trained brain surgeon so I never have to do this stinkin' job again.

The ashtrays were piled high and stinking and even with the doors open the smoke swirled in the air. Sometimes she could understand the anti-tobacco fanatics; it must be hell to be in a place like this if you didn't smoke. But wasn't it up to them to organize themselves reasonably: set up their own bars and roadhouses and stuff, advertise them as non-smoking, and leave other people alone? Of course, if anyone was damn fool enough to fall into the trap of opening a non-smoking bar they'd be out of business in no time flat. The non-smokers would still go to the usual places and still bitch about the air. You could see it at just about any party, especially if the house the party was happening at had a big No Puffin' sign on the door. The smokers would congregate on the back porch with their sinful addictions on display, and next thing you knew the damn porch'd be practically falling off the side of the house with the weight of all the people out there while inside the place the air would be clean as clean could be, the music playing to nobody at all, everyone migrated to where the jokes were. So what was that? What it was was, given a choice, even non-smokers were bored with non-smokers and their control issues.

The tables were cleared and cleaned, the towel cloths stripped off and in the big canvas sacks, the floor rough-swept and ready for the cleaners when they came in, and thank you, sweet jesus, the boss was handing out paycheques. Of course by the time they took off this tax, that tax, income tax and carpet tax you wound up doing three-quarters of your work for the fools in Ottawa. But she took it, diminished as it was, and went to the staff bathroom long enough to do what she'd been dying to do for a half an hour or more.

Prettyboy was waiting, sitting on the back steps looking as much at home as the ear-chewed tomcat who waited patiently each night for the boss to dump the bar food scraps for him. Bits of chicken sticking to the bones, bits of sparerib ditto, hamburger buns and even some meat patties and always plenty of fries. Why is it, you have six people at a table, and they all order double-duty hamburgers with fries, then when it comes they eat less than half their fries and leave the rest? Why not order three fries? Oh well, the damn cat loved fries, so he benefitted, and what he couldn't finish and the other cats didn't find the crows would clean up as soon as dawn banished the dark.

She sat in the passenger seat and let Greg do the driving. She'd have liked to have him do the talking, too, but he seldom said very much. Maybe he was shy. Well, at least he wasn't shy in bed! God save us from those ones.

The whole front of the place was changed and altered just because Little Miss Wonderful wanted her own place. Suzie Creamcheeze and her chalet! How did they wind up with someone like her in the family, anyway? Doreen at least had the politeness to get herself to hell and out of everyone's hair when she decided she wanted something other than what the rest of them had. And Brady, well, say what you want, there was someone who knew what she wanted and was willing to go where it was, then lay claim to it. But bloody Colleen, it was as if she was starving or something, wanted it all, live at home, have all that, and still have the pisspot sports car, the fancy clothes, the swish job in town.

Her and her damn clothes. Her and her damn *mine, mine, mine* stinginess. Like that when she was a kid, too, raising shit about her bike, as if it was anything more special than anyone else's, until finally the old woman said they all had to keep their mitts off it, Or Else. No matter if your chain broke, you don't touch darling Colleen's bike. No matter if you had a flat, don't so much as look at the damn thing. "I never touch your stuff so don't you touch mine." How many times had Miss Priss come out with that one?

And now she comes home with that blue tin box. Talk about pissing on your posts! She's worse than a male dog with a bladder infection. And just look at the place, trees whacked way back from where they had been, ground all cleared and levelled, even a huge chunk of the slag heap pulled out and spread around until the place looked like a bloody tennis court or something. Just so Whiny Whimper could have her way.

Darlene was too keyed up to sleep. You can't go ninety per, hour after hour, and then just shut 'er off and go to dreamland. But that's why she'd brought Greg home in the first place; whatever else you had to say about it there was no better way to smooth out the wrinkles, get rid of the hyper and ease you into a slack-muscled relaxed mood that welcomed the sandman. And a helluva lot more fun than a sleeping pill, too.

In the morning she actually managed to catch up on some sleep. They'd maybe all worn themselves out with all the to-ing and fro-ing of the day before. It was the smell of ham, eggs, and pan fries wakened her, not the screech of engines or the raah raah of chain-saws or even the squabbling of kids. She left Greg sleeping and went to the kitchen. Singe was busy at the stove. The kids were setting the table, except for Tommy, who was running herd on the toaster.

"What you doing drinking coffee?" she grumbled at him. "You're gonna stunt your growth."

"Good," said Singe, laughing. "That way he won't hit ten feet tall after all. Leave the man alone, he's not allowed but two cups anyway."

"Man? That'll be the frosty Friday."

"You get paid last night?" Singe asked her quietly. She nodded, and he waited.

"Cheque. Haven't had a chance to cash it yet."

"That's fine." He patted her gently on the shoulder. "We'll wait until Monday."

"Maybe you'd like to come into town with me, hold my hand until I've cashed it and handed it over to you."

"Why, thank you, darlin', then I'll take you to the pancake house for breakfast, how's that sound?"

It was so hard to stay miffed at Singe. Part of her wanted to tell him to go shit in his hat, and the other half, the half that won out, wanted to sit in a booth with him and the kids and take on a dou-ble order of Belgian waffles with fresh berries.

Couldn't exactly fault him, though; she was the one had pulled the booboo. And all she'd intended to do was sit down and play a couple of cards, maybe have a good laugh, unwind a bit. Instead, she kept getting to within one or two numbers before someone else screeched Bingo, and the next thing you knew she was playing three cards, then five, and was back the following day to play again until it was time to go to work and the next thing after that the whole damn paycheque was gone. And she hadn't won a bowl of peanuts. She'd already been three months behind because of Dorrit's broken tooth and the dentist bills for that, and when she came up short again, Singe stepped in.

"You gonna bust your ass to build me 'n' Dorrit a house, too?" she asked.

"If that's what you want."

"What I want is this place fixed up," she corrected. "It hasn't had a coat of paint in years."

"You think there's something we could trade the paint store for what we'd need?"

She shrugged, she wasn't getting into that one with him. He'd just rub her nose in it in that enraging quiet, reasonable, logical fashion of his, and one day he'd end up with a hatchet between his ears because of that attitude.

Colleen got up and had breakfast with them, then had to ruin it all by organizing the kids. Couldn't she ever just take things as they were?

"If you go to your rooms and rustle up all the dirty clothes, then wrap them in bundles with your sheets and pillow slips, I'll do a big laundry. And," she gave them the rah rah team smile, "I'll make the beds for you."

They were off in a flash and Darlene could only shake her head and take her coffee out on the porch. The rest of the world was barely awake, and Colly had to once again show what an absolute wonder she was. When she went back in for another cup of coffee, the table wasn't cleared, the dishes weren't done, and Singe was sitting rolling a smoke. She almost hollered for the kids to come do the dishes, but then she saw how Singe was watching her. They'd already had the reminder about money; she wasn't ready for another go-round about who did and didn't do their share of work around here. And that damn Maude, not even out of bed yet! And useless when she was.

Darlene stacked the dishes in the sink, gave a squirt of detergent, ran hot water, then let the dishes soak so the egg yolk would soften while she had her next coffee, but as soon as she'd got to the bottom of the mug she started in on the sinkload. Singe said nothing, just smoked a couple more home rollies, then went outside to check on the cement pad.

When Darlene had the dishes done and the kitchen tidied, she went into the living room and picked up. Socks—god—big ones, little ones, and half of them fit for nothing but throwing away, which she did. The place needed dusting, too, but before she did that she'd get one of the kids to vacuum; maybe Jessie, she was good at it. But Jessie did it most of the time, and Tom had worked with the men yesterday, so that narrowed the field to Dorrit and Little Wilma. Which really narrowed the field to Dorrit because Little Wilma probably couldn't even drag the cannister at the end of the hose.

"Hey, Dorry." She grabbed him when he came in the house for a drink of juice. "I have a twenty-five cent job needs done and you're exactly the first choice."

"Okay." He smiled up at her, and she cuddled him, rocking him gently. "What is it?"

"You get to ride the vacuum," she crooned. "My little cowboy."

"If I find pennies, can I have 'em?"

"You sure can so. And nickels and dimes, too."

Darlene looked through the freezer, found two very big venison roasts and brought them out. They were rock hard but would thaw while roasting, and if she did them on the propane grill the house wouldn't wind up like a sauna. No more than get one meal cleared away and it was time to start another. Did everyone spend so much of their life concentrating on food?

🖈

Tony came into the kitchen yawning, and behind him, Greg, guarded and more quiet than usual.

"That kid's gonna suck the floorboards up the way he's going at the living room," Tony said, laughing.

"Oh, jesus, I nearly forgot." Darlene reached into the penny jar and took eight or nine of them. "I gotta scatter these for him to find."

"Smart move," Tony agreed, smiling. She wished he'd put his tee-shirt on and not wander around with his chest hairs showing. How did men manage to get muscles like that? He even had muscles from his neck to his shoulders, like little triangles, and his belly looked like he had beer cans under his skin. No wonder Greg was surly; if positions were reversed and one of his old humps was walking around the kitchen in a string bikini, with tits that wouldn't stop and hair till hell wouldn't hold it, she'd be in a bit of a snappy mood, too.

Jessie came in with a bucket of eggs and put them on the counter for someone else to wash. Darlene almost told her to do it herself, but the way the kid turned for the door it was pretty clear there was something else needed done outside and an adult waiting to make sure she did it. So Darlene took the pennies to the living room, tiptoeing quietly although she could have ridden in on a Harley and not been heard over the noise of the vacuum. Dorry was concentrating on the big chair: he had the cushion off and the end of the hose shoved against the crack where the seat met the back. She slipped some of the pennies under the cushion on the sofa, where he obviously hadn't been yet, and dropped the rest on the carpet, then tiptoed back out of the room and went to wash eggs.

Singe was digging spuds, putting half of them in one bucket, half in another. When both buckets were full, he brought one into the house, put the other in the bed of the pickup. That could only mean he was going to Lucy's place. Darlene got a supermarket bag and went out to the rhubarb patch, pulled stalks, broke off the leaves, and piled them along the fence to mulch and keep down the long grass.

"You take this, too, you hear?" she called. "You know Lucy loves rhubarb." When the bag was full, she handed it over the fence to him, then picked an armload for the house. Maybe she'd make a stewed pudding or something. Or a nice big grunt, they always enjoyed a grunt.

Darlene saw Colleen in the garden picking pod peas, after filling both clotheslines full of sheets, pillowcases and just-about-worn-out clothing. Darlene could as good as see through the backsides of several pair of Dorrit's faded shorts, and the girls' underpants were so worn they looked like see-through silk. She supposed some of it didn't matter too much, summer and all, but still, they were on the verge of downright immodesty. Mind you, Maude would never notice, she wasn't around home long enough or often enough to pay attention to stuff

71

like that. At the rate she was going she'd show up one of these times and her own flesh and blood would ask who she was.

Darlene hadn't cared for Maude the first time she saw her. Even then she was like an overripe pear: looks gorgeous, but when you go to pick it up it's all mushy and good for nothing but wasp food or maybe compost. Some plums get like that, too, especially the big old-fashioned golden ones. They look like the best ones on the tree, but when you pick them you find the skin split at the top and juice thick as syrup leaking out, some of it already crystallized. Be careful of those or you'll wind up stung, as often as not there's already a wasp gone in through the crack, gorging itself, ready to stab anyone who seems to be stealing its treasure.

Al wasn't the kind you could say much to, though. He might be quick to give his opinion, but that didn't mean he'd welcome anyone else's. And he'd got stung, no doubt about that.

Not that she could hold Maude entirely at fault, much as she might like to. Al was the first one to trot off out the back door and go poaching in someone else's playpen. Actually, he'd lasted longer at faithfulness than anyone had expected. Maude was lugging Tom on her hip and was big with Jessie before Al had started to stray. You'd have thought Maude knew nothing about it, patient as a damn spider when it came to deviousness. She waited right up until Jessie was, oh, maybe a year old, and then one night after supper Al headed off saying he was going to help someone fix his furnace, and no more was he gone than there went Maude, too, and no way anyone would believe anything about furnaces the way she was dressed. She got home before Al did, but not by much.

And then one night Al didn't get home at all. Not that he'd intended it that way, but there he was, parked in the back alley of his townie floozie's place, and someone cracked open the hood and ripped loose all the wiring and took the distributor cap. He couldn't fix it at night, so he had to wait until morning, *and* get his brothers to come in to help, at that. His story was the pickup had stalled and just wouldn't start up again six or ten miles up the Lakes Road, but nobody believed that, although Maude had put on an innocent enough face through it all. At the time, Darlene had thought Colly had rocks in her head because Colly believed Maude was the one

72

who had trashed the car. Darlene had been of the opinion Maude didn't have the gumption, for one thing, or the knowledge, for another. Now, though, with a few other examples of Maude's don't-get-mad-get-even mentality, she suspected Colly had been right. Of course hell would freeze into a solid lump before she'd say so!

They'd split up soon after, Maude moving into town with the kids. She wasn't there more than a couple of months when she came home from the bar and the kids were gone, the babysitter asleep on the couch. Al had the kids, of course, and Maude showed up to get them, of course. See-saw, marjory daw, back and forth and up and down, and so before it got totally ridiculous, Maude moved back in, but only back into the house, not really back into Al's life. Not really. Now it looked as if Maude wasn't in anyone's life, maybe not even in her own. For all Tommy and Jessie saw of her she might just as well be the truant officer.

And why aren't there such things nowadays? The old man used to tell tales about the truant officer rounding up kids and frog-marching them back to school, like it or lump it. Now, the malls were full of truants, the arcades overstuffed with them; people moaned and groaned about the drop-outs, but nobody did zip-all about it. Speaking of zip, that's probably why; if the truant officer tried to impose his will on any of them, he'd probably be turned into the human sieve, little holes through him from the zip guns.

Singe drove off with his spuds, rhubarb, and a big cardboard box of something that required him to close the flaps into a lid and then duct tape them shut. He waved at Darlene, and she waved back, then moved over to have a closer look at what the hoorah had been about over where the alder clump used to be and was no more.

From what she could see and figure out, what had started out being called a shack gave every promise of turning into one of those damn monster houses that were cluttering up the north end of town. The cement pad looked just about big enough to be used as a roller-blade rink. The ground was already hard packed in spite of all the stumps being hauled out and taken back behind the rim of trees and stacked; it would take a hundred years for them to rot away. In the old days, say ten years ago, you could have just soaked 'em in diesel and set them ablaze, had it all over and done with in a week. Now, not a chance, with worries about the ozone layer, and yet the mill continued to belch tons of stuff into the air every day, so the cleanup seemed to be on the shoulders of the little guy, as usual. In Seattle they even had restrictions about when you could burn your fireplace. But don't inconvenience industry!

She watched Colleen leave the garden, rinse her hands at the hose and head for the house. Who else would wash up before going to the basin to wash up?

Darlene followed Colleen into the house, saw her heading upstairs with an armload of sheets. Oh well, what the hell, might as well, and ain't life swell. She trailed behind, to help make the beds. The kids' rooms didn't look too bad, as long as you ignored the archaeological digs under the beds. At least there weren't any summer socks festering in the sunlight.

"Really appreciate the help," Colleen grunted, shoving Tommy's bed back against the wall.

"I'm so glad it's Sunday, the day of rest," Darlene said.

"Remember Gran saying, 'Six days shalt thou labour and on the seventh thou shalt work like a mad fiend'?"

"And what was that other one? 'If a thing is worth doing, it's worth putting it off for a year or so'. She'd liven this place up if she was still here."

"Maybe she is, in a way. Don't you ever look at Jessie and think of Gran?"

"No. I look at Jessie and think she's probably headed for trouble."

"Jess? No, she's not going to wind up in trouble, she's too level-headed for that. Of course, she might well wind up causing trouble!" And they both chuckled.

The door to Maude's room was open, and the bed, rumpled and messy, was empty.

"Well, there you go," Darlene sighed. "I thought she was sleepin' in, and instead, she ain't in at all."

"Wasn't here long at all this time," Colleen concurred.

"Oh, well, maybe she'll think to drop by for Christmas dinner."

"Should report her to the bloody welfare."

"What good would that do? All's the welfare is is a place where the government spends god knows how much money doing sweet fuck all. They just stand in the hallways and gossip with each other."

Darlene walked into Maude's bedroom, peeled the covers off the bed, took the sheets and left the blankets on the floor.

"Maybe we should at least . . ." Colleen began.

"Oh, piss on that! She's got the life of goddamn Riley around here."

"She's Al's woman."

"Was, you fool. Was."

"Well, she's the mother of Al's children."

"We hope they're his."

"Now now, you know . . ."

"Shut up, Colleen," Darlene said casually. "Just shut up, okay."

Darlene was halfway to the door, then turned, went back to the bed, tipped the mattress off the frame and leaned it against the wall. "If she bitches," she grinned wickedly, "just look as innocent as hell and say, 'Gee we thought we were doin' you a favour, airin' out the room and all'." And she reefed the window wide open. "Lookit the damn mess on the floor," she nagged, scooping up crumpled and probably soiled clothes. "Bad as a bloody kid."

Colleen looked at her but said nothing.

⁂

They made sandwiches and juice and packed them in the laundry basket with towels and sun screen, and were trying to figure out the best logistics for getting it all to the creek with a minimum number of trips in the pop can when Singe came back with the pickup, followed by the firewood trucks and a crew of Lucy's relatives, including a half-dozen kids. Any and all plans went out the window. Instead, all the kids were put in the bed of Singe's pickup, the laundry hamper and food went in the front with Colleen and Darlene, and Tony opted out of the trip altogether. Greg had faded after his initial cup of coffee; he just suddenly wasn't to be seen, and neither was his car.

Kids hooted and hollered, yelled and shouted, splashed and screeched. Colleen swam leisurely, and Darlene tried to snooze on the rock. After a while she gave up and went into the water herself for a while. The kids inhaled the food, drained the juice and had such a great time Dorrit managed what his mom hadn't been able to and fell sound asleep. Little Wilma stubbed her toe on a rock and then freaked out at the sight of her own blood. Jessie was so disgusted by the display she tossed the kid into the deep part of the pool and then had to go in herself to drag the hysterical brat out again.

By the time they headed home Darlene felt exhausted. Any more fun like that and she'd probably die. But no rest for the wicked: the roasts were just about ready and the spuds wouldn't be enough for a crew this size, so while Colleen made chili, Darlene made lasagna.

They took the table outside and set it up at the side of the house, with all the plates piled on one end and the cutlery jumbled beside them.

"Best we load the kids' plates first and get them to hell and gone out of the way," Darlene suggested. "Otherwise they'll push 'n' shove and get in the way and wind up getting a crack on the ear or something."

The kids took their plates to the front steps, ranged themselves without any dispute and, as if they hadn't already made short work of three loaves of bread made into sandwiches, started at one side of their plates and worked their way to the other side.

The men were shy, but not so shy they couldn't pack their plates high with food and then find places to sit and eat. They were all sweaty, and the swath cut into the bush from where the alders had been was well started. Singe saw Colleen staring at it, puzzled.

"We're gonna fell the big ones and firewood 'em, then the boys are bringing the skidder up, prob'ly tomorrow. With it and the earth mover, shouldn't take long to get a good swatch done. Gonna head back toward the old pit and see if we can reef out enough coal for fuel for the winter."

"Hard to think of fuel for the winter when it's this hot."

"Them old workings ought to be good for something," he mused. "I mean, there might not have been enough left for the company to haul in the profit they were used to, but christ, the price of coal then was peanuts alongside what it is now."

"It's dangerous," Darlene said. "You know what the old man said, it wasn't prices being low, it was safety measures costing so much. Stinkin' gas and all."

"Worth a try," Singe insisted.

It was hard to believe so much food could vanish so completely but the proof was in the empty dishes. Without being asked the kids collected plates and took them in to wash, but that still left the pots and pans, glasses, mugs and cutlery.

"You ever have nightmares about sinks full of dishes?" Colleen asked.

"My worst one is the one where I don't have any hands," replied Darlene. "I seem to be fine, I mean, I'm walking around and doing things, it's just I don't have any hands, my arms end at my wrists. Nobody seems to notice, though."

"With me, it's teeth. I have this stupid dream where I'm sitting at this huge banquet table, sort of old-Italian-y. There are a bunch of other people around, all dressed to the nines, and each of us has like four different crystal glasses and more forks and knives than hell would hold, candelabra down the middle of the table, I mean this is all very swish! And me? Well, I reach up, and I pull out a tooth. No pain, no strain, no muss, no blood, I just pull out this tooth, rinse it in my water glass, polish it on my napkin and put it back in place again. People are talking—conversing I guess you'd call it—and paying no attention, and I'm up at the end there, taking out teeth, washing and polishing them, and putting them back in again. And that's all there is to the dream."

"That's it?"

"That's it. Weird, eh?"

"Yeah, but you always were." And they laughed together, finishing the dishes, cleaning the kitchen, sweeping the floor.

Colleen went up to the coop and picked up a bucketload of eggs. It looked as if the barred Rock-y ones had gone back over to Bob's where they'd probably wandered off from in the first place. They seemed to be down to the original couple of dozen, although from the number of eggs you'd think there were two or three times that many.

She had the eggs washed and in the bowl in the fridge when the cop arrived. He came to the back door, poked his head in and actually tried to smile. "Hi." He took off his hat, rubbed his scrubbing brush hair. "Singeon around?"

"I don't think so." She moved to a window and looked outside. "No, I don't see any of them, actually. They'll be back, but I don't know when."

"Well, maybe you could help me?"

"Depends what you need help with. A drink of water, sure, I can get you one, but catching bank robbers is a bit outside my field of expertise."

"Chickens."

"I beg your pardon?"

"You neighbour claims to have lost thirty." He frowned, got out his little notebook, flipped the pages and peered. "Something-or-other velders."

"Something-or-other-velders? What is a somethingorothervelder?"

"Some imported breed of chicken, as I understand it. Says he paid five dollars each for day-old chicks, plus air freight out from Quebec, and now they're all gone."

"Bringing something from Quebec is now considered 'importing'? Jeez, I 'imported' some food from town, if that's the case."

"Guess the guy in Quebec imported them from Europe."

"So what's worth five dollars for a day-old chick? They got four legs or something?"

The cop shrugged. Colleen shrugged.

"You mind if I look around for them?"

"Well, of course I mind," she said, smiling sweetly. "Unless you have a search warrant, of course."

"No, I didn't think I'd need one. You said the other day his chickens wandered all over everywhere, and I just thought well, maybe they'd be, oh, I don't know, over where the raw dirt is, maybe, looking for bugs or something."

"Do you see any of them over there?" She laughed. "Tell you what, you and I will go up to the henhouse together. And that's it for searching the joint, okay? If you find even one chicken with an Air Canada boarding pass stamped on its arse I'll give it to you, no charge at all."

He followed her past the garden and up to the coop. She opened the door and went inside; he followed, stooping to get in. One or two of the hens peered idiotically from the laying boxes. They looked at the cop, the cop looked at them, then shrugged. Colleen left the coop, cop following, and went to the open gate of the hen yard.

"We open this gate first thing in the morning and let them out to free range." She was starting to feel quite ticked off. "At night someone closes the gate. By then the hens are in their coop. We close them up because of raccoons and because of neighbours."

"You've had trouble with your neighbours?"

"We only have one neighbour. And the day that stingy bugger pays five bucks for a one-day-old baby chick is the day I'll buy stiletto-heeled shoes. You have to understand something; the guy is a lunatic. If you believe every accusation he makes, well, you might as well rent one of the upstairs bedrooms and move in here full time because he'll have you running out here five times a day looking for things he never had in the first place. Crackpot Bob, everyone calls him."

Suddenly, the cop lurched sideways, his face registering shock and horror. Colleen stumbled, grabbed at a fence post, barely managed to keep her feet under her. Every tree on the place swayed, and the chickens took hysterics. The gate to the hen yard slammed shut, then swung open again. The noise was like one huge reverberating clap of thunder, and from the corner of her eye Colleen saw the chimney sway, then crumple, the bricks tumbling to the roof, slamming, sliding and rolling off to land on the grass. And then everything was so quiet a person might think she had gone deaf.

"What the fuck was that?" the cop blurted.

"Earthquake," she replied weakly. "Thank god it was short."

They didn't talk on the way back to the house. The cop stood useless while Colleen stared miserably at the scattered bricks. She looked up at what was left of the chimney, then looked back down at the rubble. "Well, shit," she said, finally.

The cop seemed to have forgotten about the purportedly missing something-or-other-velders. He didn't seem to know what to do with himself. Eventually, he sauntered off to his car, got in it and drove off.

For lack of anything else to do, Colleen began picking up bricks and stacking them behind the house. The broken ones she just dumped in a pile. She wished she knew where everybody was, wished she knew they were safe. Silly, because of course they were! Unthinkable that they weren't. So why did she worry? Why? Because Mother Earth had just belched, that's why.

Darlene came out of the bush carrying Dorrit, stroking his back, holding him tight. Colleen stood waiting, praying the kid wasn't hurt.

"He's okay," Darlene called. "He's fine."

"What about the others?"

"They're fine, too. Everything's okay."

Well, of course it was. Silly of her to feel so frightened. It was just, well, the truth of it was, they were so damned frail. Just think about the back of their necks, that skinny little column, you could easily grab it in your hand, it wouldn't take much of a shake to dislocate everything, snap the spinal cord, paralyse or even kill them.

The rest of the crew arrived shortly after Darlene did. They were all laughing, talking about the tremor, each of them with stories about swaying trees and jiggling moss. She was so busy trying to calm them down she almost forgot to tell Singeon about the visit from the cop.

"Only something-or-other-velders I ever heard of are Lakenvelders," Singe said casually. "Doubt if old Bob's got any."

"Even if he had them at one time he doesn't have them now, I guess," she said, turning away, relegating the entire silly episode to the memory dustbin. "I wish that guy would get a life. One that didn't include us."

She felt as if she'd done more than enough for one day and left the others to their own devices. She started the bath water, got her housecoat, took it into the unfinished bathroom, locked the door, and got into the tub. Maybe one of these days someone would take it into their head to finish the place. The walls weren't really there, just two-by-fours, and on the far side of them the boards that were the wall of the kitchen, with the pipes for the sink showing. Above her head the heavy green-insulated electric wires showed, the fixtures in place, everything safe and tickety-boo, just no ceiling to hide any of it.

At one point, overwhelmed with something she couldn't name, she'd bought gyproc, intending to do the bathroom herself. She stored it in the shed, and three days later it was gone. Turned out Singeon had thought it was just left over from something and had taken it down to Lucy's place to fix up her bedroom and living room. He'd replaced it, but before it got put in the bathroom, Maude got one of her boyfriends to use it on the walls in her bedroom. Mind you, it never did get painted.

And no use fooling yourself into thinking Maude would one day replace it, either. Maude had the idea she was the milkmaid of all creation, designed for nothing more than draining tit. Somewhere, somehow, someone had forgotten to tell her you don't get milk without feeding the cow.

She fell asleep quickly and easily, waking only slightly when Little Wilma crawled into bed with her.

"What you doing here?" Colleen asked.

"Will there be more earthquakes?"

"Probably not. Unless you jab me with an elbow or something, then the earth will shake because I'll throw you out the window."

Wilma snuggled down in bed, then rolled and twisted and finally curled up against Colleen's back. Colleen yawned and went back to sleep, and when she awoke again it was light outside, the birds were singing, and she could smell coffee.

She got herself a cup of coffee and looked around the downstairs to see who had made it, but she was the only one awake and up; Singe must have set the automatic maker before he went to bed.

She had two cups of coffee and three cigarettes on the porch, then got herself washed, brushed and spiffed, and drove to work, hearing boring report after boring report about the earthquake. Four point five on the Richter scale, centred between Nanaimo and Bowen Island, the third rumble in five days. Some expert was yammering on about a period of intense activity and, of course, more blether about how the Coast was way long overdue for the big one. Yeah, yeah, she thought. Yeah yeah yeah, been hearing about this incipient big one my entire life and never anything any worse than yesterday. There'll be a big one, and it'll come about the same time as world peace.

She was the first one at work, used her key to let herself in by way of the side door. She turned on her computer, and while it was creaking and groaning its way back to life, she did the coffee grounds and water thing at the maker.

Someone had tried to access her files. Heh heh heh, go ahead and try, you sneaky fucker. Heh heh heh. There is diddly-squat on the hard drive. What do you think I am, weak-witted? She snapped open her briefcase, took out her little plastic storage box of disks, and put in the one she needed. Stan, my man, you don't fool me, you wouldn't hesitate to raid this old bazoo, swipe my work, then pass it off as your own. That's how you got where you are, riding on someone else's back. But not my back. Not then, not now.

She got coffee and settled herself to work. She had more than an hour all by herself before the first office staff arrived. She smiled at them, waved by waggling her fingers, and briefly joined in the "Did you feel it?" discussions.

She took her disks and briefcase with her when she ducked out to go to the donut shop and buy a box of assorteds. She took them back to the office, made sure she had a couple for herself, then left the rest of them by the coffee machine. The blast of sugar energized her, so when she made her first phone calls she sounded like the chipper chickadee.

Appointments confirmed, she completed the last of her presentation, then stored it to disk, twice, because she had a backup disk for everything she considered to be her own. By the time Stan arrived, Colleen was working on general material, some of it almost interesting.

"Anything new?" he asked, his face close to hers as he peered at her screen.

"Just working on this," she answered easily. "They'll be in to see you this afternoon, remember? I thought I'd have the stuff ready for you so you can brush up a bit before you see them. They're renewing." She wished he'd stay up to scratch on his own stuff for a change. "And they want to extend by five percent."

"Appreciate it," he said, but she knew he didn't. He took it for granted. Well, you just keep on doing that, boy, and one day you'll find out the road is not smooth, after all, and the paving crew hasn't even been notified, let alone started work.

She went for lunch early and enjoyed every bite of her fish and chips. That was one good thing to be said for skipping breakfast: lunch always tasted so good. When she had finished eating she ordered a pot of tea and lingered over it, waiting for the acetaminophen to work on her headache. That was one of the down sides of skipping breakfast, your blood sugar got out of whack.

Darlene could easily have slept until it was time to go to work, but the kids were up and clattering in the kitchen, and nobody else went in to ride herd on them, so she hauled herself down and cracked a few of them on the side of the head to smarten them up. They glared but shut up, and she got coffee. Singe came in when she was less than halfway through and looked as if he was surprised.

"You just about ready?" he asked pointedly.

"Sure am," she lied, rising and taking her cup with her.

"Where we going?" Dorrit asked.

"Can I come?" Little Wilma was already dressed, although her hair looked as if the sparrows nested in it.

"Brush your hair and we'll see," Darlene said, yawning, and headed to her room to get dressed.

Singe drove, Darlene sat by the door, with Dorrit between them and the other three in the crew seat, nagging.

"Shut up," Singe said quietly. "Next one I hear nittering, nagging, bitching, complaining or arguing will be put out to walk."

"It's cramped in here," Jessie whined.

"Of course it is, it's a crew-cab pickup, not a fuckin' caddy limo," Singe said.

"Well, my knees are jammed."

"You knew how big the space was before you got in."

"How come Dorry doesn't sit back here? He's got short legs."

"Want to walk?"

She didn't, and shut up, but sat looking sulky. There was room back there, Darlene thought. My god, adult men rode in crew-cab trucks and didn't fuss up, but Miss Jessie Kiss My Ass wanted to ride up front all the time. Taking her turn seemed to be beyond her.

Darlene cashed her cheque at the credit union and handed half of it to Singe who put the money in his pocket and nodded.

"Anything you need to do?"

"I have to go to Wal-Mart."

"Can we come?" Jessie asked.

"Are you going to whine and whinge the whole damn time?"

"No, Auntie," Jessie promised.

None of them whined, none of them whinged, and not one of them tried begging or scamming. Darlene gave them each two dollars to spend and threatened to leave them behind if they weren't waiting for her at the checkout in fifteen minutes. "And try not to convince everyone in here that you're trash, okay?"

She got boxer shorts for the boys, six each, and packages of sport socks, four to a plastic baggy. The girls got cotton underpants, three solid colours each, three with flowers. And, of course, plastic bags of cotton socks in pastel shades. She got each of them two tee-shirts and two cut-off jeans/shorts, and a new bathing suit each. Some people would probably let the kids choose their own, but how much time did a person want to spend in Wal-Mart with the voice coming loud from the overhead speakers, "Shoppers' alert! Special on watering hoses for the garden in aisle seven thousand nine hundred and eight." She pushed the cart over to the shoe display, where big "sale" signs were hanging from the ceiling. She wasn't sure if she should get them sandals or sneakers, so she wound up getting both.

They were waiting, and they hadn't attracted a crowd of disapproving onlookers, so they must have been behaving. Of course, they each had candy. What else would a kid buy with two bucks, anyway?

God, it doesn't seem like much when you're looking at it one item at a time, but add it all up and it hits you between the eyes. Oh well, that's what it was for, to spend.

"We goin' home, now?" Dorrit smiled up at her, and she could have swooped him up and kissed his face off.

"Might as well," she agreed. "We're broke all over again."

"You want some candy?" He held his bag of licorice up and smiled again.

"No, thank you, darlin', you eat it all up, you deserve it, you've been a good, good boy."

"I been good, too," Wilma countered.

"I know you have. You're one of the best girls in town."

They paid no attention at all to the stuff being taken from the cart and put on the counter for the cashier to ring through. They didn't expect to get anything for themselves; they had their candy, after all. It wasn't until they were back home and the bags were on the table that they realized she hadn't been shopping for herself at all.

"Oh, Momma!" Dorrit held up his cut-offs and beamed. They looked just like blue jeans, only short-legged, and he'd been wanting a pair since last year, just because the big guys wore them.

"Thanks, Mom."

"Thank you, Auntie." And Jessie grabbed Darlene in a big hug. "Thanks."

"You okay with boxers instead of jockeys?" she asked Tom.

He looked up, grinned, then blushed. "Yeah. And these are real cool."

"I'm a cool cat," she teased.

Tony came in with something more or less roundish and thick with grease. He showed it to Singe and they began to talk Mongolian. She looked at the kids and pulled a face, they laughed and grimaced back at her.

"What?" Singe smiled.

"You guys." She cuddled him from behind, her face between his shoulder blades, her hands crossed on his chest. "It's like igpay atinlay."

Nothing would do but the kids whip off to their rooms, strip to the skin and start pulling on new stuff. When they came back down again, prancing and proud, they looked like new people; even Little Wilma had brushed her hair again. For once it was free of tangles.

"You all look so diddly tickety-boo," Singe picked up Dorrit and cuddled him, "that if you want to drive back to town you can come with us. We have to go to the machine shop and get this reamed out and a new one packed in."

"What's wrong with it?"

"Feel inside. Feel those little gritties in the grease? Bad news. Means something is scouring at it. That means it's likely just a tad off-centre, not turning smooth, the way it should. Don't wipe your finger on your clothes!"

They raced back to the pickup, and this time it was Little Wilma sat up front between Singe and Tony, who had the mystery bit wrapped in some newspaper to keep the grease off the inside of the truck. The silence when they were gone was so wonderful Darlene almost felt as if she was in some other place, some place not home, some place civilized and wonderful. She filled the tub with hot water, stole some of Colleen's bubble bath, not much, just enough to put a bit of lilac scent to the room. She lay in the tub enjoying the peace and quiet, feeling so comfortable and so pampered she wouldn't have called the queen her cousin. She wasn't sure she could explain that expression to anyone, but Gran had used it when she was feeling particularly pleased, or when someone had given her a gift, and that was good enough for Darlene. She missed Gran. For that matter she missed the old woman, too. Not in the same way, perhaps, but nothing is ever the same.

When the water cooled, she took Colleen's bathrobe off the hook behind the door and wrapped it around herself. Colly would raise holy old hell if she knew, but then Colly was always raising Cain about some little thing or other. Darlene made sure she hung the terrycloth dressing gown over the door, so it would dry and air, and no one be any the wiser.

There were probably half a dozen things she could do, but the bath had made her realize how tired she was. Thank god she had Monday nights off! She could catch a nap, get up bright-eyed and bushy-tailed, catch up on the few chores and still have some part of her day off to herself. God knows tomorrow would come soon enough and bring with it more BS than a person should have to endure.

She wakened to the gleeful shrieks of kids, followed by the roar of a piece of equipment. A person could be assured of a long life around here, it was so noisy you not only couldn't sleep, you wouldn't be able to die! Lord, and old Ponce de Leon had gone off in search of the fountain of youth, wound up lost in the swamps of Florida, and all he'd ever have had to do would be stay home and help Mrs. Leon run herd on a pack of kids. He mightn't have stayed young, but his life would have seemed overly long, and checking out of it would have been welcome.

*

Colleen made her presentation, showed all the facts and figures, the ins and outs, and could tell before she got to the end she'd made another coup.

"So, where'd you learn so much about logging equipment?" the manager asked.

"Some of it from my brother Singeon—he works for you when the bush isn't closed—some of it from my brother Jewen, and a lot of it from the research I did when I was preparing the prospectus for you."

"Singeon's your brother?" he said, smiling. "I didn't realize you were one of those Lancasters."

"See, that shows you aren't originally from around here." She smiled back. "People from here know us from a half mile away."

"You ever decide you're tired of working for that total asshole Stan, you let me know. There's always room here for someone who's willing to take some initiative."

"Thank you. I appreciate your confidence in my work."

She could have gone back to work stepping from cloud to cloud but instead chose to drive back in her pop can. Maybe she'd do a bit more research into the entire logging industry. It would be nice, better than nice, it would be vindication to walk out on Stan on Friday and on Monday start a new job, especially a job where she might be more appreciated.

For that matter, maybe she should also do some research into the construction business. Not houses or apartments, but what about highway construction and road building? She liked the idea of working for the logging contractor, though. Of course, people said things they didn't mean, you always had to keep that in mind.

She didn't let Stan in on the good news until after she'd sent everything off with the courier. He resented it, and this time didn't try to hide it.

"Seems to me it would be much more professional if I knew every step of the way what it was you were doing," he snapped. "You're overstepping your position."

"I'm very sorry you feel that way," she replied carefully. "I'll certainly try to do better in future." But she had no intention of changing the way she was doing things; if it ain't broke don't fix it. And he'd swipe her ideas. He'd done it in the past, and she'd vowed then he'd never get another chance. It wasn't ego, it wasn't a need for recognition or praise: in a job where your pay packet depended, in part at least, on commission, swiped ideas were the same as swiped dollars.

When she got home, the swath into the bush was well started, and a new piece of gear was parked in the yard. It looked like a mammoth dinky toy with a big digger on the front. What next, and where was all this gear coming from, anyway?

She changed from her good clothes into jeans and tee-shirt, thick cotton socks and high-tops, then put the spuds on to cook. She wasn't sure how many people were going to troop into the house so she used the biggest pot they had and all the spuds in the bin. She put a reminder on the bit of blackboard: someone, probably herself, would have to dig more spuds tonight.

She picked all the pod peas she could find and raided the carrot patch as well. The carrots were small, and she'd planted them so close together she could easily afford to pamper their tastebuds with the super sweet babies. She'd take every second one, that would leave room for the remainders to grow, and the next time she'd take every second one, as well.

There were beet tops, and the chard was ready, too. She took the peas and carrots into the house and got scissors and a colander and went back out to clip greens. The turnip greens were going to seed already, and the spinach, well, what a waste of time that was once the sun started to shine. She'd heard that some people were planting their spinach under cover, keeping the sunshine off it to stop it from bolting. Might be worth a try. On the other hand, it might not be anything other than another make-work project, and she was beginning to feel she didn't need to make herself any more work than she already had.

She opened two quarts of government mutton and put them on to simmer with the peas and carrots, then washed and spun the greens and made a huge salad. She had no idea where Darlene and the kids were, but the pickup was parked over near her cement pad, so they weren't off in it.

When the spuds were ready she drained them, then added margarine and a shot of olive oil, sprinkled plenty of chopped garlic chive on them, and put them in the oven to stay warm. She turned down the heat under the government mutton stew, and took a cold beer out to the porch. She yawned, then arched her back to take some of the tightness out of her shoulder muscles.

She had finished her beer and was contemplating another when everyone came back to the house. The first thing to arrive was a skidder, with Dorrit sitting on the driver's lap, steering the huge thing and as proud as a peacock. Tom was standing on the side step holding a small chainsaw and talking to the guy who was supposed to be driving the rig. Colleen felt the familiar lurch of panic and squashed it down. How else was a kid supposed to learn, and it must be safe or Singe would never have agreed to let him try.

Next came the earth mover with the bucket turned so the kids could squat in it safely. And just how safely was safely, anyway? Tony was driving it, as casual as if he'd been pushing a wheelbarrow.

Behind the earth mover the two firewood trucks appeared, loaded to the very top with split alder rounds. And behind that, a log truck from the sawmill, with Singe riding in the passenger seat. And here came Jewen, walking behind the log truck, with something wrapped in his shirt.

The something turned out to be two puppies, one male, one female, both black and white and obviously terrier. They looked to be about a month and a half old and were still totally unafraid.

"Found 'em," said Jewen, grinning. "They were sleepin' on the moss just outside the mouth of one of the old tunnels. Mother must'a whelped inside."

"I thought they sealed those goddamn things!" she exploded.

"Well, wood rots, Colleen, you ought to know that. And a terrier, well, the only thing that'll keep one of them out is something that'll keep water in. Or vicey versey." He handed her the male. "This is Spot." Then he held up the female. "And this is More Spots."

"I don't want this dumb thing," she said, but she knew she was sunk. The pup was as good as grinning at her, wagging its tail so hard its entire back end wiggled.

"Maybe a bowl of milk?" he suggested.

"Doubt if there's any milk in the house." She took the female, too, and headed for the kitchen. "Come on, Cleo. There's a good boy, Faro, that's it, you'll be fine."

She broke bread slices small and poured venison stew over them, put the pups in the backroom with the plate of food and left them to it. They didn't know plate from backside of the moon, and they'd probably never had bread or any kind of cooked food before, but they didn't hesitate; they were gulping and almost choking when she closed the door on them. She didn't believe the story about the mother whelping in the abandoned tunnel, though. These pups looked as if they were pure terrier, and their tails had been docked. No hiding-out homeless bitch can dock her pups' tails, you need people for that. She was sure if she took the time and bothered to look she would find either a tattoo or a lump that hinted at an implanted identity nub. She was willing to bet one of the fools had bought them and deliberately planted them where they would be almost immediately found, knowing, of course, that nobody was going to leave them there or, for that matter, get rid of them once they'd seen them. Devious, every one of them. Moving each other around like chess pieces or something.

"Jewen," she said quietly, "those pups' tails have been docked."

"Well, now that you mention it." He nodded, trying hard to look as if he hadn't noticed.

"Did you stash them out there?"

"Me? Stash them? Why would I do that?"

"Okay." She shrugged. "Fine, then. Be that way."

The lumberyard log truck headed off, following the firewood trucks. The equipment was parked side-by-each in the yard and the kids were busy scrubbing up at the back sink. "Where's your mom?" Colleen asked Dorrit. He looked up at her, smiled and shrugged.

"So who's been looking after you?" she asked. They all looked at her as if they didn't know what she was saying. "Jeezly," she sighed. "Jeezly weezly."

Darlene and Greg wandered in just as the others were finishing supper. There wasn't enough of anything left to feed a midget let alone two adults. Darlene checked the leftovers, shrugged, and sauntered to her room. Greg stood around shifting from foot to foot to foot again, until Colleen wondered if he was trying to get his feet out of his shoes.

"For chrissakes," she snapped, "sit down and quit fidgeting or I'll get hives just watching you."

"Hives?" He sat, though. Some people are just about as smart as the far side of a muddy ditch. If his hair was the right colour, he'd be the epitome of every dumb blond joke she'd ever heard.

Jewen poured tea into a clean mug and put it on the table in front of Greg, who looked at it as if he was afraid it would bite him. Well, if you can't figure it out for yourself, to hell with you, Colleen thought.

After a while Darlene came out in fresh clothes—her own, thank god—and before anyone could ask her anything she kissed Dorrit, dropped a bag of Kraft caramels on the table and was heading for the front door, waving goodbye. Greg got up from the table and hurried after her, his tea untouched.

"I hope when them pups is growed," Singe said quietly, "they're as well trained as he is."

"I'll do the dishes," Colleen said, "*if* the kids do the chores marked on the board."

"What's the third one?" Jewen peered. "Slug patrol?"

"I want an angel to come from heaven and blow or something. If we don't find a way to get rid of them we aren't going to get any squash, cucumbers or tommytoes from the garden."

"Where's all the new kinds coming from, anyway?" Singe asked. "Seems to me when we were kids there were just those greeny-grey buggers with black blotches. Now there's white ones and orange ones, and I swear to god the other day I saw one was black and looked like a hunka ribbed rubber."

"There's yellow ones, too," Jessie added. "They look like bananas, they really do, except bananas aren't all slimy."

There weren't enough scraps for a dwarf, but she scraped what there was onto a plate and took it to the backroom. The pups went at the food as if they hadn't already had a meal. When she took the empty plate to the sink to wash, she put the pups outside, and no more did their feet touch the grass than they were squatting.

"Thank you, god," she said conversationally. "Very kind of you."

When she heard the roar of the lawn mower she looked out the window. Tom was riding on it, taking it along the fence line around the garden, cutting the long grass and weeds. He didn't have the hopper attached, and she wondered if any of them would ever again bother with the stupid thing. Unless the grass was totally bone dry and no longer than a fingernail clipping, the hopper plugged just where the plastic tube came up off the mulcher.

Jewen was making spears out of pieces of branch with a nail set in the end. The kids walked behind the mower, spearing and jabbing viciously, each trying to collect the most slugs.

Singe was digging spuds and Tony was taking the rototiller between the rows, whapping down the few weeds and turning the dirt, aerating it. She wished she had a video camera: it was like the opening scene from a Walton's programme, each and every one of them busy, busy, busy. So much endeavour just to try to stop the slugs from wiping out the vegetable patch!

The kids were in bed asleep, the adults sitting with a pot of fresh tea and some fresh-baked peanut butter cookies when the southbound bus stopped outside, then started up again. They all looked over at where the pups were curled on a worn-out discarded jacket, then each of them shrugged.

"Maybe a raccoon," Jewen said, yawning.

"Think the driver'd know enough to go right over top of the little bandit-faced freak." Singe checked his watch. "Well, enough of this hilarity, I'm going over to Lucy's."

"You take her a bucket of spuds," Colleen suggested. "And maybe a couple dozen of the cookies, too."

"Oh, hell, I near forgot." He reached in his jeans pocket and pulled out some money. "Here, this is from Darlene, for house expenses."

"Good job you reminded me." Jewen reached in his pocket. "My paycheque came through."

"Seems to me I ought to chip in, too," Tony said quietly. "I been eatin' like a total oinker ever since I got here."

"You been working like a dog, too," Singe said. "That ought to count."

"You been working right alongside me."

"Yeah, but . . ."

"Shut the fuck up," Jewen snapped. "Let the man pay his way; he don't want to feel like no freeloader."

They all handed money to Colleen who nodded and tucked it in her jeans pocket without counting. The hydro bill was due, they'd need groceries again before the end of the week, she'd have to pick up milk and cheese and stuff at noon the next day, and the insurance payments were coming up soon.

They didn't hear the footsteps on the stairs and porch so when the front door opened they were all startled.

"Christ, is this all you guys have got to do?" Al asked, walking in with a garbage bag of stuff in one hand and a grin a mile wide. He caught sight of Tony, grinning at him from the sofa. "Found the place, did you?" Al laughed softly. It explained a lot. Not everything, but a lot. Maybe they'd shared the same cell.

CHAPTER THREE

For days the kids walked as if their feet weren't touching the ground. Dad was back. Even those whose dad he wasn't were caught up in the glory. Dad was back, and so every one of them had to squeeze in the crew seat of Singe's pickup and head off to the bike store. He even got a heavy plastic jobbie of a bike rack, so there could be no excuse for any of them to leave their treasure out where someone might drive over it or, worse, trip on it and break a bone or two. Little Wilma wanted training wheels, but Al told her if she couldn't ride the bike she'd just have to do without one. She got all set to whine, took a look at how indifferent about it he was, and gave it up as a bad job. She was beginning to realize it only worked on her mother, and her mother was seldom in the picture.

Then off to Wal-Mart, and it was a Gameboy each, then to the fish and chip shop for a whopper of a meal. One day he borrowed the truck, drove into town on his own, and came back with two inflatable boats and four life jackets. "Tommy does the oars on this one, and Jessie does 'em on the other one," he said sternly. "You small tads, you're only allowed to row in real shallow water, and then only if one of the big kids promises to spot you, understand?"

"Yes, Dad," said two of them.

"Yes, Uncle," said the other two.

There was, of course, no way to warn Maude that Al was back. Nobody had the slightest idea where she was. Darlene hoped when Maude showed up she'd arrive by herself; there was always the chance that, if she showed up with a drone in tow, Al would wind up gone away for another couple or three years.

Al went into town, again by himself, again borrowing Singe's truck, and when he came back he had new steel-toed work boots, four pair of new red strap work jeans, a dozen Stanfield's tee-shirts and three flannel macs. He also had at least two dozen pairs of work socks, not just grey ones but blue and green ones as well. He got back before noon and was out working in new duds before one o'clock. When the Prince of Wales and his assistant/son arrived to start rebuilding the chimney, Al was as work-stained and dust-encrusted as anyone, grinning widely, already relaxing inside, where self-preservation had tightened and hardened him while he did his time.

A week after he arrived back he got Singe to drive him to Cranberry where he handed over an envelope stuffed with cash, then took possession of a nine-year-old crew-cab. It had about enough gas in it to get to the Petro-Can, and once there a check of the dip-stick showed it needed oil, too, but the tires were good, and even Singe couldn't find anything much wrong with the engine or tranny. The kids were excited and acted silly because there was a tape deck in the brown Chev, with speakers set in under the crew seat, and even a little box with a collection of Willie Nelson and Kris Kristofferson.

🏹

Not a week later there was a dump truck parked beside the house, and Al busy with socket sets and wrench sets and odd-looking bits and pieces of stuff only Singe and Jewen seemed to recognize. Tony watched, and once in a while nodded as things started to make sense to him.

Tony's behaviour and attitude around Al was somewhere between best buddies and the kind of awe usually reserved for hockey players who have a habit of getting hat tricks. Colleen knew he and Al had known each other long before Al came back; there were shared references to other men about whom she knew nothing, and sometimes someone would say something and only Al and Tony would burst out laughing. But they never said anything about where they had met, or how, or even when, and it didn't really seem important enough to ask questions; people meet other people all the time. Sometimes they even share the same cell. You never know.

When the dump truck was working to Al's satisfaction he got a magnetized plastic sign for both doors: "Al's Aggregates." He and Singeon had a good laugh at that, and even Jewen chuckled. There was a phone number on the sign, too, and when, on impulse, Colleen dialled it from work she got what was obviously a machine telling her to leave a message and Al would get back to her. She left a message and her number at work, and two hours later Al called her.

"Yes, ma'am." He was grinning; she could hear it in his voice. "I understand you have some need of aggregates?"

"Yes, sir." She played along with him. "I'd like the aggregate total of the square root of five times sweet diddly-squat, please."

"Yes, ma'am, that would be bugger-nothing in a brown bag."

"I'll take two, please."

They chatted briefly, told each other see you later and love you, and the rest of her day seemed brighter because of the call. On her way home from work she stopped at the Dairy Queen and got a gallon of vanilla, and took it home, put it in the freezer while she rushed around making supper and six pecan pies. Al was nuts about pecan pie, even when it was made with walnuts, which was all she had.

Whatever it was he was doing with aggregates, the dump truck was busy enough. The loader seemed to rumble back and forth between the gravel bank and the slag heap, filling the dump box. Then Al would drive the truck off, taking either or a mix of the two and delivering it somewhere, for some reason or other.

He began to tan again, and his laugh and squint lines showed more clearly, paler against the increasing dark of his skin. A couple more weeks and he would once again look like she remembered him.

The firewood trucks were hauling sacks of coal now. She wasn't sure who was buying it or how much they were paying for it, but everyone on this end seemed more than satisfied. Darlene said they had shored up the roof of the old tunnel and had a salvaged diesel-powered donkey rig to pull flatcars out of the shaft. Colleen took her word for it. She had a thing about the mere idea of a coal mine: it gave her the heebie-jeebies to think of people willingly stepping down into one. Too many old stories of explosions, cave-ins and floods, and too much like thumbing your nose at the devil and daring him to do his worst.

She couldn't believe how quickly her little shack was taking shape, or how little resemblance there was to anything either small or thrown together.

"Doesn't take any longer to *do* it than it takes to half-do it." Jewen chewed his toothpick and smiled at her.

"But three bedrooms? Jewen, I don't need . . ."

"Sure you do. No law says you have to put beds in 'em. Set up your own computer stuff in one, for example."

"I don't have any computer stuff at home, just at work."

"Sure, there's no room in the old place for it, and the kids'd just spill pop down it or something. But here . . . no problemo."

When next she spoke about the size of things, it was Singeon she cornered. "The living room is big enough for a ballroom dance competition," she dared.

"You know you're going to enjoy the space. Don't deny yourself, Colly," he said with a laugh. "You're too Scotch, that's your one little fault. You've been crammed into a cubbyhole of a bedroom too long, you've been spending hours every day in a ditsy little office space, you couldn't swing a kitten in most parts of your life, and once you get a TV of your own in one corner and some good speakers set up for a sound system, well, you'll fall in love is what you'll do. Music needs some room to fill, it needs . . ." he waved his arms, then shrugged, "space."

She bought groceries, she cooked suppers, she tried to organize the kids so the house and chores were kept up to snuff, and she did her best to sidestep Stan at work. He was getting careless about his strategies in his private little war against her. She knew she was going to quit soon. It was either quit or engage in a war of her own and take his job from him. And she didn't want his job, mostly because she wasn't willing to expend the energy it would take to wage war, especially since she wasn't allowed, by law, to kill the sucker.

Maude walked right into the middle of it. She showed up at suppertime, and it was obvious from first glance that she not only had been drinking heavily, she had something else floating around in her as well. She saw Al, gasped aloud, and put out one hand to steady herself against the kitchen door jamb.

"Pull up a chair," Al invited cooly. "There's lots."

Maude mumbled something that might have been hello, or might have been thank you or might have been the first line of a Beatles song, and made her way to the chair Tommy vacated for her. He took his plate and cutlery with him, then darted for clean ones for her. He set her a place, poured her a mug of tea, and squeezed himself onto the same chair as Dorrit, who didn't mind at all.

"How you been?" Al asked easily.

"Good. You?"

"If I was any better, I'd have to be twins just to hold it all. We were starting to think you'd got yourself lost."

"Lost? No." She shook her head no when someone offered to pass her the bowl of corn on the cob. And as if her movement was a signal, a car horn sounded from outside. Maude looked suddenly terrified.

"Tom," Al said clearly, "go outside and tell your mother's friend to come in and join us for supper."

"What if he says no?"

"Tell him to lay off the fuckin' horn. It ain't polite, and your mother isn't a dog to come just because he whistles, okay?"

He put two slices of deer liver on her plate, and ladled gravy. "You always were partial to deer liver." He smiled. "Should'a known the smell of it would bring you back. If I'd'a thought, we'd'a had it two weeks ago, then we'd'a seen more of you. Spuds? They're fresh picked today."

"Just one," she whispered. Dutifully, she picked up her knife and fork and began to eat the deer liver. The taste of it seemed to remind her body that it hadn't had nourishment for hours on end. "It's good." She looked better, her surprise and fear wearing off. Obviously, Al wasn't going to pound the shit out of her because if he had been going to he'd be doing it already.

Tom came back in, followed by Brewster Johnson. Colleen quickly picked up a cob of corn and started to eat it, hiding her grin behind it. Brewster Johnson was so completely dumb, a person would have been forgiven for thinking he was nothing more than a wart on the arse of the average toad.

"Hi, Brew." Al flicked his eyes at Jessie, who took the hint immediately and gave up her place for the visitor.

"Sit down, fill your plate, there's lots."

"Thank you kindly." Brewster grinned and set to with more enthusiasm than wit. "Didn't know you were back yet," he said cheerily. "How's everything going?"

"Real fine, Brew. Fine as silk. Here, try some of these hot biscuits; Colly made 'em, and you know she's the best biscuit maker for miles."

Brewster ate with the appetite of someone who took most of his meals in a diner, and Maude cleaned her plate but said no thank you to seconds. Not Brew: he took seconds, and then was Johnny-on-the-spot for dessert as well. "Fine meal," he grinned, his round face reminding Colleen of a tomato. "What do you think, we going to get thunder?"

"Oh, I'm sure we will," Jewen agreed. "Wouldn't be surprised if we got lightning right along with it."

"Been too hot and dry for too long." Brewster was always convinced he was right up there with the great conversationalists of the world. "Bush is closed down and has been for a while; now they're talking of watering restrictions, and the forest fire hazard is so high they say they're going to close down the access roads to the lakes and rivers."

"Bush has been closed for more'n two months," Jewen agreed.

"Helluva thing." Brewster was spooning berry grunt into his mouth, maundering on as if he didn't know he was talking to a room half full of loggers. "The way it rains all damn winter until everything's soggy, and then the next thing you know it's so hot and dry people's out of work. Makes me glad I don't have to depend on logging."

"Makes me glad, too," Jewen agreed, but it went right over Brew's head.

Brew worked at the chain supermarket in town and seemed to think it was a white-collar career. Mostly he stocked shelves and changed the little plastic tabs that told the price of things. Sometimes he trimmed the wilted ends of celery or stripped off the browning outer leaves of lettuce, but mostly he pushed dollycarts of cereal or women's sanitary supplies and refilled the displays.

He was so dumb he probably didn't even know that Maude had a buzz on from more than just one or two beer.

"Surely do appreciate your hospitality," he said, apparently quite unaware of the incongruity of chatting amicably with the husband of the woman he'd been boffing.

"Oh, anytime, Brew, anytime." Singeon got up and went to fill the kettle, then put it on to boil for another pot of tea.

"Soon as you kids've finished, you can clear the table, wipe it down, then neatly stack the dishes in the sink and put 'em to soak," Al directed quietly. The kids nodded. It didn't take much from Al to get them all in line. "Then you can go outside to play with the pups. And don't you set foot on the path back into the dig, you hear?"

"Yes, Dad," said two.

"Yes, Uncle," said the other two.

The plates got scraped into the big plastic bowl, and Little Wilma was given the honour and glory of taking it out to the pups. Dorrit got to wipe off the table, and did such a good job Singe grabbed a tea towel and dried the top.

"Thanks," Dorrit said, smiling, and once again, Singe melted.

"Any time, boy." He tossed the wet towel to the kid, who caught it and burbled with glee.

"More tea, anyone?" Singe moved to the stove.

"You been back long?" Maude asked, looking at her mug, not at her husband.

"Nearly three weeks. Feels good."

"I, uh, guess we should, uh, maybe, well, have a talk or something." Her eyes skittered from the mug to Al's chest, then to the sugar bowl in the middle of the table.

"Why'n't we just take a coupl'a beer with us and go for a ride together?" Al turned to Brew. "Only way a person gets any peace and quiet around here is to leave." But that, too, went over Brew's head. "Tell you what," Al rose. "Why'n't you watch you some TV in the living room, Brew, have yourself a beer or something, maybe another dessert, whatever. Me 'n' Maude won't be gone long, then you can be on your way, how's that?"

"Fine by me." Brew nodded and pushed his mug where Singeon could refill it with fresh tea. "But I think I'll just have tea if you don't mind. There are more cops out on the highway than there are fleas on a dog. I mean to say, we must have seen what, Maude, eight or nine different cop cars on our way out here."

"Well, then, maybe Maude and me should pass on the beer." Al grinned. "Hate like hell to get on the wrong side of Johnny Law."

Maude didn't seem too keen and eager to leave with Al, but she was the one had more or less suggested a chat to clear the air, so she tailed after him, leaving her shabby purse hanging by its strap over the back of the chair. The strap had broken at one point and she had fixed it with a staple gun. The metal staples made the purse look even more worn-out and weary than it was.

Colleen took over at the sink and washed the dishes. At one point Brew started to get up from his chair, saying something about lending a hand, but Jewen shook his head and spoke quickly.

"You get in her way and she'll raise hell," he said, as if it was anywhere near true. Brew believed him and sat back down again.

"Do you allow smoking in the kitchen?" he asked hopefully.

"Oh, hell, man, you can smoke anywhere's you like in this place. Here, have a rollie?"

"I've got some pre-mades. Maybe you'd like one of mine?"

"Why, thank you, Brewster."

101

Colleen didn't understand the way men talked to each other. Sometimes two or more strangers would meet and talk together so casually and easily you'd think they'd known each other since Grade One, and other times, like now, there was this strangeness, this over-politeness that extended past the stranger and included even Singeon and Tony. Although Tony didn't seem to know all the rules.

"Maybe I should go out and . . ." Tony never got to say what it was he had in mind to do because Singeon shook his head and Jewen said, "No." Just that, flat, emotionless and certainly not the least bit threatening or confrontational, but Tony sat down again, hurriedly.

"So how's things at the store?" Jewen asked.

"Fine." Brew looked comfortable enough to take root. "Just fine. And you?"

"Fine. Been shut down a couple of months, but there's always plenty to do around the place."

"I imagine so," Brewster agreed. "Been busy my own self, had the plumber in to redo the pipes, and all. Hauled out that old cast-iron tub and knocked out a wall so's they could install one of those new fibreglass jobbies with the swirl thing."

"Big job?"

"No, the wall only went to what used to be a sort of a linen closet or something. One of those stupid goddamn things with hardly enough room in 'em for a tube of Preparation H."

"You got the piles?" Singeon asked sympathetically.

"Me? No." Brew blinked, hesitated, then decided against expanding on the subject. "Got rid of it, anyway." He was obviously referring to the closet. "The tub fit in good once that was gone. It's got one of those shower attachments, you know, you can play with the dial and get what they call the pulsing stream, in case you got, for example, muscle ache."

"You get muscle ache, do you?" Again it was Singeon.

"Some of the time. My job has me bending a lot."

"Know what you mean. With me, for some reason," Singeon ran his hand along the outside of one leg, from bulging calf upwards, "it aches all the way up into my butt muscles. I tell people I got a chronic pain in the ass." He grinned. "So what happened to the big old tub?"

"Just chucked 'er into the backyard for now. Have to get rid of it, though."

"I'll come by with the truck tomorrow. We can haul 'er up with the winch, load her on back, get her out of your way, no problem."

"Appreciate that. Big ugly old thing."

Colleen was just about ready to shriek by the time Al and Maude returned. Al seemed totally unchanged; Maude seemed half a step from hysterics, but all she did was tell Brewster she'd only be a couple of minutes, and she left the kitchen and headed upstairs.

After a while they heard her come downstairs and go outside, then she came back in and they heard her go back upstairs. Then down again, and then up one more time. She was upstairs a fair while that time, then came down again, and a few seconds later Colleen saw through the kitchen window that Maude was cuddling Tom and Jessie, talking softly to them, and they were nodding. Maude gave them each a big hug and walked back toward the front of the house, then the car horn sounded.

"Guess that's for me." Brewster smiled, stood up, shook hands with everyone, even Al, and walked out the back door and around the side of the house. He stopped, spoke to the kids, reached in his pocket, brought out some money and handed it to Jessie.

They just sat in the kitchen until the sound of the car died away, then Al stood up, reached for his smokes, and stretched. "Maybe take the kids for an ice cream," he said.

"I can get in another hour or two before it's time to pack 'er in," Singeon said.

Colleen stood alone in the kitchen, wondering why it all of a sudden seemed as if the shabby purse dominated everything. It wasn't a big purse, god knows, but it seemed to be just about all she could see, the staples like some kind of meek accusation.

She took the purse and headed up to Maude's room with it. The mattress was still leaning against the wall where Darlene had flipped it. The closet door was open, the empty hangers moving slightly in the breeze through the open window. The bottom drawer of the dresser was half open, the drawer empty. Colleen checked everything, and Maude was gone, even her deodorant stick gone from the upstairs bathroom.

Colleen hung the purse by its stapled strap from one of the hangers in the closet. Then she shut the closet door, but even with it closed she could still picture the purse, swinging slightly.

When Darlene came home from work without Greg, Colleen heard her and wakened.

"Maude's gone," she said.

"Gone? Maude? You mean dead?" Darlene gasped.

"God, no! Just gone, as in moved out. Her room's empty."

"Won't be for long. I'll move into the bugger myself, first thing t'morrow."

"You? First thing? Your idea of first thing is ha'past noon."

"Don't get started with me, Colly, I'm in no fuckin' mood for it, okay?"

"Jesus, Dar, get a grip." And Colleen rolled onto her side, her back turned to her sister.

Darlene hauled off her clothes, pulled on a clean tee-shirt and crawled into her messy rumpled bed. Well, if it wasn't one damn thing it was another. That damn Greg was just up and gone halfway through her shift. "Have to go see someone," he told her, no sign of a smile. "Won't be back tonight but maybe I'll see you tomorrow for a while. But if I don't, don't worry, I'll be back soon."

"Where in hell you going all of a quick?"

"Got a chance at a bit of a job." He kissed her cheek briefly and that was all he wrote; he was gone, and she had to catch a ride home with Barb, who, of course, was full of questions like: Did you have a fight or anything? And gee, you don't think he's got a squeezie, do you? Why was it the less people had to say the more they talked? And if the yahoo didn't show up tomorrow it'd be back to weasling one of the guys to drive her to work in Singe's truck, then another lift with Barb Yackety-Yack. If it wasn't one damn thing it was another.

🕊

Colleen was changed and in jeans and tee-shirt and thinking of what to put together for hungry people when someone started playing with an air horn. The sound bleated, blasted, then repeated, and she shook her head, wondering why kids seemed to think noise meant fun. Or was it the other way around, you had fun only when there was noise? Someone must have yelled at them, though, because the uproar stopped, for which she breathed a sigh of thanks to the heavens.

The cop showed up again when Colleen was washing the makings for salad. He rapped on the front door, and when she hollered for him to come in, he called back, identifying himself.

"Well, come on in anyway," she laughed. "We're not proud around here."

"I uh, am here on, uh, official business," he answered.

"Yeah? Well, come on in anyway."

"I have a search warrant."

"You have a who?" She left the sink and hurried to the front door, wiping her hands on a tea towel. He stood on the porch, looking uncomfortable, another cop standing behind him and two more waiting beside a second car. "Jeez, all this for old Bob's chickens?" she joked.

"I'm afraid it's a bit more than chickens this time." He handed her the blue paper; she looked at it, and shrugged.

"It says here you're looking for 'stolen property, drug parapha' . . . you guys spelled that wrong, you know . . . and," she started chortling, "'apparatus for the manufacture of illegal alcohol'. You mean a still? Hell, we shut that down weeks ago. I guess you want me to show you around?"

"That won't be necessary. Is Singeon here?"

"Singe? He's over working on my house."

"Is Albert here? Or Jewen?"

"Cuttin' stove wood, I think, unless they're delivering slag 'n' gravel for someone's driveway. You could save yourself a lot of tramping around if you just sat on the porch for a while and waited; they're expecting supper in a coupl'a minutes, and they've never missed a meal yet."

"Is Anthony Brandeis here?"

"Who?"

Before he could answer, the air was smashed to smithereens by the sound of an old mine whistle. The cops nearly jumped out of their uniforms.

"What was that?" one of them demanded.

"Those kids," she sighed, shaking her head. "Honestly, you could tell them a million times and they'd still . . ." The horn sounded again. "Cut that out!" she yelled, but it sounded a third time. "Earlier on, it was an air horn of some kind. I don't know where they find all that junk, so help me, but sometimes it's about enough to make you want to be deaf. They'll quit when they've had enough, I guess. Want to come with me, I'll take you to Singe, and then I've got to get back to making supper."

Singe knew the cops were there: the cars were in plain sight of where he was working on the house. He just kept working, waiting for them to make their way to where he was.

"Says he wants to see you," Colleen said with what seemed like easiness.

"What can I do for you today?" Singeon half turned away, spat out his snoose, wiped his mouth, then turned back to face them.

The cop had another copy of the search warrant. Singe took it, looked at it, then took his reading glasses from his shirt pocket, carefully fitted them to his face, and read the entire search warrant from top to bottom, both sides.

"Well," he said, laughing, "good luck." He waved easily. "There's near two hundred acres here, most of it in second- or third-growth with a lot of brush, slash and blowdown. Be careful about holes in the ground, you might fall through and down an old mine shaft. And if you're gonna bring in the dogs, could you make sure they stay away from the hen coop?"

"It would facilitate matters greatly if you would assist us."

"Well, I'd like to, I surely would, but the thing of it is, you're barking up the wrong tree. There hasn't been a still on the place since, oh, hell, it's got to be at least twenty years. The old man made his own, right up to the day he'd no more than walked away from the thing than it blew up. Scared him so bad he quit drinkin' for damn near a year. As for the drug stuff, well, your helicopters fly over here about three times a day, just above tree level; if we were growin' anything other than what Colly's got in her garden, you'd already have it spotted. And there's nothing around here that's stolen. And that's about all the help I can give you." He pulled his round can of snoose from his back pocket and tapped the lid. The cop stared at him, then nodded.

"Mind if I take a look inside?" He gestured at the partially built house.

"Help yourself. There's a sack there for wipin' your feet." And he took a pinch, stuffed his bottom lip, and tamped it into place.

The cops walked around inside the shell of Colleen's house, picking up the tools, looking at serial numbers, putting tools back again. Singeon didn't even try to get any more work done; he walked to the shed, dug in his pocket for the key to the padlock, unlocked it and opened the door wide, propping it with a block of wood.

Colleen came from the house and moved to the propane barbecue with a platter of hamburger formed into patties. She looked at Singe; he shrugged, then turned aside to spit. He hauled his hanky from his back pocket, wiped his mouth, put the hanky back, and went into the house to wash his hands. When he came out, he had a load of plates which he set on the back steps.

He brushed off the top of the picnic table Jewen had made, and stacked the plates at one end. He had the cutlery and condiments out and the salad in the middle of the table with a tea towel over top to keep out the yellow jackets and hornets, when the kids came drifting out of the bush with the puppies. Spot, sometimes called Faro, was sleeping in Dorrit's arms, but Morespots, a.k.a. Cleo, was still on her feet, although plodding instead of dashing and leaping.

The pups were in their yard, flopped on a couple of old sacks, and the kids were scrubbing their hands clean—there would be a tidemark at the wrist, but at least the hands and fingers wouldn't look like a load of landfill—when Jewen and Al came out, carrying chainsaws and splitting mauls.

The cops came over and spoke with them, but Al wasn't of a mood to stand in the backyard jawing. He headed for the wash basin in the house, two of the cops walking casually with him, polite as hell, but persistent. Jewen turned on the hose and sluiced his head and face.

"Christ a'mighty," he breathed, "I don't think I died, but it's at least as hot as hell." He smiled over at Colleen. "Something smells just about good enough to eat."

"I'd like you to answer my question, please," the original cop insisted.

"What question was that, son?" Jewen wasn't going to make it easy.

"Whether or not you have seen two beef steers and a pig."

"Can I see that there search warrant again, please?" Jewen took it, peered at it as if he were Mr. Magoo, then smiled. "I don't see a thing here about livestock."

"Stolen property." The cop was just a slight touch testy, now.

"Oh, they been stolen? From where? By who?"

"Have you seen them?"

"No, haven't been any stray critters wandering around here that I've seen." He looked at his hands. "Want to come in the house with me while I scrub the dirt off my hands? And," he sniffed, "I think I need to get out of this sweat-stinkin' shirt, too, or Sister there won't feed me."

The cop nodded. Jewen headed for the house, and the cop turned to Colleen. "You?" he asked.

"Me, what?"

"Did you see two steers and a pig?"

"No. You must think we're an outpost of the SPCA; no more does a creature wander over a fence line than you're out here looking to see if it came to our place."

"What's in that shed?" He pointed.

"Well, Singe unlocked the door and left it open, so I guess you can go in and see for yourself. I haven't been in lately, but the last time I was, it was a tool shed. We keep it locked because kids seem to have a fascination for tools and a habit of cutting themselves with them."

"Are any of these *your* kids?" he asked. Colleen laughed freely.

"I should say not! My heavens, I don't even fuck, let alone breed."

His eyes widened, as if he had never entertained the notion a woman might call it what it was and not hide behind the "love making" label.

Al came out of the house carrying the mammoth-sized casserole dish. He put it on the picnic table and the heady aroma of macaroni and cheese lifted from it with the steam. "Smells wonderful," he told her.

"I cooked the broccoli in with it," she said, smiling. "This man was wondering if any of these kids were mine," she added.

"Two of 'em's mine." Al did not smile at the cop. "One of the others is my sister's, the other's my brother's. They aren't here, sister's at work, brother's at work, too. So's his woman."

"Mind if I look in that shed?"

"Look in 'em all far's I give a shit." Al was obviously angry. "You guys really do make my arse ache, you know. Here, you kids, sit down on the bench and sit quiet or you'll go to bed hungry. Grabbin' at stuff like you never got told about manners and politeness. Jessie, you fix a plate for Dorrit, and Tom, you fix one for Willy, okay? Thank you."

Jewen and Singe came out, followed by bored-looking cops. The cops looked at their colleague, who gestured at the shed, and they all moved over to have a look at shelves of hammers, screwdrivers, wrenches and spare parts.

The family was eating supper when the stovewood truck drove out of the bush. Lucy's cousin honked a few times, waved and drove past the cop cars as if they weren't even there. The cops came out of the tool shed, one of them waved, but Lucy's cousin preferred to misunderstand and waved back, then honked.

"Who was that?" the cop demanded. "And where are they going?"

"Who it was, was my woman's cousin, came to get some stovewood. And where they're going, well, I suppose probably going home with it, but you never know, they might take it into their head to go to the Dairy Queen, hard to say."

"Do you have a firewood permit?"

"I don't need no goddamn government permit to cut down my own alder on my own land and give it free gratis to my own goddamn in-laws." Singe laughed. "And this *is* our land. And those *are* our alders."

"Do you declare the income on your tax returns?"

"What income? I told you, they came to get stovewood. I didn't say I sold it to them. Hell, you don't charge family!"

The cop turned away, and he and the others spread out, looking in, behind, under, in front of and on top of just about everything. They huddled together, talking, then headed down the skidder road to see where the stovewood truck had been before it drove off with a load of wood.

"Christ, don't hardly need the stove or the barbecue with all the heat here," Al groused. "Singe, you been up to anything?"

"I thought it was you."

Eventually, another car arrived with two more cops and a hyper German shepherd. No more did the police dog jump out of the car than both pups started raising hell.

"Best we feed those little buggers," Al decided. He left the picnic table and got the dog dishes, half-filled them with kibble, then dropped generous dollops of macaroni and cheese in, with a hamburger patty for each pup. "Here." He opened their gate, put the food bowls on the ground. "Eat this and shut up. Jeez, it's just a police dog, it's nothing to get upset about."

The dog was on a long leash and at a word from the handler it put its nose to the ground and started weaving around, sniffing.

"Well-trained dog," Singe noted, "but awfully nervous and silly."

"You'd be nervous and silly if you had to spend all day in the company of the Outriders," Jewen answered.

"I don't like big dogs," Dorrit announced. "They push you down all the time."

"Well, some of them do. But when I get my hunting dog, it won't push you down." Al reached over, tapped a piece of broccoli on Dorrit's plate. "You pretending that isn't there? You pretending it's invisible?"

"I don't want to eat it," Dorrit answered, smiling at Al. "And Auntie Colly said I didn't have to eat it as long as I ate extra salad."

"Okay." Al speared the broccoli. "I'll eat it for you, how's that?"

"That's good. Did the dogs eat all the hamburgers?"

"Here, I'll get you one."

The kids cleared the picnic table and put the dishes in a sink full of hot water to soak, while Colleen whipped a quart of farm cream and brought out the dessert.

"Grunt," Al sighed, smiling widely. "I love it. You just sit down, load your plate and eat until you grunt like a pig."

"Oink oink," Singe agreed.

They were just starting dessert when the cops came back out of the bush with the police dog off the leash. The pups started raging again, and the police dog rushed their pen.

"Get that fuckin' mutt on the leash!" Al roared.

"Lance!" the handler called. The dog stopped, turned and headed back obediently.

"There's little kids here," Al lectured. "Goddamn dog's a trained killer and you let it loose around little kids?"

"He's under control." The handler was angry.

"Yeah, he is *now*, but he didn't look under much fuckin' control when he charged the pups."

The cops didn't answer. They headed for their cars, got in and drove off, watched by dessert-chewing Lancasters.

🦅

"More grunt?" Singe asked hopefully.

"But not blackberry, it's rhubarb and apple."

"Oh, shit, how awful." Singe laughed. "Nothing but rhubarb and apple? What's the world coming to anyway?" He went into the house to get the other dessert, and before he came back with it, the air horn sounded again, brash and harsh. Obviously, the kids were innocent: they were stuffing themselves with grunt and not an air horn in sight.

They had finished dessert when Tony came sauntering out of the bush, grinning widely. Nobody said anything about his prolonged stay, and nobody mentioned the blasting of the horn. He washed up and sat down to a huge plateload of supper, as if it was an everyday occurrence to move into an abandoned mine shaft and stay in the dark.

"Excellent hamburger," he said quietly. Al snickered. Singeon laughed. Jewen grinned and spooned whipped cream onto his grunt.

Colleen went into the kitchen to put on the coffee maker, and while there she washed the plates, glasses and cutlery in the sink, emptied the dirty water, rinsed the sink, then refilled it and put in the next load to soak.

At two-thirty in the morning Colleen was awakened by the clatter when the last of the brothers, Norm, and his wife Wilma, brought Darlene home from work.

CHAPTER FOUR

Colleen pulled three thousand dollars out of her savings account and handed it to Singeon for building materials. He told her it was too much, but took it anyway. Five days later the well diggers arrived and started checking over the place with their willow wands. They had their drilling rig in place when Colleen came home from work so she matter-of-factly increased the amount she cooked for supper and invited them to stay for the meal. They agreed readily, and even offered to help with the dishes, but Big Wilma and the kids had that under control. Big Wilma was about the size of one of the terrier pups and had only acquired the Big after Little Wilma was born. She quite cheerfully admitted she couldn't cook to save her life but could clean up like go-to-hell. When she was home, which wasn't often, she also took care of the laundry, even going so far as to iron shirt collars and cuffs, something Colleen thought was a total waste of time if you didn't *have* to be gussied up for work.

Darlene had two chums, now: Greg some of the time, and Larry some of the time. Greg hadn't taken the change very well, but Darlene asked him who'n hell he thought he was. "If you can't be here all the time don't complain if someone else takes your place."

"That's a great attitude, Darlene!" he blustered.

"Well, that's my attitude, like it or lick it," she answered.

Larry's main charm seemed to be that he had a car and didn't mind finding his own way on the nights when Greg was available.

"I'm not walkin' home in the rain just because *you* aren't here," Darlene snapped at Greg.

"It's not as if I'm running around on you; it's just that my jobs come . . ."

"Yeah, that's what *you* say."

"What'n hell kinda work does he do, anyway?" Norm asked.

"Oh, damn'f I know. Told me one time he did stocks 'n' bonds, but not full time. Drives truck sometimes, I think. Whatever it is he does, it isn't steady, and it's always at night. Maybe he cleans office buildings," she added.

The well diggers had a room in the motel just down the highway and headed off to it after supper. They were back first thing the next morning and setting up for work before Colleen had finished her coffee. By the time she'd put on her office drag and done her face, the noise had begun, a steady rhythmic ker-chunk *thump* ker-chunk *thump*. Darlene came into the kitchen looking like fury.

"What's that fuckin' racket?"

"Well diggers."

"What'n hell're we doin' with well diggers? We got water."

"Ask Singeon, he's the one told them to come."

"Probably something to do with that monster mansion they're putting together for you. For your hot tub or something!"

"I'm off to work." Colleen reached for her briefcase. "Don't forget, the kids need school clothes, soon."

"Oh, jesus, that again."

"School supply list is on the reminder board."

"Can't you take it in with you?" Darlene poured coffee. "Save me a trip," she wheedled. "Buy you a chocolate bar?"

"There's still the clothes."

"I know, but I can't do *both* in one trip."

Colleen took the list with her and stopped off at Wal-Mart at lunchtime. They had the supplies pre-packaged, even had individual displays set up for the different schools. The store was jammed with people going from Bayview to Hillside, from middle to high school, picking up bundles and lining up for the cash registers.

She had enough time to get the supply bundles and hit the tee-shirt display as well. How many each? Four? Better get six; there were five school days in a week, and what if the laundry wasn't ready in time? More underwear, more socks. She'd leave the jeans for when she had the bodies with her; she couldn't remember who liked zipper-front jeans, who liked button jeans, who had begun to refuse to wear the jeans with the elastic in the back. She'd leave the shoes, too; who knew how much their feet had or hadn't grown lately.

On the way back to her car she passed the sports shop. A clerk was adding to a display of clothes. Colleen stopped, looked in the window; coordinated tracksuit-looking things in some kind of nylon or something. Brand names and designs in contrasting colours. A person could get dark blue, light blue, green, black or even shades of pink and purple. She looked around, realized at least a third of the kids in the mall were wearing Nike, Adidas or Umbro outfits.

She nearly choked when she saw the price, but jeez, it was, after all, back to school. She'd headed back too many times without anything new, and no way was she going to stand by and let that happen again. It matters. People talk about self-image and self-esteem, and all too often none of that can even begin to happen because the kid knows full well she's wearing worn-out shoes two sizes too big. Colleen could remember how she felt when she'd had to wear someone else's gumboots, and they were so much too big for her that they flopped and made fart-sounding noises. So her feet were dry, so what? She'd felt like a freak, felt stupid, would have preferred to be drenched to the knees and shivering rather than go around like that. She had a good job, she made good money, and for sure, you couldn't take it to heaven or hell when you went—which you could do in the blink of an eye—and maybe Wil's parents weren't around often enough to have the chance or inclination to notice kids' fashions, and maybe Darlene could barely afford to put lowest-priced jeans on Dorrit's little butt, and Al probably thought his kids were totally gorgeous regardless what they had draped on their bones. But she was their auntie, she had noticed, and thank you dear god in heaven, there is money. And while it's undoubtedly true money cannot buy happiness, the lack of it certainly guarantees a hell of a lot of misery.

When she got home after work the drilling rig was still making its monotonous racket, and the kids, bored by waiting for something

115

and seeing the next best thing to nothing, were doing something on what little was left of the front slag heap. She managed to get Tom's attention, then waved her arms and pointed at her car. Tom nodded, nudged Jessie, and all four of the kids came down off the slag and moved toward her, looking as if they were arguing with each other about something.

All the guys were busy building at the new house. The roof was on and finished, the doors were on, and Jewen was putting board-and-batten siding on over the vapour-guard plastic sheathing the outer walls.

Colleen went into the house and changed, then she went over to the new house to have a look, and to dream. The bathroom was done, the floors were down and sanded, the kitchen was done and just waiting for the stove and fridge, and her bedroom was ready. She stood in the doorway to what would be her living room, admiring the fireplace built by the Prince of Wales and his son. They might be an odd pair, with almost as many tales hanging off them as "those Lancasters," but the work they did was past excellent to inspired.

"Can I move in yet?" she asked for the umpteenth time.

"Nope." Singe hugged her. "Not until the weekend. We're vacuuming all the dust and stuff up tonight and putting the sealer on the tiles. When that's dry—be a day or two at least—we'll move in the fixtures and all, and then give the floor another coating. Probably be lugging in your stuff by the weekend."

"So I can tell them to deliver?"

"Tell 'em to bring it, oh, what do you think, Jewen? Friday morning?"

"Better make it Saturday afternoon, just to be sure."

Big Wilma seemed her usual cheery self, but Norm had a hair across his ass and wouldn't say why. He was a moody bugger at the best of times and Colleen had never understood him. Oh, he was her brother, all right, and she loved him, all right, but he must have come from a different cut of cloth than the rest. Everyone else just let it hang out: if they were griped they said so, and why. Norm, he never let on one way or the other. He'd be hard-nosing you or ignoring you to beat all hell, and you could ask him why and the most you'd get was: you know. For years Colleen had gone over every word, every gesture, trying to figure out what it was she had said or done that had Norm in a mood, and then she just got sick of it, sick of assuming the blame, of accepting the idea she was responsible for his moods and emotions. Now when he got something up his nose, she just left him alone. He didn't seem to notice. Just about the time you started to feel easy with his grumpiness, he'd explode. Even then you probably wouldn't find out *why* he was going up like a skyrocket. Once, years before, in the middle of one of his fits, Al had yelled that he was a moody son of a bun. Jewen said moody was one thing, psychotic something else, and Norm had gone at him with such fury the rest of the boys had to intervene, knock him to the floor and sit on him until the madness passed.

At least he didn't go into one of his patented episodes while the well drillers were still there. He left before they did. He just finished his meal, got up, and without a word to a soul, left, still in his work clothes.

They got the kids into bed by nine-thirty, then sat on the porch with a citronella candle burning to ward off mosquitoes. Big Wilma made tea and brought out the cupcakes and muffins.

"What's wrong with your old man?" Al asked.

Big Wilma shrugged.

"He's got something riding him," Al persisted.

"Well, he's got him a squeezie," Big Wilma said, her voice breaking, her eyes suddenly damp. "And she's got a husband with no sense of humour at all."

"Jesus christ almighty," Al grated. "Are we off on one of them again?"

"He promised." Big Wilma cleared her throat, and her voice strengthened. "He said last time there wouldn't be any more, but . . ."

"Fuckin' tomcat," Al muttered.

"I'm not exactly sure what I'm going to do." Wilma poured tea, her hand steady. "But you can be sure I'm not just sitting like a lump on a toad's back waiting for things to sort themselves out again."

"Be a shame if you moved," Jewen said firmly. "Better if *he* did, really. I mean, it's not fair to Little Wilma, for a start. She lives here."

"And so do you," Singeon concurred. He dusted cupcake crumbs off the front of his shirt, stood up and stretched. "Prefer it if you decide to stay." He bent and kissed her cheek. "So I'll see you in the morning." He tapped his pocket, checking his pickup keys, then kissed Colleen. "Take care. Sweet dreams." They watched him head to the truck, then Jewen reached for another cupcake.

"He's right."

"Of course he's right," Colleen agreed. She turned to Big Wilma. "Please think about it, about staying. And not just because of Little Wilma. We want *you* to stay, too."

"I don't know if I can. Not if Norm . . ."

"I'm getting a cup full of Norm, lately," Al said, yawning, but not because he was tired. He was like a big cat, and the yawn was preparation for a roar, a confrontation, an attack. Not a lion or a tiger, nor even a jaguar: Al was a big round-headed tatter-eared alley tom, basically wanting only to be left alone, to bask in the sun peacefully, the smell of overripe sardine still clinging to his whiskers. "Seems like all his life Norm has bossed this family with his antics."

"Controlled our behaviour with his misbehaviour." Jewen nodded.

"First time he doesn't get it all his way, it starts. First he sulks, then he pitches himself a fuckin' tantrum. By me, it's time for him to grow up."

"Singeon says . . ." Colleen began.

"Singeon isn't right *all* the time." Al yawned again. "Good kick in the arse might put Norm's brain in gear."

Colleen wasn't going to argue with Al, but she couldn't really see much difference between the way Norm operated and the way Al did with his yawning as good as an open threat. Except, of course, with Al you at least knew why he was in a state. She didn't say anything, though; she just headed off to the bathroom to brush her teeth and get ready for bed.

In the morning there was no sign of Norm's new truck. Colleen ate her toast and drank her coffee at the kitchen table, and tried to figure out what she could do, or say, that would clear the air and get Norm back where he was supposed to be.

She had no ideas at all. Wilma came into the kitchen dressed in her work gear and looking as if she hadn't slept much, or well. She smiled and moved to give Colleen a kiss on the cheek, then got coffee and started packing her lunch.

"Are you going to let me pay for the stuff you got Willy?" she asked.

"No." Colleen made it sound very casual. "It's just a back-to-school present from a doting aunt."

"Thank you. I think she slept in her track suit last night."

"They'll have them half-frapped before school starts," Colleen chuckled softly.

Wilma looked out the window, checked the presence or absence of trucks and cars, and shook her head slightly. "Now *that* pisses me off." She looked on the verge of tears.

"I'll drive you," Colleen said hurriedly.

"Thank you. I'll be ready in a jiff." Wilma turned from the window, and for a moment the look on her face was enough to scare a person's hair white. But she didn't say anything, just hurried to finish her lunch, fill her thermos, then put on a replacement pot of coffee.

She didn't say much on the way to the freight yard, either. Colleen would have felt better if Wilma had raged, or wept, or both. The air of calm detachment was too much like dissociation, Scarlett O'Hara deciding not to think about things until she got back to Tara.

"You gonna be all right?" she asked.

"I already am all right. Tickety-boo," Wilma lied.

At noon Colleen went to the furniture and appliance store to make the arrangements for the delivery of her new stuff. Phyllis Thatcher was waiting, and why not: she was on a small salary plus commission, and she knew Colleen had deliberately chosen her over either of the two male clerks. Phyllis had two kids to support, as good as on her own. Oh, Marty paid child support sometimes, but how far does the occasional hundred dollars go when stacked up against the heap of things kids need? Little luxuries like food and basketball sneakers, nothing extraordinary. Probably one-third of the kids in town had several sets of fancy track suits, the best of sneakers, and more than one pair at a time. They belonged to swim clubs and tennis clubs and took more lessons than hell would hold, piano and skating and hockey school, and rode mountain bikes that cost close to a thousand dollars, or they even had their own horses. Another third of the kids knew by age nine there wasn't any use dreaming about any of that; they'd be lucky to get enough to eat at suppertime. Oh, but it's a classless society, she fumed, with equal opportunity for all.

She wrote a cheque and gave it to Phyllis, then stopped by the bank on her way back to work and transferred savings to her chequing account to cover the amount. She looked at the balance and frowned. Seemed to be more in there than there should be. She asked the teller to check again, and the teller smiled and assured Colleen the total was correct.

"Nice to be so rich you don't know how much you've got," she teased.

"Oh, it's a dreadful burden," Colleen answered easily. "And it clutters up the landscape as it flutters out of my pocket and blows off on the breeze."

She endured an afternoon at work, ignored Stan as much as she possibly could, and left Johnny-on-the-spot at quitting time. She drove to the freight yard, but Wilma wasn't there. One guy said she'd already gone home; another said she was probably still in her truck.

She wasn't, at least not in the gravel truck. She was home when Colleen got there, and in the driveway was parked a Travel-all. It wasn't new, of course, but it looked good: the paint job obviously new and not a sign of a dent or scratch. Wilma came out on the porch, grinning. "What do you think?"

"I think people will begin to suspect you run a daycare; kids will fight for a chance to ride in it. Of course," she pretended to scold, "you couldn't get the damn thing for summer holidays, oh no, we had to cram them into my little thing or rattle out their teeth in old pickup trucks or something. You're a real nice guy."

"Yeah, I am, and I've got a real nice bazoo, too."

"I wouldn't know. I've never been allowed anywhere near your bazoo to see if it's nice or not."

Norm came in as they were finishing supper, and he was in a total fury. "You bitch," he roared. "Did you think I wouldn't find out?"

"Leave me alone!" Wilma was off her chair and backing away from him, her hands raised in futile defence.

"I went to the damn bank and guess what? Just guess!" And he took a swing at her. He missed, and that could only mean he had been threatening and not yet ready to really hit her.

"Stop it!" Al stood up. "You're scaring the shit out of the kids."

"Do I care? Take a guess, big guy. Do I fuckin' care?" And he was so angry at Al's interference, he took another swing at Wilma and this time hit her, knocking her to the floor.

"Momma!" Willy yelped, and jumped off her chair. She didn't run to her mother, though, she stood in front of Norm, defiant and brave. "You leave my momma alone!" she screeched.

Norm hit her, hard enough to send her sideways. Jewen was off his chair in a flash and Al was right behind him.

"Come on," Al said, and Tony was moving, too. Colleen wished Singeon had come home for supper, but he was at Lucy's.

Wilma got up from the floor, ran over to Willy, who was weeping and holding the side of her face. Already the kid's eye was swelling shut, turning blue. "Easy, baby, easy," Wilma soothed, checking Willy's ear, her jaw.

Norm struggled, cursed and hollered, but he wasn't up against three townies, and he was quickly hustled out of the kitchen. The other three kids sat stiffly, staring at their plates, Dorrit trying hard not to puke.

"Go to the bathroom, Dorry." Colleen took his hand, led him from the table. He moved as if boneless, his eyes huge, his face pallid.

"That bastard," Wilma said dully. She looked out the window to where the struggle was still going on, Norm bellowing wordlessly. "That bastard!" Her tone changed. She rose and headed for the doorway. "I'll show him!" she said.

Colleen left Dorrit on his own and tried to catch up to Wilma, but all she managed to do was get herself a ringside seat. As Wilma went past the growing woodpile near the back door, she reached out and grabbed the first thing that came to hand: a splitting maul, heavier by far than an axe, one end of it flattened, like a sledge hammer, the other wedged like a thick and bulky axe.

"You bad-tempered goddamn weasel!" Wilma raged. "You scared the kids, you hit Willy, you hit me and . . . you stinkin' puke!"

Norm broke free, backed away from his shocked brothers, who stood staring with disbelief. Tony made as if to intercept her, then thought better of the idea and stepped back out of the way.

Norm took off, heading for the bush, past the chicken coop, moving at top speed, certain every hound in hell was about to feast on his flesh. Without any change in her attitude at all Wilma veered, no longer interested in trying to run off the fleeing Norm. She went at his new pickup.

Nobody moved to stop her. They just watched. And there was plenty to watch. She started at the tailgate and worked her way down the driver's side to the front grille, then up the passenger's side to the tailgate again.

"Jesus christ," Jewen breathed.

"You stop her if you want. I'm not getting in her way." Tony laughed. "Damn, but that's one helluva woman!"

Colleen moved to stand beside Al. He put his arm around her, hugged her close, then chuckled. "Don't be scared, Colly," he told her. "It ain't us she's mad at."

When the pickup truck looked as if the earth mover had gone over top of it, Wilma moved to her own vehicle, tossed the maul in the back, then got in and drove off, slag and gravel spurting from her tires.

"Remind me to watch my P's and Q's when she's around." Colleen headed back to the house. "I have to try to settle the kids."

But they were fine when she got back. They even had the plates scraped and piled in the sink, but the dishes weren't done; they'd been watching out the window while Wilma demolished the pickup.

"Fun's over," Colleen told them. Through the window she saw

Norm coming back out of the bush, his face registering total disbelief. Nobody said anything to him. He went to his truck, even walked around it, then looked helplessly at Jewen.

"Gimme a lift?" he asked.

"Maybe it'd be best if you took your stuff," Al suggested. "You sure as hell don't want to be here when she gets back. Or until she cools down."

"Fuck her," Norm blustered.

"Somehow I think your chance to do that just drove off with her hair on fire." Jewen punched Norm's shoulder. "Come on, get some black garbage bags, and I'll help."

"The woman's crazy!"

"No, she's just mad. What did you expect? You can't act like a spoiled kid and not expect people to get fed up with you."

"Why should I pack? Let *her* pack, I bloody well live here."

"Well, thing of it is, see, we all talked it over, and we'd rather you hit the pike than the two Wilma's."

"You're kidding. Aren't you?"

"No." Al's voice was cold and hard. "Thing of it is, see, we've all had a gutful of you and your rages and furies. You don't even try to behave. Whereas Wilma and Willy are easy to get along with and, believe it or not, they actually help out, which is something can't be said about you."

"I was *born* in that house!"

"Oh, don't be an asshole, you was born in the hospital like the rest'a us." Jewen laughed easily. "Come on, get your gear and get gone before she comes back and finishes the job."

Norm took four stuffed black plastic garbage bags with him when Jewen drove him off in Colleen's little car.

"Trust that bloody Singe," Jewen said. "Takes off with his pickup the one night we need it."

Just before noon the next day the tow truck arrived to haul the heap of dents to the body shop. After supper that night Singeon drove Jewen and several more garbage bags of stuff to the motel unit where Norm had checked in.

"How 'n hell 'm I supposed to get to work!" Norm raged.

"Shank's pony? City bus? Taxi? See if the body shop has a loaner?

I don't know as, were I you, I'd even show up at work, what with Wilma still having that damn maul in her car and all."

The body shop, it turned out, had a loaner, and Norm swallowed his pride although he nearly choked on it. He went by the works yard to pick up his paycheque, and the timekeeper managed to hang onto a straight face until after Norm left in the bright pink Volkswagen. Then he howled with laughter and hit the CB so every driver within range would know to keep an eye out for the bug. Wilma heard the call but didn't bother to acknowledge it. She didn't even promise herself she'd drive the loaded gravel truck right over top of the pastel nightmare.

On Saturday afternoon, closer to two than to one, the furniture truck arrived with Colleen's stuff. An hour later she was strolling from room to room with a look on her face that suggested she'd passed the pearly gates and was on her way to at least one of the Seven Cities of Cibola. The hydro was connected, the fridge running, the new freezer wasn't plugged in yet; the movers had suggested she give it twenty-four hours for the fluid to settle. She wondered what unsettled fluid was like. Maybe it frowned a lot, or sighed constantly, maybe it paced or chain-smoked hand-rolled cigarettes.

All she took from the big old house were her clothes, and a couple of cherished souvenirs. She had a new bed, new dressers, new bedside table, new lamp in her bedroom. The living room seemed bare with just one couch and two chairs, a TV, a CD player and a VCR, and the kitchen was past bare to barren, with a small wooden table and four chairs. The cupboards were empty, nothing but her favourite coffee mug and a sugar bowl her Gran had given her for her playhouse when she was six. The new coffee maker had more buttons, knobs and digital displays than the cockpit of a jet plane, and when the toast popped it flew all the way out and landed on the counter. But it was all hers.

She had supper at the old house, as usual, and cooked most of it herself. But once everyone was fed and given a tour of the new place, she had it to herself. She sat on her couch watching her TV until she was ready to go to her bathroom. That's when she remembered she hadn't brought a towel or face cloth from the big house. At least she'd thought to buy sheets and bedding. And when she crawled into bed she couldn't believe the expanse of it. She'd spent her entire life sleeping in a single bed, not much more than a cot, really. And now there was room for two or three others to sprawl beside her. But the best part was there weren't two or three others, there was just her, in her own place.

🕊

When Colleen told the CEO's secretary, Bev, she was going to tender her resignation, there was silence on the other end of the phone.

"You lasted longer than I expected," Bev finally sighed. "What if we counter with an offer along the lines of we'll transfer Stan and you'll get his job?"

"I don't want his job." Colleen sighed, too. "There's no fun in this anymore. I've waited too long, you see. I've worn it all thin. But I had to be able to tell myself that I'd given it my best shot."

"You're sure?"

"I'm at the point where everything is an imposition. The others in the office seem like huge pains in the ass, the clients all seem like idiots, and I work as hard at not sounding like a snarly turd as I work at actually doing my job. Time to move on, I think."

"If you decide you want to come back, you phone me. Don't even bother going into the office over there and putting in an application; just phone me. Thank god the old man's in Europe for the next week. By the time he gets back and hears about this, it'll be old news."

Of course, she had another job to go to. Somehow, her casual daydream had become reality. Her resignation took effect on a Friday, at the end of the work day, and on Monday she started at the logging company. The best part of it all was her work in no way resembled what she had been doing. She had all the excitement of a new job, with new people to get to know and new routines to establish; she also had the challenge of learning the new job from scratch.

"I'd'a never thunk it," Singeon teased her. "My own sister, for chrissakes? It's humiliating! How am I going to explain it to my crew?"

"What's an environmental impact assessment person?" Tom puzzled.

"Mostly I just go around and tell people like your uncles to clean up the damn mess they've made. Here, you," she pointed at Jewen. "Get half a dozen guys and get that slash away from that creek. And you," she pointed at Tom. "You go over this place with a fine-tooth comb and pick up each and every oil can, gas can and any other kind of can you find."

"And they pay you for that?" Jessie laughed. "Sounds like a good job to me."

There was, of course, more than that to the job. Much more, in fact, and none of it made any easier by the need to pick her way through reams of government rules and regulations, all of which seemed in a state of flux and apt to about-face at any minute. An innocent bystander might well think the entire forestry policy—and possibly even the department itself—had been put together by a pack of bureaucrats who had never even set foot on a wooded path, let alone actually gone out into the bush or talked to those who lived so many hours of their lives out there.

The company provided her with a four-wheel-drive Chev pickup, and she didn't have to wear drag anymore. She bought her own steel-toed work boots, and was issued a white hard hat with the company logo stencilled on one side and her name on the other side. Singeon must have contacted someone about it because the name was "Collie," and beneath it was a rendering of Lassie's face.

"Best lookin' hat in the bush," Singe teased.

"And of course I'm not supposed to know they're already calling me 'the bitch', right?"

"Nobody's calling you the bitch."

"I bet they're not."

She was up earlier in the morning than ever before, and at first needed an alarm clock to wake her. No more sipping coffee and maybe nibbling a slice of toast, she had a breakfast fit for a logger. Usually she packed her lunch the night before and only had to get her thermos ready in the morning, and when she left her house she closed and then locked the door. The feeling of satisfaction that swept over her when she heard the deadbolt click into place was more than reward for the dent in her bank account.

She wore red strap work jeans, warm woolen socks, her insulated safety-toed boots, a tee-shirt, a mac over that, and as the weather cooled she added a down vest; she didn't need it when she was in the truck, but once she was at the site she was outside, in the weather. Before the end of the second week in October the storms were on them, harsh and blasting wind driving big drops of near-icy rain, and she needed a dryback jacket of stiff oiled canvas and several warm toques so she could hang the wet one off the car heater to dry after a sojourn outside in the anger of the west coast rain forest late autumn. Every day the light arrived later and weaker, the clouds and fog hung on longer and thicker. By mid-November the first snow was gathering in the upper levels, and the workies were muttering about being shut down soon. Of course, the recreational skiers were practically orgasmic with joy, and why not? They were, for the most part, city workers whose annual income in no way depended on weather.

Once the decision had been made as to which area was to be logged, the location of the site and a forest survey map were given to her. She went out to check for sensitive areas. And that meant walking up and down slopes, looking for streams, looking for signs of bear habitat, looking for eagle nests, osprey nests, and trying to guess correctly whether spotted owls or marbled murrelets used the area. Even though she knew the bears were bedding down for the winter, she worried about them; city people and townies might think bears were beautiful creatures willing to mind their own business if left alone, but the truth wasn't always what was presented. Any bear, with or without cubs, challenged or left alone, was as apt to charge as it was to saunter off tending its own affairs. She started taking Morespots-Cleo with her, because if there's one thing can send a bear running it's the yap-yap-yap of a small-sized dog. A big dog might wind up lunch, a small one probably won't.

Morespots, of course, didn't know she was there as defence against bears that were probably sound asleep; she preferred to try to dig up marmot tunnels or find squirrel dens. At least she came when she was called, and she was good company on the often long drives to and from the sites. Colleen didn't worry about the marmots. The poor little terribly endangered fuzzy balls were deep in their dens by now, curled up for their long winter sleep; the terrier wouldn't get within a quarter mile of them, probably. Singeon had told her a marmot tunnel might well be two, three, even four hundred years old, generation after generation of the once numerous now almost rare little beauties adding to it, digging and scratching side tunnels, extending the length, the width, even the depth of the warren. She wondered how it was, in a region that got so much rain for so many months, the warrens didn't flood and drown the hibernating creatures. Almost enough to make a person wonder if, small as they were, their brains were big enough, or complex enough, or hard-wired enough to have an instinctive talent for skilled engineering.

Usually Colleen ate her lunch in the truck, but if the sky wasn't leaking down the back of her neck or the wind trying to blow her off her feet, she might spread a piece of tarp on a log or stump and sit there, sharing sandwiches with the dog and checking the landmarks against the map. She had what seemed an endless supply of spray cans to mark trees that were to be left untouched. As best she could she marked them on the map, too. There was no rule, regulation or subsection that covered "culturally modified trees," but any time she found one, she marked it. Some of the CMTs had branches trained to grow out straight and strong to support the burial platforms, although nobody put their dead on platforms anymore; they had them cremated or embalmed and buried in the churchyard or municipal cemetery like everyone else. Some of the trees had big bare patches where, years before, the bark had been stripped to make baskets or woven hats and regalia. Every now and again she'd find one with an entire chunk missing, and she wasn't sure what caused that, although there were some academic types who said it was where someone, decades past, had "borrowed" wood for a plank, or a serving tray or whatever. Colleen didn't really believe that, but who was she to argue, especially since she had no theory of her own with which to counter, and when she asked the almost-relatives they just grinned and made daft jokes, teased her by insisting the trees had been hit by lightning, said the X-files were alive and well and that little grey aliens had swiped samples for their cloning research.

Once the logging started, she was back often, on an irregular basis, to check that the sensitive areas were left untouched. The company had several shows going at once, in different areas, under different conditions. One day she might be trudging through sodden moss, puddles the size of small ponds, and thick, usually thorny, underbrush. The next day she might be clambering a steep wet slope, rocks twisting underfoot and rolling and clattering, bouncing and slithering behind and below her.

As autumn marched on grey and drizzly, Colleen added a pair of dryback trousers to her work gear. She climbed into them as she left the truck, climbed out of them when she got back in again, and by Christmas she had bought a second pair of boots: safety-toed rubber gumboots. They were hard to walk in and so heavy that at first the muscles in her calves ached at the end of the day, but at least they kept her feet dry. Twice a day she changed her warm woolen socks: her feet sweat in the gumboots until her socks were so wet she might as well have been walking barefoot. Often she took off her dryback jacket and down vest in the truck and discovered her tee-shirt was wet with sweat. She tried leaving off the down vest and found herself shivering, her stomach muscles cramped against the cold.

"At least sweat is warm," Singe told her. "Wear the vest. Unless you trade it in for a pair of thick wool Stanfields."

"I can't wear the wool ones," she confessed. "They itch and itch, and then I get a rash in my inner elbows and under my arms."

"Well, then, it's the down vest, I guess."

"Gee, and to think I used to go to work looking *swish*."

Usually it was dark when she left for work and dark again by the time she got back home. Often she stopped at a diner or café and bought supper rather than face the thought of having to start cooking when what she really wanted was a hot bath and an early bed.

Some days her job seemed totally mindless, even silly. Other days she went home with a belly full of liver and onions, mashed spuds and gravy, feeling as if she'd more than earned her pay and done something worthwhile in the bargain. Often she fell asleep and dreamed of the trees she had marked and thus protected, dreamed of them reaching for the cloud-thick sky, their boughs heavy with rain and mist, their trunks huge, bark ribbed and thick.

Darlene didn't like to think of Colleen's new house. Every time she did she felt insulted and slighted. So she concentrated on feeling good about having her own room, with a more-or-less newish double bed and two dressers plus a closet. She even managed to keep it on the close side of tidy, partly because she didn't really have all that many clothes to dump on the floor since the arrival of the blue tin trunk which had been moved over to the new house, but mostly because she came home from work one morning and found a brand new wicker laundry hamper between the bed and one of the dressers. She never did find out who had bought it for her, so she thanked everyone for it, even those who denied any knowledge of its origins.

The day she got Greg to help her move from the downstairs room to what had been Maude's room, she took down the old blanket and Salvation Army Thrift Store drapes that had separated the room into two inadequate spaces. Once she was settled into the upstairs room she worked for three days scrubbing the downstairs one: walls, ceilings, floors, woodwork, doors, windowsills, even the inside of the closets were scoured clean. She waited the rest of the week for it all to dry thoroughly, then she painted. It took her days. And she managed to outdo every pratfall joke she'd ever seen or heard of, even to stepping back and putting her foot down in the paint tray, crushing the roller so she had to get a new one.

When the room was finally finished—paint dry, floor washed and waxed, then buffed to a dull gleam—Darlene moved Jessie and Willy into it. They went off to school from one room, came back and found their stuff elsewhere.

"Oh, wow," Jessie breathed. "Oh, *thank* you, Auntie!"

"Damn nice of you." Al gave her a hug. "You should'a hollered for some help with it."

"Oh, and when would *you* find time," she scoffed. "I'm not sure you have enough time to pee, the way you've been working lately."

It was true Al was working like the proverbial sheepdog. Singeon and Jewen were back logging, Norm didn't bother to show his face at all, and yet the trucks moved slag and gravel regularly, while other trucks took away sacks of coal, and still others came to turn scrub maple, alder and wild cherry into stovewood. And where Al went, Tony did, too.

Darlene had more to do than ever before, and it wasn't easy. She didn't have to haul herself out of bed first thing in the morning to get the kids off to school because Al and Tony were up and getting ready for the day's work. But she had the shopping to do now that Colleen didn't pick stuff up on her way home from her town job. And didn't that cost an arm and a leg? Everyone chipped in—even Singe, who was as good as living full time with his woman and her kids—but it still put a hole in the paycheque; and, of course, there was the hydro bill to deal with, and the satellite dish company, and insurance, for the house and the vehicles. As if that wasn't enough to have to keep track of, there was the constant cooking, and she really began to wonder why Greg was hanging in the way he did. Gone were the fun afternoons playing pool or going to bingo, gone the drives to the city for window-shopping. She had to get some kind of supper started, and even if she wasn't there to eat it, others would be, and if she didn't do it, the kids wouldn't eat until who knows when. She wouldn't have blamed Greg if he had decided it was all getting just a bit too mundane, but there he was, still smiling, Johnny-on-the-spot to drive her shopping or to help prepare the casserole.

🖋

Wilma waited until the weekend when they were all at the supper table, except for Singeon who was at Lucy's. "I've been offered a long-distance haul," she said quietly. "I'd be gone four days, home three if I'm lucky, two if I get held up somewhere."

131

"Held up how?" Jewen asked. "Like 'your money or your life'?"

"Like blown radiator or wonky differential. Besides, if anyone ever says 'Your money or your life', I'm going to answer 'Take my life, I need my money'."

"Jesus, don't joke," Tony admonished. "There's ay-holes out there will send you to glory for less than that."

"Little Willy's no problem." Al took a second helping of deer chops, then passed the platter to Tom. "Half the time we don't even know she's here; other half, we're overjoyed she is. Right?"

"Right," the kids replied. "Willy's okay."

"I thought maybe with some of the extra money, I could, like, hire someone to come in and, well, *do* around here a bit."

"Do?" Jewen had the platter now. He took two more chops, then passed the platter on to Wilma. "I guess I've never thought about what all there is to do. I guess it's a lot."

"Understatement, Jewen," Wilma smiled. "I'm damned if I know how Colleen did it all. The laundry is a full day's work on its own." She passed the platter on to Colleen, who took one chop and handed the rest to Tony. "I guess I never thought to tell you thank you." Wilma blushed. "I guess I was too wrapped up in my own stuff. No wonder you moved out!"

"Wasn't that." Colleen was blushing, too. "It was never having privacy, and never getting the chance to just be alone. I mean I love you all like crazy, okay, but . . ."

"Some people do okay in solitary," Al said. "Others go nuts. Me, I like a crowd."

"Me too," Jewen added. "I was never partial to being on my ownsome."

"So, would that be okay? Getting someone in to do?"

"I'll chip in on it." Tony said, surprising them all. "I mean here I've been living the life of Riley: good food every day without fail, clean clothes all the time, roof over my head, place to rest my bones. At first I didn't have a pot to pee in nor a window to chuck it out of, but I'm flush now, and it's only fair to let me put some in. I been takin' long enough."

"I'll chip in, too," Jewen offered. "Same reasons."

"Got anyone in mind?" asked Colleen.

"No. But seven out of ten in town are out of work. Someone will be glad of the job."

Norm arrived in time for dessert, but refused the offer and wouldn't even sit down and have a cup of coffee with them.

"I came to talk to Wilma." He was surly, already halfway to an explosion.

"So talk," Wilma said easily.

"In private."

"This will do."

"In *private*, Wilma, dammit!"

"I'm not going anywhere alone with you. You can talk here and now with your family, or you can talk in a lawyer's office, but you're not getting me somewhere alone so you can scare the shit out of me or start hitting again."

"Sure you won't have a coffee, Norm? There's a fresh pot."

"Don't push me, Al. I said no."

"Suit yourself. Me, I'm having another. And some more of that pie, too. Who made the pies? They're great."

"Auntie Colleen made the crusts and we did the filling. She told us how," Dorrit piped up, smiling. "We put in more sugar than she said, though."

"Shut up about the fuckin' pies, okay?" Norm snapped. Dorrit's smile vanished, and he looked down at the tabletop, eyes blinking rapidly, tears welling.

"Well, Norm, you see, it's like this." Jewen stood up, taller than his brother by several inches, heavier by fifty pounds, and none of it settled around his waist or arse. "You just don't talk like that to the little ones, okay? I mean, look at Dorry now. He's scared. He's just a button, and he's scared. I'm not. But then I'm not three feet tall, either."

"I want to get things settled with Wilma. I want Willy to stay with me on the weekends, for a start."

"I want you to pay child support, for a start. Three hundred a month."

"Kiss my arse on three hundred. I got the body work on my truck to pay off. When that's paid off maybe . . . just maybe . . . I'll pay child support. But *you*, bitch, you won't get one red cent!"

133

"I don't want your money. I don't need your money. I was feeding my own self before I met you, I fed myself the whole time we were together, and I can just keep on feeding myself. I been feeding me and Willy since you ran off, and I could keep on doing it, too. But if I have to do the whole shot, don't you start telling me anything about visitation because, by me, it ain't a right, it's a damn privilege."

"She's my kid!"

"You say that half the time. The other half you accuse me of steppin' out on you."

"If I don't get to see her, you won't get a penny."

"If you don't pay child support, you won't see her back as she walks away from you."

"Three hundred? It don't cost no three hundred to keep a sliver of a kid like that."

"Why don't we go to court, see what the judge says."

"Why don't you lick my ass."

"Because it's sitting on your shoulders, Norm, and I can't reach that high."

"You owe me damn near five thousand dollars for the body work."

"I paid for half the truck and never did get to drive it much."

"You paid for half? In a pig's eye you paid for half!"

"I did so and you know it. Then you had it registered in your name only. I bet you were already planning on hitting the road, and you wanted to hit it in style. Well, fine, it's your truck, you pay for the body work, no skin off my nose."

The bickering and nattering went on until Norm stormed out, vowing he'd ride to hell on a boom of logs before he'd let *her* squander any of *his* hard-earned money. Once he was gone, the kids dared move from the table, but before they could settle themselves in front of the TV there were dishes to do, table to clear, counters to clear and wipe, stove to clean. They didn't even bother complaining anymore; it did no good at all, and in the time it would take to lose the debate, they could have the chores finished.

Big Wilma put up notices on the bulletin boards at the laundromats, on the notice board in the Four Corners, the convenience store a mile and a half down the road from the house, and ran an ad in the local paper.

✸

Lottie Docksteader had four grown children, all of whom were married and with children of their own. She could have been kept busy knitting cardigans, mittens, warm socks and toques; she could have filled her days with peanut butter cookies and rumballs; she could have visited this one for tea, had lunch with another, supper with a third and an evening visit with the fourth. And she had no intention of doing any of that for the rest of her life. She could have had a job pumping gas at the Petro-Can; she could have short-order cooked for the Grill, but she preferred to *do* for the Lancasters.

Lottie was close to six feet tall and had what they called big bones. Over the years she'd covered those bones with a padding of muscle and just enough evidence of whipped cream, mashed spuds and homemade bread to round off the corners and pad the edges. She knew about chickens and compost bins; she knew about propane furnaces backed up by a wood-burning airtight; she knew to leave the windows open a thin crack even in the coldest weather or else condensation built up, ran down the glass and puddled on the sills before dripping down to the floor. She even knew it does nobody any harm at all to let the pups lick the plates or clean off the pots and pans.

She arrived for ten and put breakfast dishes on to soak, then put a load into the washing machine. While the dishes waited and the laundry swirled, Lottie headed upstairs to straighten the beds, and, if the room was tidy, to dry mop the floor and do dusting. If there were dirty clothes, socks and mess on the floor, Lottie didn't even straighten the bed, she just turned on her heel and walked out again. She was willing to *do* but she wasn't about to *muck out*. Lottie never went anywhere near Darlene's room, and Big Wilma's room was always so neat and tidy there was no use going in and looking for something to do because it was obviously already done. The men caught on in a hurry that if they wanted anything *done*, they'd better make sure they cheerfully danced to Lottie's tune.

About the time the washing was ready for the dryer, the upstairs was as good as done, the hallway dry mopped, the stairs swept clean. That's when the dishes were ready to be washed, rinsed and left in the rack for god to dry.

Then Lottie hit the living room. By noon it was cleaner than a dentist's waiting room: the cushions on the couches and chairs turned, the windows always clean, the drapes and curtains vacuumed, the carpets, such as they were, swept. She insisted too much vacuuming of a rug ruined it quicker than muddy feet or a long-haired dog.

Around noon Darlene got out of bed, usually with Greg, but if not, with Larry. Any thoughts Lottie had about the arrangements she kept to herself. Once Darlene's breakfast was done and the mess cleaned up, Lottie had her lunch, then went to the bathrooms to scrub tubs and toilet bowls, change towels and face cloths, and shine the mirrors.

The laundry was dry by then, so it was time to fold the towels and such, and, only when vitally necessary, of course, do the ironing. And when that was done, time to start figuring out what to feed everyone.

The school bus dropped off the kids, and Lottie sent them to change into play clothes, then organized them into chore detail. There was the pups' pen to rake and the poop to bury. Eggs needed to be picked up, brought in, washed and put in the big bowl.

"You should take a dozen or so for yourself," Jewen told her, and Lottie didn't need to be told twice. She even figured out a system that worked best in her own head and was, somehow, never fully explained to anyone, but meant if there were extras, she bought them for her children. She didn't bother to tell anyone she paid two dollars a dozen for the large brown-shelled wonders and charged the kids two-fifty a dozen. They thought they were getting a deal, since similar free-range fertilized eggs in the health food store were close to three dollars a dozen.

Lottie helped with homework if there was time between school bus and setting the table for supper. She not only made peanut butter cookies, she taught the kids how to make them, too. Lottie made pies; Lottie made fresh bread; Lottie even had a grocery list held to the fridge door with a magnet that looked like a fat-faced pig.

Her meals were not fancy, but they were delicious, filling and always on time. As far as the kids were concerned, one of the best things in the whole set-up was that Lottie would not only eat supper with them, she was the one who stacked the dishes in the sink, added water and detergent and left them to soak while everyone had dessert. When that was done, Lottie left, and the kids cleaned the kitchen.

Every second day or so, depending on just about everything else up to and including the weather, Lottie washed one, sometimes two floors, usually the kitchen or backroom where the boots, rain gear, work jackets and drybacks were kept. There were scatter rugs there and the dirt and mud collected on them as if magnetized. If Lottie didn't actually wash that floor, she took the scatter rugs out and shook them, muttering to herself as clumps of the surface of the earth tumbled onto the winter grass.

Jewen had made a boot scraper out of bottle caps. He was only thirteen at the time, but it worked so well it was still in use: a more-or-less-square swiped piece of half-inch plywood had been covered with upside down bottle caps—beer bottle caps, pop bottle caps from back in the time before twist-offs. Each cap had been nailed to the plywood with at least one, sometimes two shingle nails. When someone wiped their boots, the metal edges of the bottle caps did an excellent job of scraping off mud, even of prising small rocks and pebbles from between the treads of the soles. Every day, rain or shine, Lottie upended the bottle cap scraper and tapped the end several times against the cement walk, dislodging the dirt, readying it for another home-from-work bout of duty. Then she swept the sidewalk, even if it was pouring rain, which, being the West Coast and wintertime, was almost guaranteed.

She became so integrated into everyone's life it was only natural to suppose she would join them for Christmas dinner.

"Can't do it." Lottie shook her head. "I'd like to but all four kids would be insulted half to death. They're used to coming to my place for a big dinner, it's kind of a tradition. You'll have to make do without me."

She put presents under the tree for each of the little kids and found presents for her on the back seat of her car when she went out to go home. That's when she decided each and every horror story she'd ever heard about Those Lancasters was a lie, especially the one about the old man killing his wife then blowing out his own brains with the same deer rifle.

The tree had been cut on their own property, and stood in one corner of the big living room, festooned from top to bottom with decorations accumulated over a couple of generations.

"Y'know," Jewen joked, "a person could prop a few two-by-fours, or maybe some laths, in that corner, and the kids could decorate 'em up, and nobody'd know it wasn't a tree. You can't even *see* what's under all that glitter."

"Could keep the same one," Al suggested. "Won't matter if the needles fall off, the kids'll cover the bare branches with tinsel and aluminum foil icicles and who'd be the wiser."

"No," the kids hollered, pretending to take it all seriously. "No, that wouldn't be right!"

Lottie had been baking up a storm for days, and the kids' mouths were seldom empty. She'd brought bags of her own supplies with her, then taken half the tarts, cookies and pies home for her own Christmas dinner with her children and grandchildren. Colleen had put her new stove to good use and made dozens of shortbread cookies from Gran's recipe. Darlene had made mince pies and tarts, and together they had made steamed puddings.

"If the Russian Army shows up, we'll manage," Al grinned. "Damn, but I am going to enjoy this Christmas!"

"Wonder if Norm'll show up."

"Be a shame if he didn't," Jewen allowed. "His loss, not ours. You'll never convince me his floozie can bake like this." And he popped another of Lottie's butter tarts in his mouth.

Darlene had to work Christmas Eve and worried she'd sleep in and miss the uproar when the kids started opening presents. She needn't have wasted her energy; the kids stayed up so late watching TV and eating mountains of popcorn that they slept until nearly nine in the morning. By then Darlene's own excitement had her awake, and she even had time for a cup of coffee before Dorrit arrived, grinning and carrying a present he had wrapped himself. It had just about enough scotch tape holding it together to make it unopenable.

"For you." He handed it to her, then climbed on her knee. "I found it myself, I paid for it myself, and I wrapped it myself," he announced proudly.

"It looks gorgeous," she lied, holding him tightly, kissing his neck. "Can I open it now?"

"Yeah." He was red-faced and squirming, barely able to contain himself.

She had to get up and hitch him to one hip so she could go to the hell drawer and find the scissors to cut the scotch tape. She left the scissors on the table, just in case he had wrapped other presents for other people.

"Oh, you darling, it's exactly the right thing. How did you know I wanted bubble bath and scented soap? How did you know that?" She fussed over him, cuddled him, thanked him a dozen times, and hoped to god the stuff didn't smell like dog shampoo or overripe fruit.

Jewen came downstairs in clean jeans and tee-shirt, followed by Al and Tony, then Colleen came over from her place, and no sooner was she stirring her coffee than Singeon arrived, with, miraculously, Lucy and her three kids. They had a laundry basket full of wrapped gifts which they put under the tree.

"Took some fast talking," Singeon beamed. "But she finally agreed."

"Here, Lucy, have a chair, have some coffee, have you had breakfast? Would you like something?"

"Eee-yah," Lucy laughed, "leave me alone or I'll go home again."

"Tie you to the chair."

The kids came into the kitchen, too excited to speak, and everyone surged to the living room, coffee mugs in hand, to watch.

"Let's see." Jewen hunkered by the tree. "Look at the loot. Why, here's something for Simon!" He held it out, and Lucy's eldest stepped forward, grinning. "And something for Dorrit, and something for Tom, and something for Peter, and something for Jessie, and here's one for Carol, and something for Willy, and look at this, there's something for *me*!"

"Here's a big one for Big Wilma." Al handed it over, kissed her on the cheek. "Merry Happy, Wil."

Colleen sat with a notebook and pencil, trying to keep track of who got what, and in which colour or size.

The new bikes—bigger, brighter, fancier and more expensive than the ones Al had bought mere months ago—were on the front porch, with name tags hanging from the handlebars. Lucy's kids' grins got wider and wider until, Singeon said, they were just about able to swallow the entire house.

"Here, now, if you're going to ride that bike you need to get some clothes on, you're not heading out in pyjamas to catch your death of cold," Darlene nagged.

There was a rush for the bedrooms to get dressed, and that meant Lucy's kids, already clothed, were first to ride their bikes.

"The last thing I expected was more bicycles," Big Wilma said quietly. "Seems to me the paint on the others isn't even really scratched up, yet. No wonder they were blown away."

"Santa, huh?" Singe laughed softly. "And what name does Santa go by this year?"

"I got the bikes," said Al, laughing. "Jesus, do any of you remember the year we all got bikes? I thought of that and I thought hell, it's not every day you get the chance to help make a memory."

"Thank you," Lucy said quietly. "It was really decent of you to remember my kids, too."

"Hey, they're family, right?" And Al dared go over and kiss Lucy on the cheek.

"I'm taking my new camera out there and getting some pictures." Darlene jumped up and headed off to get dressed.

"And I'm going to start making stuffing or the bird won't be ready until New Year's." Colleen felt totally overwhelmed, surrounded by too many people who were excited and laughing, talking and not listening. She almost longed for the peace and quiet of her own place, then felt traitorous and guilty.

She also felt worried and knew she would never in a million years be able to talk about it with any of them. You didn't have to be a rocket scientist to know Al had spent a small fortune on Christmas. New twenty-one-speeds for the older kids, new top-of-the-line standards for the younger kids and a new camera for each of the adults. And she knew the cameras were not cheap. Each came with its own aluminum case and attachments, close-up lenses, distance lenses, and none of them cheap, either. And yet all she knew he did for money was sell slag and gravel for driveways and fill. She didn't believe he made much doing that. So what else was he doing? And Tony, too. She touched the bracelet on her left wrist, knew they weren't standing on the street handing them out free gratis, knew she had close to five hundred dollars on her arm. She wanted to protest it was too much, wanted to refuse it, and knew she couldn't.

Colleen had the stuffing made and was just getting ready to put it in the body cavity of the turkey when the taxi drew up in the muddy front yard. She had no idea at all who it could be. And then the men were clattering down the front porch, whooping and hollering, and a woman was getting out of the cab, waving and shouting, "Surprise! Surprise!" Any worries Colleen had about money or how some people in the family were making it vanished in the rush of uneasiness she experienced when she realized the capering woman was her sister Brady.

"You see who that is?" Darlene asked from the doorway.

"Yeah. Tell me I'll be okay about this."

"If you promise to tell me the same thing."

"You'll be okay about this."

"You'll be okay about this, too."

"Wonder if it's especially sinful to tell lies on Christmas Day?"

"If it is, we're both going to hell."

"No, hell is coming to us."

🌲

And it did. It came through the front door swathed in an ankle-length fur coat, with fur-lined cossack-style boots to ward off any chill. On its head, a fur hat, like a round-shaped fuzzy basket.

"Colly," it cried, "my darling! Dar, you angel!" And the big hug enveloped them both, the scent of perfume overpowering even the smell of the stuffing. "Surprise!" it crowed repeatedly. "Caught you off guard, didn't I?" it celebrated. "Pulled a good one on you."

"This *is* a surprise," Colleen managed. "You should have let me know and we'd have . . ."

"I love surprises! I just love surprises!" Brady repeated. Tony kept looking at her and grinning hopefully, and Greg seemed unable to believe his eyes. Colleen hoped Darlene wouldn't notice, get jealous and kick off a go-round.

The men brought in the luggage.

"Jeez, Brade, for cryin' in the night, you must'a needed your own freight train!" Darlene blurted.

"Oh, most of this is just my costumes and stuff," Brady said, waving casually, her diamonds catching the Christmas lights and reflecting them. "Just dump it anywhere it'll be out of the way."

"You can put it in my room," Big Wilma offered. "It won't be in my way."

Up the stairs they went, taking boxes, suitcases, bags and more boxes.

"You've changed *everything*," Brady mourned. "Nobody's even in the same room they used to be in. Wallpaper's changed, rooms are painted different colours, I can hardly believe it's home!"

"Well, christ, Brady, you been gone long enough," Darlene said, already falling into the old pattern. Colleen vowed she wouldn't, not if it cost her the end of her tongue, from biting down on it so hard.

It was easy to stay out of the uproar. All she had to do was stay in the kitchen and work on the big meal. With the turkey stuffed, trussed, and in the huge roaster, in the oven, she could turn her attention to cleaning up the mixing bowls and cereal bowls, although she couldn't remember when anyone had taken the time to eat cereal. There were mandarin orange peels to put in the compost, there was more discarded wrapping paper than a person would believe, and candy wrappers until hell wouldn't hold them.

She was glad when Brady got the idea that it wasn't Christmas without some snow. That hint alone was enough to galvanize the kids into hauling on an extra layer of sweaters, finding gloves and toques and heading out to the storage shed to hunt up the sleds and the plastic slider-boards.

"You should come, too, Colly." Singeon came up behind her and cuddled her.

"Singe, darlin', I am up to my arse in snow just about every working day of the week." She made it a joke. "And right now my idea of heaven doesn't include slipping, sliding or landing in a drift with snow down my neck and my backside getting wet. Off you go. I'll be happy as a flea on a shaggy dog."

"You don't know what you're missing," Brady lectured. "If you'd spent as much time as I have in places where it hardly even rains let alone snows, you'd know just how precious it is."

"Don't imagine it would do the slot machines and roulette wheels a lot of good to be covered in snow," Colleen said.

"Well, then, get your toque."

"I'll pass. If I own any share of the snow, I'll give it to you as a welcome home gift."

The silence when they left was so complete she could imagine she heard her heart beating and her pulse pounding. She was glad of the five pounds of brussels sprouts that needed to be washed, wilted leaves picked off, brown spots excised and stems trimmed. There was something so calming about a stainless steel sink half full of little floating miniature cabbages, something mundane and unchallenging, soothing in its very boredom.

When they were done and soaking in salted water, she started in on the carrots and swede turnips. She peeled spuds until her hands ached and the skin on her fingers puckered. Then she took a break and went into the living room to try to find some space in the midst of the chaos.

She made piles for each and sorted through the gifts, moving Lego sets from the coffee tables and remote-controlled monster trucks from the big chairs. She plugged in the battery charger and loaded it with the run-down ones from the sleek racing cars which had only made it up and down the hallway a dozen times before whining to a stop.

She consulted her list, but in all the furore there were things she hadn't noted. She didn't know who belonged to the life-sized poodle that, when wound up and switched on raised and lowered its head, barking a metallic noise guaranteed to make a body's brains dribble out its ears inside of two minutes. She could guess at what clothes were whose because of the sizes, but she had no idea who owned the lovely big metal dump truck or the equally lovely big metal skidder. She made an extra pile for the unidentifiable. She took wrapping paper, torn boxes, discarded cartons and two of the boxes the mandarins had been packed in and went to the burn barrel with them, then went back and checked the turkey.

She decided not to bother making a salad, there was already more food planned than they were going to be able to eat. She started whipping bowls of cream, and put them in the fridge. She got the other table from the backroom where Jewen and Al had stored it the night before, after they'd hauled it in from the shed, and she used two new pale blue unfitted sheets for tablecloths.

She opened jars of homemade pickles, other jars of pickled beets, jars of corn relish and a quart of zucchini chutney. She brought in the extra chairs from the shed and from the bedrooms, she even brought in folding picnic chairs, and still she had to get some alder rounds and set them in place. She brought her own dishes and bowls from her place, brought her mugs and cutlery, too. Thank the good lord she'd had the foresight to get several packages of plastic-coated throwaway plates or they'd be eating out of tobacco can lids!

She took six packages of frozen whole cranberries out of the freezer and very carefully made her sauce and set it on a countertop to cool. One year she'd put it in the fridge and forgotten about it and everyone else was too polite to ask so it didn't get put out; afterward everyone had laughed good-naturedly, but it wasn't the kind of mistake a person wanted to make twice.

By the time the others got back, red-faced, chilled and wet, the turkey was as good as done, the vegetables were cooking, and Colleen had been home, had enjoyed a nice long hot bath and had changed into clean clothes. She was sitting in the big chair, enjoying the break, when the trucks pulled up, their beds heaped high with snow.

She watched through the big window as the kids piled out and, wet or not, started off-loading snow and packing it into lumps that became snow people, a snow palace and even a snow dog. And, of course, each person needed a carrot for a nose, and nothing would do for the dog but a round orange.

Then they came inside, shivering, and the rush was on to haul off the sodden clothes, get kids into hot tubs of water, dry them off, stuff them into clean clothes and try to find a place to hang wet towels, wet jeans, dripping socks.

"Just throw it all in the laundry room and I'll deal with it," Big Wilma insisted, and finally, someone listened to her.

With the washing machine chugging in the background and carols coming from the television, they finally sat down to a huge meal. Bowls were passed, bowls were emptied, bowls were refilled and passed again. And then Brady began to weep.

"You don't know," she sniffled, "how *glad* I am to be home."

"You don't know how glad we are to have you home," Al said, patting her hand. They all nodded and said welcome home, glad to have you back, even the ones for whom it was a total lie.

The meal was fantastic, and the visit to the mountain snow had honed appetites to a nearly desperate eagerness. Everyone ate hugely, then ate more, and the compliments to the cook flowed as freely as the gravy.

"I've eaten in some of the most expensive restaurants in two countries," Brady couldn't help bragging—it was just something that was so much a part of her that Darlene often called it Bradying—"and this is probably the best meal I've had since the last meal I had at this table. Colly, you could get a job in *any* of those places and improve the menu."

"Thank you." Colleen smiled and passed the stuffing bowl to Brady.

"I'm going to eat until midnight, then fart until dawn." Brady laughed, and the kids all chortled happily, storing it away in that place kids have for what they consider to be gems.

"If I eat another bite I'll split down the midline and spill myself on the floor," Tony said with a sigh. "I'd like to thank you all for the kindness." He looked over at Al and something private passed between them. "I haven't lived with *real* people for a lot of years. Mostly army barracks and oil camp bunkhouses and . . . like that. And being here, with you guys, is really special."

"Glad to have you," Singeon answered.

"Uh, me, too." Greg cleared his throat, spoke hesitantly. "I mean, I haven't been in the army or in an oil camp but, yeah, it's special, all right."

"Ah, maybe not in the army or an oil camp," said Jewen. "But you did spend about four years in Wainwright, that counts."

Greg looked at Jewen, and opened his mouth to say something. Nothing came out. He looked at Al, who was looking at Jewen, then he looked at Tony, who was watching him closely.

Colleen wasn't sure what was going on; men had some very strange ways of communicating with each other. Sometimes they'd be talking about something totally unimportant and boring and then later on you'd find out they were actually talking about something else, something hidden in their casualness and off-handed easiness.

Except there was nothing easy about what was being communicated here. She didn't want it to go any further, so she got up from her chair and started clearing off empty plates. Jessie made a move to get up to help, but Colleen smiled and shook her head, and the girl relaxed, flashed a grateful grin.

"Just about dessert time," she said.

"I was pretty sure you'd figure it out." Greg leaned back in his chair, seeming to relax.

"Oh yeah." Singeon leaned over and tapped Peter on the shoulder. "You don't have to eat it all, Pete," he said. "You save some room for dessert."

The kid nodded, looked over at his mother, who nodded at him. "I took too much," the boy whispered.

"Well, of course you did," Singe replied. "It's Christmas, you're allowed to take too much. In fact, it's expected."

Colleen put on a pot of coffee and scraped the plates into the dog dish. It was almost full; they'd have stomachs on them like pot-bellied pigs if they made their way through the whole thing.

"I am so *full*!" Brady chirruped. "There goes the old diet right out the window."

"I'm not on a diet, but I might have to be by the time I've packed on the lard that's sure to come from a meal like this," Big Wilma said. "I can see me filling the entire seat of the truck, layers of me, mounds of me, jiggling with each bump in the road and the boss wondering why the fuel consumption just went sky-high. Even with the truck empty I'll hit the weigh-in station well into overweight."

"Everyone's bein' silly," Dorrit said, laughing. "I like that."

"Oh yeah." Tony didn't smile; he hadn't taken his cool gaze off Greg since Jewen had dropped his little bomb. "And some of us are more silly than the rest."

The steamed puddings were hot, and there was enough whipped cream to float the royal yacht. They piled it on thick and dug in as if they hadn't already turned a farm-raised wild turkey into a stripped carcass.

"We should do what Singeon is always saying we should do," Carol piped, "and move in here."

"What? You think every day is Christmas in this house?" Lucy teased softly. "You'll soon enough find it's not. Think of the stack of dishes you'd have to do, all these people."

"There's lots of us to help," Tom told her. "But," he added honestly, "there's lots of other chores to do."

Colleen didn't join them for steamed pudding. Instead she got the first sinkload of plates and cutlery washed, rinsed and in the rack. Then she dried her hands and went to the table for coffee and a butter tart piled high with whipped cream.

"They'll have to reinforce the dance floor," Singeon warned, passing the mince pie to Brady.

"Oh, hell with 'em," Brady laughed shrilly. "I'm about sick and tired of all that, anyway. Maybe I'll just phone 'em and tell 'em to find someone else to pick on for a while." She looked up, defiant. "Maybe I'll just move back home."

"Yeah?" Darlene shrugged as if it wasn't any kind of surprise to her. "Well, as they say, time flies. For myself, well, I still have my hourglass figure, it's just that the sand is shifting."

"I could get a job." Brady sounded as if she thought she had to argue the point with someone. Maybe herself. "There's lots of stuff I can do."

"Sure there is," Jewen agreed. "And you could always go to the college and take one of those job preparation courses, learn computers or something."

"Sure I could," Brady agreed.

The kids got the night off chores, and Jessie insisted that was the best Christmas present of all. Colleen wasn't allowed back near the sink; she took coffee into the living room and sat in a big chair, feeling as if the next thing she was going to do was fall flat on her face.

After a while, Singeon came in, grinning widely. "They kicked me out because I did the driving up to the snowline." He sat on the sofa, leaned back, stretched his long legs in front of him and patted his stomach. "Feel like I've got that entire turkey sitting in there, maybe writing a letter to his relatives, telling them of his adventures."

"How's he going to hold the pen with no bones and no beak?"

"Magic." And he tossed a cushion at her. She caught it, tossed it back.

"So, what was that little byplay with Greg?" she asked.

"Oh, just Jewen's way of letting him know we know he's a spook."

"Him?" She laughed, unable to believe it.

"Yeah. Friend of ours has been keepin' an eye on him." But Singe didn't say who the friend was or why he was tailing Greg, and Colleen knew not to bother asking.

"Does Darlene know?"

"She might know now, although she didn't seem to pick up on the Wainwright thing. She sure can pick 'em. Good job our noses are clean, eh?"

"Are they?" She didn't smile, she just watched him. Singe grinned and nodded, spread his hands innocently, and she had the uneasy feeling he was lying in his teeth.

"Of course, Colly, dear. Hell, we haven't even fired up the old man's still. We're the most reformed bunch of rangytangs you're apt to meet."

"Can we finish the snow in the truck?" Tom spoke and the other kids ranged themselves behind him, waiting for the word from on high.

"You make sure you're all bundled up," Singeon said with a yawn. "And *no* chuckin' snowballs, you hear? Too many little ones in the bunch and they're liable to get hurt. You got that, Tommy?"

"Yes, Uncle."

Colleen almost got up to supervise the mitten-and-toque thing, then decided to hell with it, they had parents, it wasn't her brood.

She yawned. "Well, maybe the best part about Christmas is it only comes once a year. God, I'm bushed!"

"Yeah, well, you would insist on doing it all." He got up and moved to check that Lucy's kids had their jackets buttoned, their gloves on, their heads covered. She watched him tucking Carol's hair under the knit toque, making sure Peter's scarf was in place. It was like when she was young and Singe had been the one to do those things for her. He finished tucking in the scarf and his big finger flicked twice, tapped once on Peter's chin, again on his nose. Colleen remembered that, too, and how much like a caress it had felt.

The kids trooped outside and the noise level dropped by more than half. Jewen turned on the porch light and the big security yard light, so the kids could see as well as if it were broad daylight. "That ought'a finish wearin' 'em out," he said hopefully. "God, I'm glad I don't have any."

"That you admit to." Brady plunked herself on the sofa, smiled a challenge at Colleen. "So, am I sleeping in your new palace?" she said baldly.

"I don't have a spare bed." Colleen couldn't believe how panic-stricken she felt, her stomach suddenly lurching as if she'd been in the back seat of a car, going over an unexpected bump. "I don't even have a foamie."

"Why do you need all that room to yourself?" Brady was settling in for a real debate, and with Brady a debate was an invitation to a fight. "The boys could lug a spare mattress over in no time at all."

"Oh, you get my bed." Big Wilma sounded casual and easy, and Colleen could have kissed her. "Your stuff is already in the room," she reminded her, "and I buzzed up and changed the sheets and stuff."

"And where *you* going to sleep?" Brady looked suspiciously at Wilma, and Colleen knew nothing had changed: Brade was still as sharp as a tack and as paranoid as a person could be without winding up in a rubber room.

"Well, you see, the thing of it is I'm back on the road day after tomorrow, so my room would be empty anyway. Just seemed the least complicated way to do things is all."

"Yeah?"

"Sure, and that way you can be back in your own home, with your family, which is why you came back, isn't it?"

Colleen nearly sagged with relief. This was twice in one day Wilma had demonstrated a genius for dealing with Brady. First the luggage, now the sleeping arrangements. She knew the second-to-last thing she wanted was to have Brady get a toe in her door; once installed, Brady wouldn't be moved out except with a stick of dynamite up the fundament. The only thing worse than having Brady invade her space would be to have Darlene do it. Brady, at least, wouldn't ignore all the boundaries and raid the clothes closet. But she'd make a stalwart try at running every aspect of Colleen's life. And probably the main reason she wouldn't just take over the clothes closet was none of the clothes would fit her: she was too tall and had too much silicone in her chest. It *had* to be silicone or something like it, because no natural boob could be that size and still stand up so insolently. Unless, of course, she was wearing Wonder Woman's brass-plated strapless bra.

The byplay might have continued but Tony's cell phone rang and Brady reached for it as if it was her own. "Yeah?" she drawled, "it's your nickel." She listened, then grinned, but there wasn't much humour in it. "Well, as I live and breathe," she increased the drawl until she sounded like a total you-all. "If it isn't the Colonel herself. What*ever* could we do for you? We got no towns to burn, villages to raze, women to rape, countrysides to pillage or cities to plunder, but we'd do our best and maybe send you some mince pie."

"Doreen?" Darlene asked. "Let me talk to her. Brady, you stop being a bitch and let me *talk*."

Everyone had their turn, mostly saying the same things over again: miss you something fierce, wish you were here, where are you, my *god* it must be cold there this time of year, when you going to trade in your uniform and come back home where you belong? Brady sat watching them, her smile mocking, her eyes glittering with what might have been jealousy, or it might have been scorn.

When the call ended and the remember-when's began, Colleen excused herself, pleading exhaustion and went out the back way. They were winding up the "Remember the time Doreen took the old man's pickup truck and drove us all down to the store for pop and ice cream that she put on the bill," and Colleen knew the next one would be either the time Doreen dove from the top of the bridge and not even the big tough guys would follow her or "Remember when Doreen got caught necking with the mayor's daughter and the old fart just about had himself a conniption, sent Iris off to Queen Margaret's School for Young Ladies and she ran off the second night she was there?"

She was almost asleep when Jewen and Al carried in the spare mattress and took it to one of the bedrooms. She didn't hear Singeon and Lucy leave with the kids and was surprised in the morning to waken to the smell of coffee and find Wilma already in the kitchen. "I must have gone out like a shot," said Colleen, yawning.

"No wonder. Look how much you did while we were all building Frosty and his friends. That was one *hell* of a job getting that meal together," said Wilma.

"And just think how lucky we are: we get to do it again for New Year's."

"You okay about me bunking in here? I mean, I can easily make do on the couch over there; I just figured, well, seeing how it's Brady, and in view of the stuff I've heard over the years and . . ."

"My gratitude is such," Colleen sipped coffee, nodded, then grinned, "I can easily put up with you. I don't know how you pulled it off; usually Brade can manage to chisel people into doing things the way she has decided they'll be done. You got around her, and . . . maybe I should take lessons because I never could. Ordinarily, Brade would have pushed and pushed and pushed to get herself installed here if only because she knew I didn't want her. Plus, well, it's new and it would make her feel she'd got a good one up on Dar, plus . . ." She shrugged. "Hell, you don't need a rehash of an entire childhood of me feeling as if I wanted to bash in Brady's head."

"She's something else again, for sure."

"I wonder if all families are . . . I don't even know the word I want . . . but like Singeon and Jewen are just about wonderful and Norm has always been a pain in the ass. Doreen, well there's nothing much wrong with her as far as I'm concerned but both Dar and Brade go up like skyrockets at the mere mention of her name. I could get along fine with Dor, even if she lived here, but the other two, I couldn't be easy with them if *they* were the ones off doing their patriotic thing with the Canadian Secret Intelligence Service. It's almost like at some point early on we formed teams. This bunch will get along just fine, and this other bunch . . . you know?"

"I've got one sibling," Wilma laughed. "A brother. Three years older than I am. I doubt if I've heard ten words from him in the past dozen years. I don't dislike him, and I don't think he dislikes me, we just have nothing to talk about. Family is really just something that happens to you. If you get along, great, and if you really love each other, wonderful, but if not, so what?"

"You make a good cup of coffee." Colleen stifled a yawn. "So good, in fact, I'm grabbing me another one."

CHAPTER FIVE

Singeon let them all know days ahead of time that he wouldn't be on hand for New Year's dinner. "Lucy came here for Bah Humbug, only fair I show my face at her folks' for Auld Lang Syne."

"You know they'll take that to mean you're settled," Jewen warned.

"Yeah, well, I kind of been thinking of moving some of my stuff over there," said Singe as he poured coffee, then looked at it in the mug as if he'd never seen any before in his life. "She's a good woman."

"She is that. You okay about the kids?"

"They're nice kids."

"You planning any more?"

"Ought to be another one in about five months." Singe grinned. "That feels good."

"You're sunk. That's it. Freedom shot to hell. Taken the bait, swallowed the hook, and you don't even care you're getting reeled in."

"Your turn's coming."

"Yeah? I can bank on that, can I?" Jewen sounded wistful. "Thing is, the ones I like are already taken, and the ones I could get wouldn't make life any nicer or easier. How'd you luck out, y'old fart, and get someone like Lucy?"

"Luck. Best luck I've had since the old man blew his brains out."

Colleen stayed home New Year's Eve and supervised the kids while they made bowls of popcorn and a big tray of fudge, then sat watching TV parties until the countdown began at midnight. The kids raced out on the porch with noisemakers, whistles, pots and lids, and fireworks Brady had bought in the States and brought across the border illegally. As the strains of the familiar song began to drift from the television, the first of the rockets went off, filling the sky with what looked like streamers of sparkling white light.

"Wow!" Tom shrieked. "That was a thirty dollar one, I bet!"

Colleen waited until the light had dimmed, then set off another, and another, and the kids screamed with excitement and screeched "Happy New Year" to the coons in the trees out back. The pups, almost dogs by now, went into their hoochy and stayed there.

Promises were made, vows were sworn. Colleen brought a blanket to the sofa and lay down on it, not intending to go to sleep. She did, and the kids watched the tube until one by one they faded totally and headed to their beds. By the time the first of the celebrants wove home, only Dorrit was awake, watching something totally unsuitable.

The others came in soon after, and the house party was in full swing when Colleen went out the back door and across the wintry yard to her own place. She made sure both front and back doors were securely locked, checked all her windows and went to bed fully clothed; she did not want uninvited guests of any kind or sort.

She was gritty-eyed and tired New Year's Day, and the big old house looked as if the Khmer Rouge had visited. But she got the ham in the oven and the vegetables ready before any of the hungover ventured down for coffee. Several people she did not know were crashed in the living room, the luckiest one on the sofa, the others on the floor.

"You seen Greg?" Darlene asked, puzzled and badly hungover. "He went to bed with me when I went . . . I think . . . but . . . he's not there now. Nobody else is, either."

"Haven't seen him." Colleen smothered a yawn. "And he isn't passed out in the backyard. Checked the bathroom?"

"He's not there."

Colleen couldn't give the first part of a damn, and Darlene was really too hungover to be able to muster anything much except confusion. It was at least three in the afternoon before either of them thought to see if Greg had fallen asleep in his car. "Well, there you have it." Colleen turned back toward the house. "The car's gone, too."

"He was too hammered to drive." Darlene stared stupidly at the place she had thought the car was parked. "He as good as passed out cold as soon as he flopped on the bed."

"Must'a woke up, then."

The kids were tired and subdued but picked up dozens of empty beer cans and more liquor bottles than made any sense. They washed the liquor bottles and put them in the backroom; they'd be useful when the run was ready. The beer cans they rinsed, then removed the pull tabs and added them to the big pickle jar that held their collection; one day they'd have saved enough that the guy at the garage would be able to send them where they were supposed to go and they'd have the satisfaction of knowing they'd provided a wheelchair for a kid who needed one. Some of the overnight guests managed some coffee, said thanks for a wonderful time, and drifted away; others stayed, not yet ready to dare attempting to face the world, handle traffic, or walk into whatever was waiting for them at home, if they had homes.

By the time supper was ready, people had managed to defeat their hangovers; they simply went to work on another one. Their booze consumption didn't interfere with their appetites though, and the ham disappeared as if it had evaporated. Even Darlene, both worried and angry because of Greg's vanishing act, managed to do justice to the huge meal. The food and drink seemed to revive the near-dead, and by the time Dorrit had his bath, the ones few seemed to know had left, one of them grabbing people one by one, hugging them fiercely and vowing endless friendship. "You'll never know how much it means," he insisted repeatedly, "to be included in the family celebration. When a guy's away from home and hasn't got a chance of getting back, something like this can be the difference between heartbreak and hope." And off he went, damp-eyed and emotional.

"Who *is* he?" Big Wilma asked.

"I don't know," Darlene said wearily. "I thought he was with you."

"Me? Christ, I hope not. I thought I came home alone. Well, 'cept for you and the boys."

"You seen anything of Greg?"

"Who? Oh, him. Not since before countdown at the O-Hey Corral."

"Really? I could'a swore he came home with me."

"Fuck, I thought it was Larry came home with you."

Christmas break ended January 3, and it was back to the grind for the kids on the morning of the fourth. Lottie was back *doing* for them by then, and Colleen handed over the reins and responsibilities gladly. And sent a prayer to heaven that Brady not rub Lottie the wrong way and cause her to quit.

Surprisingly, Lottie and Brady got along famously. Lottie took one look at the stripper wigs, false eyelashes and makeup and knew everything she needed to know. Brady watched the competent way Lottie moved around the kitchen and breathed a sigh of relief. She had never pictured herself as Suzie Homemaker and knew only too well how much went into keeping a step ahead of the Board of Health. It wasn't a job in which she had any interest at all; besides which, she had other things to do, other fish to fry, other cats to skin, and had to get on with her own life.

The first thing she did was whack off her hair. It was her only New Year's resolution, and she'd made it standing in front of the mirror in the women's washroom just before midnight, staring at her own reflection. For more years than she wanted to remember, she'd spent hours at the hairdresser's, getting her mane teased, curled, stripped, bleached and piled into fanciful and sometimes even beautiful arrangements and creations. The results were starting to show. Even with the expert ministrations of the best camouflage experts she'd been able to find, her hair was thin, weak, dry and brittle, with more split ends than roots. She no longer had any idea what her own colour would be, and she knew that however much money she poured into the endeavour, there wasn't going to be anyone in a four-hour drive who could work wonders and fart miracles with her mop. At the New Year's Eve bash they'd attended she'd taken good hard looks at the hair around her. There were some dos that looked pretty fancy compared to the rest, dos that wouldn't have caused a glance, let alone a second one, in the venue from which Brady had so recently departed. The rest of the women had, more or less, virgin hair. Well, not virgin, but in comparison with what Brady was used to, you might as well say so. She also studied the makeup, or near lack of it, and the clothing. She was miles ahead on garb, no doubt about that, and could have given lessons on how to apply war paint. But when it came to hair and nails she was not in the ball park, and knew it within seconds.

So New Year's Day, just before they sat down to the bang-up meal, Brady got the hair clippers, went into the bathroom, closed and locked the door, opened the window, lit a joint and got herself blasted, then went to work on her dome. It was easy, all she had to do was start at the front and work back, then start at the back and work toward the front. Giggling and more ripped than she'd been in years, she surveyed the end result of a half hour's mind-numbed psychedelia. "I've seen golf balls with more fuzz than that," she snickered. "It makes a peach look downright hairy. Change my name to Chiquita Chihuahua. What do I care? I've got more wigs than Whoopi has."

She didn't put on a wig, however. She went to the table *au naturel.* The only comment came from Jessie. "A bit more makeup and some platform shoes and you might pass for Michael Jordan. Except, of course, for the basketball. Or is that what you've got balanced on your shoulders?"

"Watch it," Darlene warned. Jessie nodded and withheld further comment.

After the meal was finished, the kitchen cleaned, and the several uninvited-but-present-all-the-same guests had finally departed, Brady sat on the sofa with toenail clippers and did a number on her nails. When she was finished she looked at her fingers and for a moment sheer panic hit her; they could be anybody's hands, for chrissake. She felt as if she was going to start bawling like a little kid. The layers of lacquer were gone, the long cost-a-fortune-to-keep-up nails were gone. She was left with well-cared-for cuticles, and plain, ordinary, everyday fingernails that barely hid the ends of her fingers. They looked, in fact, the way they had looked when she first left home all those centuries ago.

"Don't worry." Jessie sat down beside her, patted her knee. "They'll grow."

"They're too short, aren't they?" Brady mourned.

"Better too short than too long. When they're too long women use their hands funny. Like they can't really pick something up, you know?" The girl looked at her own hands, then looked at Brady's. "Could you show me how you do that? Get them looking so . . ." she paused, trying to find the right word "so much the same as each other. Mine are . . ." She gave up trolling in a vocabulary suddenly inadequate. "See?"

"It's the cuticles. The little beds." Brady reached for her nail kit. "We won't get them tickety-boo right off the bat," she chattered. "You don't want to bruise them or damage the nails. And you have to oil them, soften them, before you start working on them. That's what this stuff is for, see. And after we've soaked with this, we use this little stick. You do *not*," she said sternly, "*not ever* shove or jab at them with the end or the edge of a nail file, okay? Either you use one of these or you do *not* touch them."

"Yes, Auntie."

"Lookit Jessie!" Tom screeched, pointing and laughing. "Lookit Jessie tryin' to pretend she's . . ." And that's as far as he got with it. Al's kick wasn't hard, but it was well aimed. More of a push than a real kick, it sent Tom stumbling into the hallway with a shocked look on his face.

"That's the last time," Al said quietly. "Nobody's razzing you about using my razor. Which, by the way, you need like you need another asshole."

"Don't argue with him," Brady said sternly. "It only encourages them."

"He does it all the time!"

"When he does, you come and tell me. It's not tattle-tale-ing, it's lessons in survival. I'll talk to him and if it doesn't stop, I'll tell his father. And *he* will deal with it, won't you, darlin'?" She smiled at Al, who as good as melted, and smiled back at her.

"I'll boot his arse so hard it'll look like he's wearing shoulder pads," he promised. "Tom," he turned to his first-born, "you aren't a baby and you haven't been for a long time. So reach out and catch on, okay? There's stuff you're trying out, and there's stuff Jess is going to try out. You're tryin' out man stuff, she's going to try out woman stuff."

"Auntie Colleen doesn't bugger around like that."

"You didn't know your Auntie Colleen when she was the same age Jess is now. You rag on Jess and I'll make mention of the zits you get sometimes. I'll make a big deal about it if you pong a bit. Which, incidentally, is something you have to start payin' attention to: use my deodorant stick after your bath or shower. And zip the lip!"

"Auntie Colleen used stuff when she had that other job," Jessie corrected. "It's just since she got her new job she hasn't worn it."

"Auntie Colleen hardly used *any*," Tom denied. "You couldn't even really *see* it when she wore it."

"We could work on your cuticles, too, Tom," Brady suggested. Tom recoiled as if he'd been shot with salt. Wordless, he walked to the kitchen and sat at the table reading a comic book.

"Guys don't do their nails," Jessie whispered.

"Jess, there's something you have to learn right now. In this world, shit heap it can be at times, guys do whatever in hell they want to do. And one day, so will we."

The winter rains drenched the world unendingly. Swollen rivers cut into their banks, eroded them, the mud and rocks slipping, tumbling into the current, staining the water. Creeks and streams became uncontrollable torrents, culverts washed out, water crept up and over the roads, the best bottomland flooded, ducks, wild geese and trumpeter swans swimming where hayfields were supposed to be. Twice Colleen got stranded on bush roads; the first time, her knobby tires failed her on a curve, the rear end slipped and skidded sideways, one wheel winding up in a churning ditch. Even with four-wheel drive she had trouble, and she began to think she was going to have to hike her way out on foot, but eventually she dug enough muck out from under the stuck wheel she could creep back over the lip and onto the slick mess that was pretending to be a road. Covered in mud, she made it home only three hours late. She stripped off her filthy clothes and rain gear on her back porch, skin blue-tinged and goose-bumped, and went into her house in her underwear. Even her panties were wet and mud stained. She began to wonder if she'd been halfway around the tip when she'd changed jobs. Stan might have been a pain in the jaw, but he'd never once caused her to leave work with her pants wet.

She used the hose to get the mud off her rain gear, brought in her filthy clothes and tossed them in the washing machine, then hung up her drybacks over the warm-air vent in the backroom, and got into a tub of hot water, pondering the question of the day: how can a person get soaking wet and covered with mud inside a dryback suit? Oh, well, sir, the answer to that question is: go scrabbling around in a ditch, with water going up your leg, down your neck and under your rain jacket by way of the same place your arse sticks out!

The second time, she got stranded for real and spent the night in her truck, her CB and cellular both reassuring her the road crew would get to her lickety-split. They got to the other side of the washed-out bridge by one-thirty in the morning, but it was nearly noon before they had her and Morespots on their way to hot food and fresh clothes. "You sure you're okay, lady?" the grader driver kept asking.

"Just racking up the overtime, that's all," she said, yawning.

"Ain't it the truth," he agreed. "Myself, I always got me a sleeping bag in an extra plastic bag tucked under the seat. And I got a raft of them high energy bars and some trail mix, too. I got stuck once hell and gone up on the Summit going into Tahsis, spent two miserable bloody days caught between a washed-out bridge and the big hole behind me where the road used to be before it went careening down into the creek some hundred feet or more below me. Vowed then: never again. You want some of them energy bars? You're shiverin' like hell."

160

"I think I'll wait for a real meal, thanks. I'm not really hungry, but I could drink another cup of your thermos coffee if you've got any."

"You just help yourself. Nothin' like it, eh?" He laughed as if he had never known anything but the finest of circumstances. "You hang on. She gets rough a bit up ahead, but after that we'll hitch up with the rest of the gang and you can switch from this bucket of bolts to a real live pickup truck with a heater. Nice dog, terrier, is it?"

"Nothing better than a good terrier," she agreed, sipping the warm brown mess that had possibly at one time or another been coffee. It tasted wonderful!

The snowline crept down until the logging company manager decided it was ridiculous to even pretend they could still operate economically or efficiently. They shut 'er down for snow season.

"You going some place warm and dry?" Darlene asked enviously.

"I'm going to bed," Colleen answered.

"If I was you, with the money you make and the time off you've got, I'd head for, oh, I don't know, Reno or maybe Mexico, some place where the sun shines warm and it hasn't rained in at least two weeks."

"Dar, did you ever stop to think that you've got hours every day where you could go to school, like Brady's doing, and wind up with some kind of training that would get you a job where you wouldn't feel so . . . cheated."

"Don't you start in on me. All's I said was if I had a job that paid me big money to sit in a truck all night listening to the damn radio and talkin' on a cell phone, I'd do more than sit around on my ass reading books nobody else can understand."

Colleen did a lot more than that in her time off. She went to the complex every day, worked out on the machines in the fitness studio, soaked in the hot tub, then swam laps until she was so tired all she could do was go back into the hot tub for a while. She visited the library, she went in and out of the several furniture stores looking at what was available in case she decided to do something about the still-empty rooms. She signed on for and took a course in advanced computer mysteries, she took Morespots to obedience training, and every day she rented a couple of videos. When the kids caught on to that they started showing up at her place as soon as the school bus dropped them off. "Homework first," she insisted. "You just line yourselves up at the table here and get it done. I'll check it."

"Then there won't be time to watch anything before supper's ready."

"Ah, but it'll be done, and when you've finished your chores you can whip over with a clear conscience and watch the video then."

Even Dorrit and Little Wilma had homework. Colleen personally thought this was so close to child abuse the difference didn't matter. *She'd* never had homework when she was in grade one!

"I guess there's just so much more stuff for them to have to learn," Al said. "Can you believe it? The old man, idiot that he might have been, could understand goddamn near everything going on in the world when he was, oh, say, twenty-five or so. I mean *everything*! If he ran into a machine that wasn't working, he could pretty much figure out how to fix it. Now? It's like living between the pages of one of them science fiction stories. Do you know they've got eavesdropping stuff that can zero in on you from a half mile or more away? I saw a thing about it on TV. No shit. They could climb a tree, oh, to hell and gone down at the other side of Bob's place, for example, and put this itty-bitty box in place, and then leave and go sit in their nice dry office and hear everything that gets said here. Now if that ain't science fiction I don't know what is. They can jigger with your phone so they can tape record everything that's said; even when the phone isn't working they can hear oh, who knows, Lottie vacuuming or someone takin' a leak or . . . you'd never believe what they can find to waste tax money on, babe."

"What's that got to do with homework in grade one?"

"Well, it's more stuff for the kids to have to learn about, isn't it? Way I understand it, each and every one of those kids is already learning the Salish language, and now they're going to teach 'em all sign language so they can talk to the deaf. That's something I'd like to learn. Maybe get Tommy to show me. Nobody ever thought of teaching us deaf-talk, might'a come in handy."

🦅

Wherever it was Greg had got to on New Year's Eve, he stayed there. Darlene was worried at first, then insulted. "Inconsiderate bugger," she mourned. "You'd'a thought he'd'a had at least enough polite-ness to phone and say, 'Won't be comin' to see you no more'. At least have said *why* he was packin 'er in and hoofin' off down the road. But not a word. Just gone like he'd never been here. Well, and see if I care." But she did, you could tell by the way she didn't even bother with Larry for at least a week and a half. "Be nice if I knew what I'd done to send him packing."

"Probably doesn't have a lot to do with you anyway." Tony pat-ted her hand. "Men and women are different, doll. Now you take you 'n' me. We got a good thing started and then, well, it all changed, right? If we'd'a stayed on the way it kicked off, we'd'a probably not even been talkin' to each other by now. Instead, it changed and here we are, and we're good friends. Which isn't to say I wouldn't be grinnin' from ear to ear were you to snap your fingers and say, 'Fido, heel'. But that's probably not going to happen and I know it, so I'll be happy with what I get."

"What's that got to do with anything?"

"See? Now what I said would make perfectly good sense to just about any real man on the face of the earth, and to a woman, it's a puzzle. That's how we're different."

"Really? Is *that* how we're different." She was grinning, the old flirty note returning to her voice, displacing the bewilderment. "Here I thought it all had to do with plumbing and hormones and the odd gonad or two."

"I didn't know my gonads were all that odd, actually."

"Take it from one who knows, Tony. Some's long and some's thick, but it's odd to have them long *and* thick."

🐀

Al didn't talk it over with anyone; he made all the moves himself. Maude and Brewster were just sitting down to a supper of roast pork and applesauce, potatoes, gravy, hot biscuits and frozen peas when Al walked up the few stairs, knocked on the back door, then walked in without waiting for anyone to invite him.

"Al!" Maude exclaimed and paled.

"Hi, darlin'." He moved to the kitchen table, leaned over from behind, kissed her on the cheek, grinned at Brewster and then sat at an empty place. "Hi, Brew, how's it going?"

"Good." Brewster stood up, went to the fridge, got two beer and a can of Sprite, came back, put the Sprite down in front of Maude and a beer in front of Al. "How's yourself?"

"Fine. Just as fine as silk, actually."

"To what do we owe the honour?" said Brewster, taking a sip. "Would you like some supper?"

"No, thanks, Brewster, but you go ahead. I won't be long. Appreciate the beer. Maudie, the kids miss you. You haven't been to see them since you left. They've still got your Christmas presents wrapped and waiting, and here it is goddamn near March."

"I didn't want to butt in. I mean . . ." She looked panic-stricken.

"Now, Maudie, I told you, all you had to be was sober, and all you had to do was let me know ahead'a time. I never said you couldn't see 'em, and I never said you hadda stay away from the place."

"You serious?" Brewster asked.

"I was talking to Maudie about it." Al's eyes narrowed.

"Well, I understand that," Brewster nodded. "Thing is, you see, she's kinda scared of you."

"And you ain't?" Al mocked.

"No." Brewster smiled again, and Al wondered if maybe the guy wasn't quite as stupid as most people figured. "No, I'm not afraid of you, Al. If you'd been going to kill me, you'd'a done it already. Maudie, she misses those kids. Sometimes she cries over it. But we didn't phone or do anything about it because we didn't want any trouble at all."

"Won't be any trouble as long as she doesn't make any." Al sipped his beer. "When's the baby due?" he asked suddenly.

"Easterish," Maude whispered.

"Well, don't you think you should let your other kids know they're going to have a baby sister?"

"Or brother," Brewster bragged.

"Whatever," Al said. He drained his beer and stood up, then reached out and patted Maude's head. "Don't you punish yourself no more, you hear? I'll have the kids ready at ten Saturday morning." He looked across the table at Brewster. "And I want them back by six Sunday night."

✶

Colleen watched from her living room window as Jessie and Tom followed Maude and Brewster from the house to his new car. They were dressed in their best clothes, and she knew they were also wearing their best company and go-to-town manners. Maude looked as if she couldn't quite believe any part of it, and Brewster, poor dumb bugger, looked as if there was nothing the least bit out of the everyday. He opened the passenger's door for Maude, helped her into the car, waited until she was settled, then closed the door, and moved to the driver's side. The kids got in the back seat and sat stiffly, not even waving as the car took off and nosed almost silently down to the highway.

✶

Things weren't settled as easily with Norm. Month after month went by without any sign of child maintenance. That didn't mean he wasn't a regular and annoying presence in Little Wilma's life. He showed up at her school and put her in his car, took her to McDonald's, then to the complex, where he bought her a new bathing suit and a set of swimmer's goggles. By the time he brought her home Big Wilma was halfways to frantic and Jewen was actually considering phoning the police to report the child missing.

"As if she wasn't my kid!" Norm roared. "Well, she is, and I'll haul 'er outta school if I so please. You already deprived me of my brothers 'n' sisters. I'll be go to hell if you're takin' my kid, too."

"If you're so worried about your kid, try supporting her for a change!" Big Wilma yelled.

"Why'n't you come get her every second weekend?" Jewen said, trying to mediate the screaming match.

"Don't you try to tell me when I can see my own kid and when I can't, Jewen. It ain't up to you. It's got nothing at all to do with you.

You want to play the violin about some kid or another, make one of your own, but don't get into it with mine."

"Stop the yelling, Norman. We don't need the whole tribe awake and scared half outta their wits by your noise."

"Don't try to tell me what to do, Al. You can't even run your own goddamn life so don't try runnin' mine. I picked up the kid offa the playground at recess, and we had a great day together. She had fun, I had fun, and that's all any of you need to know, okay?"

"The school was worried sick."

"The school can kiss my arse. You's can *all* kiss my arse."

He wasn't satisfied to raise hell at the house; he went down to the school, arrived unannounced and unexpected, and bent the ear of the principal for fifteen minutes. "And *when* I take her, I'll let you know." He really thought he was being reasonable and cooperative. "So's you won't worry, which they tell me you did the last time. But when I want to see that kid, I'll see her, and that is that."

And after all the fuss and uproar, it was the last time he went by the school to pull Little Willy out of class. Instead, he took to showing up at the place just before supper, scooping her up, throwing her in the air, catching her before she hit the floor, swinging her by one arm and one leg, anything to make her laugh. The nights he stayed for supper could be divided into two categories: the quiet and pleasant ones when Wilma was on the road, and the other kind, when she was home and they all had to listen while he nagged her about being gone half the time.

"It's not natural," he said, pointing his fork at her, "and you know it. A mother should be with her kid, not off delivering tons of cedar shingles to California. When you're coming back with a load of out-of-season vegetables is when you should be here, with her, looking after her or something. That's what a *real* mother would do."

"A real father would support his kid," Wilma answered.

"Would anyone like more green beans?" Lottie acted as if nothing at all was going on, as if it was the most natural thing in the world for everyone to have to listen to the sniping.

Colleen missed most of the on-going go-round; she made sure she didn't go near the old house when she saw the refurbished pickup truck parked outside. Darlene was glad she had to go to work, usually before Norm arrived, but she heard about it from Brady whether she wanted to or not.

"Someone's gotta *do* something about it," Brady lectured. "It's enough to ruin a person's digestion."

"Tell you what, Brady, *you* do something about it," Darlene said. "I can't."

"What can I do? Norm doesn't listen to me."

"Norm don't listen to a soul. He'll get bored, he always gets bored. He'll find himself a new squeezie and be too busy for this horseshit."

The rain continued, and even soaking with diesel oil couldn't make the burn pile do what it was supposed to do. The kids tried; they pulled at the pile, started any number of small fires. The idea was supposed to be that the small bonfires would dry out the wood, the combined heat would spread the flames, eventually two or more bonfires would become a respectable blaze, and the mess would be ash. Except it didn't work that way. Finally Al got sick and tired of the whole go-round and headed into town after breakfast. He was back in time for lunch, and after he had eaten his fill, he and Tony unloaded and then set up the heavy-duty industrial-sized chipper/shredder, which some people called the stump muncher.

The kids were overjoyed. "Can I try?" they piped, almost coming out of their skins with excitement.

"Not in those clothes," Al lectured. "You're still in your school stuff. Go change into work grubbies and then we'll see what we see."

The little kids got to drop in little branches, the bigger kids restricted to the heavier limbs.

"Otherwise it's not fair. It's an all-day job for the small tads to get their-sized branches in there; and there's no way they could handle the bigger ones. If you two lumps put in the small ones, the little kids don't get no turn at all," Tony said as he grabbed a chunk of waste wood and dropped it in the feeder. "Stand back, now, and watch what it does to a hunk that size."

The noise was incredible, the stream of chips poured from the spout, the little kids cheered happily, and the two older ones nodded approval.

"None of you, and I mean *none*, are to go near this thing on your own. Don't need someone going down the chute here and comin' out the other end as sausage meat."

"As if there wasn't enough noise around here, what with this machine, that machine and the next one," Lottie nagged. "Now we got one of *those* damn things bleatin' and growlin'. Might's well live in a boiler factory."

But the heaps of branches diminished, the piles of chips grew, and every few days or so someone went at the piles with the earth mover, filling the bucket, driving back down the skidder trail with the load, dumping it in the gumbo near the slag heap and gravel bank.

"Gonna have this place tickety-boo before Easter time," Singeon complimented them. "They'll be sending someone out from Yard Beautiful to take pictures."

"Right, with you standing there like a scarecrow," Brady scoffed. "Nothing, and I mean *no* thing will make this damn yard look nice!"

Darlene was in the bathroom, getting herself ready for the St. Patrick's Day green-beer bash and not particularly looking forward to any part of it because even the Ukrainians thought they were Irish on Paddy's Day and the place would be jam-packed and noisy. Lottie was making shepherd's pies in the kitchen, using up the leftover roast of government mutton, putting the cooked meat through the grinder with plenty of onions and enough garlic to wipe out the vampires of Transylvania. The knock at the back door surprised her, she hadn't heard any sound of a car.

"Yes?" Lottie opened the door, the wickedly sharp butcher knife still in her hand.

"May I speak to Miss Darlene Lancaster, please?" the cop asked politely.

"You got a search warrant?"

"No, ma'am, I'm not here to search," he said, smiling. "Just a few routine questions."

"Well, you just wait the routine wait here at the routine back steps and I'll see if you fit into her routine," Lottie snapped. She closed the door, hurried to the bathroom and rapped on the door. "Ms. Darlene? There's a cop at the back door says he wants to ask you questions."

"Well, let him in, then."

"You let 'em in and they can poke around all they want with or without a search warrant," Lottie warned.

"Jeez, and for this I pay taxes? Well, let 'im in. I got the submachine guns hid where he'll never find 'em and I tied the hand grenades to the tree branches so's they'd look like pine cones; they'll never find 'em."

She took her time and finished her face before going to the kitchen. The cop was sitting in a chair, his notebook on the table in front of him, and Lottie was working overtime at ignoring him.

"What now?" Darlene got herself a cup of coffee, did not offer one to the cop, and sat at the table, pointedly checking her watch. "I don't have long, I'm due to go to work soon."

"It won't take long," he assured her. "I wonder if you could tell me when the last time was that you saw Gregory Duncan?"

"New Year's Eve," she said promptly. "He was here and then—poof—he wasn't."

"Do you have any idea where he went?"

"Not a glimmer." She shook her head, her mouth tightening. "Never said word one, just buggered off. No fare-thee-well, no bye-bye for now, just poof."

"What time did he leave?"

"I don't have any idea, I was asleep."

"Had he mentioned any plan to leave?"

"I told you, not word one."

"Do you have any idea where he might have gone?"

"I told you, not a glimmer."

"Did you report him missing?"

"To who? I don't know anything about his family, not even if they're still alive or not. All's I know is where he lived, and I've gone there a dozen times and never got any answer."

"Did you report it to the police?"

"Well, can't you check your own records? Of course I never reported it to the police. It's a free country. The man can come and go as he wants. Although he better not come back by way of this place, because I'll rip his face off if I see him again!"

"And you have no idea where he might be?"

"Jesus christ, man, your shoe size must be bigger than your IQ! I already *told* you, not the faintest foggiest notion. Why'n't you go check where he worked, see if they know."

"Thank you for your help, miss." He put away the notebook, picked up his bus driver's hat, and holding it in his hands, made his way to the back door. "If he should contact you, perhaps you could let us know."

"Yeah, yeah, sure," she nodded. "Ohmigawd, *look* at the time! If I'm late the boss'll nail me to the front door." And she got up from the table and hurried to her room. Lottie kept working on the shepherd's pie. The cop blinked a few times, then left, and nobody said goodbye.

The kids were in bed, the adults watching TV and drinking tea when the cops came back, to question the rest of the family.

"I'm not sure I saw him after, oh, maybe ten at night." Al laughed. "Mind you, after ten that night I couldn't see much of anything. Jewen had to be designated driver."

"And that only lasted until we got back here." Jewen laughed as well. "I'm not sure, but I think he came home with the crowd. We had a *lot* of people here that night. Front yard was full'a cars."

"And Greg was here?"

"Well, I think so, but I'd hate to have to take an oath on it. Well, fact is, I couldn't take an oath, could I, because I'm not sure. I know he was at the bar because he was drinkin' like hell, which is something he didn't usually do, and I suggested he catch a ride home with the rest'a us but he didn't want to do that. He was too drunk to be driving, though."

"But you aren't sure he came here?"

"No. Now Darlene, she was convinced he did; in fact she said she had to drive because he was so smashed all's he could do was slump against the door and drool. But she wasn't exactly too fit herself, everybody'd been buying her drinks all night and she wasn't feeling any pain at all."

"And you?" The cop looked at Tony, his eyes suddenly hard.

"Me? Oh, man, I was shit-faced." Tony laughed. "The Queen herself could'a shown up here and you'd never prove it by me. I do know he wasn't here New Year's Day."

"And you haven't seen him since?"

"Don't really expect to." The laughter was gone, and Tony's eyes glittered as fiercely as the cop's did. "If he's got any sense at all, he'll stay away from here because Dar's mad as a wet hen and he probably knows it."

"And why would she be mad, do you suppose?"

"Because your boy dumped her, right?"

"Why do you call him my boy?"

"Aren't you the one looking for him?"

The cop just stared at Tony, his eyes flat and snake-like. Tony stared back, and then smiled slowly. "A manner of speaking," he added.

"And nobody has any idea where the young man is now?"

"You might check and find out where he worked." Brady looked and sounded like someone who was only trying to be helpful. "We just thought he'd like, well, maybe got fed up, you know. I mean, what with Larry, and all, being in the picture."

"Your sister had . . . has . . . more than one . . . interest?"

"Interest?" Brady nodded, grinning. "Oh, well, you might call it that. But, yeah, she wasn't tied down to just one guy, eh? Maybe Curlytop got fed up. That's what I called him, Curlytop."

The cop left the big house and went over to Colleen's place. She was expecting him: she had seen the car leave the highway and park by the front steps.

"Yes?" She stood in the partially opened doorway and did not invite the constable into her house. He nodded, went into his spiel about just a few questions, looking for a possibly missing person, wondered if she had seen blah blah blah.

"I'd think it was probably close to four a.m. when they got

home." She stifled a yawn. "I didn't go out, I stayed with the kids. I think we started fading just after midnight. I know I was asleep on the sofa when the animals arrived, and I wasn't up for a party so I just came home, here. I'm not even sure I saw Greg. In fact, I'm almost sure I didn't see him. I saw Darlene, but only as I was heading for the back door."

"So he might not have come back at all?"

"I can't say one way or the other. I didn't see him. Not that I remember, anyway." She yawned openly. "Excuse me," she said, smiling. "I get up before the sun, so by this time of the evening I'm on my way to bed. Usually. Have you looked for his car?" she asked suddenly. "Like on TV 'calling all cars, be on the lookout for so 'n' so', that usually only takes five or ten minutes."

"Right." He grinned. "And the case is solved inside the half hour."

He thanked her for her time, wished her a good night and walked to his car. She didn't wait to watch him go, she just headed for bed, and in the morning she awoke to the "click" that sounded just before her alarm went off and her radio began to play. She cooked sausages and eggs, ate them with lightly toasted white bread made by Lottie, drank two cups of coffee and put the rest of the pot in her thermos. Her lunch was already packed; all she had to do was take it out of the fridge and put it in her metal kit.

They were back at work, and her time at the fitness gym had saved her from aching muscles when, after a couple of months lay-off, it was time again to trudge up and down slopes, picking her way over deadfall, with Morespots trotting beside her.

🦅

The cop showed up at the house before Darlene was out of bed. Brady was off at the college in town doing her upgrading course, and Lottie was well into her housework. When the cop knocked, she answered the door but then stepped out on the porch. He sighed, wondering who it was ran on ahead of him telling people they did not have to invite the law into their homes unless presented with a search warrant. The fact he had one didn't impress Lottie at all.

"The men are gone," she said peevishly, "and Ms. Darlene worked late last night. And I'm not sure I got the right to . . ."

"We aren't interested in the house," he told her. "Not now, anyway. We want to have a look around the grounds."

"Well, I guess there's no way I can stop you," she said grudgingly, "but you might's well know Mr. Singe and Mr. Al aren't going to be too charmed about all this harassment." She pronounced it ha-*rass*-ment, which was the way the cop had said it before his training had systematically and deliberately removed all trace of individuality and regional accent from his speech.

He turned, waved at the cars parked in the driveway, and almost as an afterthought, presented Lottie with her copy of the search warrant. She didn't even look at it, just watched as the dogs were brought from the kennel van. "Are those snarly little terriers on the place?" the cop asked.

"No. One's with Miss Colleen, the other's with Mr. Al in the truck. But you make sure those dogs don't chase the chickens or there'll be hell to pay, make no mistake about that. Damn chickens," she said, frowning, "they rule this place, so help me if they don't. Never saw such go-round over a few hens just about ready for the old-age pension."

She left the cop at the bottom of the stairs and went back into the house hoping the cops didn't make so much noise they wakened Darlene. Wouldn't take much to set off those poorly socialized mutts. Why a body would actually go out of his way to train an animal to behave as badly as those ones did was a puzzle, straining on the leash, hyper and silly as they were, just waiting for the chance to pull down some poor jaywalker and savage him into submission.

The cops were in the bush for more than three hours. When they came out they were soaked to the skin, all shine gone from their boots, and the dogs were ready for a good long sleep on a blanket in the corner of a cell or wherever they were kept. Two of the cops were smeared with mud; heaven only knows what they'd been up to, but whatever it was hadn't improved their outlook on life.

Al and Tony were back by then, the dump truck parked on the side of the road because the driveway was full of police cars and the kennel van. They were having lunch and talking with Darlene.

"Guess I'll go speak to them." Al got up, carrying half a sandwich.

The cop saw him coming, sandwich in hand, jaws busy.

"Find who you were looking for?" Al asked, looking at the exhausted dogs. "You maybe should contact Rhys Williams," he suggested. "He's got coon hounds, trained and all; they'd do better in the bush than those poor things."

"They aren't used to bushwhacking," the cop admitted. "They're more used to working streets and alleys and such."

"Those dogs of Rhys's," Al said, finishing his sandwich, "they can go all night without poopin' out on you. Maybe give him a call. Any sign of wotzisname?"

"Gregory Duncan."

"Yeah. Greg. What do you figure, he wandered off drunk or something, got lost in the bush? He could'a, I guess, but . . . where's his damn car? It's a puzzle, for sure."

"That skidder trail doesn't seem to go anywhere."

"No, it's just access in to the firewood lot. Gets us to the slag heaps where we get some of our crushrock, for driveways and fill and such."

"Would Mr. Duncan's vehicle have been capable of negotiating that road?"

"Greg's car? On that? Well, I suppose anything's possible in this world, but if he'd'a done that, wouldn't you have found the car? I mean, once the road ends and the slag heap begins there's nothing could go any further. And then there's the mud and the potholes and all, I doubt if right now anything much smaller than a good four-wheel truck could go far without getting bogged down. We got no trouble with the gravel truck, but I'm glad you boys didn't try to drive down there, we'd'a been towing you all out until midnight."

"Could he have driven into that old mine shaft down there?"

"Well, like I say, anything's possible, although that's pretty iffy. Those old shafts, they're dangerous as hell, eh? Roof might fall in, bottom might fall out, you don't have any idea what you might encounter. Been thinking of blowing the shafts shut tight but it'd cost a lot and why doesn't the law make the damn company do it?"

"We'll probably be back with spelunkers with breathing gear, just in case." The cop waited to see how Al would react, and when he didn't, the cop tried again. "They'd have a good chance, don't you think, of really getting in and finding out what was in there?"

"I suppose so." Al shrugged. "Helluva waste of time, though. They might call them shafts, but really, all they are is holes, and you know what a hole is, it's nothing. You really figure Greg went in there? With his car?" He shook his head again. "Well, you're the experts, I guess."

He watched as the cop cars and kennel van drove off; then he went back into the house and poured a fresh cup of tea. "They seem to think he drove his car into the old mine shaft," he said quietly. "Talking about bringing spelunkers out, with breathing gear and everything."

"Crazy people," Lottie decided. "You'd think they had better things to do with their time. Maybe go out and catch some of those drug dealers they're always going on about on the TV, or catch some of those murderers and rapists. Drive a car into a mine shaft. Right. Then fly to the moon, I suppose."

"Well, much as I'd like to stay and chat forever, as the man said," Al drank his tea hurriedly, "the truth of the matter is, time's a'wasting and we've got two more deliveries to make this afternoon."

Darlene helped clean up the lunch dishes, then set up the ironing board and got her clothes ready for work that night. Since she already had the board out and the iron hot, she touched up shirt collars and cuffs, and made sure Dorrit's clothes were properly folded and more or less wrinkle-free. And while she was at it, she checked Little Willy's stuff as well. There was no reason she couldn't do Tom and Jessie's, too. She supposed Colleen would pitch a damn fit when she found out Darlene was taking her car today, but enduring the fit would be a lot easier than hoofin' it. She and Larry were on the outs and that was fine by her, she was just about fed up with him, anyway, moody bugger that he was. She was just going to have to figure out a way to somehow scrape together enough money to get herself a car of some kind. Even Brady had a car, and she'd hardly been home long enough for her hair to grow out a bit. Of course, she came with a fair bit of money put away; maybe that was the clue. Maybe Darlene should stop waiting tables and start shaking her boobs: seemed to be good money in it. And she had a lot more boob to shake than Brady ever had, even considering the silicone or jello bags or whatever they'd used.

Colleen pitched a fit, but Darlene wasn't there to get on the receiving end of it, and all the others did was blink, then turn their attention back to the boxing matches on TV.

"And do I have to get Singe to build me a damned bank vault? The bitch used a drill and bored out the lock on the garage door!"

"Well," Jewen half laughed, "you know what they say: where there's a will there's a way."

"I'm tempted to phone the cops and report my car stolen." Colleen was white-faced with fury. "And as long as the rest of you act as if what she does is no big deal, she'll just keep on doing it."

"Why do you get so bent out of shape about it?" Al asked. "Jeez, Colly, you weren't going to be using it anyway."

"It isn't hers? She just *presumes*, Al! She drilled out the goddamn *lock*!" And she left, slamming the door behind her. Dorrit looked down at the floor, blinking rapidly, twisting his fingers together.

"It's stealing," he whispered. "Momma said shouldn't steal. But Momma stole Auntie Colly's car." And he began to weep.

"Jesus christ in heaven," Al sighed. He picked up the heartbroken little boy, sat him on his lap, and stroked his leg. "Momma didn't steal a thing," he insisted. "Auntie Colly's just tired, grumpy and upset. All's your momma did was borrow it, is all. So she could get to work. She didn't steal anything. Stealing is when the thing never comes back again. And you'll see, when you wake up tomorrow Auntie Colly's pisspot will be parked right by the house."

In the morning, sure enough, there was the pisspot. With a broken headlight and a crumpled fender. Al supposed it was god's own luck the bashed-up side was turned to the old house so when Colleen left in the company pickup, her headlights would have shone only on the undamaged part.

"Goddamn," he sighed. "I wish to god Dar would smarten up."

"Might not have been her doing; you know what them parking lots is like," said Jewen.

"She shouldn't have taken it."

Al had two cups of coffee and went out to Colly's pop can. The keys were still in the ignition. Damned Darlene, that alone would have been enough to get up Colly's nose if she'd noticed. Without saying anything to anyone, Al got in the car, started it up, sucked his teeth impatiently when he saw the gas gauge registered nearly empty. Colly never got that low on gas. What had Dar done, taken off on a joy ride? Jesus, talk about going out of your way to find trouble!

He drove directly to Fred's Motors, and took a quick boo around the lot before going in to talk to Fred himself.

"Al. How's things?" Fred wiped his hands on a filthy rag, stuffed it back into the pocket of his blue-striped coveralls.

"Dar pranged Colly's pisspot." Al tossed Fred the keys. "New headlight, new fender, probably have to work on the driver's door, it seems wonked, doesn't close easily. Nor open, either." He grinned. "Complete tune-up, the works, up to and including a new paint job. Gotta make it worth Colly's while or she's going to pull Dar's hair out, roots and all."

"I get more goddamn work from your family, I tell you," Fred laughed. "I'll pay a year's university tuition for my daughter on what I made on Norm's pickup. Je*zuss* but Willy did a job on that!"

"Yeah, well, you know how it is, Willy's got a temper and Norm was out of line. Still is, dumb bugger. Is that '92 Ford out there in decent running order?"

"Not bad." Fred took off his glasses, breathed on them, wiped at them with the tail of his shirt, put them on, didn't like what he saw and tried the whole thing over again. "About the same shape as that Chev I sold to Brady a couple of months back. How *is* Brady?" He grinned hopefully. "Hot damn, she's better looking than ever!"

"Keep dreamin', pal. You got no more chance with Brade than anyone else in a three-day walk. How much is the Ford?"

"Oh, I can make you a good deal on it. Considering that I'm going to ream it out of you for the bodywork and paint job. Import cars and all, you know how it is."

"Your brother still doing marine sales and service?"

"Yeah." Fred took off his peaked cap, turned it upside down and from beneath the sweat band took a joint of homegrown. He put the hat back on his head, lit up the joint, sucked on it, then handed it to Al who nodded and inhaled. "He's doing okay. Working like a dog with rabies, but that's the only damn way he's happy, anyway. You lookin to buy a boat?"

"Might be. Work boat, not one of those fancy plastic jobbies. Been thinking about maybe going beachcombing. Or something," he added vaguely.

Fred closed up the place and drove Al down to the insurance agent to register the Ford and get insurance coverage on it, then drove him back and helped put on the plates. "You tell Colly I'll have it ready as soon as I can. She gonna need a loaner, you suppose?"

"No. She's got the company truck."

He drove the Ford to the building supply store and bought a new lock unit for Colly's garage door. When he got back to the house Darlene was up, drinking coffee and looking defiant.

"Well." He glared at her. "You sure the shit ripped it this time."

"I'll get it fixed."

"What the hell did you do, run into a goddamn tree or something?"

"Or something," she agreed.

"Dammit, Darlene, the whole fuckin' family is getting fed up with this bullshit of yours! Drilling out the lock, for chrissakes!"

"I'll buy her a new one."

"With what? A dollar down and another when she catches you? What in hell were you thinking, anyway?"

"I needed to get to work."

"So what part of that is Colly's problem? Why didn't you arrange for a ride?"

"I *hate* askin' people for a lift all the time!"

"But you don't hate stealin' from your own sister?"

"I never stole nothing. I just borrowed . . ."

"Yeah, that's what I tried to tell Dorry last night when he started crying." And Al brought her up to date on that. "Poor little bugger, sitting surrounded by his own damn family, cryin' his eyes out because his old lady swiped a car."

"Ah *shit*!" Darlene started crying. "I'm sick and fuckin' *tired*, Al! Jesus, if it ain't one thing it's another, and when it concerns me it turns to shit."

"That ought to tell you something about your choices in life, you goddamn moron." He tossed the keys to the Ford on the table in front of her. "Here, registration's in the glove box. She's licensed, insured, and I forged your name so she's yours. And don't even *look* at Colly's stuff again, you hear? You so much as touch a gumboot and I'll beat the shit right out of you. I mean it. Not so much as a gumboot. Don't go within fifty yards of her place. The whole lot of us have had a gutful of this bullshit, you hear." Darlene gaped, and Al cut loose. "One more episode and you're gone, Dar. I mean it. You keep your light-fingered hands to your own damn self. You don't 'borrow' a damn thing. Because if you do, you'll find yourself living somewhere else and visitin' Dorry on the weekends. The entire family is fed up, so you clean up your fuckin' act!"

Darlene was up from the table and off to her bedroom, sobbing loudly. Al pounded the tabletop. *"Jesus aitch christ!"* he roared.

"Oh stop the noise." Lottie sounded bored to tears. "Look what you done now. You cracked the entire tabletop. Lookit. Another wallop like that and she'll be in spoon-sized pieces all over my clean floor. Now how am I supposed to fix that?"

"I'll fix the bugger."

"Oh, just reef it off the legs, right? Just kick it back together again, right? You got about as much finesse as a bear shittin' razor blades, Mr. Al. *I'll* fix the table, you go find something to kill or something."

Al stomped outside and headed across the yard and down the skidder trail, hands stuffed in his pockets, eyes squinted in anger. Now it was the goddamn table. And who was the old bitch to talk to him as if he was a ten-year-old who needed to be scolded? Wasn't a real table, anyway, just a goddamn door if the truth be faced, something Singe had tossed together as a make-do and nobody else ever got around to actually replacing. So, if it was cracked, so what?

Tony was loading the dump truck, a bucket of gravel, a bucket of slag, the big old loader rumbling contentedly, the huge tires making easy work of the gumbo. He waved and Al waved back but kept walking, past the mess and machinery, over the lip of the slag heap, down the other side, to the mouth of the mine shaft.

Still mumbling and muttering to himself, he went into the shaft, got the big flashlight and turned it on, then walked along the shaft, past the side tunnel where Singeon's in-laws came to cut coal, past another tunnel heading in the opposite direction, all the way down to where the main shaft stopped suddenly, blocked by a cave-in. Al stared at the wall of coal glittering in the beam of his light, then he turned left, and moved into a small side tunnel.

The tunnel continued at an angle, but Al felt along the wall, found the fissure, then turned sideways, sucking in his gut. He squeezed through the jagged crack, moving slowly and carefully, easing his way along, sucking air through his teeth with a little hissing sound. No matter how often he came here it still made him feel edgy. There was a wider, much easier entryway, but they used it as seldom as possible, and then only when both expedient and safe. This was what, as kids, they had called the shortcut. Back then its secretiveness thrilled them, like whipped cream on your ice cream, because the really *big* secret, of course, was that they were in the shafts at all.

The crack widened suddenly, and Al pushed his way through to the ballroom-sized cavern or pavilion made when the coal was hacked out and sent to the surface during World War I when thirty percent of the company's product was shipped to Germany to be used in the manufacture of weapons raised against the sons and brothers of the very ones who had toiled in the mines. The enormous cross-ties and support beams were scored with initials and names; his own grandfather's name was up there: George Lancaster, whose brother Peter had been crippled for life when caught in a shell burst. Al could remember old Uncle Peter, legs gone, his torso perched in a wheelchair, his mouth organs shining in the special leather carry-pouch made to hang off one arm of the chair. Mouth organs of every size, tone and pitch, and the old man telling him it was easy enough to become an expert on them, all you had to do was have nothing much else to occupy your time for thirty or forty years.

He switched off the flashlight and put it on a shelf. He didn't need it here. Singeon had figured out how to harness the stream that ran year-round through the sloped tunnels. He couldn't remember what Singe had called it, some kind of wheel, basically a glorified version of a juice can whirling in the running water, a bigger version of the generators that fit on the rim of a bike wheel and make the headlight gleam.

The lights were on all the time. It hadn't been easy getting the materials here, but given time and perseverance almost anything can be accomplished. They'd brought them in through the ventilation shaft a good mile and a half beyond the house on the side closer to Crazy Bob's place. They'd simply waited until the mad fucker was at work, driven the trucks in as far as they could without leaving sign, then hiked in with the gear over their shoulders. Took a couple of months, and Singe had to cozy up to Bob's woman and keep her occupied so she wouldn't hear or see the loaded pickups, but bigger prices have been paid for lesser gain.

The hydroponics were state of the art, now. The Indica grew lush, the pungent smell of it just about all a person would need to get ripped out of his gourd. Cash crop, they called it. *Cannabis sativa.* The devil weed! One puff and you're on the slippery slope, halfway down the road to hell and damnation. Rot your brain. Make your armpits smelly. Next stop total dope addiction, complete with fangs and an unslakeable thirst for the blood of newborn babies.

And beyond the plants, back toward a different air vent, the roller frame. The parcels were put down the vent shaft, slid and slithered along the rollers, came off the end to form a pile on the floor, then the hole was covered again and there it waited until the time they opened the parcels, added the cut and repackaged it in smaller quantities for distribution to the mules. Let them bring their goddamn trained sniffer dogs around if they wanted. The ventilation system didn't send air out the old vents anyway. By the time the air was routed, rerouted and sent through the shafts there wasn't enough smell left to interest a buzzard. And if the fuckin' mutts did find their way in they'd be lost faster 'n a person could believe.

The problems were small when you were dealing with the hydroponics and the imports; it was doing something with the money was the challenge. It meant you had to include people, trust people you ordinarily wouldn't even look at twice. It meant having accountants and lawyers on the payroll; it meant the most pain-in-the-arse network of blood-sucking flunkies and bum boys with off-shore accounts and bearer bonds and more goddamn rigmarole than a person could stand. Tony was good at that kind of thing. Not the actual doing, but the finding of the people who could do. Tony and those friends of Brady's, although he didn't trust those buggers enough to let them have even a hint of this place. Didn't tell Brady bugger-nothing, either, not that he didn't trust his own sister; it was just that the fewer people the better, the less known the safer. And no telling how friendly her friends really were or for how long.

He checked the hydroponics and for half an hour walked slowly, as content as any farmer with his bumper crop. And no need to worry about drought, hail or locusts, not down here. If a person had sense enough, what better place for year-round garden produce than an old mine shaft or pit? Temperature was constant, the environment easily controlled, small risk of bugs, airborne moulds or fungi. What could be better? If a person had that much sense, you'd think the person would grow weed instead of lettuce, but some people, like Colly, for example, are born already conditioned into a law-abiding mind-set.

He made himself coffee and sat drinking it and just looking at the set-up in the pavilion. Amazing, really, what a family could acquire in only a few years. The old spirit of Scots enterprise: the business sense that built the Hudson's Bay Company and established the sugar trade in the Caribbean. Oh, and incidentally, although it isn't spoken of in polite circles, of course, brought boatloads of slaves from Africa and, in later years, the wage slaves who had carved these shafts and pits. Just figure out what people wanted and find a way to get it to them, and the profit, like the blood of the lamb, shall flow.

Damn, but there was still the matter of the table. Well, hell.

He drained his coffee cup, rinsed it with clean water from the bucket and tipped the water onto the floor, then put the mug back on the shelf Jewen had made long ago. They used to keep crackers on the shelf, protected by a half-dozen rat traps because the entire place was seething with the furry-backed naked-tailed little shitters. It hadn't bothered them to have to finish off the broken-backed rats and toss the bodies down the tunnel before eating dry crackers and pretending they were feasting on beef. Rats didn't bother him at all, then. Now the mere thought of them gave him the heebie-jeebies.

He squeezed his way back out through the crack and made his way by the light of the torch back to the mouth of the tunnel. He stood blinking for a moment, adjusting his eyes, then went to the cellular, kept safe from weather in an insulated picnic cooler. He wasn't going to get the phone put back in at the house, and he wasn't going to let the rest of the mob know there was one back here. That damn Darlene would have the long-distance operators working overtime.

Tony parked the truck and got out, stretching, arching his back to ease out the stiffness. "I saw a little white flower, so help me god," he said.

"No, over at the old house."

"One of Grandma's snowdrops, probably. In a while the place will look like it's carpeted with green leaves and white flowers. And after them, the crocuses. Used to be planted in beds but they're wild, those things, they refuse to be confined, and they spread, man, how they spread."

"Cops pulled me over for a roadside check this morning."

"Fuck!"

"All's I had on was slag and gravel so I let 'em escort me to the weigh station, and I was underweight by about five hundred pounds. They checked all the permits, papers and probably what I had in my thermos, and then tailed me down the road. So I stopped and told 'em where I was delivering and asked if they'd like to come supervise the unloading, just to be sure. Damn, they did." He laughed. "Most of the time you tell 'em that and they'll just take off, but no, there they were, standing in their silly suits, watching as the stuff poured out the truck and landed on the lumberyard loading lot."

"It's that goddamn Greg." Al hitched his jeans, shook his head. "As big a pain in the arse now as he was when he was underfoot all the time."

"Do you believe in hunches?"

"What's yours?"

"That we do some landscaping around here. We've been a bit, well, sloppy." He pointed at the tire tracks. "They're apt to wonder why we been drivin' around over there."

"You're as paranoid as a person can be and still dare whip 'im out to pee, but yeah, I believe in hunches. Why'n't we shove the dirt around a bit with the bucket, and then park the equipment there. Make it so damn obvious they don't even see it. That's what you do with a stovepipe, you know."

"Shove the stovepipe, you hillbilly fool."

"Shove *you*!"

They got back to the house not ten minutes before Manson's Furniture drove up with the new table and chairs. Lottie looked at Al and shook her head. "You're a horse of a different garage, you are," she told him.

"Well, I bust the other one, didn't I? Only right I replace it."

"You'll be working overtime for two months to pay for this."

"Maybe it'll teach me to hang onto my temper," he said, grinning. "If it did, it'd be cheap at twice the price."

"Your mother should have spanked you for it."

"My mother," the smile vanished, "beat the shit out of me with a kindling stick and all it did was make me even madder."

As the new table was being brought in the front door, Al and Tony took the old one out the back door. "Now why'd you go and do this?" Tony asked mildly. "It was a perfectly good table."

"It'll make a perfectly good one again. Hoof 'er out to the workings, we'll use 'er for a work bench."

"T'hell with it. Too much like work." He dropped his end of the table. Al lost his grip on the other. The table hit the ground, the split in it widened. Tony almost cursed, but Al's sudden gesture for silence stopped him. Al leaned over, his eyes narrowing. The table lay ruined, legs poking upward, splayed and twisted. Al pulled something from the wrecked mess that had been the mounting bracket, held it out for Tony to see, then carefully placed it on the underside of the tabletop and stepped on it with his heavy boot, twisting and crushing.

Together they picked up the ruined table and carried it to the stump muncher. A few whacks with the maul and the shattered door was pounded away from the mounting brackets and the pieces were stuffed in the hopper. The machine was turned on and the roar was ear-shattering. Tony took the maul and attacked the mounting brackets, hammering them into shapeless lumps.

"Hope the fuckers go deaf," Al said, but was unable to hear his own words over the noise.

Brady headed in to school every morning and did her level best to learn her lessons, pass her tests and work toward her grade twelve equivalency. She figured at the rate things seemed to be going she'd be ready for old-age pension before she was qualified for a well-paying job. Of course, she didn't *need* a job—she had steady money coming in from the enterprise—but she needed a way to account for it. She felt as out of place as she had when she was in high school and burning with the rumours flying in the corridors and cafeteria, rumours about "those Lancasters" and their wild goings-on, rumours that might or might not have had some basis in fact, but which, really, had nothing to do with her. She wasn't the one making and selling moonshine; she wasn't the one got in a fight with two cops; she wasn't the one got all liquored up, went to a dance, put the tap on a married woman and then had to scrap with her husband and two of his relatives. Then, she didn't even have a car, let alone was able to drive it at speeds well in excess of the limit. She wasn't known as a good-time girl, a party girl, an openly sexual easy feel. But it all stuck, like catshit to a new wool blanket; even if you managed to scrape off most of it, the stain would remain.

None of that was hanging from her now, and the town had grown large enough quickly enough that there were other people to occupy the target in the gossip shooting gallery. She was enrolled as Brady Marsh, the last name she'd picked up in an insane and probably record-making short-term marriage to a guy whose face she could no longer remember. He was young, and so was she at the time; he was in the US Air Force, had curly blond hair and told her she was on her way to fame as a singer-dancer-actor. They got married in Reno, so fast neither of them would have had time to catch the flu, and she didn't even know anything was wrong between them until the special delivery postie brought her the large manila envelope. She signed for it, opened it and found the divorce papers. She walked around the apartment and wondered how in hell she was going to make the payments on the furniture they'd chosen. She went into the bedroom and checked his dresser and his half of the closet. Empty. But she'd known it was: he'd been called back to camp two days earlier. He had cuddled her, kissed her nose, told her he'd be back on the weekend. Said he was going to apply for and get a house or apartment near the base and they'd be together. He admitted his parents were going to be rabid at the thought of him getting married, but so what—as long as they had each other they had everything. And then the special delivery postie. He must have known, even at the time. It still stung.

As Brady Marsh there was a measure of anonymity. Mind you, there weren't a lot of women named Brady in the world, let alone a surplus of them in the same town, but most of the women in the upgrading class were from other places anyway. That was a surprise to her, at first. Hardly any of them were from around here, almost all of them were from out of town. The ones from here either had jobs or didn't want them.

To judge by the personal disclosures of the others, women wound up in this class because they had come here with husbands who were looking for work, usually semi- or unskilled labour. It didn't seem to matter whether the men found that work or not, the stories assumed a tiresome sameness of increasing tension, arguments, usually physical abuse, with or without alcohol involvement, and then either he left or she did and took the kids with her. Virtually all were on welfare and living in basement suites or little old houses where the wiring was condemnable, the plumbing laughable, and the kids were all crammed into one small bedroom because even if he'd left, she couldn't afford the rent on the original place, not on what welfare paid, not with the cost of sneakers and jeans, not with the price of hamburger.

Brady didn't have to count her change and make some frantic mental calculations before deciding if she could afford a can of

Orange Crush with her lunchtime sandwich. Brady didn't have to embrace casual workie appearance and show up in faded jeans and two-year-old tee-shirts. But she did. She didn't want to seem totally different, even if, perhaps especially because, she knew in her heart she was.

"What kind of nonsense is this!" She was near tears. "I'm *never* going to understand this muck."

"Let's see." Tom left his homework and came around the table to stand beside Brady. "What's your problem?"

"How'n hell'm I supposed to know what an *integer* is?"

"You don't know?"

"No, I don't know. If I knew I might not be so close to hysterical."

"Go back to the start of the chapter," said Tom, flipping pages. "They must say something about it somewhere," he continued, his tone soothing. "They're shitheads but they don't cheat."

"Lookit this!" She pushed back from the new table, rose to her feet and started pacing around the kitchen. "I'm here like a dummy, and the *kid* is helping me with my homework? And when I finally ace this stuff, I'll be fully qualified for bugger-nothing! I can register for more courses that I won't understand! I can try to get myself trained for something I probably don't want to do anyway! And if I *really* buckle down, who knows, in only another who-knows-how-many-years I'll be qualified to be a hairdresser!"

"Don't give anybody else the same cut you gave yourself," Jessie teased.

"I can't find anything about any integer," Tom admitted. "Maybe it was in the chapter before this one."

"Maybe it's a typo," Tony suggested. "Is there anything you *do* know that in any way resembles the word you don't know."

"Shut up." Brady sounded dead casual. "I've been known to kill for less."

"I'd heard that about you but was praying it wasn't true," he said, laughing. "Go for the throat, I heard."

"Integer. What a stupid word. Integer. It'll probably turn out to mean 'number' or something. You'd think they'd just say what they mean." She went to the coffee pot, checked it, muttered and emptied the last cold inch of brown mud down the sink. "God, I wish I'd stayed in school while I had the chance. I think a person's brain must be like a muscle or something. As long as you're using it regularly, you've got a chance of learning; stop studying and your brain, I don't know, turns off the part that you need to remember things. If you keep on in school you stay tuned up, like an Olympic athlete; and if you quit, then go back years later, you have hell's own time because first you have to get your brain in shape." She stood watching the fresh coffee drip into the clear glass pot. "My brain," she decided, "needs to go to Jenny Craig. And it needs some aerobics or something. So as soon as I've had a cup of coffee, I'm going to the swimming pool and if anyone else needs to exercise their brains they better be ready when it's time to go, homework done." She frowned. "I warn you, now, homework done. Not having any of the rest of you turn out as flabby-minded as I've become."

But she stuck it out, integers and all, and when Peter Cottontail hopped off down the bunny trail with his basket of eggs, Brady had the equivalent of grade eleven, and was hopeful she'd have grade twelve by year-end.

"Some system," Jessie griped. "They're going to make me go to school for *years* to get grade twelve, but the equivalency ones get it in months. Maybe *I'll* drop out for a while and then sign on for that easy ride."

"Maybe you'll ride the toe of my boot if you drop out," Al promised.

"So why am I going to school?" Jessie asked. "I'm not trying to be fresh. I really want to know. If I keep on going for *years*, I'll have grade twelve, and with it, *if* I'm lucky, I can get a job in the supermarket with old Brew. Or maybe I can sit down at 758-PUPS and dispatch taxis to beer parlours. Or I can take my life in my teeth and drive cab so every junkie for miles can try to rob me."

"Or you can go on to university and make something of yourself."

"Make something of myself? Hey, I already *am* something."

"Good girl," Tony agreed. "You sure are something. What, we're not sure, but for sure it's something. Something good, too."

"Ever think of being oh, I don't know, maybe a nurse?" Al said. "Maybe a doctor?"

"Takes a long time to be a doctor," she fretted, "and it costs buckets."

"Listen, if it's money you're worried about, stop worrying. I'm working. And as long as I've got money coming in, your way is paid."

"Know something?" Brady interjected. "I felt like that when I was your age. Concentrated so hard on 'Why should I?' and 'What's the use?' that my marks went down, and that bummed me out so I spent even more time convincing myself it was a waste of time. So then I dropped out, and for a while I slung hash but then they found out how old I really was, and it wasn't old enough, and they canned me. So I went to the fish plant. And after a while I got so fed up I took off and wasted a whole bunch of time at shit jobs, and then I started dancing. And do you want to know something, darling? *If* I'd stayed in school and done some real work, by now I not only would have my doctor's papers, I'd have my own office and everything that goes with it."

"What was it like, being a dancer?"

"It was shit. You want to know how good it was? Well, what I'm doing now is about ten thousand times better. But if you want to find out for yourself, so's you'll know for sure, first thing you do is go on a diet because they want them slim and trim. No candy, no chocolate bars, no ice cream, no sandwiches, just rabbit food. Then you have to spend most of your money on rent and hair and nails and costumes and the chiropractor and dance lessons. And then, maybe, just maybe, you might get a job hoofin' 'er in the chorus line. And you'll have to wear support stockings even before you need them so's you can ward off varicose veins and . . ."

"Don't forget all the men pawing at you," Al included.

"I was coming to that. And you can't even punch out their lights or you'll get fired. You have to smile, smile, smile. Or instead of all that you can be living in a dorm with a bunch of other people your own age, going to classes, playing on the basketball team, or the tiddlywinks team if that's what you're good at, and working toward something *better*."

Big Wilma took Norm to court for non-payment of child maintenance. So Norm came out to the house with blood in his eye and
acid on his tongue. He yelled and hollered, ranted and raved, and
vowed vengeance of every possible sort. In the midst of his tirade,
the cops arrived. Since there was nobody in the house at the time
except Norm, Big Wilma and Lottie, Norm assumed it was Lottie
who had called, and cut loose with a few vows and promises in her
direction. "It couldn't'a been Wil," he roared, "I was with her."

"Wasn't me," Lottie insisted. "I'm only here to do, I'm not here
to get a whip and a chair and try to tame the animals."

"Bullshit!" he shouted.

"The phone doesn't even *work*!" Lottie yelled. "Now shut up and
leave!"

And he did.

Big Wilma took out a peace bond on him, even though she knew
the paper wasn't any protection at all. "I want it on record," she
said. "Just in case."

"It wasn't me," Lottie insisted. "Honest to god, it wasn't me.
Most of the time I was in the kitchen with them, minding my business, making peanut butter cookies. When I wasn't there, I was
doing laundry."

"Don't worry about it, Lottie," Jewen sighed. "It doesn't much
matter one way or the other."

What did matter, to all of them, was that not only did Peter
Cottontail bring chocolate eggs and bunnies, he brought Singeon's
first acknowledged child.

"She's the spitting image of her momma," he said, grinning.
"Black hair and lots of it, and her eyes will be dark, too."

"She got a name? Or are we going to call her 'she' all her life?"
said Jewen.

"Lucy likes the name Kathleen, and that's fine by me. She's as
cuddly as a cat, and about the size of one, too."

Nothing would do but that they all troop up to the hospital to
stand in front of the big glass window staring in wonder at seven
and a half pounds of scrunch-eyed and puffy-faced baby.

"Gorgeous," they decided. "Lovely," they agreed. "Just about the best ever." They were unanimous, and Little Willy had to be picked up so she could get a better look. "Can I hold her?"

"Not yet," said Jewen. "Gotta get her home, first. They won't let anybody but nurses in there with them right now."

"I'm going to be a nurse," Willy decided. "Then I can be there, too."

"I'll be the doctor," Jessie put in, "and you'll be my nurse, and we'll mostly do baby stuff."

"The rest of us," Jewen said with a laugh, "will do our level best to try to make sure you've got lots of business."

They were still oooh-ing and aaah-ing and waiting for Singeon to walk Lucy down the hallway to join them in their idolatry when Brewster and Maude arrived on the maternity floor. Maude was in a wheelchair pushed by a nurse, and Brewster walked proudly beside the chair, holding Maude's hand.

"Hey, Al," Brewster said politely, beaming widely.

"What's shakin', Brew?"

"Maudie's in labour," Brewster bragged. "How come you're all up here?"

"Singeon's woman had a little girl."

"Busy night all round." Brew seemed to take some kind of extra pride in the notion. "I'll let you know," he promised.

"Yeah, hope it all comes out okay." Jewen kept a straight face. "You want to visit with your mother for a while?"

"No, not yet." Jessie was still staring at Kathleen. "She's got Brew, she doesn't need us."

"Maybe later on." Tom shrugged. "See how she has her hands curled up like little fists? Maybe she's going to be a boxer."

Brewster phoned at three-thirty to tell them Maude had given birth to a girl. "Nine pounds," he bragged, "bald as a cue ball. Probably means she's going to have blond hair, huh? Going to call her Mavis. It's a bird," he explained. "Supposed to have a real nice song."

"Congratulations, Brew," said Tony, stifling a yawn and trying hard to sound interested, even enthusiastic. "You give Maudie our best, okay? Tell her . . . oh, tell her she did a real good job and we're proud of her."

In the morning Al phoned "Bouquets" and ordered two flower arrangements, one for Lucy, the other for Maude. When asked if he wanted anything special on the card, he thought fast. "The one for Lucy White should have 'Love and Best wishes from the entire family,'" he dictated, "and the one for Maude Johnson should have 'Congratulations from Jessie and Tom'." The clerk wrote the messages on two different slips of paper, but somewhere between her pen and the bedside, something went scroogee. Lucy got flowers from Jessie and Tom, and Maude got flowers from the entire family. The switch confused Maude and went a long way to convincing Brew he'd been accepted totally.

"Appreciate it, Al. Really appreciate it." He pumped Al's hand repeatedly. "Means a lot to me, to both of us. Well, actually, all three of us now."

"Oh, any time, Brew," Al said, not having the slightest clue what it was Brew was going on about; until he went over to visit with Lucy and saw the card that had come with her flowers. By then he figured, all things considered, it would go better to leave things alone.

Lucy and Maude took their babies home, and a week later Norm was in hospital, although not on the maternity ward, and not for any little blessed event. His squeezie's boyfriend went after him with a foot-long fish basher, a length of wood shaped like a small baseball bat, with a central core bored out and stuffed with a lead plug. The riggin's was supposed to be used to finish off fish once they were finally landed, but the boyfriend hadn't hooked a twenty-pound salmon and couldn't have cared less about the Marquis of Queensberry. He used the basher on Norm.

"Ever think you might be in better shape all round if you went after single women?" Singeon held the wheelchair steady while Norm made his painful way from the bed.

"Don't start on me," Norm managed, his lips swollen and purple, his face held together with sutures and bandages. When he spoke, he lisped, the result of the sudden removal of several of his teeth.

"I'm not getting started on you. Not enough of you left to start in on—the guy did a real job on you. I'm just suggesting if you stayed away from married and otherwise hooked-up women your health might improve."

"The ones who aren't hooked up aren't worth looking at. Besides, they expect too much. The hooked-up ones aren't looking for anything long-term or heavy; they don't want commitment, all's they want is a fun time."

"Yeah, you look like it was real fun! Any bits or pieces of those teeth still stuck in your mouth?"

"They fished 'em out. Took X-rays to be sure."

"Hell, you've had so many X-rays the toilet bowl is going to glow in the dark after you pee."

"If I ever get to the point I can pee again," Norm said. "Kicked the living devil out of m'kidneys and cracked a rib, too."

"Fun, ain't it."

They went down in the elevator and then across the waiting foyer and through the front doors to where the big ashtrays ruled under the rain overhang. Singeon lit a cigarette and passed it to Norm, who took it, inhaled deeply, then sighed.

"Jesus," he breathed, "that's good."

"When I was in here," Jewen lit up, too, "they let you smoke in the TV lounge. You could even smoke in your room as long as the person in the other bed wasn't on oxygen or allergic or something. Now, christ, they take you in, patch you up and you wind up here for a smoke, risking pneumonia, bronchitis and probably the flu, as well."

"Just another form of Prohibition," Al sympathized. "Get us used to being controlled and regulated. Once they can say what you can stick in your mouth or up your nose or in your arm and where you'll go to do it, they can train you for other things. Didn't learn bugger-nothing from that other thing in the States. People just started making their own and going blind from it. It actually worked against them, set up a mood of rebellion. It's what gave the Mafia it's real start, and they're still trying to clean up that mess. So they dropped Prohibition and had the good sense, for a change, to put heavy taxes on the booze so's they could dip their beak, too."

"If it worked to their advantage, why didn't they enlarge it?" Singeon lit up, and leaned against the wall.

"'Cause they're stupid. They got no sense at all. This big 'war' on drugs? Make a person laugh. What it's really for is to get us all used to having helicopters over the house or landing in the cow field, guys in combat suits running around looking for weeds in the pasture, arriving any hour of the day or night with bits of paper that allow 'em into your house. Small step to giving them machine guns to carry while they do their silly-bugger business. How serious are they? Well, when was the last time you heard anything about Noriega? Supposed to go on trial, be a public example, rah rah rah. What did we get? Fuckin' football player with an attitude and a boxer with a hard-on. Both of 'em dark complexioned, too, or did you miss that part of it? Meantime, the public example, who was, after all, a damn CIA puppet, just sort of slides off the front pages, and for all any of us know he's living in a mansion in Bel Air."

"Goddamn, but when you get going, you can talk a blue streak." Singe grinned. "There's times I could just listen for hours. Where *is* that guy, anyway?"

"He'll be here in a minute. Don't get your water hot."

"How's little Wil?" Norm asked

"Starved to death in the ditch. Soon's we save up enough money for a casket, we'll bury her."

"Stop the shit."

"Well, what do you care? You been so busy chasin' nooky you haven't had time to buy her a pair'a sneaks. Didn't even get a chocolate bunny from you at Easter. You're makin' yourself look bad, bro."

"If I was sendin' money to *her* I wouldn't hold back. It just pisses me off no end that first I got to fork out big dollars to get m'damn truck fixed and then I'm supposed to hand over more money to the one who wrecked it."

"Well, you *did* piss her off. I mean get a grip, guy."

"Here he comes."

Tony arrived with a small box in which nestled four large-sized styrofoam cups with plastic lids. Nestled among them were a collection of little plastic cream jugs and small paper packets of sugar.

"Place is jammed," Tony explained. "Lineup goes damn near all the way around the room. There's more crutches and wheelchairs there than in the physio rehab area, people gimping on canes and with walkers. Jeez, half the town must be fallin' apart."

"Well, if this don't beat it," Singe said, laughing. He lifted his coffee. "Look, for god's sake, it's latte!"

"No wonder the place is jammed." Norm took his, removed the plastic lid and inhaled the aroma. "The stuff they bring on the trays is one of them chemical mysteries. Lukewarm, brown and tasteless. You wonder where they get it and what it is."

"Part of their rehab programme," Al joked. "They want people up and moving around as fast as possible so they put real good coffee in the cafeteria in the basement and then only allow you to smoke outside, and the next thing you know even the quadriplegics are on the move."

"Stings." Norm winced, his tongue moved gently across the swollen purple mess that was his mouth. "But good. Might save my life."

"If it does it will only be so some other pissed-off logger can take a round or two out of you. You gotta wise up, guy. We're all gettin' just a bit fed up with it."

"Ah, Singe, chrissake, who'd have expected the guy to get so raunchy?"

"So what's in it for them?" Singe asked Al. "The law and what you were saying, I mean."

"Money, you dinkhead. You saw that thing on TV last year. All those boxes stuffed with money, remember? They bust into that empty room and found who knows how much? Well, why bother with the whole rigmarole about collecting taxes and all when you can just walk in and take the whole friggin' thing? And then not have to account for it. So where did it go? How much of it didn't even get back to the cop shop? How much of it did they put aside to divide up amongst themselves later?"

"Anyone got another cigarette?" Norm squirmed in his wheelchair, trying to find a comfortable position. "My mouth hurts," he moaned. "And my balls are the size of watermelons, only purple. I'll be lucky if they still work."

"We'll be lucky if they don't," Singe argued. "Might keep you out of other people's apple trees."

"Jesus, it's cold out here."

"Wanna go back? No problem?"

"No, I want another smoke. You didn't think to bring anything else, did you?"

"Nope." Al stared at the parking lot. "You know the liquor store's closed. Besides, the last thing you need is to get yourself boozed up. Kinda luck you been havin you'd fall outta that chair and fracture your skull on the floor or something."

CHAPTER SIX

Colleen took the old rototiller out to the garden area and tried to start it up; no matter what she did, the engine wouldn't kick over. She took out and replaced the spark plug, she cleaned the carburetor—she was ready to try arcane incantations—but the machine just sat, unresponsive and cold. Tony had a try at it and couldn't get it going. Al gave half a dozen tugs on the starter cord, then just walked away from it, got in his truck and drove away, disgusted. She was still fighting with the old machine when Al came back with the new one perched in the bed of the pickup.

"See," he said, grinning, "you don't have to walk behind it, either, you just put your pretty little fanny on this seat, turn the key and there you go. Move this to the right and the tines turn. Shove this up here and the lawn mower works. Got a hitch on the back where you can connect that cart in case you want to move stuff, weeds or whatever."

"This won't do the corners." She pretended to be critical but was stroking the hood of the silvery grey wonder.

"Darlin', I will personally dig the corners for you. And this poor old thing" he touched the handles of the old machine "is going to sit up on a big block'a wood with baskets of flowers hangin' off her."

Tilling the garden had never been easier. The new machine had more attachments than a cat has fleas, each with its own lever. She could use the breaker plow, then the rock picker, then the roto-tines, then the power rake and listen to music at the same time. Part of her wanted to bust out laughing, but a bigger part looked at the soil when she was finished experimenting with all the gadgets and wallowed in satisfaction.

Of course, Tom had to try it out, too, and after him, Jessie. Then it was only fair that Dorrit and Little Wil have a try. When Singe brought Lucy and the kids over for a visit, out came the rotovater; and weeks before it was time to plant, the garden looked ready, the dirt tilled to the consistency of potting soil.

She bought two hundred dollars' worth of sterilized steer manure and worked that in, then let the rain do its thing, after which she waited to plant the garden. The early spring mildness vanished overnight: the wind howled and screeched; rain lashed almost sideways; puddles formed, spread, joined up with each other and became little ponds that overflowed and sent runoff streams raging around looking for a place to empty themselves. The culvert down the road near Bob's place washed out, the ditch water spread along his driveway and he was as good as cut off from civilization for two days. Then Jewen realized what was going on and went over with the front-end loader.

"Surly son of a bitch," he said mildly on his return. "I fished his culvert pipe out of the mess, I cleaned his friggin' ditch, I got the whole shiterooni back together for him and he barely said a word to me. I wasn't expecting no bouquet of roses, but I wasn't expecting to be hard-nosed either."

"The old man should never have sold the place to him," Al said. "He's been a pain in the ass for years."

In spite of Jewen's efforts the water won again. The culvert washed out again, the driveway flooded, and old Bob's front yard began to look like a lagoon, complete with wading Canada geese and a few swimming mallards. Jewen went back down with the loader, and this time Singeon and Al went with him. The cleanup happened quicker with more people busy with shovels, but by the time the culvert pipe was back in place and the water began to drain again, Bob's front yard was a mess of mud, stones, goose shit and duck feathers.

"What I ought'a do," Bob raged, "is burn the house flat to the ground and hike off down the road. I'm s'damn sick of this place! Coons get the chickens no matter what I do; fuckin' sheep wander off and the cougars eat 'em; fattened up a coupl'a pigs and the bear ripped the back door off the shed and took 'em both! A man," he announced mournfully, "gets a gutful after a while."

"Let me know when you're ready to stop talkin' about it and actually do it," Jewen told him. "I'd be interested."

"Yeah? How interested?" Bob shivered, stuffed his cold-swollen hands into his pockets, hunched his shoulders against the monsoon. He was wet to the arse, coated in mud and obviously totally dispirited.

"Get the assessment guy to come out and put a price on it."

"They charge a lot," Bob hedged.

"I'll pay for it."

"Great place to grow rice," Al said, laughing. "You could fertilize it with goose shit."

"Geese'll eat the rice before it's ready." Bob seemed a bit more cheerful, although he was getting colder by the minute. He sneezed three times, violently, and sniffled. "Fuck, now I'm gonna catch a cold." But he grinned.

"Catch a cold!" Al said later. "Stupid son of a bitch couldn't catch a housecat if it jumped up and bit 'im on the butt."

The storms blew themselves out, the weather became mild again, the fruit trees blossomed and the bees actually got a chance to get to them. Colleen checked the garden and shook her head: the pelting rain had pounded the earth flat and it would have to be tilled again; but first she had to wait for it to drain or she wouldn't get the tiller out before summertime.

She was actually thinking of giving it a try when the storms came back again. The bees cowered in their hives, unable to get outside in the high winds, bitter cold and teeming rain. The blossoms on the trees were torn off, fell soggily to the ground, turned brown and began to rot. Two more weeks of rain, and then the weather began to change again. The assessment guy toured Bob's house and buildings, looked at the land and wrote his report. Bob protested the price was too low, Jewen volunteered to add ten thousand to it, and Bob shook hands with him.

"Helluva price for ten acres of gravel, rock, spread-out slag and trash bush," said Al, although he didn't sound angry. "Place was a bloody swamp before the old man backfilled it with slag from a coupl'a heaps."

"Not interested in trying to turn it into an agricultural miracle." Singeon laughed. "Just be nice to get crabby old Bob to hell 'n' gone out of our faces. You able to handle this okay?"

"No problem. Bank manager loves me. I'm workin' steady, I've taken out a coupl'a small loans and paid 'em back on time, no sweat."

✦

The autumn weather stopped, spring returned, the garden drained enough so there was no threat of the tiller getting bogged down, and Colleen took it back into the garden and retilled the weather-flattened soil. When the clouds cleared, the sun was warm, but when the sky darkened again, the air was cold and damp. The second crop of snowdrops ventured out of the mud, followed by crocuses and grape hyacinths. Buds formed on the forsythia and the first hint of leaves showed on the wisteria. Colleen got the beans and peas planted and put in her spud patch. Then the rain hit again, and by the time it cleared she had to retill the unplanted area. But the yard was bright with daffodils and that made up for a lot. The weather channel map showed the eastern part of the country was still shivering through blizzards and sub-freezing temperatures. "Yeah, well, at least we don't have to shovel it," they told each other when the rain started again.

The weather cleared one more time, and they went over to help old Bob move. It didn't take long. When a person has had enough, the person has had, after all, enough, and Bob had decided he had lost enough money trying to save on the cost of meat by raising his own. The mere sight of a chicken feather, he said, could send him into nervous near-collapse. "And I'm gonna make sure I don't change my mind," he cackled happily. "Man, I could'a easily gone to Mazatlan and stayed a year with what it's cost me on bear and coon food.

"No," he shook his head cheerfully, "I won't need a single one of those tools: the condo setup has a guy who does all that, fixin' door latches and cuttin' the lawn and all. All's I need is a few garden tools and even they prob'ly won't get used but once or twice a year. Oh, just the socket set and a coupl'a wrenches." He waved easily. "These new cars, with all that computer stuff in them, a person can't do their own tuneups and repairs anyway. Most'a this stuff won't fit into the place," he said, momentarily mournful. "I don't know *how* I collected all this stuff. Who did I think was going to use the other four bedrooms, and why did I furnish them, anyway?"

His condo was brand new, with three big bedrooms and what could be a fourth but was called the hobby room. Small chance of Bob taking up sewing or weaving, smaller chance of him deciding to become a world-famous painter or novelist. What they didn't know to put where, they put in the hobby room for Bob to unpack later on. They moved his bedroom, everything that was in the kitchen, the living room and one of the spare bedrooms, and put a case of Kokanee in the fridge as a house-warming present.

Then they went back to Bob's place and sat on what were now their own front steps, drinking beer from cans and grinning at each other. "Got 'er all back again," they said repeatedly. "Place is complete again."

A week later, they moved Singeon, Lucy and the kids into what had been Bob's place. "How'd you get her to agree?" Jewen asked.

"It wasn't that she was dead set against leaving the reserve," Singeon answered, "it was that she had no intention of moving into the big house with the whole family. Likes her privacy, Lucy does."

"I suppose some do," Jewen said. "Look at Colly, as an example."

The weather stayed mild and reasonably dry; the peas grew, the beans grew, the spud tops showed taller every day, and Colly planted her chard and spinach. The columbine flowered and the hummingbirds came back, the kids put out feeders and the ants tried to get to them, crawling up tree trunks, along the branches to the cord holding the plastic bottle full of sugar-water. They went down one side of the cord to the little nipple-like holes, drank their fill of nectar and trudged back up the other side of the cord to return to their underground nests with a few drops each of honey and water mix.

🕯

And then Darlene got fired. Some poor sap with a most unfortunate misconception reached out, put his hand on her inner knee as she cleared the empties from the table, then stroked upward, grinning fatuously. At about the time his hand reached her crotch, the tray dropped, the empties smashed to the floor, and her fist connected with his nose. Actually, Dar wasn't aiming for his nose, she was aiming for the back of his head, trying her level best to send her clenched mitt through his entire face to reach her goal.

Not satisfied to do a job on his face with one measly blow, her left hand, freed from the burden of the tray, grabbed his hair as his head lurched backward. She yanked forward, redirecting his phiz, and about the time his chin cleared the rim of the table, her knee, aimed at the ceiling, connected. It was enough to cost her the job she didn't like very much anyway. It also cost him. Worse, from the point of view of the boss, it promised to cost the insurance company a real whack, which is why Dar joined the ranks of the unemployed.

"Fine, then," she said, shrugging, "be that way. This is turning into a real low-class joint, anyway." And she didn't even wait long enough to help pick up the shards of glass, the jugs, the shattered bottles or the small change scattered on the wet floor. She just took off her apron, tossed it to the boss, went and got her jacket and left.

"Son of a *bitch*!" she screeched, coming into the living room. "I am so *mad*!"

"Easy, easy." Jewen sat up, hair rumpled, eyes bleary. He had taken to sleeping on the couch, claiming it was more comfortable than his bed. "What's wrong?"

She sat on the couch and snuggled against him, until she calmed enough to tell him what had happened. It didn't help her mood that he laughed.

"Shut up, okay," she snapped. "To top it all off my knee hurts like a bugger."

"Let's see." He made himself quit laughing. "Maybe you bruised it."

Darlene tried to roll up her pant leg, but it wouldn't go far enough to bare her knee, so she stood up, undid the button and zipper, and let the pants fall to the floor. Her knee was red, swollen and streaked with blood. There was also a purple lump the approximate size of a dime in the skin just over her knee cap.

"You just sit here," he said, patting the couch. "I'll go get a cloth."

"Peroxide, too, maybe?"

He was wearing nothing but his boxers, black with a white stripe, and when he came back from the bathroom with a hot cloth and the first aid kit, Tony was sitting beside Darlene, handing her tissues, patting her hand and hearing the tale of the vanishing job. Jewen knelt on the floor, and put the cloth on the knee. Darlene winced and hissed air through her teeth.

"Fuck," she breathed. "Now it isn't just hurting, it's throbbing."

"There are scores of *soft* places on the human body, darling," Tony told her, "and no need at all to hurt yourself on the few hard places. You probably got him bang-on flush. Next time, try for the side of the jaw, it'll do just as much damage to him, and a lot less to your pretty self."

"I'm going to put peroxide on it," Jewen warned. He lifted the cooling cloth, looked closely at the knee and made a soft 'tut tut' sound. "Looks like that lump might actually be something." He bent to examine it closer, then, frowning, felt the knee carefully. "Grab her hands," he said conversationally. "I don't want her decking me." And his fingers pinched.

Darlene jerked and cursed; then Jewen was grinning and offering her something. "You got a souvenir," he chortled, holding up a broken tooth. "You can wear it on a chain around your neck."

"Bit me. He *bit* me." She took the tooth, looked at it, then at her knee. "Now it's really bleeding. Oh, *why* does everything have to be so *grotty*." And the tears flowed freely.

"Come on, darlin' Darlene." Tony put his arm around her shoulder, pulled her close and patted gently. "Come on, you're tougher than that. It was a shit job, and you're worth way better than that. Come with Tony."

Jewen finished putting the band-aid on Darlene's knee, and Tony helped her across the living room and up the stairs. Jewen grinned to himself, cleaned up the slight mess, put the first aid kit away, and lay back down on the couch. In minutes he was asleep.

Larry might have accepted the same kind of first-come-first-served arrangement he'd been part of with Greg, but Tony had other ideas. The first time Larry came around to see if the story he'd heard about Darlene blowing her cool was true, Tony met him before he got to the front steps of the house. The conversation was polite, to the point, and explicit. Larry looked at the muscles bulging under the blue cotton work shirt, then at the size of the hand holding the cigarette, and he nodded agreeably. He even waved as he got back into his car and drove off down the road.

The big change wasn't the loss of the job or even the reestablishment of the relationship between Tony and Darlene. The big change was in Dorrit. He was on his way downstairs for breakfast when he looked through the partially open doorway and saw his mother and one of his favourite people in bed together, curled in a coziness of tangled arms and legs. Instead of continuing on in search of cereal and milk, Dorrit walked into the bedroom and climbed on the bed. Tony roused, lifted his head, and was looking almost eyeball to eyeball with a very hopeful little boy.

"Are you gonna be my dad, now, or somethin'?" Dorrit asked.

"Or something," Tony agreed, sitting up and yawning.

"Really? Or just for a little bit."

"I guess that depends on you. I didn't know you wanted a dad. I never much cared for my own."

"You don't need any damned dad," Darlene disputed sleepily. "You've got more uncles than you know what to do with."

"I don't got no dad," Dorrit insisted. "Everybody else has a dad." He stared at Tony. "You had a dad."

"That's true. He wasn't much, but I had him. Probably still do. You're sure you want one?"

"You." Dorrit nodded.

"Well, we'd have to negotiate, I guess. I don't want a kid who's cheeky, or lippy or whiny or anything like that. If I was going to be somebody's dad I'd want him to be nice to me. And if he was nice to me, I'd be nice to him. And we'd talk politely to each other. But the main thing would be I'd want my kid to be cuddly, even when he was a big boy, and I'd want to have good times with just him and me, sometimes. Know what I mean?"

"No."

"Well, I'd want to do things just him and me. No mom, no cousins, no uncles, nobody else at all, just my kid and me."

"You watch your damn self," Darlene said, sitting up, eyes hard and glaring. "Don't you go setting up something with my kid that you aren't prepared to handle for the rest of his days. No hairy-assed drifter is dumping my kid! Better he have nothing and get used to it than think he's got something and then see it walk out on him."

"I haven't walked anywhere since the night you brought me home from the bar." Tony reached for his cigarettes, lit two, and handed one to Darlene. "Even when you moved that ridiculous narc in here I still hung around, didn't I? Well, didn't I?"

"If you dump him I vow to god I'll . . ."

"Well, just don't you jump up and start hollering that I'm not allowed to see him or have him for visits. I mean it's got to work on all sides."

Dorrit moved closer, and Darlene grabbed him, pulled her to him. He cuddled her and wriggled himself to a spot in between the two of them. "We could sleep," he offered. "We could snooze."

"We could," Darlene agreed, "but we aren't going to. Don't you have school or something?"

"I could stay home."

"Magnanimous little fart, aren't you?" Tony laughed. "Come on, I'll do you some bacon or something."

✻

Jessie and Tom had no need for a stepfather. They had Al, and he was as much a dad as anyone could have wanted, needed, or for that matter, survived. But they did think Dorrit was lucky.

"He's got both, now," Tom explained.

"You've got both," Colleen countered. "You've got your dad and you see your mom on weekends."

"She's busy with Mavis. Mavis this and Mavis that, and she says she's the best little baby anybody ever had."

"Everyone says that about babies. Babies aren't supposed to just *be*, you know. They have to be the best, the cutest, the sweetest, the happiest. Just because they're babies."

"Yeah?"

"Yeah." She knew he wasn't convinced. "She said the same things about you."

"A long time ago." She couldn't detect any hint of jealousy; it was something else, and she wasn't exactly sure what, something very much like mourning or grieving for something or someone long gone. "People get a car and it's the best," he said, examining the beds of his fingernails. "And then, even if the car is still working, they get a new one. Jess and me, we're the old cars."

Colleen went to see Maude, to try to find help with Tom's sorrow. Colleen knew she had no workable ideas, no magical insights. For all the loads of diapers she'd washed, the meals she had cooked, the cough medicine she had spooned, she wasn't a mom. Maybe with labour pains came some kind of special awareness, some kind of instinctive knowledge or biological wisdom. She hoped so, because otherwise, life for moms must be terrifying.

The house wasn't new, but it was decades younger than the one Maude had lived in when she was with Al. Set back a reasonable distance from the sidewalk with only a small backyard and the front yard grass to the house itself, it seemed plunked down rather than set. Not a rose bush, not a flower bed, not even a flowering shrub or an ornamental tree. Just grass, as if the occupants really yearned for the open prairie, fell asleep at night pining for miles and miles of nothing but miles and miles, an uncluttered horizon, no untidy mountains or often shabby forest to intrude.

The front steps were cement, painted red; the house itself was white, unremittingly white, no coloured trim of any kind. The shingles on the roof were ordinary asphalt, black, and the handrail was made from what had, in a former life, been metal pipe. The front door was white, and there was no doorbell or buzzer. Colleen knocked, then knocked again. She fully expected Maude to answer the door dressed from top to bottom in white.

Maude was wearing skin-tight purple leotards and a purple (with multi-coloured splashes) top. Her hair looked like she intended at any minute to step before the TV cameras to do a commercial as Chiquita Banana, and she had more bangle bracelets on her wrists than anyone ought to be caught out in.

"What a surprise," she said, her voice falsely cheerful. "Come in. We'll have coffee."

"Thank you." Colleen stepped into the house, closed the door and followed Maude down the short hallway to the kitchen. As she passed the living room she looked in through the doorway. She had never seen a room so determinedly clean, neat and tidy in her life.

The kitchen looked as if it was only used on alternate Tuesdays. Every surface was clean, and shone. The taps and spigot at the stainless steel sink were shiny, and free of tattle tale spots; they had not only been washed and rinsed, they had been dried and polished. Set right in the middle of the kitchen table was an African violet. It looked overwhelmed by the burden of its duty.

They didn't talk much until the coffee was made and they were sitting together at the table, as stiff and formal as foreign delegates at the UN.

"It's Tom." Colleen decided she might just as well dive in and get it over with.

"Tom?" Maude sounded as if she had little or no idea who claimed the name. So Colleen recounted the conversation, as close to verbatim as she could. Maude stared at her. Maybe she'd forgotten how to speak or understand English; maybe she was waiting for a translator.

"What am I supposed to do?" she asked, and waited for someone to give her instructions.

"I was hoping you'd have some ideas."

"Ideas?" She didn't even seem to know what ideas were; the concept seemed to have escaped her experience.

"He thinks he's lost you," Colleen tried again.

"Don't be silly, he knows where I am."

"He isn't happy, Maudie. He feels as if you don't love him any-more."

"That's silly. Of course I love him, he's my son."

"Maudie, maybe we can come up with some way to, well, like, let him *know* that."

"Oh, you guys, really." Maude sipped her coffee, then got up abruptly, left the kitchen for a moment, came back with an ashtray, cigarettes and a lighter. She sat down again, lit a cigarette and watched the smoke rise from the tip. "You Lancasters have some really weird ideas," she said, so matter-of-fact she sounded like a different woman than the one who had answered the door. "The whole time I lived with Al I felt like I'd been put down on Mars or somewhere. You could *see* things when you were all together, like real things, only floating in the air. At first I thought I was crackin' up, but then I caught on to what it was. Emotions. The whole lot of you, yourself included, with everything just hanging out: this one's happy, this one's feeling goofy, this other one's bummed out, and another is angry. And everyone of you knowing how the others felt, not a word needing said, like as if you were mind readers or something. And you all *insist* on being happy. Happy? Nobody in their right mind expects to be really *happy*. And the kids when they came, it was the same. Well, you expect little babies to be jolly, what do they know, anyway. But kids are supposed to learn what the world is really like, and neither Tom nor Jess ever really caught on. And why should they? There I was trying to teach them to be reasonable, and there were all the rest of you insisting on being bloody *happy*. So, of course, the kids thought I was the odd one, the grumpy one, the one who looked for the fly in the butter. And when Al went away, well, it just got worse. I should have moved to my own place then. But I was scared. And the rest of you stepped in to take up the slack, every day in every way more and more involved in my kids' lives, and every day in every way they became more and more like strangers I'd met waiting at the bus stop or something. And I got lonelier and lonelier."

"We're talking about Tom," Colleen reminded gently.

"That's what I'm talking about," Maude insisted. "He thinks I left him? He left me long before Mavis was born. Years before. He left the crib and started turning into a Lancaster. He stopped being *mine* a long time ago. And Jess, well, she never was, mine I mean."

Abruptly, Maude left the table, went to the fridge, opened it, then opened the little freezer door and brought out a bottle of vodka. She put it on the table, went for glasses.

"Not for me." Colleen smiled and shook her head. Maude shrugged, poured three or four ounces in a glass, tossed it off as if it was water, refilled her glass and sat down again. She lit another cigarette, and her hands trembled.

"And yeah," she went on, as if there had been no interruption, "yeah, I was stepping out and messing around. So? Sue me. What difference did it make? Whether I was there or not, life went on."

She reached out to tap her ashes in the ashtray, and her trembling fingers missed the mark: the ashes fell to the tabletop. She stared at them, brushed them to the floor, lifted the cigarette to her mouth and inhaled greedily. "And then Al came back. And when we went for that ride?" Her eyes welled tears. "He didn't waste any time or make no bones about it, he just put it to me. Told me he'd take my kids away from me, said he'd go to court and prove I was a mess; he knew I'd been drinkin' heavy, he knew I'd been using, he knew everything, and it was enough and I knew it. He said if he had to go to court I'd never see 'em or hear from 'em again. Or I could fuck off, no problems and no trouble, and Brewster wouldn't get hurt."

"Have you told any of this to your kids?"

"No, and I won't ever do that either. Why wreck their lives anymore'n they've already been wrecked."

"Tom thinks all you want to do is fuss over Mavis."

"Mavis? He thinks . . . Why don't you come and see Mavis."

The baby's bedroom was dim, the blinds drawn, the curtains pulled. Soft music played in the room, volume low. The baby lay in her bed, eyes blinking slowly, looking half asleep and very much like an elf. Every now and again she would raise one fist, suck her thumb a few times, then lower her arm again.

"Hey, baby." Maude leaned over the crib, her voice crooning, and very slowly the baby turned her head, focussed on her mother's face. A faint smile flickered, and then the head turned away again, eyelids fluttering shut.

"That's the best she gets." Maude straightened, shook her head and moved from the crib, walking toward the doorway. "She never really goes to sleep, and she's never really awake. Taken one at a time, everything works: eyes, ears, hands, feet, the whole thing, on its own and by itself works just fine. But up here," she tapped her own head, "something's scrambled or something. They don't really know. It's been one test after another since before we left the hospital."

"Haven't they found out anything?"

"Boozing. Using. She'll learn to sit up, she'll learn to walk, she'll even learn to talk but . . . you tell me how I explain that to my other kids. You tell me what I'm supposed to say to them. They come here and they chatter away, talk talk talk to me, talk talk talk to Brew, questions about this and questions about that. Brew takes them to the store with him at night and they're right in there, piling stuff on the shelves, marking prices, chatter chatter, and he loves every minute of it. He knows *his* kid prob'ly won't do any of that. Take her there she'll prob'ly knock stuff *off* the shelves. He don't blame me. When I get hard on myself he says, 'Hey', he says, 'I was there, too, okay? We both done it to her. I was drinkin' right along with you, I was popping same as you, don't take all the blame, how were we supposed to know'. It's nice of him, but it doesn't help any."

Colleen didn't want any more coffee, she didn't want any more talk; she just hugged Maude and left the clean house in the featureless yard.

After supper she loaded kids in her crew-cab pickup and drove to the river. It was too early for swimming or wading or even for sitting on the rocks, but there were tadpoles for Dorrit and Little Wil to hunt, and the first pussy willows for them to break off and take home. Colleen walked with Tom on one side and Jessie on the other and, as gently as she could, told them about Mavis's affliction.

They listened, they even understood the explanation, and they accepted it so calmly she wondered if they had understood anything at all.

"And so that's why your mom spends so much time with her," she finished. "She *has* to because, well, something could go wrong really easily."

"Something's already gone wrong," Jessie said flatly. "Sounds like she's a total retard or something."

"Retard isn't a very nice word," Colleen corrected.

"Nice? The not-nice happened before the kid was even here." Tom sounded so much like Jewen it made Colleen feel out of place and time. Jewen had stood by the kitchen sink, leaning his skinny flat butt against the counter, face white with shock, eyes seeming huge and sunken, and even the silly servant from the welfare had to pay attention to him. *Don't be ridiculous*—his voice had been so soft, and had been heard by all of them. *We aren't the ones who committed any crime so we don't need to be punished. Of course we're staying here and of course you're going to agree. Singeon is old enough, Al is old enough, and of course we can look after the little ones.* She'd gone to him then, even though she had to wrench herself from the grasp of the child care worker. All he'd done was put his hand on her shoulder and she knew she was safe. *She's lost enough already,* he said. *Can't any of you see that?*

"You're a good kid, Tom-oh." She put her arm around his shoulders and hugged him, amazed to realize he was almost as tall as she was.

"So it was boozing did it?" He slid his arm around her waist, matching his steps to hers. "And they know it, like, the doctors and all know what it does?"

"We can probably get a book about it, or something."

"So how come they just keep on selling it?"

"Money," Jessie interjected, coming out of her deep silence and moving to walk on the other side of Colleen, sliding her arm around Colleen's waist, linking them like Siamese triplets. "They make a bundle of money off it, don't they, Colly?"

"Tons."

"Yeah? But how much does it cost them when they get a kid like Mavis? I mean, she's gonna cost a bundle, sounds like."

"Ah, but not today. Right now they're pulling in tons of money and they won't have to spend any of it until some time in the future. And by then it won't be their problem."

"Idiots." Jessie sounded older than god's molars. "Make you wonder, eh?"

"It would that."

"But Kathleen's okay, right?"

"Kathleen is just about totally perfect. She's like you two were, real keepers."

Kathleen had a shaggy mop of black hair, huge dark eyes that slanted at the outer corner, and a soft little mouth that seemed to know only two expressions, either a wide grin or a wide-open chortle. She was long and slender, and spent hours in her jolly jumper, suspended in the doorway between kitchen and dining room, where she could see just about everything. Spot loved to go over for a visit because he could scoot past the jumper, dodge the baby's eagerly grasping hand, then whip around and come charging back again. Neither he nor Kathleen showed any signs of tiring of the game. Every now and again, just to keep interest flowing, Spot would walk over slowly, then stand pressed against the baby's legs, suffering her pudge-fingered grasp.

"That dog is nuts," Lucy decided. "He acts more like a cat."

Old Bob's house, now Lucy's house, was big and well built with gyproc on the walls of the rooms and heavy lino throughout. Simon and Peter shared a big upstairs bedroom. Carol had chosen a smaller one downstairs and kept her door closed even when she wasn't in her room.

"Oh, she keeps it clean," Lucy said easily, as close to bragging as she would ever come. "I don't have to do much for that one. If she doesn't want me going in there it's no skin off my nose; she's not hiding anything, she just likes her private space is all. I've got a sister like that."

"She could be doing anything in the world in there!" Darlene protested.

"I doubt whatever she's doing is dangerous. I mean she isn't going to blow up the house with the rest of us in it. She probably just reads her books or something."

Just past Carol's bedroom was another room that seemed to have been added as an afterthought. The linoleum on the floor was a different quality and a totally different pattern; the ceiling was higher at one end than the other, following the slant of the roof line, and the only window was a small one, heavily curtained. This was where Singeon installed the second TV and hooked up the video game machine and a VCR. He bought a sofa and several stuffed chairs, and put up shelves to hold the growing pile of movie videos. "There." He patted the boys on their heads, teasing them. "Now we don't even have to see your faces, right?"

"Right," they agreed, secure in knowing they were welcome anywhere in the house at any time. "And we don't have to be bothered by you."

"You could have got them second-hand stuff," Darlene told him. "They don't need new, they're just kids."

"Ah, it was on sale," he lied. "Out-of-stock pattern or something." But he saw the hunger in her eyes and understood it only too well.

Al took them all with him early one Saturday morning. "Not telling you anything," he said, laughing. "Follow along behind and find out."

Tony knew what was going on, but not even Darlene could get it out of him. They piled into vehicles and drove off like a cavalcade of nutbars, down the road to the highway, then south to the outskirts of town. At the marina, Al parked where there was just enough room for the others, and together they trooped to the locked gate. Al had a key, usually reserved only for members, and he let them through the gate. They walked along the wooden plank dock and played If I Had the Money.

"This one," Dorrit said. "It's got sails *and* a motor. And I like the colour."

"This one," Little Wil countered. "It's got a house-thing on it."

"This one." Al stopped beside a big wooden craft that had spent its life as a fish boat. "We're gonna turn the fish hold into, like, living space, so we can all go out and spend a few days fishing or whatever and not need to come in at night. You can put down sleeping bags and foamies and just crash right on the boat."

"You're kidding!" Big Wilma's smile could have gone twice around her face. "I've always wanted a boat. My god, it's like a dream or something."

"Is this for real?" Darlene asked Tony.

"Oh, it's for real all right. Gonna have a good summertime, babe, if it ever gets here."

They trooped on, and Al took them out for a three-hour cruise. He explained over and over how everything worked, even let the kids take turns at the wheel, pointed out the radar screen and the fish catcher. "See, you turn this on and there she is, that's what's on the bottom. See how it goes up a bit, down a bit, just like the yard at home, and see, over here, those bright dots are fish. If we were all set up we could just drop our lines over the side and see if we could get one of them interested enough to drop in for supper."

"Oh, man," Big Wil breathed. "I can feel it already. The sun will be shining, it's going to be just about hot enough to boil water on the sidewalks in town, and I'll be stretched out on the deck back there near the rail. I'm going to get me a brand new beach towel, one of those that are like five feet long or something. I'll have my suntan lotion, I'll have me a cooler of cold cold beer, and I'm going to just barbecue myself out there. Maybe a bit of music, maybe not. If I get too hot I'll just yell 'Stop the boat', and I'll be over the side, have me a swim, get myself back up on deck, lie myself down again and bake some more. Jesus, I'll be the colour of milk chocolate in no time flat."

"I'm going to have one of those lawn chair dealies that are more like couches than a chair," Darlene agreed. "I'll put 'er on deck and the first person who wakes me up is apt to perish. I don't really care if I never catch a fish, there's going to be plenty of fools doing that. I don't really care if I don't get a tan. What I'm interested in is doing nothing at all, although I do like that idea of just yelling, 'Stop the boat so's we can go swimmin'."

"I'm catchin' fish," Dorrit told her. "I'm catchin' *lots* of fish."

"Can we go exploring?" Jessie asked. "Like go, uh, up there?" She waved her arm, encompassing the world. "And could we, like, stop at places where nobody else is, and look at what's there? And at school they said there were, like caves, and the waves carved them out of the rocks. Could we go there and see them?"

"No end to what we can do," Al said.

"Prawn traps," Lucy said firmly. "And crab traps."

"We could do whale-watching tours," Brady decided. "And tourist stuff. Advertise on the internet, have 'em flown in from Seattle or Anacortes; they'd love the whole seaplane thing, landing in a spray, the throat-clutch thrill as they teetered around getting from the plane to the deck of the boat. Take 'em on a cruise, maybe see if Lucy's family would be interested in doing some 'traditional' stuff, maybe salmon barbecue, a bit of dancing."

"Right," Lucy said sarcastically. "Anytime you need a tourist attraction, bring out the savages with their drums and dances. What about some of you milk-faced bastards doing the dog and pony show for a change?"

"We could," Colleen conceded. "Get Paddy O'Reilly and his gang to do, like, Celtic jigs and reels and clog dancing, and maybe they'd even do that thing they're learning, the morris dancing, with the ribbons and sticks and tinkle-bells."

"If they bring out the ribbons and bells," Lucy laughed heartily, "I'm sure I can get my cousin Joe to haul out his bagpipes. Wouldn't that blow 'em away; he could wear Grandaddy's kilt with some Salish regalia, and caterwaul on the pipes and give 'em some real cultural schizophrenia."

"Would Joe do it?"

"Oh, pay him enough and he's apt to do anything."

"Hey, you guys, I'm serious," Brady snapped.

"Brade, babe, you been away too long. *We're* serious, too." Singeon gave her a gentle push on the shoulder, then hugged her. "Lighten up, give yourself a chance."

"Well, I could always dance for them." She winked at him. "I've got all those damn costumes packed away in trunks. I could do the feather dance and the fan dance, and for that matter we could get some maple leaves and place 'em in strategic positions and I could pretend to be the freakin' flag."

When they got home again, the cop cars were parked from the

roadside to a spot in front of Colleen's house. The doors to both houses were open, search warrants were thumbtacked to the door frames, and the place was crawling with burly men in black coveralls. Police dogs slobbered on the ends of their leashes, sniffing obsessively.

"Guess Dudley Do-right got bored, or something," Al growled.

"Guess we better go over and see if they're at our place, too," Singeon said from his pickup. "I'll be over after they've gone."

"Well, just get out the transfer of title papers," Jewen spat. "Prove to 'em we bought old Bob's last few scrawny hens when we bought the place."

Colleen raced across the yard and up the steps into her house. A police dog was sniffing at the cupboards in the kitchen. "Look at the floor!" she screeched. "Get that muddy mutt out of my house, he's tracking dirt all over the place. Just *look* at the rug in the living room! Your mothers never teach you to wipe your oversized feet?"

"We have a search warrant," a cop said defensively.

"I don't care if you've got an original copy of the Bill of Rights, there's no need to make a mess of my house. Didn't your mother teach you anything at all? See that cocoa matting on the front porch. You wipe your damn feet on it before you come in. And *most* of us take off our boots in the hallway. Look at the damned mess!"

She just about went ballistic when she saw her bedroom. Every drawer had been hauled out of the dresser and emptied onto her bed. Her closet had been emptied and a policewoman was checking pockets while a policeman tried in vain to get the board he had pried loose back into its proper place.

"I want your name and your badge number." Colleen was shaking with fury. "You might have a warrant to *search* but you don't have one to search and destroy!"

In the big house Lottie was sitting at the kitchen table dealing yet another hand of solitaire, a cigarette burning in the ashtray, her coffee mug half full. "One thing about it: it's damn kind of the government to send these morons out to make sure there's always something for me to do around here. By the time they're through I'm guaranteed another two weeks' wages. They've torn Jessie's bedroom apart, Mr. Al, they even pulled boards off the walls."

"Who knows?" Al said with a shrug. "Maybe they've come out to catch the mice who live in the walls. I think maybe I'll just phone my lawyer. I think we might just charge the fuck-headed pricks with harassment."

"Well, there's gonna be hell to pay," Lottie agreed, "because they're out there right now with shovels, digging holes in Miss Colly's garden."

"They'll be goddamn sorry for doing that," Jewen said, laughing. He went to the back door and hollered at the mud-streaked men in the pea patch. "You diggin' for oil or something?" he mocked.

"Jesus, here comes Colly." Al pretended to cower. "Guess I'd better make a fresh pot of coffee; we might be here a while."

"Cinnamon buns due to come out of the oven in about two minutes," Lottie said, putting a red nine on a black ten.

The cinnamon buns were gone, the coffee pot empty, and the smell of roasting lamb beginning to issue from the oven, before the garden ravagers were satisfied they were never going to find whatever they thought they were searching for and put their shovels in the trunk of a car.

"May we use your hose?" one of them asked, holding out his filthy hands as explanation.

"Shove the wet end of it up your arse for all I care," Colleen snarled. "Why ask *now*? Look at the mess you've left me with! You've ruined all the hard work, you've ruined all the young plants. Someone's gonna hear about this. I want your name and badge number," she demanded, adding it to the growing list she carried in her pocket.

Several cops came running down the skid trail, excited as kids on a Sunday picnic. One of them dove into a car, grabbed the microphone and started babbling. Someone else grabbed a camera and moved back down in the direction he'd just come. He was red-faced and puffing and Colleen sincerely hoped he'd have a heart attack with his next cumbersome step.

They had just finished a bang-up supper of roast lamb, mashed potatoes and two kinds of salad with raisin pie for dessert when the original cop showed up at the back door.

"I need Mr. Al and Mr. Jewen to come with me," he said, almost apologetically. "We'd like you to be present when we begin dismantling. And if you have a lawyer, now would be the time to phone."

"Already phoned," Al answered coldly. "Gonna sue your asses off for harassment."

"Yes, sir," the cop nodded. And then it was just like on TV, and the kids stared, open-mouthed with amazement. "You have the right to remain silent," the cop began.

"I can't believe it," Colly breathed. "He's going to *bust* you!"

It was a two-day wonder in the local paper, complete with photographs of the old vats and the coils of piping. And there on the front page were three of the four Lancaster boys, howling with laughter and pointing at the heap of junk being loaded into the police van. Big Wilma laughed so hard Colleen was afraid she'd wind up pulling a muscle or something, and Lucy stood with Kathleen sitting on her hip, smiling widely and waving the baby's hand in a bye-bye as Daddy Singeon was driven off to be fingerprinted and photographed.

By the time they had to go to court, the garden was again neat, the peas and beans flourishing, the radish and early spinach were being harvested and added to salads, and the lilac was blooming. The Crown took two days to present their case. Al's lawyer spent one morning ripping it to shreds.

"And did you examine the seized material?" he asked the expert witness.

"Yes."

"And in your expert opinion, sir, how long has it been since the equipment was last used?"

"I would think at least twenty years,"

"Twenty years," the lawyer repeated. He paused, and let the silence in the courtroom do all the talking for him. Then he turned to face the judge squarely. "Your honour, please," he sighed. "The last time a drop of anything went through those coils the oldest of these men was less than fifteen years of age. Three houses have been ransacked; we have copies of the repair bills and we have the cleaning bills because of tracked-in mud and what-have-you. We have already begun proceedings of harassment."

"Your point?" The judge was having trouble keeping a straight face.

"Well, sir, the Bible does say the sins of the fathers shall be visited upon the children," the lawyer conceded, "but it doesn't say any of them have to go to jail because their late father made his own moonshine. These charges should never have been laid. Taxpayers' money and everyone's time has been wasted."

"Helluva thing," the judge agreed.

They all went for fish and chips for lunch, and regaled each other with silly jokes and what at the time seemed like witty remarks.

"For this they brought out the spelunker club," Singeon chortled. "God help us if they bring out the archaeologists, no telling *what* they'll uncover."

"Yeah, Great-grandma's broken crockery or something," Colly agreed. "You never know, there might be some real finds for the bottle collectors."

"So where *was* the damned thing?" Big Wilma asked.

"Oh, not very deep in at all," Al explained. "They walked us into a hole just past where we've been hauling out slag. Couldn't have been much more than, what would you say, Jewen, maybe a hundred paces, hundred fifty?"

"'Bout that," Jewen agreed, reaching for the platter of cod. "Maybe a bit more."

"And there was this alcove sort of thing, and there they were, proud as hell with this, like, junkyard dealer's wet dream. And me, I just bust out laughin'. I mean, the only puzzle I have is how the old man managed to not blow up the whole damned shiteree!"

"Wonder how many people wound up either half blind or walkin' sideways because of the mess he turned out with that thing."

"Sky-high. I mean it, you never saw such a plumber's nightmare in your life!"

"And all them cave explorers disappointed because they hadn't got to go in deeper. The cop is telling us about being under arrest, and other cops are asking us questions about How does it work, and the spelunkers are asking if we'd mind if they explored deeper, and one of them assuring us we don't have to worry about any of 'em getting hurt because they have their own insurance, and I vow to god I heard the old man laughing."

"That wasn't your old man, you fool, that was *me*!" Tony poked Al in the ribs. "Just think, they didn't even bother charging me because, they said, I was only a visitor." And he started laughing again. "I could get away with murder, I suppose, and they couldn't charge me because I'd say, 'Who, me? Oh, I'm just visiting'."

CHAPTER SEVEN

The reporters were waiting when the acquitted got back from the fish and chip shop. Questions were called to them; answers were ignored, mistranscribed, misquoted and taken out of context; and the cameras flashed. When the first noisy scrum had satisfied itself, the local community programming TV volunteer stepped up with a video camera and asked basically the same questions as the print media.

"Justice has been done," Singeon said.

"We were confident from the very beginning," Al said.

"I think a public investigation is in order," Jewen stated. "And I don't think any good would come of the police investigating themselves; that's too much like putting the fox in charge of the security guarding the henhouse."

"I'm just a visitor," Tony said, smiling. "I wasn't charged. I was there to support my friends in their time of need."

"Me?" Brady managed to look both totally innocent and utterly believable. "I've never been inside any part of it. As far back as I can remember the place was out of bounds. Mom told us there were boogers and goblins lived in it. And I'm not ready to find out if she was right or not."

"I didn't even know the hole was there," Colleen said with a shrug. "We've always tried to block up any we found. The company was supposed to do it, but . . . you know what companies are like. And, anyway, the entire area is riddled with tunnels, and I suppose they'll collapse from time to time and cause new holes. Personally, I wish the police would stop dinking around bothering people over nothing at all and get to work earning some of that money they get paid. Taxes go up and up and up and what do we get for it? We get people charged for something they didn't do and that hasn't happened in two decades anyway."

"I don't want to talk about it," Darlene said firmly. "I've been scared stiff ever since they showed up with their guns and dogs, and I'm still scared stiff, and I don't think it's over: they'll keep on at us until they drive me to Prozac, and even thinking about it upsets me so I don't want to talk about it."

"A picture of it?" Singeon smiled as he spoke. "You're sure? Well, I suppose so, but only if you promise not to go in very far because it's really not safe down there." He winked and the TV camera volunteer got it on tape. "You might trip over a cop or get bit on the bum by a police dog or something."

They watched themselves on the local channel and made jokes about their small screen debut. When the interview ended and the screen showed the man with the collection of spoons he clattered in time to music played by a child who could hardly be seen behind a huge accordion, they changed channels and watched a movie about a handsome scalawag who ran moonshine in the mountains and was chased over twisty, dangerous dirt roads by federal revenue agents.

"Jesus," Big Wilma complained. "How come he's such a hero and your old man is suddenly next thing to Dillinger?"

"Well, Dillinger is a hero now, too. And so's Alvin 'Creepy' Karpus. All the bad guys become good guys in time. God, Nixon's being canonized and Ollie North never *did* get what he had comin' to him."

"I gotta go pack." Wil left the sofa. "I'm off at the very crack of tomorrow. If that bugger Norm shows up while I'm gone, tell him he's behind on his child support and this time I've put the lawyer on it from the very get-go."

The community station replayed the interview and the shots of the maw leading into the shaft where the still had been found. Those who hadn't seen it the first time had heard versions from friends who had watched, and by noon of the third day, the whole town was laughing. Even those cops who had in no way been involved in the great moonshine bust walked with their eyes down, trying to pretend their uniform had been issued by the bread company or the dairy delivery. The laughter turned to anger when two local businesses—one of them the bar where Darlene had worked—were torched and the police had to admit they had no clues at all.

"Damn," Darlene exclaimed. "Well, I don't feel so bad, now, I'd'a been outta work, anyway."

"They should stop harassing innocent people and get to work catching a few crooks for a change," one of the town councillors ranted. "It's time the tail quit waggin' the dog. We're going halfways to broke paying for protection and we aren't getting any!"

The police, pushed almost to controlled fury, managed to even the score, and Al and Tony almost had a ringside seat for the incident. "Cops Come Through" the headline in the local paper read. The sub-heading was "Massive Seizure Off Plum Point." The local pro-gramming TV station got their video to the wharf just in time to capture the arrival of the police boats. Helicopters hovered over-head, and in the open doorways the camera caught shots of men in SWAT suits with automatic weapons aimed at the confiscated yacht. The men in handcuffs and leg irons who trooped off the largest police boat and trudged, clanking, up the wooden walkway to the waiting police van looked like anything except sailors. They ignored the reporters, ignored the video camera, even seemed to manage to ignore the police with their guns and dogs. They stepped into the van, sat on the benches and ignored everything and everyone, including each other.

"We had the cover off the motor," Al recounted to family and reporters. "And I had the carb out and was cleaning it. First hint we had was the helicopters, whirling above us, like dragonflies, or something out of a space-horror movie."

"It was like being in the opening scenes of *Apocalypse Now*," Tony said, his face still pale from shock.

"We wondered if they'd found more pipe for Pappy's still," Al tried to joke but his smile was forced. "Then there were even more choppers and high-speed police boats, and all I could do was try to get the carb back together and pray to god it worked properly."

"Even if it hadn't worked properly, if it had worked at all would have been good enough for me," Tony said. "Man, it was scary, and coming so soon after that silly thing with the old pipes and stuff—well, listen, I was worried. They had about enough guns to win a war!"

"Did you see the actual encounter?" asked a reporter.

"No, hell, we were a good two, three miles from Plum Point, which is where they said the Yank boat was heading. We'd gone out fishing, and I didn't like the sound of the engine and, like I said, had the cover off, and then this *armada* went flyin' past. And the next thing we know, here's this whirlybird hoverin' up above us and a guy with a loudspeaker is telling us not to move so . . . we didn't!"

"Even though I was so scared my bowels were tryin' to move." Tony tried a weak joke that fell on its face and perished.

"So we had to sit there," Al said, "and then there was the sound of machine guns or something, like in a war movie, and then . . . the parade began and they told us to follow them in. So we did. Well, we had to stop to let four cops on board to search us and all but, like, it's easy to understand why they wanted to do that: they have to be sure we weren't part of whatever. It wouldn't have mattered who happened to be out there at the time, they'd have done the same thing. I mean, it wasn't just because it was *us*."

"They even hauled up the crab trap to be sure," Tony said. "They were really efficient; I was impressed. Even if I was scared stiff."

And the truth of it was, both Al and Tony were scared just about shitless. They were exactly where they were supposed to be at exactly the time they were supposed to anchor, waiting exactly as planned, with the cover off the engine just in case they needed an alibi. They had the crab trap out and the cod lines over the side mooching, and they had the other thing where it was supposed to be, too.

The other thing was an inflated, watertight and airtight rubberized storage bag in which a fortune in uncut diamonds was packed. Its twin had already been dumped in Plum Point. The plan was the Yank boat would stop by to pick up the first bag, as down payment, and when they were sure they were being paid, they would continue on, make the rendezvous, transfer the cargo, get the second submerged bag, and head off back to American waters.

The RCMP combined forces with the FBI, DEA and other groups of initials too numerous to mention, and the stuff had been tracked since before it even left the Golden Triangle. Both nations proclaimed a victory in the war against drugs; both nations made much of the James Bond aspects of the investigation. All along the route agents swooped down and scooped up co-conspirators. Had they waited ten minutes more, they would have had Al and Tony, too.

The evening news showed the cops standing around a table on which was piled bag after bag after bag of white powder, and in front of it, spread out on the table and clearly visible under the overhead lights, the diamonds. They didn't glitter or glimmer or shine or shimmer: they were uncut. But they were impressive. As usual, the police overestimated the value of the drugs and, being in so generous a mood, overestimated the value of the diamonds as well.

Al and Tony waited two weeks, then went out fishing again, this time taking with them their brand new self-contained underwater breathing apparatus and their wet suits.

The inflated rubberized bag was still there, held down by two round lead weights. The weights sat on the murky bottom, and the rubberized bag stretched upward yearningly, like a new kind of bull kelp straining toward the sun. Al grabbed the strong rope in his gloved hand, cut it, and went back up with the bag. He surfaced and pushed his face mask up onto his head. Tony was leaning over the side, grinning. Al handed him the rope, swam to the ladder and climbed up to the deck.

"I guess it's too bad about the cops finding them all, huh?" Tony asked.

"Damned shame if you ask me."

"Awful hot for the time of year, isn't it?"

"Too damned hot for me. I'm taking a vacation." And at supper he said as much to Brady, who nodded and understood completely. She drove to a pay phone she had never before used, and when she came back home again, she just nodded. The people she had contacted also understood completely. Or thought they did. Had they understood completely there would have been blood on the moon.

Brady went into town and parked behind the old arena, then walked down Main Street to the bookkeeping and accounting office. "I really don't know if I'm early or late," she told Charlie Prince, son of Old Charlie, grandson of Charles Jr., whose father Charles had first opened the business. "I've got my papers with me, see: this is my partnership agreement, and these are my stock shares. And the whole thing brings in about ninety thousand a year; that's US dollars, and that's after the US Internal Revenue has had its bite. And this," she handed a contract form across the desk to Charlie, who was too busy looking at Brady to really spend much time looking at a piece of paper, "this is the name and number for my US accountant."

She didn't bother to mention he was actually the bookkeeper for a group of people whose very existence Charlie Prince would never have believed, which was a measure of his foolishness because heaven knew he had watched enough TV police drama and drug enforcement movies. But Charlie, who could willingly suspend his disbelief when it was all happening to Arnie or Jean-Claude, complete with massive explosions and mammoth pyrotechnics, simply could not or would not believe the reality of what was going on in every town on the continent. In that, he was not unlike most other of his neighbours.

And even if a person was able to force himself to acknowledge a worldwide conspiracy to flood the population with drugs, who, for crying out loud, would ever entertain the notion that little Brady Lancaster, who had gone to school with Charlie, had grown up just down the road and taken the school bus, even played on the mixed gender softball team, would in any way be involved? Okay, so she'd gone a bit wild as a teenager, fine: we all do silly things when we're young. And yes, she'd left home and become a hoochy-koochy dancer. What was so shocking about that? Every bar and pub in the country had strippers performing for heaven's sake. It might have seemed outrageous fifteen or twenty years ago, but time marches on and we aren't in the Victorian era anymore.

And anyway, she moved home and is going to college, and so what if she invested some of her earnings when she was in the big time down there in Lost Wages. Goodness sakes, let's get real about this, she's practically the girl next door. And in any event, having her for a client could be lucrative.

"I know he'll cooperate with you in every way," she said, smiling. "In fact, I'm sure he could have found a way to do my Canadian income tax himself, but, well, you know how we are, those of us who are from here. We like to do business with people we know and do our shopping at home."

"Is that all you'll require? Income tax?" He smiled back at her.

"Well, I'd like some investment advice, too." She looked so totally gorgeous with her short hair gleaming and her long earrings swinging when she moved her head. "I mean I don't *need* that much money a year to live on, Charlie." Her laugh tinkled like little crystal bells. "Heavens, you know me, just give me a pair of jeans, a tee-shirt and some sneakers and I'm fine. And if I start yearning for a hot tub, well, there are always the old sulphur springs, right?"

"I haven't gone up to the sulphur springs since, oh, it must be since grad night." He shook his head. "Funny how a person forgets things."

"There are *some* things I'm never going to forget." She smiled, and he tried desperately to remember something . . . anything . . . that would explain what seemed to be special meaning in her tone of voice. "And here I am, depending on you all over again."

"And you can." Charlie couldn't remember any other time Brady had depended on him, but his memory was in a turmoil, and right now he didn't even seem to be able to remember he was married and the father of five boys.

"I think I'm supposed to pay my taxes in installments, or something. And if I forget, would you please drop me a line about it?"

"I can't phone you?" Charlie appealed. "*Everybody* has a phone. And a fax. And a modem," he chided. "You really *should* get properly set up."

"Oh, you just stop it," she said with a laugh. "Why would I want all that tacky old plastic shit cluttering up the house when it's going to be so much more *fun* to go to lunch with you."

🦌

Darlene, for all she'd been infuriated when she lost her job, didn't seem to be too interested in finding another one. "If you need any help with anything, just let me know," she told Lottie, who nodded but had no intention of cutting back on any of her work, because she didn't want her hours decreased or her job to vanish.

"Give me a holler if you need help in the spud patch," Darlene called, and Colleen nodded, but privately vowed she'd spray the garden with Agent Orange before she gave Darlene any reason to think she had any sort of claim to it. Darlene just didn't understand boundaries. What was hers was, of course, hers and hers alone, but what was yours was up for grabs. Like the canning cellar. Darlene had never so much as washed a jar in her life, but it was "our" canned fruit, "our" jam and "our" jars of salmon and government mutton. Of course it was *her* car that she now drove and *her* room and *her* bed and *her* rose bush, given to her by Tony, and planted in front of the house for her. Colleen watered it when she did her morning chores, and Colleen sprayed it with a powder that combatted black spot, but it was Darlene's bush and those were her roses, and hers alone.

"I don't really enjoy reading," Darlene said, shaking her head, sounding bored to tears.

"Well, maybe the complex, and some fitness training," Big Wil suggested.

"Oh, hell, Wil, really, just the idea of it puts me to sleep. Christ."

"Hell, Dar, I don't know," Brady snapped. "I find enough to keep me occupied. Why not put some thought into it yourself. I mean, there's always birdwatching, right?"

"Birds?"

"Yeah, you know, them things that fly through the air? All feathered up and prob'ly full of lice or something. People watch them."

"Watch them do what?"

"My daughter got herself a horse," Lottie offered. "That seems to keep her about as busy as a person would want to be."

"No. I'm not much for animals."

"Well, hell, take up race car driving, then!" Colleen flared. "You moan about being bored but you don't want to *do* anything. You whine about not having a job but you don't go out and *get* one. I mean whose life is it, Dar? If it's *yours*, why not engage yourself and live it?"

"Don't you talk to me that way, you damned snot!"

"Come on, Colly, give it up," said Brady. "Let's you 'n' me go lift some weights or something with Willy."

"You's can all go pound sand up your arse for all I care!" Darlene screeched. "I don't know why, out of all the damned people in the world, I got stuck with a bunch of heartless sluts like you's."

"Easy, babe, easy," Tony soothed when Darlene laid it on him that night. "Hell, you don't need a job. We've got more than enough to get by. Leave the job for someone who needs the piddly money they pay."

"But I got nothing to *do*," she moaned.

"Oh, yeah, you do." He licked her ear, traced his tongue down her throat. "I can think of a whole *whack* of stuff you can do."

"Oh, you," she giggled, her mood changing completely.

The next morning Tony went into town and bought forty dollars' worth of colour film and took it back to the house. When Darlene woke up, Tony was sitting on the edge of the bed smiling at her. He held up the camera Al had given her for Christmas, and winked. "Forgot about it, didn't you?" he teased. "Too upset and preoccupied because your little narcky boy took a hike and broke your heart."

"Oh, him." She shrugged dismissively. "I was only using him to make you jealous. It was *you* I was after all along."

"Well . . . you got me. Here, I'll show you how to put in the film."

Tony took a week off and went all over hell's half acre with Darlene and her camera, pointing out possibilities for photos, introducing her to the fanatics at the photo club, and, because he wasn't her sister or her sister-in-law or any kind of woman at all, his opinion mattered, his suggestions counted, and he was an authority on how not to be bored with your useless life. Darlene started what she immediately called her career.

"I'm a nature photographer," she said proudly, and believed it.

"Right," Colleen agreed. "And I'm the daughter of the missing Russian princess, Anastasia Romanov."

"I *knew* you were no fuckin sister of *mine*!" Darlene retorted bitterly.

The cops had done such a job on the garden patch when they went digging for whatever it was they thought they'd find that Colleen's best efforts couldn't undo all the damage. Instead of her spuds coming up in neat rows, spaced far enough she could go between them with the fancy rotovating machine Al had bought her, they came up here, they came up there, they came up damned near everywhere. She had spuds in with her beans and others coming up with the beets, she had them in the chard patch, she had them growing in amongst the corn. "What a mess," she muttered. "Just look at the bastards. I should sue and get the judge to send them out to do the weeding. I'll be *years* getting this mess organized again. There will be bastard spuds coming up in the oddest places next year, too."

"That's okay." Tom patted her shoulder. "Wherever they come up, we'll hunt 'em down and eat 'em."

"You goof."

"Me? Did I scatter spuds all over the backyard? Not me."

Lucy's relatives were digging coal again, taking it by the sackful, piling the sacks just inside the maw, ready to be trucked to their customers. They were digging in the alcove where the old man's distillery had been sitting; they were apprehensive at first but with every last scrap of the apparatus taken off by the police, there was nothing left to tie his ghost to the place, and their fears subsided, then vanished. The coal was number one anthracite, each piece shining, easily distinguishable from other, dull rock.

Tom went out every afternoon as soon as he got home from school. In the jumble of junk and artifacts in the basement, he had found a miner's old safety hat and convinced himself it had been worn by his twice-great-grandfather, whom he imagined had also been named Tom.

"You'd be safer and more comfortable in a new hard hat," Al told him.

"I like this one. It fits real good and it looks dead cool."

"Whatever." Al wasn't about to get into it; he figured all he had to do was wait a bit and the old riggin's would start to rub, or even more likely the kid would take it off and put it down, then forget where he'd left it. God knows enough jackets, hats, sneakers, even a baseball mitt had been lost that way.

During the week Tom only got in two or at most three hours, but on the weekends he got a full day's work. Lucy's brother paid him by the sack, so the harder Tom worked, the more money he made. And, of course, the harder he worked, the dirtier he got.

🦅

Darlene was taking pictures of just about anything she could find to photograph: the walls in the hallway were becoming a gallery of moody shots of rotten logs from which sprouted ferns and even young trees; shots of boggy alder bottom with large puddles and small pools flanked by moss so deep it rivalled belief, and from which grew the tiniest of long thread-stemmed flowers shaped like stars in colours of pale pink, pale blue or creamy white. One photo, enlarged and framed, had taken an honourable mention at a local showing: Spot, nose down, bum up, ears cocked, eyes nearly crossed in concentration as he examined a fat bumblebee on a strawberry flower. Honourable mention didn't even rate a ribbon, let alone a prize or any money, but it was after all better than a slap in the mouth with a dead fish, and Darlene was encouraged by the small success.

"Might not have won," she said defiantly, "but the town is full of fools whose stuff didn't even get entered."

"What do you mean you didn't win? There's a tag there says honourable mention, isn't there?" Colleen might argue, nitpick, bitch and natter with Darlene, but every once in a while she said or did the right thing. "I like it. I'd like a copy of it for my hallway, if you wouldn't mind. How much do you want for it?"

"You pay for the developing and framing and it's yours." Darlene could come through sometimes, too.

She walked down the skidder trail looking in the salmonberry and thimbleberry scrub for hummingbird nests. She had several promising shots of the birds themselves, hovering at a feeder or sipping from flowers, but if she could just find a nest, even if it was last year's and empty, she knew she could get some excellent pictures. She took pictures of salmonberry leaves on which sat tiny bright green tree frogs, almost but not quite the same colour as the thicket, and she got what she figured would be a hilarious shot of a snail, feelers fully extended, upside down on a branch.

Tom was taking a break, sitting on a damp rock, his face thick with coal dust, tear streaks showing from when he'd somehow bashed his hand with a falling chunk of sharp-edged coal. He didn't know he had tear streaks or he'd have rubbed at them with his hands or poured water on his face or even gone to the creek and washed. All he knew was his hand hurt like hell and he was so tired all he really wanted to do was lie down on the wet grass and sleep. The antique miner's hat was pushed back slightly, and he sat with his forearms on his knees, head bowed, lines of fatigue slashed into his face. Darlene started taking pictures from the cover of the trees.

The best two were taken just before and just after Tom recognized her. She had them enlarged, mounted and framed together. In one, the exhausted, filthy-faced boy was looking up as startled as if he'd just heard the cackle of death, and in the other he was smiling through his fatigue like the poster boy in a campaign against child labour.

On the strength of her honourable mention, she was invited to show some of her work at the local college. The photos of Tom counted as one entry because they were in the same frame. She also entered a shot of a mossy log with water droplets glistening, a close-up of a bright yellow skunk cabbage flower, and what she considered her best one: Dorrit with his Tonka trucks, playing on the nearly exhausted slag heap with Spot sitting in the bed of the truck, while Dorrit guided it along the road he'd made. None of those photos won anything, but the shots of Tom took first prize.

Singeon had copies made for his living room wall and for Colleen's as well. "He's beautiful," Singeon said quietly. "I knew he was cute, but I didn't know he was beautiful."

Al studied the photos of his son, then nodded and arranged for a third print, which he delivered to Maude and Brewster.

"You're workin' him too hard," Brew stated.

"Nobody told him to do it," Al retorted, stung. "He makes a lot of his own choices."

"He'll be as wore out and wrecked as the rest of us by the time he's thirty-two," Brew said hotly. "Jesus, Al, fuckin' *look* at us! Oh, I know, the whole lot of you think I'm some kind of dozy jellybelly because my job at the store isn't much. But it's about all I can manage." And he turned, pulled up his tee-shirt, exposing the scars on his back. "I was as skookum as any of you and you know it! And all's it took was one falling chunk and I was face down in the mud. Then I spent a year and a half in bloody hospital, just in case you've forgotten. Five fuckin' operations later they said, 'There you go, all fixed up'. And *nothing* was fuckin' fixed, man. You want *this* for that kid? Never mind lookin' at his face, or his big eyes, or that smile, look at the bloody hand he's got stuck out in front of him, the one with the rag wrapped around it. Don't you know that's *blood* on the rag? Take a good look at his hand when you go home. C'mere, goddammit."

He grabbed Al by the arm and tugged. Other men had tried that and wound up on their backs with their faces rearranged, but in Brewster's house, discussing Al's son, the rules changed.

"Look at her hands." Brewster lifted Mavis gently. "Look at those hands. Well, Tommy's used to be like that, okay? I mean, jesus, Al."

Al looked at the baby, her pixie face, her lopsided smile, and nodded. Goofy old Brew was right. Al could remember when Tom's hands had been like those of the damaged baby.

"Thanks, Brew." He sucked his front teeth, then nodded. "I'll remember."

At supper that night, Al looked closely at Tom's hands. "So, what you got in mind for after you finish school?" he asked.

Tom nearly choked on his venison steak. "Me?" he said. "I don't know. Uh, maybe drive gravel truck for you?"

"You could. Then spend your life reliving mine, I guess. God knows, I'm reliving my dad's life. You might spend some time looking at choices and options, Tom. It's a great big world out there, and some of the things there are to do are fun." He winked. "I mean, hell, with those eyelashes you could probably be a gigolo and get rich while having a really good time."

"Ah, stop it." Tom almost blushed but managed to control it for the first time in his young life.

"All kinds of stuff out there. I want you to go see the school counsellor about it. They've *got* to have, like, lists of all what kinds of jobs there are."

"What I think," Jewen interjected, "is we ought to concentrate on winning the damn lottery and send Tom here off to learn how to handle the money. Personally, I'm aiming for the big one. I figure I'll only win once, so why waste my luck on a measly million when I can hold out until it hits—oh, I don't know—thirty point six mil or so."

"I'm serious here, Jewen."

"I know. That's what makes you such a fuckin' drag tonight, Al. Get off the kid's case, okay? Think back to when you were his age— if you can remember that far back—would *you* have sat down with a freakin' *list* and set about planning the rest of your life? Anyway, he's gonna be a bodybuilder; he's already started himself a good set of muscles."

"I thought," Tom dared, "I'd take some lessons and be a piano player in a whorehouse."

"Ah," said Brady, flipping a spoonload of peas at Tom, "they don't use piano players anymore: they've got CDs and porno films."

"Don't *any* of you people ever take anything seriously?" Al was starting to feel angry.

"Yeah. Yeah, we do," Darlene shot back. "And maybe we shouldn't. The whole thing is just a damn crapshoot, anyway. I mean how can *we* plan anything when those hotshots at the top of the ladder can change everything on us, even the damn rules?"

"All's I asked him was . . ."

"Would you like some more steak, Al?" Brady handed him the platter and winked at him. "Put something else in your mouth besides your foot, okay?"

"What *I'd* like to know," Jessie demanded, "is why it's so important to plan Tom's future, and for all you seem to care," she glared at her father, "I don't even *have* one."

"I would have got around to you," Al snapped.

234

"No," she shook her head, "you never 'get around' to *me*. Tom, yeah, he gets to do stuff just with you. Me? I'm always part of the gang. If you do something, or talk about something, it's either Tom or *us*, all of us. Me?" She shrugged, her eyes bright with insult. "I might as well be smoke."

"Good girl!" Brady clapped and smiled. "Takes guts."

"Don't you talk to me that way," Al said.

"Why shouldn't she?" Jewen's voice was still mild, and he asked it as a puzzled question, not with any defiance. "She's a person, isn't she? She's got a bone to pick, obviously. I think she's right in what she says. Of course, it isn't just *you*, it's all of us. We kind of take old Jess for granted. Sorry about that, Jess."

"Yeah." Darlene nodded. "You spend a lot of time looking after Dorrit for me, and I bet I never did really thank you. I'll try to do better in future." She grinned and winked. "And believe me, please, you *do* have one. A future, I mean."

"I'd bet money I know what she has in mind." Brady got up from the table, hurried to the hell drawer for a ballpoint, then ripped a strip off the margin of the evening paper. She scrawled quickly, folded her guess, handed it to Jewen, who put it in his pocket, starting to grin. "And here," she put a five-dollar bill on the table.

"I'm not betting money," Jessie said firmly. "You *know* I never bet money. I don't have enough of it, and if I lose . . . no money."

"Well, I bet money all the time, and I don't need yours anyway. So it stands: if I'm right, I get my five back; if I'm not, it's yours."

"Okay, Jess, let's see if she knows you as well as she thinks she does. What have you got in mind so far?"

"I'm going to be a firefighter," Jess answered.

"You're *what*?" Brady choked out, staring.

"Going to be a firefighter. I'll be tall enough, I know that for sure. And for the other stuff, you have to be able to do so many push-ups and you have to run a certain distance inside a certain time and stuff like that so they know you could, like, carry someone out, or run in with heavy hoses or whatever. And I'll be able to do all that, too. On top of which, I don't panic."

"Well, there you have it," said Jewen. He took out the scrap of paper, looked at it, laughed, and handed the five-dollar bill across the table.

"What did she say?" Tom asked.

"Would you believe social worker?"

"Jess? A social worker?" Tom looked at Brady as if she had just sprouted a tail. "Auntie Brady, whatever gave you an idea like that?"

"In *my* day," Brady replied, "they were fire*men*. It never occurred to me that a woman would . . ." She stopped, face to face with something that obviously surprised her.

"Gee." Little Wil sounded awed. "I didn't know Auntie Brady was from the good old days."

🐦

Norm held out against paying child support. "Why should I?" he growled. "She makes better money than I do. It costs me a week's pay to rent an apartment. She lives here, in *my* family's house, for free; that should count for something. It's *my* brothers 'n' sisters is doin' all her damn kid care, what more does the bitch want? She never *did* pay me for when she wrecked my truck."

The judge wasn't the least bit sympathetic. He set the child support at a hundred dollars a month and ordered another twenty a month as installments on unpaid back debt.

"A hundred-twenty a month? Does the silly old bugger think I'm made of money? In a pig's ass, I will."

He had a two-bedroom apartment now and what seemed like an endless procession of young women with huge hair who stayed for greater or lesser amounts of time and left when it suited them.

"Ah, kiss 'er off." He grinned. "There's more where she came from. The bar's full'a them come midnight." And he seemed totally unbothered that nobody was falling in love with him, nobody wanted to try forever 'n' ever or let's save up for a white picket fence.

He bought himself a brand new top-of-the-line Harley Davidson, complete with leather saddle bags, and roared to and from work. He headed off on it to the city, was gone a week, and came back with a black leather jacket with more pockets on it than you'd think there was room for, each of them shut by a shiny big zipper. To go with his jacket he bought fancy leather chaps. When he had them on, only his butt was uncovered by calfskin, his faded blue jeans showing through. "Oh, sure," he replied to Dorrit's question, "they had 'em in pants, too, but leather on leather could be slippery and I didn't want to slide off going around a corner. Besides, they weren't very comfortable to sit down in, and to top it all they were hot, and there's parts of me I don't like to get sweaty."

He took Little Wil for a ride first, then one by one the others. Their first spin was taken on back roads and even logging roads away from traffic, where he could go slowly until the little ones got over feeling terrified and began to enjoy the trip. When they did, he increased his speed but not by much. With the older kids, he drove as fast as road conditions would allow, and each of them loved it. "Gonna make bikers out of you yet," he said, grinning.

Having issued the court order, the judge trusted in god, the angels and the bureaucracy that the money would be collected and forwarded on to Big Wil. Nothing of the sort happened, and it seemed nothing was going to be done to enforce the order. Big Wil continued to drive long-distance hauls. Little Wil went to school and lived with her aunts, uncles and cousins. Lottie showed up five days a week to do for them all. And Norm finally acquired a more-or-less steady girlfriend named Lindy.

"I never *saw* so much hair," Jess breathed.

"Is your hair naturally curly?" Little Wil asked.

"It is," Lindy said, smiling. "And before anyone asks I tell 'em: curly hair isn't all it's cracked up to be. When it rains I can't get brush nor comb through it, and when it isn't raining the damn stuff snarls up with static electricity. So I just leave it alone most of the time and it grows any which-a-way it wants."

Lindy wore brand new leather chaps and a brand new bezippered leather jacket. She also had new cowboy boots with silver toe guards and silver conchos on her clothes. When she took off her jacket, her sleeveless, low-cut fancy tee-shirt showed the tattoos on her arms and portions of tattoos on her chest.

"That must have hurt real bad," Dorrit decided.

"Nah." Lindy ruffled his hair. "Men say it hurts, but women don't seem to mind. It's nothing at all alongside of havin' a baby."

Dorrit turned away, puzzled to no end by the comparison. He

could see no connection at all between a baby and a unicorn with a rainbow spiralled around its horn.

Lindy drank coffee, complimented Lottie on her cinnamon buns and chatted easily with Darlene and Brady. Colleen joined them for a cup of coffee and then excused herself and went back to the garden.

"You from around here," Brady asked.

"No, I'm from Surrey," Lindy admitted. "I moved here about four years ago. Came by myself at first; well, by myself with my boyfriend if you catch my drift. We got a place at the north end of town and once I'd found a job and all, I went back and collected my kids from my mom. I had three of them then. Got four now."

"And the boyfriend?" Brady probed.

"Oh, him." Lindy shrugged. "It didn't work out, so we just split the sheets and he moved on."

"Is the baby his?"

"No, he wasn't very good-looking, and I didn't want a homely kid. Soon's he left I hooked up for a little while with a real good-lookin' guy. It's his kid, but he doesn't know it. It works out better that way, no complications." She looked around the yard, and nodded. "That black stuff looks nice for a driveway," she decided. "If ever I get a place'a my own, maybe I'll be back to get some from you."

Lindy and her kids rented a stucco-sided four-bedroom square box of a house on five acres of weedy grass and shared the place with a big long-haired part German Shepherd who had strayed onto the porch, then stayed with them, and whom they called Rambler. Also on site were several once-stray cats who didn't mind the dog and who didn't expect to get in the house. One of them lived under the front porch, another lived under the back porch, two shared an abandoned hen coop, and some others seemed at home in an old barn. "Feed 'em?" Lindy laughed. "Hell with that! The place is up to the eyebrows with mice and rats, so the buggers can feed themselves or starve." She had a dozen hens in the coop with the cat. "I guess it's the hens leave the eggs," she said, laughing. "Never heard of a cat doing that. Although there *is* the Easter Bunny, right?"

Lindy laughed a lot. She was easy around the kids and at home with the adults. When she and Norm left after their first short visit, she seemed almost like a member of the family.

"I wonder if I let my hair just grow and 'go' like she does if it would . . ."

"No, babe," Tony pleaded, "keep brushin' and combin', please. God, you grow hair like that there'll be no room in bed for me."

"She's sure got nice hair."

"*You've* got nice hair," he assured her. "She's got a rat's nest."

"You like my hair the way it is?"

"I like everything about you just the way it is." And he pinched her gently on the hip and winked at her. "What you got, you got well arranged, and what you don't got you don't need."

🌿

Without a word to anyone about it, Al went into town in his pick-up one day and came back with two motorized bicycles.

"What in hell are *they*?" Darlene demanded. "They aren't scooters."

"No," Al agreed. "You need a licence and all for a scooter. These are what the French call 'mobilettes'. I ordered 'em for the kids. You start 'em by pedalling like hell, and . . . Here, try one."

"You sure?"

"Exactly like a bicycle," he assured her.

She took one, listened to his instructions, then got on, pedalling furiously. The bike was heavier than an ordinary one and started off slowly, then the motor coughed and coughed again.

"Twist the handgrip," Al called. "The right-hand one."

The bike coughed again, then caught, and Darlene shrieked. She headed down the skidder trail yelling with surprise. When she came back the yells had changed to a wide grin. "I want one," she announced. "I love it."

So did the kids. Tom and Jess didn't get a speck of homework done; they could hardly be tempted to leave their bikes long enough to sit down for supper. The two little kids stared enviously.

"They don't make 'em small enough for you guys," Al explained, "but we'll head in on Saturday and find something you *can* ride."

They came home with what looked like a midget tractor and a teeny jeep. "A body isn't going to be able to hear herself think," Lottie argued. "What with lawn mowers and garden tillers, them French bikes and now those silly things, it's gonna sound like free day at the midway around here."

"Well, then, I guess we just better head out back a ways and start working on a racing track for them," Jewen said. "Wouldn't take much of that racket to make me crazy. They sound like bad-tempered bumblebees or something."

"Seems like the day before yesterday it was tricycles," Big Wil moaned, "and I guess day after tomorrow it'll be their own cars. Time flies."

Time flew fast enough that Sports Day was upon them. Those with jobs took time off, claiming the flu and, picnic lunches packed, juice coolers full, headed off to the school sports grounds to cheer on the family competitors. At the school grounds they met other flu sufferers—and a few migraine, wrenched back, bursitis and even impacted wisdom tooth sufferers—and together they sat on lawn chairs, gossiped, smiled, and at the appropriate times rose to their feet to clap and cheer. Kids ran, kids jumped up and over bars, jumped as far along the sawdust pit as their muscles and gravity would allow. Kids threw weighted plastic discs, kids strained to toss lead weights, and kids passed relay batons to each other. There were so many kids signed up for each event they had to have run-offs, with the first six in each event moving on to the quarter-finals. Three from those judgements went on to the semifinals and, finally, the elimination round. And when the winners of the elimination rounds were rested, their energies recharged with hot dogs, ice cream and cold juice, it was time for the absolute final events. By then the crowd was more than ready to call it a helluva fine day and leave, but the kids deserved their moment of glory, so everyone stayed, and the noise was incredible. The crowd cheered the winners, the crowd cheered the losers, they even cheered the judges and referees.

They took the kids to the Burger House for supper, packed them full of beef and took them home more than ready for bed. But before the adults could crash, they had to get the hyper kids to calm down, do the bathtub routine and get into their beds with books.

"Jesus god," Al sighed. "I don't know *where* the little farts get their energy."

"It must be chaos over at Singe's place by now," Jewen said.

"Damn, did you see that Simon in the 220?" Brady bragged. "I mean, did you *see* him?"

"And would you have believed our Tom could high jump like that? I thought he'd go clear over the clouds."

"I like the little ones the best," said Colleen. "They still aren't really sure what it's all about, or why winning is so important, but off they go all the same. Did you see that little guy? The one who stopped halfway down the track and ran over to the sidelines to hug his mom? They should'a given him a ribbon for *that*!"

With the track meet behind them they went back to work, miraculously cured, and their health seemed fine until the kids started to chant "Twenty-fourth of May is the Queen's birthday; if we don't have a holiday, we'll all run away." The ailments resurfaced and the only hope of healing lay in repacking the picnic lunches and heading to the school for the crowning of the queen and king of May, the Maypole dance, the Friendship dance and more events. The parents' auxiliary made, sold and handed out free foot-long hot dogs, other parents dispensed juice, and still others walked around with chilled metal bowls in which nestled slices of orange and small cubes of ice.

Kathleen sat in her stroller and bounced, trying to get out and across the grass to where Dorrit and Little Wil were dancing. When she couldn't free herself, she burped up, soaking her terrycloth bib, then she filled her diaper. Lucy hauled her out, took her to the girls' washroom, got her cleaned up and into fresh clothes, and when she brought her back, the baby was ready to sleep in the shade of the stroller canopy.

"'Atta *girl*, Carol," Singe hollered. "Way to go! Way to be, kid!"

"I vow to god," Lucy said, "it's more important to the big kids than it is to the ones goin' to school."

And time continued to fly, faster and faster until the last day of school. On the first day of holidays, time slowed to a near crawl. The kids slept in until half past eight, then charged into the kitchen to demolish the pancakes Lottie was cooking for them. "The best!" Tom told her. "I *love* your pancakes."

"Keep it up, young sir," she teased. "That kind of flattery is apt to win you just about anything you want."

Half a slag heap went into the construction of the moto track. Actually, it was a double track, one section of it reserved for the little kids, the other more challenging, with tight turns, sudden hills and bumps, even what they called the Daredevil Jump. Lottie accepted a ride down on the skidder to see the result of the days of work. "Thank god for the trees." She shook her head. "They keep all this damn noise away from the house."

When the more-or-less oval track was finished, Al and Tony put the skidder to work knocking aside whip alders, threading paths through the back bush, running a nine-foot wide track through the scrub, turning at the far end of old Bob's ten acres and looping back to join up with the extension of Singe's driveway.

"If I have to listen to those damned things," Lucy warned, "I won't bother to feed anybody at all. You make sure you do all your roarin' around 'way out back or so help me god I'll put sand in every gas tank."

"You better listen to your mother," Singe warned. "You know she's a woman of her word."

Three more of the French bikes appeared and Darlene insisted there were enough bike helmets, safety helmets and hockey helmets cluttering up the place they could open a second-hand brain bucket store. "Use the profit to buy band-aids," she growled, putting peroxide on Jess's knee. "I don't know why you kids don't have sense enough to use your damn roller-blade safety gear. Someone," she predicted, "is gonna get hurt."

Two of Tom's friends from school asked if they could bring their dirt bikes out and use the track. When they spread the word about what great fun it was, others showed up, requested and got permission; and that might have been fine except others came and both presumed and assumed.

"Who *is* that guy?" Jewen asked Tom.

"I don't know," Tom answered. "I thought *you* said he could."

"Al?"

"Not me."

"Tony?"

"No."

"Whose fuckin' business is it," the stranger snarled. "It's a public track. I guess I can . . ."

"Wrong," they chorused. "It's a *private* track."

The stranger took some convincing, as did four of his friends. Colleen sat on her back porch eating her macaroni and cheese supper and watching the punch-up. At the first sign of physical confrontation, Jess ran into the house, grabbed Tony's cell phone and called Singe, who showed up immediately, Lucy and the kids accompanying him. Lucy and the baby joined Colleen on the porch. The kids ran to join the others, dodging, weaving, bouncing on the periphery, catcalling and shouting. At one point, Tom got into it, picked up a chunk of wood and swung it like a bat. It would have been a home run, and the stalwart who had earned the whack by shoving Little Wil on her ass and making her cry, caught the wood across his upper chest and fell to the ground roaring with fury, one arm suddenly useless, the other one clutching his collarbone.

"Good god in heaven," said Lucy, shaking her head, "you guys sure start 'em off young."

"Macaroni and cheese still warm on the stove," Colleen invited. "And plenty of salad."

"Don't mind if I do," Lucy replied, and went to get and load a plate.

When the dust-up ended and the convincing was done, the uninvited left and the bruised victors set about putting up a gate they made from several old bed frames. The welding torch flared, the sparks sprayed, the beer came out and the kids grew bored and went out to the track to do their thing.

"Nah, go for it," Tom told Peter. "I don't know *whose* bike it is, but they left it here, so it must be okay for us to use it."

"What if they get mad about it?"

"They can load it up and take it home, can't they?"

"So what have we got?" Lucy peered into the gathering dusk. "Looks to me like three metal heads'a beds and two foots'a beds, but what's that thing in the middle?"

"Bedspring, I think. Thing of beauty is a joy forever, eh?"
"Some seem to think so."

The fixation with the French bicycles and dirt bikes faded as the
trips to the swimming hole increased. Colleen was laid off for fire
season and a week later so were Singe and Jewen. The bush smelled
of hot pitch and dried moss, and the garden flourished in spite of the
effects of the long cold spring.

Colleen was up by six every morning and, coffee mug in hand, she
went on slug patrol with a smooth pole to one end of which Tony
had fashioned a riggin's made from a six-inch nail. Colleen could get
half a dozen slugs on it at a time, easy, and when her spear was full
she put the pierced corpses in a plastic ice cream bucket. Most morn-
ings she managed to eradicate at least fifty slugs, sometimes twice
that, depending on how heavy the dew had been the previous night.

With the slugs rounded up and withering in a handful of salt in
the ice cream bucket, it was time to start watering. And, of course,
that required another cup of coffee and a cigarette. First, she did the
hanging baskets of fuchsia and trailing geranium, begonia and petu-
nia, then the large strawberry barrels. From there she went to the lily
bed she had started, and when the ground there was soaked she
went from rose bush to rose bush, watering, sipping coffee, smoking her cigarette and, somehow, managing also to snip off faded
blooms.

Roses done, she connected the hose to the soaker tube connector.
It was made so she could run six soaker tubes off the one hose at the
one time. About then was when the pump cut in, drawing water up
the two-hundred-foot bore hole to refill the storage tank.

She put her coffee aside, put her nippers in her back pocket, and
went up to let the hens out of their coop. Spot and Morespots came
to the gate of their run and she let them out to jump, dance and race
off in mad pursuit of nothing at all. She turned on the second tap
and four more soaker tubes began to leak water, then it was time to
get yet another cup of coffee and sit on her back porch admiring the
flowers and the vegetable garden.

Twice a week she put through a small load of wash while having breakfast. She mostly had a bowl of cereal with some berries and yogurt or toast and cream cheese with berries on top. Sometimes she thought of her huge breakfasts when she was heading off to work, but the thought of sausages and eggs was just too much when she was laid off and knew the heat of the day was going to turn the sky a bleached blue that bordered on white.

After her light breakfast she hung out her washing, then made her bed and tidied the kitchen. Housework didn't take her long, she was careful not to leave any mess behind her. That was one of the bigger blessings of having her own place: you only had to pick up after yourself.

She checked the garden for weeds but seldom found any. The first awful spring rush of unwanted dock, plantain, pigweed and smartweed was finished, the invaders defeated, but it was nice to walk along the pathways and admire the crop. The soaker hoses ran down the middle of the rows, the pathways were dry and brown, the dirt around the growing plants wet and black. Colleen liked the contrast, it soothed her to think she had at least that much control over things.

Lottie usually arrived about the time Colleen was leaving the garden. Sometimes they took time to chat, sometimes they just waved. No sooner did Lottie go in the front door of the big house than kids came out the back door, sometimes only the four who actually lived there, more often with extras, and not always Singe's kids either. They had friends from school who liked to stay overnight because of the dirt bike track, the tarzan swings in the big trees and the sure-as-guaranteed trips to the river, the swimming hole, the lake or the beach. Spot and Morespots abandoned Colleen as soon as the kids came on the scene; there was more to do in life than move quietly from water hose to rose bush, and they were off to do it with the ones who moved quickly. Bicycle races seemed to have supplanted the motorized French bicycles, dirt bikes and small vehicles, and by the time the appropriate lunches were packed, the kids were red-faced, sweaty and panting heavily.

Colleen could get four kids in the crew-cab seat of Al's pickup, and the rest piled in with Brady and Darlene. The food, towels, blankets and big juice coolers went into sturdy cardboard boxes and rode in the bed of the pickup.

"We always look like we're going to raid the Bay of Pigs or something," said Brady. "Are you sure we don't need the TV and the kitchen sink?"

The kids had to help set up their blankets and put the cardboard boxes of food in the shade before they could go ripping into the water. Brady usually won the race to the big rock where they dove, screeching, into the river. If it was the swimming hole, they cannon-balled off the bank; at the lake they raced across the bleached planks of the floating dock; and when they went to the beach, everything depended on whether the tide was full or slack.

Darlene had her cameras and gear while Brady had an endless supply of socially acceptable pornography which she read intently. Colleen had tried but just could not get into the stories: they all seemed the same, and none of them seemed the least bit realistic.

"Romance novels aren't *supposed* to be realistic," Brady told her. "They're fun. It's like reading a joke book. My god, I could *never* sit here and read the kind of stuff *you* bring along. What's that one about? Plagues?" She looked at the back of the book and shook her head. "*Jeez*, Colly, why would you want to read about all these damn weird viruses and flesh-eating diseases and mad cow disease and god-knows-what? Lord help us, last week it was that retrospective on the spread of AIDS. Now this. You trying to scare yourself to death or something?"

"Relax." Darlene yawned. "Look at it this way. If you come down with some kind of fever from Borneo or somewhere, Colly will be able to tell your doctor what you've got."

Singeon, Lucy and their kids arrived in their own vehicle, with more boxes of food, and in the afternoon Al and Tony packed up their gravel business, picked up Lottie and brought her as well. The days Big Wil was home from her run she lay on a blanket and napped, waking only to head into the water, swim and cavort with Little Wil, and come back to the blanket to dry off, warm up and work on her tan.

"You're gonna get skin cancer," Brady warned, rubbing herself with sun block.

"Probably find out there's something in that damn sun block that causes brain tumours or blood diseases or something," said Wil.

Dorrit stepped on a rusty nail and had to be taken to the doctor's office for a tetanus shot. Little Wil missed a daredevil jump on her Peppermint Patty small-sized bike and was carried home sobbing bitterly and bleeding from knees and elbows by a terrified Tom who was convinced she'd broken her neck.

And Darlene came up pregnant! She had sense enough to tell Dorrit before she told anyone else, even Tony. "And we'll have our own little baby," she promised, "and you can hold him whenever he's awake."

"How do you know it's a boy?"

"I don't. But I'm hoping. Because the last baby I had was a boy and he's just about the *best* kid in the world."

"Who will the baby's daddy be?"

"Tony, of course."

"Well, will I have to find a new one?" he worried.

"No. Jess and Tom both have Uncle Al for a dad. So you and the baby will have Tony for a dad."

"What if he likes the baby better 'n' me?"

"What a mutt," she said, cuddling him. "How could that be? Babies don't *do* anything, they're no more fun than a loaf of bread. You do *lots* of fun things with Tony, and you'll keep on doing them, too."

When she told Tony, he grinned. He didn't say anything at all, he just grinned, then turned to her in bed and held her close. Anything else that might have transpired between them was aborted by the heart-stopping uproar of the first of three helicopters.

Colleen jerked awake with her heart thumping madly in her chest. Not caring about who, what, how, why or even when, she raced for her front door, clad only in her XXL white tee-shirt with the image of a panda on the front. She jerked open her front door and stood on the porch, gawking. Several of the cops stopped their charge and gawked in return.

The helicopters seemed the size of battleships. Men came out of them with automatic weapons in hand, their lace-front boots trampling the lily bed, their faces hidden by cloth balaclava-type SWAT hoods. They raced forward, stopping only to nudge their gawking comrades, then crashed in the door of the henhouse and slammed in the door of the greenhouse. Other uniformed men with the appearance of science fiction nightmare figures poured from what looked like a postal van. They spread out, their weapons covering the old house, Colleen's house and the outbuildings. One of them released a dog, which charged around snarling and barking. Spot and Morespots answered from inside their run, enraged that any big mutt would even dare set foot, let alone lift leg, inside their territory.

Singeon's pickup came racing down the road, skidded sideways, made the turn, narrowly avoiding the van. Singe came out of it in his jockey shorts and nothing else, his hunting rifle in his hand. He took one look and tossed the rifle back in the truck, saving himself a lot of pain, possible paralysis and maybe even death.

"Jesus *fuck*!" he roared and raced for the house.

Jewen came from the house tucking his short-sleeved cotton shirt into his jeans. He was fully dressed and appeared to be in no mood at all for early morning coffee conversation. He had a cellular phone in his hand and was talking into it, eyes narrowed to slits, face frozen in fury. Behind him, Al walked out, similarly dressed, carrying a shirt he tossed to Singe, who slipped it on automatically. Tony came out with Darlene's camera and began taking pictures of imitation Darth Vaders standing in the ruin of Colleen's lily bed, of others in the shattered doorway of the greenhouse. Something had been whipped up by the rotors and hurled through the air with enough force to smash the greenhouse roof, and the dog had flipped his wig so completely he was chewing on the boot of one of the uniformed Mounties. When the dog caught sight of Tony with the camera, he charged, snarling and snapping. Tony got a good picture of the dog leaping for his face. Singe reached out, grabbed the dog by the ruff and swung it like a baseball bat, cracking its spine against the cornerpost supporting the porch roof. The dog yowled, spine broken; Singe swung it again, and its neck cracked, the noise stopped. The cops stared, horrified.

"Calm the fuck *down*!" Singe yelled. "What's up with you ass-holes? You woke the babies and now they're crying!"

"My lilies!" Colleen screeched, coming down the steps and charg-ing the men standing in the trampled ruin. One of them whirled, automatically protecting his family jewels, but Colleen wasn't about to do anything so obvious. She kicked sideways with her bare foot, got him on the side of the knee and he dropped, grabbing at his leg and moaning. "My lilies!" she repeated. "Just *look* what you've done."

Automatic weapons were levelled. Darth's voice came through a bullhorn. "Assume the position!" the voice roared.

"Oh, you're fuckin' right I will," Singe said, glowering. He turned his back, and before putting both hands on the wall of the house, dropped his jockeys and stepped out of them, mooning the law.

The police tossed the house, went through the garbage, investi-gated the dirty clothes in the laundry hamper, and sent two of their low seniority people to examine and record the cobwebs and spiders in the crawl space under the house. They tossed Colleen's house and toured her crawl space, finding only a hammer someone had left behind during construction. They confiscated the hammer and Darlene's camera, but Tony had already removed the film and hid-den it behind some of the shingles on the front wall of the house.

Cops ripped apart the tables and shelves in the greenhouse, wrecked the cucumber and tomato vines, and so terrified the hens in the coop two of them flipped in the air, fell on their sides and died of cardiac arrest. The baby peeps in the brooder room ignored the uproar and ran about twitting and scratching.

"Your heat sensors *what*?" Singe gaped.

"You fools can't tell the difference between a pot plantation and the heat lights on four dozen meat-bird chicks?" Al began to laugh.

"Oh, boy, are you up shits creek for this." Darlene was white-faced, her eyes round and wide. "Are you *ever* in for it." And she sat down suddenly, her eyes rolling, showing the whites.

The TV crew arrived in time to get all the footage they could want of the debacle, including the sight of Colleen and Brady with cold cloths and ice cubes trying to revive Darlene and stop the blood flow. They spent time on the ruined lily beds; they had plenty of time to record the greenhouse and hen coop; they got film of masked and anonymous men with assault weapons going into and coming out of the bush; and they had a wonderful time with the helicopters settled down like the creature from *Alien* in the ruination of what had been a front yard with rose bushes and flowers.

They especially rolled footage when the ambulance arrived and the paramedics inserted an IV, then loaded the still unconscious Darlene and drove off. One of the camera people even had the presence of mind to film the porch and the puddle of what was undeniably blood, just like the huge stain on Colleen's shirt, and the drying streaks on Brady's jeans. Dorrit was hysterical, Little Wil seemed numbed by shock, and Tom stared accusingly at the Mountie. "So," he asked, and was recorded for the evening news, "did you get your man? Or will you be satisfied to have killed a little baby?"

"Have you any comment, sir?" the reporter asked Al.

"All's I can say is, it's a good job our name begins with 'L' and not 'M'."

"Excuse me?"

"Donald Marshall, Guy Paul Morin, David Milgaard . . . they were all locked away on trumped-up charges, too, and it took years before science caught up to what was going on and proved with DNA evidence they were all innocent. I don't know why they got a hard-on for us, but this is the second time in less than a year they've pulled a stunt like this. And this time, they've tipped my sister into a miscarriage. It was like waking up in the opening scenes of *Apocalypse* fuckin' *Now*," he finished.

"No comment," the leader of the Emergency Response team grunted.

"No comment," the RCMP officer parroted.

"I got comment," Brady raged. "I got *lots* of comment!" And she held forth about the spread of American militarism, the creeping influence of the CIA, and the spread of fascism because of Yankee imperialist aggression. "And," she ended, "what about Manuel Noriega? Maybe he's no more guilty than we are!"

No more had the news crews begun to pack up their gear than Norm arrived, so angry he could barely stutter. Not only had the law raided the house and yard where he now lived with Lindy and

her kids, they had gone over the fence and seized three plants growing in the vacant lot. "And they're threatening to charge *us*," he
raged, "even though it's not our property."

"Well, they can't do that," Al told him. "They have to prove possession, and that means they have to prove you knew they were
there."

"I never even *been* on that place. It's just a junkyard, all rusted
out cars and tossed away bits of shit and crap. I won't even let the
kids play there because of the broken glass and all the old batteries
just lyin' around waitin' for some kid to get battery acid burns."

He was still fuming and sounding off to the reporters who had
decided to stay a while longer and get more interviews when Maude
and Brewster arrived.

Maude was in a bitch of a mood. "What in hell's going on, anyway, Al?"

"And a good morning to you to, Maudie," Al answered, immediately angry all over again.

"Are you up to something? We had cops at our place."

"No, I'm not up to something," he lied. "If they were at your
place maybe they thought *you* were up to something."

"They as much as admitted they hit us because you 'n' Maudie
used to be married," said Brew, trying to smooth things, but Al
wasn't in any mood to be smoothed.

"It might come as one helluva shock to you, Brew," he sneered,
"but Maudie 'n' me's *still* married."

"Don't be a hard-nosed asshole." Brew didn't even sound like the
old version. "You know exactly what I mean. The place looks like
the Mongol Hordes tangled with the entire Apache Nation. Even
Mavis got lifted up and moved and her crib taken apart."

"See that woman over there luggin' that camera on her shoulder?
Let's go over and you tell *her* about the baby's crib."

"The supermarket isn't going to like this," Brewster moaned.
"You get yourself in any kind of trouble at all and it's hit the road,
Jack. I'm apt to lose my damn job because of this."

"Don't you worry about it, we'll figure something out," Al muttered.

Lottie took one look at the lily bed and joined Colleen in her anger and mourning. "No excuse for that kind of behaviour," she declared. "They could easy have found some other place to land. That was done a'purpose. But what we're gonna do first is tidy the houses so's we can get some meals happening. I'll phone my daughters to get over here and help out."

"I'll get my sisters to come," Lucy put in.

"We'll meet at Colleen's for lunch." Lottie was taking over, arranging everything. "Her place isn't as big a mess because there wasn't all that much extra stuff in it to get messed all over the place. We'll all head in and do her house first, especially the kitchen. Then she can start cooking while the rest of us go over to Mr. Singe's place and get that straightened away. Then we'll do the big house and when that's done we'll go to Mr. Brewster's place."

"What about *our* place?" Norm asked.

"Well, you're last on our list." Lottie glared at him, "You don't even pay child support for that wonderful kid. And that means you don't contribute one red cent to my wages, and *that* means I don't have to do squat for you."

Brunch was hasty but supper was a bang-up affair, and by the time the dishes were done, Colleen was more than ready for bed. She slept soundly, awoke early and took her coffee outside to survey the mess that had been her garden. Even the hanging baskets had been dumped, the cedar boxes examined for hidden whatever-it-was-they-thought-they-might-find. She felt her anger growing, replacing her grief, and by her third coffee she was just about ready to take on the entire world.

Instead, she headed for her vegetable garden and began to tie up the bruised and thrashed crop of trampled beans, crushed pea plants and tromped corn. Much of it, she knew—most, in fact—would perish, but not without a good fight from her.

She was dirt-streaked and sweaty when a car pulled off the road and drove up the slag and gravel, then stopped. A woman Colleen had never before seen got out of the car and walked forward carrying a large flat of well-started tomato plants.

"I saw on TV," she said shyly. "I had these in my greenhouse and thought to myself, well, now, see, there really was a reason you planted twice as many as you need."

"My greenhouse is wrecked," Colleen mourned.

"Oh, it'll do to harden these off, dear," the woman smiled encouragingly. "We'll just take them over and put them on the protected side, then I'll give you a hand with your corn. Probably if we just cut ourselves some sturdy poles we can tie it up and keep it off the ground." She looked around, shook her head. "It's worse than it looked on TV."

Someone from the Lakeside Nursery arrived with surplus bedding plants, then a guy from work drove up with his tools and began working on the door of the hen coop. By the time Darlene came home three days after the raid, the worst of the damage was repaired. The lily bed was redug, the ruined leaves and stems removed, the bulbs replanted, and the baskets looked as if they had received only the tenderest of care.

Darlene sat in the lawn chair, face pale, eyes dark-rimmed, and Tony fussed over her, bringing her cool drinks and rolls of toilet paper. Tom took the brown bag full of used tear-sodden tissues away, and Jess kept a constant supply of ice cubes in the handbasin with the face cloth. Everyone else visited, bathing Darlene's face with cool water, putting the cold damp cloth on her forehead, telling her things would get better and she and Tony could try again.

"I know that," she wept. "But it won't be this one!"

The cops charged Singe with cruelty to animals for stopping the dog before it ripped human flesh to shreds. The family lawyer countered with animal-at-large charges and several other accusations having to do with not keeping the animal on the leash. And that was only the beginning: there were lists of broken household goods; estimated value of the garden, roses, lilies, hen coop, greenhouse; harassment; and copies of medical records including the proof Darlene had truly been pregnant.

The court fight seemed set to eat months or even years, although the lawyer insisted that there was no way they could lose; after all, not so much as one seed had been found, and the only charge against any of them involved a dog that was all set to savage someone, and they had photos of the dog charging from the film taken out from under the shingle. The snap of the dog in mid-air, mouth open, fangs ready, would have convinced anybody of anything.

Big Wil was so freaked out when she got home and learned what had happened that she quit her long-distance job and took one driving city bus. Within three weeks of her starting her new job, Chuck arrived at the front door, looking for her.

"Someone to see you, Willy," Jewen called, giving the newcomer a thorough lookover. Tall, lanky, dark hair, big hands, good teeth, jeans, tee-shirt, cowboy boots, wide leather belt with a big Peterbilt buckle and, on his left wrist, a digital watch that looked as if it was able to do everything except perhaps star in the Ice Capades.

Big Wil smiled and Jewen understood everything any of them would ever need to know. "I'll be back in a bit," she promised, and walked with Chuck toward his pickup.

"We're going to either have to wave bye-bye to Little Wil or build an addition onto the house," Jewen told Al.

"Wave bye-bye to Little Wil?" Al frowned. "Why would we do that? She lives here!"

"See that pickup drivin' away from here? Imagine an eight-horse coach like in the fairy tales."

"Other than the fact Little Wil lives here," Singe sipped his beer, "there's the matter of Norm. He's going to go up like a skyrocket if he gets wind of this. And he will! He'll do something stupid and wind up in court. We don't need that. He don't need that and the kids sure's hell don't need it. They've got enough to deal with already."

"Only reason he hasn't been totally outrageous," Al said, "is with Little Wil here, he knows he'll get his ass kicked if he tries anything dumb. If Big Wil and Whozit get together . . . hell, soon's they move in together Norm'll be there with his chest hair on fire."

"Gotta find a way to keep 'em here, then, don't we," Singe stated the obvious and sighed. "Jesus aitch, Colly's gonna have a friggin' fit!"

"Why's Colly going to have a fit?"

"Well, she's gonna have to move out of her house until we can get another one built for her, isn't she?"

"She don't have to move out," Tony dared. Usually he stayed out of family conversations, but since the miscarriage he felt secure enough to once in a while offer an opinion. "There's room there for . . ."

"Betcha she moves out instead." Al put a quarter on the kitchen table.

"Nah, she won't neither." Jewen matched it with one of his own.

"Yeah, she will," Singe guessed.

"She's not unreasonable." Tony dug in his pocket for a quarter and added it to the ones on the table.

"Maybe if we get a good start on the place *before* the lovebirds realize where they're going in that pickup, maybe . . ."

When Colleen left the next morning for a two-week vacation in the city, she had no idea changes were in the wind. When she came back, days late and so tired she was ready to spend an entire day and night in bed sleeping, the work was well underway. On the other side of the big house the bush had been cleared back, the ground levelled, the measurements marked off, the forms built and the cement poured. She parked her pop can and got out, staring. Jewen saw her, waved and hurried over, his bare chest wet with sweat.

"What . . .?" She gestured at the hive of activity.

"Hi, darlin'." He hugged her, smudging her tee-shirt. He patted his pockets, looking for cigarettes, and Colleen pulled hers out of her fanny pack. "Ah." He lit one and inhaled. "That damn Singe must'a spent one of his former lives as a slave driver. We been at 'er since seven this morning and I don't think I've had so much as a cuppa coffee. Let's go see if Lottie has one we can steal."

"What's all this?"

"Big Wil's got herself a beau," he said, grinning.

"Oh, god, Norm's going to shit bricks."

Lottie ought to have been overwhelmed by the number of workers who would need feeding, but instead she was singing along with the CD, doing a duet with Bonnie Raitt, and bustling around the kitchen happily. She gave Colleen a big floury welcome-back hug and even took time from her work to have a cup of coffee with them. But then it was back to the stove to baste the venison roast, then over to the counter to marinate the deboned halves of salmon readying for the barbecue. "We've about wiped out your spuds," she warned Colleen. "We'll be reduced to commercial ones soon."

"So what we figured"—Jewen had rehearsed his pitch several times and delivered it easily—"we don't want Norm doing something ridiculous like breaking down the door of a rented house or something. We're pretty sure he won't try anything idiotic around here, and more to the point, we don't want Big Wil moving somewhere else and takin' Little Wil with her. So," he waved, indicating the uproar and frenzy, "we figured a three-bedroom bungalow might solve the whole thing. Should be finished insid'a month."

"And Wil's boyfriend is fine with this?"

"Seems to be. Course, right now, he's so off-his-feet he'd agree to about anything you'd care to put to him. And so's Wil. If we can get 'em moved in before they start to come down outta the clouds, everything'll be fine."

"What you guys *ought'a* do," she teased, "is go whole hog and build a bloody hotel. Next thing you know it'll be Brady bringing someone home and out will come the cement forms again. Then you, and then in no time flat it'll be Tommy or Jess. If you don't build your hotel this entire place is going to be covered with three-bedroom two-storey bungalows. It'll look like Hillbilly Auto Court or something."

"You know, for a timber cruiser you have some good ideas," he teased. "Keep it up you'll be smart enough to be a hockey player so's you can go on strike because they only offered you a mere five mil a year." He leaned forward, peered, then grinned widely. "You know you got you a hickey on your neck, eh?"

"Gee." She sounded totally brain-dead. "I wonder how *that* got there."

Chuck got a job driving a mammoth gravel truck. If he felt his trucker's status had been reduced, he gave no sign of caring. "At first," he told Jess, "it's wonderful. You see all these places most people's only heard of . . . except, of course," he grinned at her and she grinned back, nodding, "for the folks who actually live there. I mean, I saw places I'd up to then only heard of in songs . . . I've driven through Kansas City," and he sang a few bars of the song, his voice on key and pleasant. "And I've seen Abilene." Again he sang and Jess joined him. "I've spent an overnight in Laredo . . ." And they sang the song from start to finish, Al watching them carefully. "I could have parked the truck and rented an apartment and stayed the rest'a my life in San Antonio. Except, good job I didn't, because I'd'a never met your Auntie Willy."

Chuck came complete with a twelve-string guitar. Evenings, he'd sit on the front porch and play quietly enough that those who were more interested in TV could watch and not be bothered by the music. Al watched Jess staring at Chuck's hands, waiting for the chance to sing along on a song they both knew. He drove into town one afternoon and came back with a guitar for her: a flat-top six-string made in Brazil. Chuck looked it over, tried it out and nodded. "Do her the rest of her life," he said quietly. "You made a fine choice."

"How much you want per lesson?"

"Oh, I think one of those barbecued salmon a week ought to just about cover it," Chuck said, "and a beer now and again."

Al had to drive back in to the music store and get a second guitar for Tom, who decided if Jess could learn to make music, so could he.

"If we ever get that damn house finished," Jewen said, tapping his mouth organ on his knee to clean it, "we can start in on a TV room."

"A music room, you mean," Al countered. "We *got* a TV room; it's called the living room, remember?"

"Says you."

"Says me."

The house came together well within the month's time frame predicted by Jewen, and Chuck and Big Wil moved in. It took much longer to convince Little Wil she should move in with them. They still all had their meals in the big house, and Little Wil saw no reason to leave the crowd, walk across the yard to watch TV as good as by herself, and then go to bed in some other place, however close it might be.

And Norm just about had a canary when he realized what was happening. "Fine thing," he raged. "My own damn family settin' up a shack-up-shack for my wife and her studly."

"Well, jeez, Norm," Jewen said in his quiet way, "who'd have guessed you'd have given so much as a hoot? I mean you've been studin' away since long before you moved out, and you've been shacked up with I don't even know how many by this time. You surely didn't think Willy was just going to sit on her fist and lean back against her thumb waitin' for you to come back, did you? I mean you're into the pubes with what's-her-name, what do you care about what Willy does?"

"It's not Willy and her doin's has me mad, you dork, it's what the rest of you are doin' gets my guts boiling. You went ahead and built a goddamn *house* for them on fam'ly land!"

"Well, dear lord, Norm, Little Wil *is* family, for cryin' in the night."

"*He* ain't!"

"No, and we didn't build a house for him. Or even for Willy. I already told you, we threw that place together so's they wouldn't hidey-ho off down the pike with Little Willy."

"And what about *me*?" It surfaced: the same kind of reaction they had learned to expect and put up with from Darlene.

"What about you?"

"Nobody built *me* a house."

"Nobody but yourself moved you out of the big one, either. You got to start taking some responsibility, Norm. You do something, there's consequences go with it. You moved out, you left Little Wil behind, you haven't paid a bean to support her, you have to live with it."

Frustrated, Norm swung at Jewen. He missed and wound up lying on his back in the dirt with Jewen sitting on his chest and laughing at him. "Norman, you just are not big enough," Jewen said. "You're the runt of the litter, remember? You're about half the size of the rest of us. We always did say you looked as if our mother had an active social life with a stubby-legged dwarf. So don't you bother trying to punch out my lights, you little mook, because you can't do it."

"Hey, Jewen," Al yelled, "if you're broke I can lend you the money to go into town and buy yourself a proper chair!"

"This one isn't very comfortable, that's for sure," Jewen answered. "And I think it might scratch at me. What do you think I should get? French provincial or Swedish modern?"

"I'll lay you out!" Norm raged.

"What's wrong with him now?" Al moved to sit on Norm's legs. "Jeez, this chair is a mess, Jewen. Get rid of it."

"He's mad because we didn't build him a house."

"Well, fuck, man, I'm getting kind of sick and tired of building houses, I have to tell you. I got an aggregates business to run, I don't got time for that other."

"I'm not building a house for some asshole who won't even feed his own kid, and that's that." Jewen lit a cigarette, passed his pack to Al. "I mean, there's not a lot in this world I draw the line at, but beating up women and not supporting your kid are on my list of how to tell a shit."

"Lindy's pregnant!" Norm hollered.

"So, don't blame *me* for it."

"Well, doesn't that kid have as much right to live here as Little Wilma does?"

"Do we have to feed it, too?"

"What happens when you walk out on that one the way you walked out on Little Willy?"

"I'll kill you, s'help me god I will."

"Oh, shut up, Norman, all you're doing is making yourself look like a bigger lugan than usual."

"The house she's renting is already too small."

"So, what's that got to do with me? *I'm* not the one dinkin' 'er."

"Get offa me."

"That's no way to talk to the guys who are sitting on top of you, Norman. You could talk like that if you were doing the sitting," Jewen lectured, "but in view of your position, I'd suggest you clean up your damned act and talk nicely."

"*Please* get offa me."

"That's better. But you start another stink and I'll tie you to a damn tree and leave you there for a while," Al threatened. "And before you get up offa the ground, you listen, and you listen good. We are fed up with the way you behave. You're setting a very bad example for my kids and I won't have it. I don't want Tom growin' up thinking this family just has babies and leaves them on the side of the damn road, and I won't have Jess growing up thinking that a man has the right to abandon his kids. Now, if you want to act like a goddamn jerk, there's not much I can do about it, but you'll act like that on some other piece of property. If you think you're going to live here, you'll behave like a human person."

"Lemme up."

"Did you hear me?"

"Lemme up, damn it!"

"Did you hear me?"

"I can hear you over here," Colleen called.

"I can hear you from inside the kitchen, Mr. Al," Lottie said.

"Hell, Al, I'm on the front porch and I can hear you," Tony shouted.

"Yes, dammit, I can hear you," Norm grumbled.

Jewen and Al let Norman up out of the dirt and sat on an unfinished bench Jewen was making for Colleen's new lily bed and rose garden.

"Obviously," Jewen said to Al, ignoring Norm completely, "we couldn't put the damned thing anywhere over on this side of the property because Norman would go out of his way to piss Big Wil off, or else he'd do something totally ridiculous like trying to punch it up with Chuck."

"We could put something in on the other side of Singe's place."

"Mind you, I'm not pounding one nail unless he agrees to pay three hundred a month support for the Wilsters."

"Three hundred? Are you crazy?" Norm argued.

"Oh, don't be such a cheap shit, you're payin' more than that for rent."

"Wilma ain't payin' no rent."

"Wilma isn't dumping half a damned basketball team on us, either. It's not like you were just moving Lindy out here, you know. We wind up with Jared, Jeremy, Jason and Janine, too."

"She know any other letter of the alphabet, you figure?"

"Funny thing is, she said she didn't want a homely kid, remember? So why'd she get herself knocked up by that stubby bugger?"

"Maybe she figured the kid would be as cute as Little Willy?"

"Dumb thought, Willy's the spittin' image of Wilma. The blockhead didn't make any impression at all on the kid. You figure that's why he'd rather live in town in a rented place than pay three hundred a month to support his first-born child?"

"*All right!*" Norman shouted. "*All right, then!*"

"Evict you if you don't," Al promised.

"Jesus christ," Jewen sighed, "I was hoping he'd stay stubborn as a sow. Damn, now I have to go back to pounding nails. And with five kids this house is going to have to be enormous!"

"See if we can hire some of Lucy's relatives again. And maybe go see a contractor because I'm not sure I know how to build a two-storey place. Be a shame to have the top half not fit the bottom half and blow off in a wind."

"Right, and I guess you expect me to pay the damn contractor, too."

"Oh, shut up, Norm," Al said idly.

"Yeah, Norm, shut up, eh."

They drove the loader to the other side of the big old house by bulling through the scrub and brush alongside the dirt bike oval. Lucy's cousins had already dropped the trees, sending the fir and cedar to the sawmill, keeping the alder, maple and wild cherry for firewood. By the time the contractor arrived with his sheaf of house plans and his skilled tradesmen, the site was ready for him.

"What's them?" Al pointed at the blue-tinged plans.

"Mr. Lancaster and his wife have been to the office several times and chosen their design for the interior of the house," the contractor said, looking at Al as if he deeply doubted this heavily tanned scruffy pup even belonged in the neighbourhood, let alone on the property.

"Lemme see, please."

"I doubt you'll be able to read them."

"Humour me. It makes life easier for everybody."

Al looked at the plans and shook his head in wonder. "Hey, Tony, c'mere a minute. You go by these and you'd think it was the Windsors moving in here instead'a more Lancasters." He handed the sheaf of drawings to Tony, then smiled at the contractor. "Appreciate it very much if you'd take the time to look around in Lucy's place, then we'll take you over to Colleen's and you can look around there. Then you 'n' us'll sit down and make some changes here."

"Mr. Lancaster was very specific that . . ."

"Fella," Al's smile vanished as he pointed at Singe. "That over there is Mr. Lancaster. The guy you were talkin' to was Crazy Norm, okay? Crazy Norm is only gonna squat in this place. Mr. Lancaster is going to pay for it."

Norm and Lindy were at the site in less than two hours. Lindy seemed puzzled but determined to be pleasant. Norm didn't know how to be pleasant and wasn't interested in taking lessons.

"You got your nerve, Al!" he blustered.

"You got cash-in-hand money to pay for this?" Singe asked.

"You know full well I don't!" Norm looked one at a time at his brothers. "I'm gonna be renting it," he said defiantly. "Three hunnert a month."

"Correction." Jewen lit a smoke. "Three hundred goes to Willy's keep. It's not rent nor payments on this place, it's child maintenance. Now you go talk to *our* contractor, and you tell him to get rid of those frills and shit. Stained-glass windows for chrissake. What you think this is, a church or something?"

"It's by way of being a dream home. Lindy always wanted . . ."

"Good, let her get a job and pay for it." Singe was furious and didn't care who knew it. "You give me one good reason why Lucy lives in old Bob's house and Lindy gets cathedral entrances and stained-glass windows and all kinds of other frilly shit. Wilma works damn hard every day driving bus, and *she* doesn't have the Snob Hill version. *Colly* doesn't have all this stuff! You go give your head a damn good shake. And how come you ain't at work?"

"I got laid off," Norm admitted sourly. "It's what they call the economic downturn. Or haven't you heard about it?"

"Right. You're on pogey but you want stained glass. My eye, Norm," Jewen sighed tiredly. "You sure do get the ideas."

"Well, if you're on pogey you can get out of those uptown dude duds and haul on some work clothes, then grab a shovel or a hammer or something and get to work with the rest'a us. You ain't sitting bullshitting over coffee like the lord of the manor while the rest'a us sweat our guts out on a place you're gonna be livin' in!"

"Christ for crabby," Norm said, glaring. "The whole bunch'a ya's crabby."

If Lindy's nose was out of joint because of the changes in the plans, she gave no sign of it. "You kids behave yourselves, now," she told them. "You play nice, and be sure to share. God," she said as she sipped her tea, "I will be glad when school goes back in again. It's been like the summer from hell. They closed the beaches at our end of town because of sewer stuff, and I have to tell you, loading that pack into my old ruin of a car and driving to the river isn't *my* idea of a great time. Jason's too little to swim and you have to keep an eye on him every minute or he'll toddle right off the big rock, and so I'd bake like a cookie in the oven and wait for it to be time to take them home again. Summer from hell," she repeated. But she was busy at the sink, scrubbing spud skins, helping Lottie get a start on lunchtime. "Are you *sure* Jason'll be okay with those kids? It's not too much to expect of them?"

"They'll look out for him," Lottie assured her. "If there's one thing those children know how to do, it's look after each other."

"Lordy, will you look at the length of that car!" Lindy exclaimed, staring out the kitchen window. "You'd need a telephone to talk from the back seat to the front one."

They all looked, and Brady stood up slowly, reaching for her package of cigarettes. "It's for me," she said carefully. "Friends'a mine from the States."

"Car like that," Lottie said, "make a person think you're hobbin' and nobbin' with the Kennedys and Clintons."

"Nah." Brady walked toward the door. "My friends are the ones who tell those low-rent bums what to do." And she left by way of the back door. The women in the kitchen laughed softly and told each other what a whacko sense of humour Brady had.

Lottie didn't know if the Yankee tourists were going to stay ten minutes or ten days, so to be on the safe side she opened several quart jars of venison stew and added that to the menu.

Brady stood by the limo and talked quietly with her visitors for probably ten minutes, then took them over to see the action as the cement trucks arrived to pour the pad for the new house. One of the well-groomed men hunkered down, took some of the wet cement in his hand, felt the texture, held it to his nose, sniffed the scent of it, then dropped it back in with the rest. He wiped his fingers on a handful of grass, then moved to where the hose dribbled constantly and washed his hands, drying them on a big hanky he pulled from his pocket. Brady introduced him to Singe and the others, and when the cement trucks were gone again, the pad smoothed and ready to set, Lottie yelled from the front door, and everyone, Yanks and all, headed to the house.

"So, d'ya need me for anything?" Norm asked importantly, mopping gravy with a thick slice of Lottie's homemade bread.

"All's we can do now is wait for the pad to dry, I suppose," Al told him. "And I don't suppose you can do much to help that along. The framing crew is gonna have the walls ready to raise by the end'a the week, and the pad ought'a be dry by then, god willing, so say Friday we expect to see your smilin' face."

"Friday's not all that good for me," Norm said, smiling nervously. "I got to go to court in the morning, and you know what that's like: they tell you ten in the morning but you might be there still waiting at three in the afternoon."

"What'n hell're you in court for this time?" Singe was ready to explode.

"Well, when they laid me off I told the foreman to go to hell, and he called me a motherfucker and punched me in the gut. So when I got back up off the ground and he tried to knock me down again, I punched the piss outta him."

"We could," one of Brady's friends said helpfully, "put him in the pad for the new house. Then he wouldn't testify and they'd have to drop charges."

"Yeah, but who wants to live your life with the foreman under the damn house?" Al teased. "They're so damned undependable the place would probably wind up higher on one side than the other and all the furniture would slide."

"Even worse," the jovial visitor said, "you might run the risk of all the family jewels rolling around like marbles or something. Rubies, sapphires, emeralds and all them diamonds clattering around underfoot."

After lunch was finished and Norm and Lindy had headed off

with her kids, and while Darlene and Lucy helped Lottie clean the kitchen and the kids took turns getting cleaned up, the rest of them, including Brady's friends, headed outside to see the bike track and the extension road down through the back to Singe's place.

"Sometimes," Al mused to nobody in particular, "the way things have been coming down around here recently, boat seizures and cop raids and helicopters and all, I wonder about surveillance bugs stuck in the damn trees. Gets so a body don't dare say anything out loud for fear some jerk somewhere is takin' notes."

"Not to worry," Brady's friend said quietly, "they're so stupid they'd lose 'em, anyway."

"Well, you may be right, but even so, after a bit a person gets paranoid, and when that happens, well, seems like the best thing to do is nothing, and the best thing to say is even less than nothing. You just sort of depend on your friends understanding how things are and not expecting phone calls or such."

"Personally," another friend said, "I detest phones and I don't trust the mail, either. I've found, in my business, that personal contact works much better than all the fax machines and e-mail and such."

"Personal contact," the cement expert nodded, "really is the best. A man gets to see the other guy's face, see his eyes, read his body language, then you've got a chance of knowing if he's bluffing or not."

They returned to the kitchen later and had coffee before Brady's friends climbed into the limo to resume their touristing. The Yanks seemed very pleased with their visit and the friendly reception they'd received. After they'd left, though, Al and Tony seemed a bit bummed out, and the way they took coffee to the front steps and sat sipping it and smoking cigarettes, a body might have thought they'd just waved goodbye to close friends. Either that or watched a king's ransom slide through their fingers.

After supper they took everyone out on the boat for an overnight fishing trip. The kids were so worn out by the excitement of getting ready and then standing on deck waving at the world that by nine they were ready to crawl into their sleeping bags and snuggle together like a litter of mismatched puppies. Lucy and Brady started a game of crib and, after a few minutes of watching, Colleen sat down and waited for Darlene to finish pouring coffee and join them.

Singe smoked his cigarette on deck and stared out across the waves at the lights on shore. He could see the bright red blinking neon sign over the new motel. Such a big fuss over it: half the town certain it marked the end of life as they had known it, the other half already planning how to spend the extra money it would bring to the economy.

"D'j'ever wish you could run an ad in the paper and let them know just *who* really owns that roach palace?" Jewen asked, leaning on the rail and reaching for his own smokes.

"No roaches on the Island," Singe said, grinning slightly. "Have to make do with silverfish, I guess."

"Well, d'j'ever?"

"Nah. I swiped a dinky car one time. We were in town, shopping with Momma and I just *had* to have that little blue car. So I swiped it. Nobody saw a thing. Few hours after we got home she caught me playing with it. Didn't say a word, just took it away from me, went out to the chopping block, put it down and used the flat end of the axe to flatten it into a shapeless lump. 'That'll learn you', she said. Just that, nothing more. 'That'll learn you'. And it did. I learned you don't swipe a thing unless you know for a fact you aren't going to get caught. Because if you get caught, you lose what you thought you'd won. I run an ad and . . . ding dong, it ain't Avon calling, it's the bad luck that'll take away everything I've got."

"It's not bad luck I'm worried about," Al said softly, "it's those fish-eyed friends'a Brady's."

"They believed you," Tony assured him. "Or said they did, which might be just as good."

"Except they made it clear they expect us to get back to full swing before New Year's, and I don't know about any of the rest'a you, but just the mere idea of doin' it gives me a cramp in my gut."

"Well, we know what your hunches mean," Singe said nodding. "So now we just got to find a way to slide out. Without winding up in a crab trap," he added.

"Strange old world." Al lit a cigarette and inhaled, then stared at the glowing coal and shook his head. "You grow and sell this stuff, you're a respectable member of society and never mind the cancer rates and the emphysema deaths."

"Here we go," said Jewen, "political analysis all over again."

"Yeah, well, maybe we all should learn to see past the ends of our noses." Tony sighed. "Not that it would change anything."

"Well, look at that gold scam. First, the government leaders of all of North America put the screws on everyone else to boycott South Africa, and that cuts off the supply of their gold and sends prices to the damn moon. Then they give huge foreign aid to the president of some flyspeck and isn't he suddenly their friend. Some little company is doing exploration down there and out of the blue finds what they say is the biggest gold strike of the century. So then this other, bigger, American company wants in, and the president of the flyspeck jumps into the picture because the big company's board'a directors includes the two leaders of the governments of North America. *They* wind up with the lion's share of the supposed biggest gold strike in history. They start selling shares and make a buhzillion dollars each. Then the guy who was in charge of testing for the little company that got screwed goes for a helicopter ride and he falls out, and we're told he was up there takin' a ride by himself, the pilot says nobody else was in there, just this clumsy corpse. Which they never did find. And *then*, lo and behold, doesn't it turn out that the whole thing was a scam, and the guy who fell out the helicopter gets blamed for buying river gold from some unidentified native and salting the core samples that convinced everyone this was the mother lode of all time. And the price of the stocks crashes, but isn't it interesting that the bigwigs, including the now former heads of the governments, have sold everything when the prices were high so they don't even get wet let alone take a bath. The investors lose more money than anybody can imagine, the board of directors, already comprised of filthy rich and very *very* respectable people, gets even richer. The little company that had bugger-nothing much to do with any of it gets the blame, and the ones who set it all up don't even get mentioned as co-conspirators and they continue to be respected, even honoured people, and us here at this boat rail, we're crooks and bums."

"Know what you should do?" Jewen threw his arm around Al's shoulders. "You should buy yourself a word processor and start writin' books." And he laughed.

"Right." Al nodded, then flipped his cigarette toward the water.

For two days they travelled up the coast, stopping in whichever small cove or bay took their fancy. They dove off the side of the boat into the cold water, swam back to the aluminum ladder, climbed up it to the deck, and got in line for another chilly plunge. They introduced the kids to face mask and snorkel. They fished for cod and cooked it on the barbecue the advertising said was portable but which had required several men to move from the pickup, down the ramp, through the marina, to the boat. The bottle of propane was easier; Colleen carried it, but, of course, she didn't have a whack of kids' stuff to help lug.

They teased each other, played cards in the evening, ate their faces off and slept quickly and well, and on the morning of the third day started home. Their first night home, with everyone else in bed and sleeping, Al sat on the porch with a pot of tea, a package of cigarettes, and both dogs for company. He watched the clouds move across the face of the enormous-seeming red-tinged late summer moon.

After a long while he got to his feet, stretched and took the dogs to their pen. He checked the water dish, slipped each of them a biscuit from the wooden box with the hinged lid, then slowly and thoughtfully he walked the skid trail, past Colleen's house, heading into the bush.

He could have made the trip in the dark blindfolded: his feet avoided the bumps, the rocks and the ruts without any help from his head. He turned and headed into the big black hole, found a flashlight and moved to the pavilion.

He ignored the grow lights, the humidity gauges, the expensive commercial greenhouse thermometers that controlled the temperatures. He even ignored the initials and names carved in the overhead beams. He spent a long time looking at the mementoes of their childhood "fort," then sighed deeply. He sat on the backside-smoothed block of wood, lit a new cigarette and smoked it slowly, then stood, rubbed his face with his hands, and moved to the entrance to what they had always called the hole-behind-the-hole.

He crawled on his belly, and as his feet left the pavilion, his arms were reaching down to the floor of the cubby. He pulled himself through, found and flipped the switch for the trouble light, then set to work.

There were eight heavy cardboard boxes, thirty-two inches long, twenty-six inches across and twenty-six inches high. There had been nine, but that was before they decided to go ahead with Lindy's house and the new motel. One by one he pushed the boxes through the short tunnel, shoving them ahead of him as he crawled his way back. He was amazed when he realized he was weeping. But dammit, he had his kids to think of, and not just Tom and Jess, there were all those other kids: Lucy's kids who now called Singe "Dad," and Lindy's kids who deserved better and more than Norm would ever be able to provide for them, and Dorrit, too sweet to be believed, and always Little Wil, who moved back and forth between the new house where her mom lived with Chuck to the old one, which she still called home.

Al knew what it was like to grow up one of "those Lancasters." He'd been one of "those" all his life. They'd been left with as good as nothing when the old fool decided to take the fast lane: an enormous chunk of bushland; a house they had no idea how to keep from falling down in the wind; back taxes chewing at their heels; the welfare snooping around looking for any excuse they could find to scoop the younger ones and put them in foster homes.

He and Singeon had managed, somehow, and when their unskilled labourer paycheques weren't enough, they became what Al now considered to be ankle-biters. They peddled off the old man's store of moonshine, and they raided two other juice-makers' storage sheds and sold their stuff, too. They set up the first grow lights and sold nickel-and-dime bags; they headed off before dawn in the autumn and scrabbled on hands and knees in farmers' fields, picking magic mushrooms; they did what they could and managed to stay together. They didn't lose the property to taxes; they stayed one teeny-weeny bunny-hop ahead of the law, more by good luck than good management, and all in all he figured they'd managed to do okay by themselves and each other. There wasn't really anything much in the past that he would change: most of it had been beyond his control, beyond Singe's control, probably beyond the control of any and all a body would care to name. He harboured deep resentment for the old fool; he could have at least paid off the tax bill before he went ahead and left a mess for others to clean. All he'd done for the six months prior to his explosive end was plop himself in his big chair and sulk. All that shine! He could have sold it and paid off the debts. Things might have been different if he had.

Well, he hadn't, the old bugger, and he didn't have to take the old woman with him, either. All she'd done was work like hell all her life; a person shouldn't get a death sentence for that. She hadn't been perfect—hell, Norm was proof of that. But everyone needs a bit of fun once in a while, a whirl around the dance floor, a sip of store-bought, some laughter and soft feelings. The old bugger had left enough of his own unacknowledged offspring, it was only fair he wind up feeding someone else's since plenty of others were feeding his.

And it hadn't been the obvious, the on-the-surface grinding hardship. It was that other thing, the beast that for years didn't get named, the placid expectation on the part of just about anybody he could name that "those" Lancasters would have been rangytangs no matter what: they had been born of hooligans, to be just another generation of the same, rough and tough and my god what will that family think of next, the messes they get into, make a body wonder what else they've got planned.

Singe had ignored it, and god knows how he managed. Al dove into it, although Singe had warned him often enough. When they finally caught him, it was like the fulfilment of something he'd been expecting. Singe offered to get him a lawyer, but Al said no, he'd take his lumps. And they had been lumps! School of hard knocks, they called it. But, by god, he got an education. When he got out after three years he was one helluva lot smarter than he'd been when he went behind the walls. No more ankle-biting for Al.

And here he was, here they all were, and it felt too much like it had felt just before he got busted that first time. One shoe had fallen, and if he paid attention he might never hear the other; if he ignored the feeling, he might not hear anything at all ever again. And it had to be something those fish-eyed friends of Brady's couldn't dispute.

He was scared of them. There wasn't much in life had scared him to the point he felt as if he was about to pee down his leg. The first week in the slammer that first time: his body bruised, his face marked, his backside throbbing and sending hot flashes of agonizing pain up inside him—that had scared him. Scared him about half as much as the fear he now felt. They probably wouldn't be satisfied with just offing him. He'd heard stories about how they would systematically slice at every member of the family and make you watch before they slit your throat. He believed the stories.

The thing with the bust and what he and Tony had hauled off the bottom was straightened out: they accepted what they were told whether they fully believed it or not. It helped that not one rock had been taken, everything was tickety-boo down to the last fraction of a fraction of weight. But it had been too close. Get caught handling that stuff, and everything you had would wind up confiscated, proceeds of criminal activity, and law'd take it all, the land, the houses, even the damned dogs, because they'd been thwarted in the past, because they were worse than the legendary elephants, never forgetting, never relaxing. They'd uproot lily beds till the cows came home, no longer caring if they actually found proof of anything, doing it for spite. Al was sure the biggest difference between them and Brady's friends was the Yank contingent was into free enterprise and those other lugans expected the taxpayers to pay for the bullets.

One by one he got the boxes through the hidey-hole in the ceiling, and one by one he packed them to the box-car-sized rusted tank that had been his own special hiding place, the one he had never shared with anyone, not even Singe. He wondered where Singe's special place was. Everyone had one, a place all their own, where sobs went unheard and a person could curl up in misery and just let the eyes leak until the pressure was gone from the chest.

He rolled the rock out of the way, remembering the story his mother had tried to teach them, about rolling away the rock at the mouth of the tomb or finding it rolled away or something. He pushed the boxes through the rusty gap one at a time, and then, grunting, got the rock shoved back in place. Good enough as a temporary measure, but he'd have to figure out something better.

Maybe something as simple as renting one of those storage lockers. Who'd know? What kind of records did they keep?

He walked away from the drum, wondering what in hell it had ever been used for in the first place. The old bugger used to joke that one of these frosty Fridays he was going to clean it out and use it in his shine business. Hold a lake of it, he'd said; instead of bothering with the BS of jugs and stoppers we just take their money and let them swim in it, haul 'em back out when they start to float face down. They'd all joked about how if the heart wasn't beating very well they could always just hook 'em up to the jumper cables, like old what's-'is-name, and rev the truck a bit. Send 'em home glowing in the dark with their hair standing on end and sparks coming from their eyeballs.

The key to the powder shed hung around his neck, and the moonlight was bright enough that he could see to get the key in the padlock without fumbling. Out in the bush, behind Singe's place probably, a big owl hooted four times, paused, then hooted five more times. Small creatures stopped moving, the background rustling in the brush halted, the night became still, almost eerie.

By the time the eastern sky was starting to lighten, Al was almost ready. He was on his way back to the shaft mouth when something began to nag at him. He turned on his heel, headed back to the huge rusty drum and rolled the rock aside roughly. Quickly, almost running, he pulled out the cardboard boxes and took them to the van. The nagging slowed, eased, then stopped. He supposed he could spend the rest of his life moving it from place to place, like a feral cat changing her den every couple of days.

He ran back to the shaft, feeling lighter than he'd felt in weeks, maybe even lighter than he'd felt in years. No, by god, his kid wasn't going to wind up raw-end receiver on the slammer football team! No bloody expectation of that or of anything except maybe one day getting a package in the mail and opening it to find the first CD of Tom and Jess Lancaster, guitar and vocals.

He knew some part of him had been planning this a long time. He even had two brand new Big Ben alarm clocks still in their boxes, the warranty papers folded between the plastic face and the cardboard box.

✒

They awoke to the smell of bacon and sausage and the sound of Al singing as he whipped the eggs. "See them tumblin' down, pledging their love to the ground."

"*Shut up!*" Darlene yelled. "Jesus aitch, Al, gimme a break here."

"Coffee's ready," he called. "Up and at 'em, daylight in the swamp. Wakey wakey, tea and cakey."

"I'll kill the bugger."

"Tom?"

"Yes, Dad?"

"Haul on your jeans and go over to Auntie Colly's place, tell her it's loggers' breakfast happening over here. Jess, you phone Uncle Singe and Aunt Lucy, tell 'em to get over here or I'll go over there and sing 'em awake."

"Anybody ever punch you out and lay you flat for stuff like this?" Tony asked, coming into the kitchen barefoot and sleepy-eyed. "For cryin' in the night, man, it isn't but maybe eight o'clock. What did you do, pee the bed and had to get up?"

Lottie arrived in time to take over at the toaster. If she was puzzled she did a good job of hiding it. The house was full, kids sitting on the front porch with plates of food, kids sitting on the steps, jaws moving. As fast as she buttered the slices they disappeared, and they could easily have used another three or four pounds of bacon. You'd think nobody'd had a bite to eat in a week! It did her heart good to see them all, so easy with each other, tossing casual insults that weren't really any such things but verbal expressions of trust and love. She'd told her daughter just last night that it was a shame Mr. Al didn't have a good woman to brighten his life. Of course, she had her own reasons for saying that: her daughter's husband was just about as much use as tits on a teapot and a mean-minded bugger at that. Don't tell her little Fred had got that bruise on his arm from tangling himself in the swing rope. The rain might have fallen last week but Lottie hadn't fallen with it; she'd seen those marks before in her life. Glenda had eaten just about enough of the shit sandwich, too, you could tell by the way she talked. Just last night she'd asked if Lottie knew

273

anybody who was doing after-school babysitting. Glenda was thinking about looking for a job.

Lottie figured, number one, she could do the babysitting herself: Glennie could just drop the kids off here or have 'em ride out after school on the same school bus as the tribe. Number two, the way things were going they'd need someone else out here soon to help do. Glennie was good at that. Lottie was pretty sure Mr. Al would be like every other man who looked at Glennie; after all, that bright yellow hair, straight as straight can be, hanging down her back in a thick braid, shining in the sun, and that face, although it hadn't been smiling much lately, well, they'd be good for each other and no doubt about that. As for the kids, well, what's three more in a crowd like the one hung around here.

Colleen finished her breakfast, took her plate to the sink, tapped Lottie on the arm to get her attention. "I'll do toast," Colly said. "You get some breakfast before you fade away to a shadow of your former self."

"Right, be a shame if I was to wither to the size of the average mountain, I suppose. There was a time people said I had 'big bones' . . . well, they don't say that anymore."

"Lottie," Al said, laughing, "there's something you should learn before you get any older. What you got is enough for two men, so the man you start courting is sure to be twice as lucky as most."

"Listen to you," she laughed. "Old Silvertongue. If you like what you see so much, wait until you see my daughter Glenda. You want to talk about enough for two men? My Glennie's about a third the bulk of me but what's there is prime."

"She's married to that . . ."

"You got it, Mr. Al. *That*. And you 'n' me's too polite to say that *what*, right? Jeez, the mistakes some people make when they're young and foolish."

The big old clock on the living room wall sounded nine. Al picked up his coffee mug and sipped, but he looked as if he was either listening for something or deep in thought.

"Goose on your grave?" Lucy asked him.

"Just thinking about something, Luce, that's all." He smiled and ignored the muted whump, ignored even the way the knives and forks began to clatter on the new kitchen table.

"Kids!" Colleen yelled, racing across the trembling floor toward the startled tribe.

"Momma!" Dorrit hollered.

"Coming." Darlene was up and following Colleen.

The new brick chimney came apart as if it had been put on the roof without any mortar; the dogs, who had been waiting patiently for scraps, raced into the kitchen, terrified, to cower under the table.

"She's a big one," Singe shouted. "C'mon, Lucy, move your sweet self."

Somewhere in the maze of abandoned shafts, rock struck rock and the resultant spark set off a large pocket of gas. The explosion heaved the earth and cracked the windows in Colleen's house. The roof of the big house sagged, and the noise was like nothing any of them had ever heard.

"Out!" Al shouted. He dropped to the floor, reached under the table, grabbed the dogs and followed the others out into the yard. Trees whipped back and forth, the tops of some snapping off; others leaned, leaned, leaned, then fell, their roots coming up out of the dirt in bus-sized balls. More gas pockets exploded, the earth heaved, the big old rusty tank that had dominated the backyard for longer than any of them had been alive vanished. One moment it was there, the next moment it was sagging and twisting, and the one after that it was just damn well gone. A three-foot-wide-at-least crack in the earth appeared, running a jagged diagonal line that barely missed the henhouse, cut through the middle of Colleen's garden and separated her place from the big house. It continued across the front yard, splitting the highway and entering the bush on the other side.

Colleen was so scared she wanted to run, but if the earth was going to drop into the old mine shafts like that she wouldn't be any safer moving at top speed than she was standing where she was. The powder shed was gone, the tool shed looked as if someone had just pulled the walls out and dropped the roof into the middle of it, and the whump of exploding gas pockets continued. Hydro poles snapped, trees fell, rocks bounced and rolled as if they had a life of their own, and the old house collapsed on itself.

"There goes the new kitchen table, I bet," Lottie mourned.

"Buy you a new one, Lottie, I promise." Al put his arm around her shoulders. "We're okay," he told her, "we're fine." But really he felt some foolish: he hadn't even thought of the gas pockets, hadn't even thought of the stories of sudden violent explosions, lives lost, bodies never recovered. He wanted to tell them all he was sorry, he hadn't intended anything as big as this; all he wanted to do was get rid of the pavilion and the parts of the shaft those snake-eyed desert dwellers had seen.

The rumbling slowed, almost ceased, but the muffled whumps continued in the parts of the shafts out back. Nothing looked anything like it had.

"My porch is wrecked." Colleen's voice was thin and high with fear. "And the old house is . . . toast."

"Don't think the toaster will work," Brady tried to joke, "the electricity seems to be off right now."

The kids clung to their parents and shook. Dorrit wept quietly and Little Wil howled loudly. "My *bike*!" she wailed. "And my *bed*!"

"Don't worry, Babe," Singeon managed. "We'll clean up the mess."

"Singe," Big Wilma touched his arm, spoke quietly to him so the others wouldn't hear her words. "There's a helluva lot of water in that big crack between here and Colly's place. I mean . . . one *hellu*-va lot of water."

"My grandad said the old shafts used to flood. They hadda keep the pumps running all the time, and even so, the guys worked in water to their arses. Must'a been an underground spring or river or something."

"You think this place might flood out?"

"No way of knowing, Willy. Maybe we'll just wind up with our own creek or river or something. How do you like the sound of Big Willy Falls or maybe . . ."

"Sudden River," she said, leaning against him briefly. "You okay, Singe?"

"Scared shitless but otherwise okay."

"Fuck, Singe." Al came over, his face ashen, his eyes huge. "I mean, like, what *now*?"

"Now? Well, you know what the old woman used to say, 'When in puzzle or in doubt, run in circles, scream and shout'. What else can we do? Start picking away at the mess with the equipment, I suppose, and pray to god whatever's going on, it stops."

"I don't even recognize the place." Al lit a cigarette, his hands shaking.

"Anybody hurt?" Wilma asked.

"Chuck's managed to twist 'is ankle is all. A few bruises but nobody got brained by a brick or anything serious. Of course, I'll have to burn my underwear because it's never going to come clean."

"I just hope I can get some of the load outta my damn boot," Singe said.

CHAPTER EIGHT

Singe's house was standing, looking miraculously untouched in the midst of rubble and ruin. The trees were down, most cracked and broken by the weight of other falling trees, and the barn and outbuildings Crazy Bob had built were in the same shape as the old house; the walls gave out, the roof fell, and there probably weren't two unbroken boards in the mess. The ground had been changed and altered: the garden was at the bottom of a new hill and the pavement was cracked and heaved but passable. A dozen cars were stopped, the people standing, staring, as wide-eyed and terror-stricken as any of the family.

"What happened?" one of them yelled.

"Old mine shafts caved in," Singe answered. "You can see the rest for yourself. You okay?"

"Hell, no, I ain't okay," someone snapped. "You don't look very okay yourself."

"Me? Okay? If I could find someone bigger 'n' me I'd sit on his lap and bawl on his shoulder."

Even knowing the road was out and there was no way they were going to be able to continue on to town, nothing would do but that the travellers make it over the fractured blacktop, avoiding as best they could the potholes and bits of smashed tree and broken hydro pole. They wanted to see the crack in the earth. Unthinkable to be this close and not make the extra bit of effort and actually *see* the birth of a ravine.

What they saw impressed them so much they stood mute. There wasn't going to be any convoy of trucks dropping in gravel to back-fill a hole. This was going to need the engineers, a large crew of workers and enough time to build a full-sized and serious bridge.

"God only knows what's going on at the other end," Big Wil worried. "You figure that split goes all the way to the shoreline? Pray to god there weren't any houses in the way or all the people in them will be . . ."

She was so worried they decided to check on things. After all, there wasn't a lot they could do at the old house until things started to settle down and stop wiggling. Al drove his van closer to the mess that had been the house, made sure all the windows were rolled shut and the doors locked, and started off after the others. He got across the road and almost to the bush, then looked back; someone was peering in a van window.

"I'll stay here," Al called. Singe looked back, puzzled. "The voting public is apt to walk off with anything that isn't already wrecked." Al waved at the crowd that had left the roadside and was now moving curiously around the totally altered place. He went back, muttering to himself, and walked over to the van. Someone had a piece of wire and was trying to get the driver's door open. "Excuse me," Al said, "Maybe you'd like me to use my key; it'll probably be easier on the door than what you're doing."

"Wanted to check it out," the guy said, glowering. "Might be someone hurt inside."

"No, I checked before I locked it up." Al smiled. "Nobody hurt in there. Real nice of you to be concerned, though."

"This is yours?"

"Such as it is, yes."

"What happened?"

"I d'one 'er," Al laughed and the potential vandal grinned. "Just got up in a real owly mood and thought to myself, Now what in hell can I do to kind of shake things up here a bit."

He wanted to yell at them to get the hell away from the house, to keep their grubby mitts offa *his* stuff, to tee off and go home, but he was one person and some of these people looked about as proddy as he felt. They were scared: they'd been driving down the highway minding their own business and all hell bust loose and, by god, they wanted to know why. He sat on the ground next to the van, leaning against a back wheel, and did the only thing he could do: he waited.

A woman came across the lumpy ground with Tom's guitar in her hand. There might have been scratches on it, but it was basically fine. "Someone said you lived here," she said as she held out the guitar. "It looks like it's okay."

"Thank you." He felt shy. "That's great. It's my son's guitar. I think you just saved him from a broken heart."

"You were very lucky." She patted him on the head as if he was only six years old. He wanted to bury his face against her and weep.

"Yeah," he said, nodding. "I didn't think so when it was all happening but when I see how close it came . . . yeah."

Someone else brought a chainsaw; the chain was gone and the bar was bent but you can always buy a new bar, people do it every day. Great-grandpa Lancaster's shotgun came next, and from the way the salvager stroked the old gun Al knew the guy was fully aware of how much it was worth. "Man," the stranger sighed, "you could adopt me and gimme this as a birthday present."

"Ain't it something? Be great if you could crack 'er open, look down the barrels and see what it saw here the first time the old man took aim at a deer with it."

"Must'a been something, all right. Before they started diggin' out this and cuttin' down that and screwin' it all up. Used to be good hunting here. Or so I'm told," he said with a grin. "My dad used to claim he hunted here."

"If he did he must'a been a friend of *my* dad because there weren't many people the old man would let on the place. And if he was a friend of my dad's, likely his hunting stories were action-packed adventure yarns they dreamed up while sitting under a tree with a jug of rocket fuel. Was your dad a drinkin' man?"

"Dear god," said the stranger. He pulled out the makings, rolled himself a cigarette and handed the pouch and papers to Al. "So did they tell you about the buck deer with a rack so big . . .?"

"And all they could do was stare at it and think what a shame it would be to drop a big daddy like that?" And they laughed together, admitting to each other they had believed the story when they were kids but had grown to wonder if the monumental set of horns wasn't, maybe just maybe, really nothing more than the branches of a young alder or maple, or even a total and utter hallucination caused by the consumption of booze.

"Not much skill needed," Al admitted.

"Was it your old man made the rocket fuel?"

"Yeah." Al felt it start, the dull ache he suspected was either shame or embarrassment, and which always turned to defiance. "My old man, the bootlegger."

"Jeez," the guy said. "I wonder if those other action-packed adventure stories were anywhere near true? Did you hear about the time Pete Bolton's lighter ran out of fuel and he put some of your old man's hooch in, never really believing it would ignite, and the bugger went up and he couldn't put it out and it fused his Zippo into one solid lump?"

"Hadn't heard that one." Al felt the grin starting. "But I heard about the guy who spilled some on his shoes and went home barefoot."

"God," said the newcomer as he sat beside him, lit his smoke, handed the matches to Al. "You know, I grew up kind of scared of my old man. Well, 'kinda' hardly tells it. And the thing of it is, he never really went at me, he'd just whirl around and glare and I'd damn near pee myself. I thought he was big fuck'a the mountain. Couple of years ago I realized I was a good few inches taller'n he'd ever been, and now I realize he was a gas bag and full of jokes."

"'Of a particular and peculiar kind'. I heard my mother say that once; I don't even remember what she was talking about, but when she said that, 'of a particular and peculiar kind', I realized there was music hidden in everyday talking."

"This," his new acquaintance said, sighing deeply, "is one hell of a mess. You're gonna need help. I'll be down in a coupl'a days. I've got a backhoe . . . might come in handy."

"Appreciate it. I feel like I could bawl like a baby."

"Small wonder."

🟆

281

The newborn ravine became a gully and the gully spread, eventually disappeared, and the uncounted tons of water gathered in the bowl of the valley where the illegal drag races happened. The area could have been prime farmland but had been ruined more than half a century before by the coal company, which had used it as a shipping yard, stockpiling coal and sending it by train down to the colliery wharf where it was loaded onto barges and into the bellies of ocean-going freighters for sale abroad. Year after year of traffic, of heavy equipment, of ton after ton of glittering number-one anthracite had altered forever what had originally been. Lucy's relatives said this had once been good deer pasture, before it was taken and misused.

The water spread out, filling the bowl, and there was no doubt which way it was going to go on its quest for the sea.

"There go the plans for the new airport," Colleen breathed. "She'll go right through the middle, then hook up with the river. Probably flood this end of the new golf course, too. There isn't room in the riverbed for that much extra water."

"Could be nice here if the water stays," Big Wil said. "Nobody wanted the damned airport here anyway. Actually, nobody wanted the damned airport period."

"Too cold for swimming," Dorrit said. "And too dirty!"

"The dirt will settle, Dorry. Tell you what. Once things settle down and we can get to town and all, we'll get us some nice goldfish and put them in here. Or maybe get some baby trout and bring them down."

"This is still *our* place, isn't it?"

"Oh, yeah," said Singe. "Your great-grandpa got hisself a reputation for being crazier 'n a coot when he bought this place. He had the idea he was going to haul all the slag heaps from around the house and dump 'em here."

"So it will be *our* lake?"

"Yep. Best get ourselves back, see what's shaking at the old place."

"See what's shaking?" Lucy groaned and pinched his cheek gently. "You stop it."

The police and emergency crews were at the house and busy with their radios and cellular phones, trying to explain to the authorities in town what had happened, just how extensive the damage was. Singe watched them for a moment, then went to sit beside Al and stare at the ravine. "Well, it's gonna be a while before we can get ourselves north," he said, yawning.

"At least there's a south." Brady sat next to him. "So what do we do, head south and check into a motel or something?"

"Good idea." Al started laughing, almost uncontrollably. "We'll go to the new one. I bet we can get a real deal on the rental."

Colleen couldn't get across the ravine to her place so she had no idea what things were like. The place looked okay, seemed to be on its foundations, and the section of porch that had come off the building could be easily enough replaced. But all her stuff was inside, and anyway, she wanted to check her house.

She rented a four-wheel-drive pickup and headed up the secondary road until she figured she was well past the workings, then she took a logging road and headed more or less northward on it. That road intersected with another, one she knew ran down to the highway— she'd been up here, marking trees. It was a mean road, but unless there were other cracks and fissures newly made by what the family was calling The Burp, she was sure she could make it. The rented pickup wasn't as trustworthy as the company-issued one, but only god in her mercy had any idea where that one was. It had been parked near the big old rusted vat or whatever it had been. Both were gone now, and no sign of either, just raw earth, freshly exposed gravel and lumps of coal the size of a small cow.

Two and a half miles from the intersection the clearcut began. Colly slowed the pickup and drove past the slash and mess. She hadn't heard word one of any plans to cut here. Not that the boss needed to check his every move with her; she had a rung or two up the corporate ladder to scale before that happened. But still, usually a person hears a thing or two. This had been fully mature second-growth, no culturally modified that she could remember, but she'd marked several eagle-nesting sites and had marked a section as being a marmot colony.

She might as well have stayed home those three days she'd spent here. Nothing was standing. Where the marmot colony had been, the ground was gouged and scarred, turned up and chewed by the tracks of a mammoth piece of equipment. She hoped at least some of the marmots had been able to save themselves, and wondered how many babies were buried dead in their dens. A mile and a half farther on the trees again flanked the roadway, but behind the screen of evergreens she could see the light and patches of sky and knew the shaving continued, hidden from public view. Anyone driving past would see a fraction of the show and think that was all that had been done. In reality the devastation was probably ten to fifteen times as big.

She was so angry and so insulted she felt sick to her stomach. Stubbornly, she continued along the road until she reached the highway. She turned right, to head back toward the family place, but just over the bridge the barriers were up, the orange lights blinking, the DETOUR signs huge. She followed the detour route for fifteen minutes and found herself back on the highway, headed north, back toward town. Two auxiliary cops stood beside their parked cruiser, ready to answer questions if any of the frustrated had any. Colleen stopped, got out, went over to talk to them, and at some point in the brief conversation she revealed she had come from the other, southern, side of the new ravine. One of the cops asked her how she'd managed to get across; she explained she had avoided it by using logging roads above the mine workings.

"I'll be going back that way, too," she added. "I only came over to see if there was any way I could get to my house."

They weren't interested in her house, but they were very interested in the possibility of a route south. They talked quickly to the voice on the other end of the police radio, then got in the cruiser and followed Colleen back the way she had come. The trip took longer because they kept stopping and tying bits of bright orange plastic ribbon-tape to tree branches and stumps.

She left them where the logging road intersected the secondary road. They were once again talking into their mike and didn't even wave when she tooted the horn and drove off again. She fully expected tomorrow's front-page story to tell her that diligent investigation by Constable Apple and Constable Plum had revealed an alternate route south and once minor repairs were made traffic would be directed rah rah lah de dah.

She was still livid when she got back to the motel. She looked up Singe and told him, then found Al and Jewen and bent their ears, too. They listened, they said all the right things, they understood her insult at how her work had been ignored, and they weren't the least bit surprised.

"It's like a ballet dance or something," Jewen said. "There's all these rules and regulations like big posts or pillars or whatever. Then there's the company and its suits, consultants, lawyers, you-name-'em. And it's their job to find a way to tippytoe in between, around and behind the posts and pillars. They fill out all the forms, say all the right things, and send off Xerox copies of your work. Somewhere else the same kind of yahoos look at it all, then stamp them, send copies back and file other copies, and move to the next big brown envelope and forget all about what they just did. A few months later, business as usual, and in go the crews. Nobody's gonna come and check. When you write the letter you're prob'ly gonna write, someone will read it and e-mail someone who will fax the minister's office and a bell will ring. Someone will fill out a pink slip or something, and if you don't do any more than that, the pink slip will gather dust. You keep on raising hell and someone who don't know what he's lookin' at will drive up to take a boo. Oh, he'll say, no sign of marmots or eagles and anyway there's been seventeen new trees planted. Then he'll go out for a big fancy dinner with the foreman or the office manager or such."

"Then why do they even bother to send me out?"

"There's a regulation says they should." He put his arm around her shoulder and hugged her. "Shoot, Colly . . . I'm sorry."

"I'm mad!"

She knew exactly what she was going to do, too. They'd pay. Through the nose, until it bled.

🌲

Singe and Lucy moved their kids back into Crazy Bob's place; the others continued staying at the new motel. They had several family meetings about the mess that had been the old house, trying to decide where to start the cleanup.

"I don't know as there was ever a law passed in heaven saying that was the only place we could build," Jewen insisted. "We been squatting in that one place all our lives. I think we'd be idiots to try to build there again, there's apt to be other shafts ready to collapse."

"Wondered about that," Singe said.

"Maybe we don't want to stay there," said Colleen as she took Singe's cigarette package from his shirt pocket, took a smoke, replaced the pack, then reached into her jeans pocket for her lighter. "Place might have boogers, now."

"Don't start," Singe warned.

"What kind of boogers?" Lucy demanded.

"Oh, shit," Singe sighed. "The old guys claimed there were gremlins and boggards and all the rest living in the old workings. They always said cave-ins and such were because the boogers got to looking for a way to get out of the darkness, bust through to the surface and move into people's houses."

"Well, one thing about it, wherever we decide to build, we got enough goddamn dead 'n' down to do it. All's we got to do is get it to the mill," said Al, sighing.

"Float it down Sudden River to Lancaster Lake," Chuck suggested. "Fish 'er out the lake, take 'er by way of the detour road. Or," he looked at Lucy questioningly, "take 'er from the lake by way of the old road, down to the bay and boom 'er up there, see if someone with a boat will tow it to the mill."

"Work work work, honest to christ, you guys are obsessive," she teased.

"Well, hell, we can't just live in woodsheds and leaky-roofed shacks," said Brady, pouring more coffee for everyone.

"Why not? The government made *us* do it for generations," Lucy answered, and nobody laughed; this, they knew, was no joke.

Despite the rubble and ruin, despite the problems and worries, the world went on about its business. School started up, and every morning the school bus stopped at the motel to pick up part of the tribe, then the others trooped on at the crossroads, where Lucy had driven them. She waved and honked her horn, waited for the bus to head off up the secondary road, then drove back to Crazy Bob's place to help Lottie and Darlene. There were lunches to cook, then cleanup, then time to start making supper. Grocery runs were organized, laundry had to be done, there were cakes to bake and pies to make and little kids to babysit.

Lucy's family came by way of back roads, skidder trails and logging roads to help with the salvage. Chainsaws roared, blue exhaust drifted, logs were piled in heaps according to length, and the equipment roared steadily, pushing an access road down to the new lake. From there it was easy to connect to the two roads that had already been built in preparation for the start of the new, unneeded and unwanted airport. By Remembrance Day the slag-covered access was ready, the trucks already taking the logs to the mill. Colleen moved back into her own place, and for a while Big Wil, Chuck and Little Wilma bunked in with her. The foundation had to be repaired on the new house the family had built for them, and they couldn't move back in until the structural engineering firm had finished checking the place.

As the logs were hauled away and the cleanup continued, with truckloads of firewood taken and sold, Colleen started her own project. She put on ear protectors and fed waste wood into the chipper, and when the pile was big enough, Al used the bucket to load one of the cousin's trucks. He drove the aromatic shavings and sawdust to whichever of the farmers had won the draw of the day. They used the freebie on the floors of their barns and stables and were grateful for the gift.

By Christmas the mess that had been the old place was gone, what could be salvaged was piled, and the rest either chipped, burned or hauled off to the dump. Big and Little Willy moved back into their own place with Chuck, who was off crutches and back at work again.

They had their Easter egg hunt at Singe and Lucy's place, then walked the now unfamiliar land. The bike track was gone; the log salvage crews had made significant progress in taking away the trees and logs, but Colleen knew she couldn't live long enough or have enough chippers to do anything much about the litter of branches and tops. She was feeling increasingly bummed out about the trash when she noticed new greenery showing from between the discoloured needles of the mess.

"Look," she said, pointing. "And over there, too . . ."

"Son of a gun," Jewen said, grinning widely. "Now if that isn't something!"

"I'm gonna take some pictures tomorrow," Darlene said excitedly. "Just think, we've got a chance to record the changes. I got some shots of the absolute mess just a few days after it happened, and I can pick a place and just keep coming back, getting pictures of the little trees coming up, growing . . . By the time Dorry's grown up this'll be beautiful . . ."

"So what do you think, we start clearing and levelling down at the lake?" Al asked.

"I'd just as rather we slap up a place down by us." Singe said.

"I'm staying where I am," Colleen said quickly.

"You'll go nuts over there by yourself," Darlene objected. "Hell, you have to drive three miles to get to the access road. Nobody'll be able to just drop in on you for a cuppa and a natter."

"I know," Colleen smiled, "but I can live with that. And I'll have the Willies to wave at across the river. Maybe we'll learn semaphore or something."

"Me, I like to have people around me." Darlene leaned against Tony, smiled up at him. "More the merrier, I say."

"We gonna be able to afford it?" Brady worried. "I got some money saved up, and you're welcome to it, of course, but . . ."

"Oh, hey, we're fine," Al said. "Look at the bright side of things for a change. Insurance companies are generous, don't you know."

"I didn't know you had insurance."

"Hell, yes," he lied. "See, it's always silver lining time."

"Yeah." Singe laughed heartily. "Norm won't be moving out here, he's scared he'll drop into a hole or something."

"Poor bloody Norm," Jewen agreed. "It ain't falling into a hole has him worried. He's scared stiff he might trip over some work if he comes out here."

🌴

Colleen came out of her house and moved to the four-wheel-drive crew-cab pickup. She walked past her little car, up on blocks and waiting for the highways department to finish the bridge. Until then the little piddlepot was out of commission: the access path the guys had pushed through to the spur road that linked with the logging road was too rough, too bumpy, too raw for the small car. The four-by had no trouble, although there were times when the rain was highballing on overtime that Colleen worried she was going to rattle some part of her own anatomy loose.

The ground was damp, the lingering winter chill touched her ears and nipped at her nose. She thought of it as the nagging time, this last sullen hanging on of the cold. Once the sun was up and doing her job, the chill would retreat, muttering and sneering, sending the occasional gust of cold wind, girding itself for the evening return. But there were crocus spears showing and the anemone leaves were already lacy, especially along the front of the house. The columbine was back, no flowers yet, but no need to be impatient.

Across the split the Willies' house was still dark; she imagined them snuggled warm in their beds, sleeping deeply, their dreams pleasant. Down the road Singe would be up, padding sock-foot, checking the kids, pulling covers in place before going down to switch on the coffee maker and sit at the table, having his first cancer stick, probably with a cat on his lap. He'd be at the house site when the others arrived; he'd tease them and call them slackers but there would be coffee waiting for them, and when the noise of the construction wakened Norm he'd waste as much time as he could before showing up, briefly, to slam a nail or two and then head off to work. Norm liked to appear as good as run off his feet with burdensome responsibilities. But really there wasn't much of that, when all he had to do was drive a truck from one address on his list to another, unloading boxes of cartons of eggs, a dozen dozen in each box. By lunchtime, if he was on the ball, the truck would be empty, and he could drive back to the yard, eat his lunch while the swampers refilled the truck. You'd think he was driving state secrets from one clandestine operation to another.

She started the truck, drove as slowly and as quietly as she could around the side of the house and down the challenge that was generously called Colly's driveway. Maybe one day it might be. Right now it was a horror. She missed the company of the terrier. But she

289

knew if she were a dog and had to choose between a house without kids and a house full of them, she'd have moved in with Singe and Lucy, too. After all, any good dog knows about priorities and duties. Maybe she'd go looking for one of her own. If she did she might not get a terrier, there were other kinds she might like just as well.

She stopped at what she considered to be her real job and slid a brown envelope through the slot. Helluva note when your mail winds up in a bombproof metal box instead of just landing on the floor, like in what Dorry called "them good old times."

Back in the truck she put on a Joe Cocker tape and drove the speed limit until she pulled in to the all-nighter and got a double latte in a paper cup with a plastic lid. She pulled the tab and sipped carefully as she got back in the pickup again and eased her way carefully onto the highway. Two miles farther she swung west and headed up toward the mountain.

She could have quit. She was so enraged she almost did. If she hadn't already had so much on her plate she probably would have driven in, invaded the boss's office and run off at the jaw. But by the time she cleared her decks and made the time to do it, she had thought things through several times and cancelled the idea. For the time being. A hiatus, so to speak.

Now she kept two sets of records—well, three if you count the Xerox copy: one for the company, one for herself, and a Xerox to Greenpeace. A bunch of volunteers doing what the government-paid bureaucracy couldn't pull together! While out spotting and marking environmentally sensitive areas and looking for nesting sites or culturally modified trees, she also watched for other things. Twice now she had found evidence the company was fudging, and twice she had used her camera to record the damage, then sent copies of the photos and the exact location to the tree-huggers. She could even tell them which map, sent which day, numbered such 'n' so. And each time the fat had hit the fire, the TV cameras were on site and turning before the government had time to pull up its pants and let the dog go back to her kennel. Both incidents were now, as the newspapers like to put it, before the courts. She wished she could let the marmots know, but she doubted they'd get any satisfaction from it.

Nothing looked the way it had for so many years. Sometimes, taken off-guard, perhaps because she'd been daydreaming or engrossed in what she was doing, Colleen would look up and for a few uncomfortable seconds she wouldn't know where she was. She could almost feel her brain give a lurch, much like changing gears on the garden tractor. In that brief flash of time it would seem as if she could see the way things had once been, overlaid on how they were now like a double exposure photo. But then things would steady-up and the feeling of dislocation would pass, she'd know she was still at home, however different home was now.

Singe and Lucy still lived in Bob's house, but it didn't look the same; after all when you're up to your eyebrows in building crews, what's another month of noise and seeming chaos? The inside was repaired, refurbished, refinished, and what the contractor called gentrified. The outside, like all the other places, was cedar board and batten, and the newly done roof was sheathed in blue painted metal with matching gutters running to brown downspouts. The place was level now with a proper driveway, and Lucy had planted several ornamental trees, flowering Japanese plum and cherry, catalpa and lireodendrum, and several good-sized magnolias. There were climber roses, too, and proper trellises for them to climb. The driveway followed parallel to the highway, leading from Singe and Lucy's place to where Norm lived with his new brood. He was as changeable and snarky as ever, but either Lindy didn't notice or she didn't care. The morning after Griffon was born, Jewen, Al and Singe presented Lindy with a legally drawn-up paper giving her rent-free occupation of the house for the next twenty years. Norm just about took a conniption. He figured if anybody got such a paper it should be him.

"It's for the boy," Singe said calmly. "Not takin' any chances of havin' him taken off to Surrey or some other damn hole just because you're pullin' stunts. If things go sour with you and Lindy, well, fine, can't do anything about that. But you'll be the one hittin' the pike, not her and the kids. Griffon belongs here with us."

"Jesus, how did I wind up with such a pack'a grouches for family?"

"Well, the way I heard it," Al said, "Mother had herself some good times with a short-ass midget."

"Dwarf, I heard," Singe corrected. "Not the seven hi-ho hi-ho guys, but maybe one'a their cousins."

"Yeah," Jewen nodded, "the hi-ho guys were off to work they go, and no sign there's been much'a that in the inheritance soup."

"Troll, more likely." Al frowned, as if concentrating on the problem. "Going by the disposition, I mean. Hope Griffon isn't like that. Snarly, I mean."

"And lazy," Jewen added.

"I ain't lazy!" Norm raged.

"Some might believe that, but not me."

"Just because you can't think of anything else to do with yourself but get dirty and sweat a lot, it doesn't mean we're all like that."

"Mouthy little turd, ain't he?" Jewen pretended to yawn. "If he could suck in as well as he blows out he could go from house to house doing the vacuuming."

"I don't think Big Wil would let him *in* the house, let alone let him open his gob."

Lindy's kids fit right in with the rest of the mob, and, somehow, that and the easy acceptance they got from the instant aunts and uncles made her feel more at home than she'd felt since she'd made the mistake of moving out of her mother's house. To show her appreciation she practically turned herself inside out to participate in and contribute to the family ventures and goings-on.

The new big house was built between Lindy's place and Big Wil's place, which were, of course, really Griffon's place and Little Wil's place.

"Need a demilitarized zone," Tony chuckled. "Damn Norm can't stop post-pissing."

"What's he done now?" Darlene yawned and snuggled closer.

"Went over there and went inside when they weren't home. Said he was just checking to be sure Little Willy had all the bedroom stuff she needed. Phoned 'em later and suggested they should get fire extinguishers in every room—worried about the kid's safety, he said."

"Charge him with trespass," she mumbled. "He'll keep it up if she doesn't."

"And if she does, he'll use it as an excuse to kick off a huge go-round," he said. "I'm glad you don't get into stuff like that," he added, apparently willing to either forget, overlook or revise the set-to's Darlene kicked off with Colleen at least once, usually twice, a week.

They had the entire second floor of the big house to themselves, and in Dorrit's bedroom was what looked like a pirate's treasure chest Tony had built to hold toys. The third bedroom, complete with a brand new crib, was already set up and waiting for the baby, due in the early summer. Tony fussed over Dar, doing his best to reassure her but the memory of their first, lost baby haunted them both. Dar seemed as healthy as a proven white-faced cow but she'd seemed like that before, right up until the helicopters started coming out of the sky.

Jewen, Tommy and Al had rooms on the top floor, with Jess and Brady in the ground floor bedrooms. But if things between Al and Glenda continued the way they'd been going there were going to have to be changes made, probably an addition to the back of the house. Jewen could pretty much picture it in his mind: move Glenda's boys into what right now was Al's room, and put Al and Glennie into the new part, build it big enough there was a room for Caroline and with luck a couple of rooms for Lottie, too, although each time the subject was broached, Lottie said she already spent more time than was good for her mental health surrounded by "those Lancasters." "I'd sooner move into a left-over bomb shelter," she pretended to grumble. "I know what you're up to and it won't work. I'm not being grandma to this army of uncontrollable heathens."

But she'd been renting all her life, and the closest she'd come to being attached to a place was here, especially since she'd been involved and included in the planning of the new big house. It was her idea to have a built-in vacuum system.

"No more changing the bloody bags," she said, "just poke in the hose jigger and blow it outside so all these feet can track it back in again."

"Blow it outside? That's not how they work . . ." Colleen smothered her grin, not sure if Lottie was joking or not.

"Huh? They don't?"

"No, there's this . . . like a chimney thing . . . or a pipe effort goes through the walls, kind of like heating ducts, only different . . . and it ends at a thing like a cannister . . . a central cannister."

"And you have to empty it?"

"Yeah. Maybe not as often as changing a bag, but, yeah, you have to empty it."

"That's dumb. Why don't they just send it out the wall, like the vent on a clothes dryer?" Lottie paused, frowning, "Maybe I should write to them, and suggest they do it my way. Just . . . blow it away . . ."

"Might work real well out here but I don't think the townies in the suburbs and such would particularly appreciate it. There's more than dust gets picked up . . . gum wrappers and . . . and what about the cigarette butts and . . . you think they'd like their lawns two-inches thick with dust buggers?"

"If they hate the emptying the bag part as much as I do they'd be fine about it. Besides, the rain'd wash it away."

And then they were both laughing, hip-bumping each other, giving little pushes and shoves that were almost like cuddles. "Some of your ideas," she said.

"I've got good ideas," Lottie answered easily. "I could be a real idea person, if I wanted."

The kitchen was her design, as well. "As plain as plain can be," she asked. "All those pretty little whirls, whorls, carved-in ivy designs and stuff are just places for dust and dirt to build up, and I've got better things to do with my life than go around with those little ear-cleaner thingies trying to keep the germs at bay."

So, plain it was, but of the finest material available. And sometimes, with a bit of time to call her own, she would sit with a cup of tea and just look at the way things were laid out—the gleaming wood, the butcher's block countertops, the built-on knife rack—and she would yearn and then argue with herself. What difference did it make if she *owned* it or not? She was here all day Monday to Friday, and everyone called it "Lottie's kitchen." And so what if she *was* renting space in what used to be a side-of-the-highway motel that had been converted to long-term rental units? She was only there to sleep anyway, and to have a few hours to herself. She had cherished those few hours of peace and quiet for quite a few years but lately, what with all the changes and all, and watching the builders putting things back together, and seeing her kitchen ideas being incorporated into other kitchens and the hustle and bustle, and Glennie coming in every day to help—the kids getting off the school bus with the rest of the pack and whipping around as if they, too, were full-timers here—there was a tug she couldn't describe when she left, and the time to herself began to seem more like exile than solitude.

That crazy coot of Glennie's had only showed up the one time, and all's he'd done was take one look at how everybody quietly moved together, a whack of scattered people becoming a bunch without a word being spoken, and he didn't even so much as get out of the damn car, he just drove off looking as if someone had put razor blades in his beer and he was trying to pee 'em out. Not the nicest guy in the world, god knows why Glennie hadn't seen through him, but there you have it. No explaining things like that. Probably it would turn out to be some kind of inherited weakness, god knows Lottie hadn't made the best choice in the world, although nobody outside the bedroom knew about it. And it wasn't his fault if he wasn't an ambitious man, not in the way people meant when they talked about getting ahead and going up in the world. How many people in this day and age get a job and keep it right up until the day they drop dead doing it? He never complained about being underpaid or not having enough holidays or being worked too hard, he just got up and got dressed, ate the breakfast she made for him, picked up his lunch bucket and extra thermos, kissed her on the cheek and always, invariably said, "Good breakfast, Lottie, you're a wonder. See you later." There was only that one day he hadn't come back from work looking reamed out, dirty and as tired as an old work horse. Instead of him, it was his foreman, standing in the doorway, looking like he'd give both balls to be anywhere else, and she knew before he opened his mouth. The surprise was that it hadn't been an accident. She'd expected some kind of accident for years. Seeing a man head off into the bush was like seeing him put on his army boots and head into combat. She remembered the foreman's words: "Sitting with the rest of us eating his grub and drinking his coffee, and then he fell over. Just kinda leaned sideways, Lottie, and . . . first aid man couldn't do a thing for him."

Nobody else knew about the stupid things he did, spending money as if they actually had buckets of it, and never anything much to show for it either. Even she didn't know where it went. Sometimes she'd wondered if he had another woman set up somewhere, except he wouldn't have ever seen her: he came home from work, had a bath, had supper and then watched TV, reading his newspaper during the commercials. Oh, there was the top-of-the-line set of encyclopedias for the kids, a five-day wonder: they'd pored over it at first, then lost interest and it was just something else to dust. Bikes, again top of the line, as if they were doctors' kids instead of being who they were. More damned power tools than you could shake a stick at, and whenever she asked what he intended to do with them he'd talk about how one day he'd be building them a house with those tools. And trips to the movies, with enough popcorn to sink a battleship, then off to the fish 'n' chips shop, as if she couldn't make them herself for a fraction of the cost.

And no good in bed. She didn't talk to him about it, and sure as hell didn't talk to anyone else about it, but to herself she would think of wry little non-jokes like, You could count the number of kids she had and know how many times he'd got it up.

Not the best choice, but far from the kind of worst choice Glenda had made. Maybe it was the outward difference, the big I-Am forever talking about this or that plan to improve his situation in life: Build and open his own garage, do car repairs at night after work. Build his own prawn boat, get a licence and head out to haul 'em in by the ton. The big I-Am, and he didn't do any of it, not only didn't make any extra money but took the money he did make and gambled with it, as if anybody with brains would ever believe a person could win their way to riches. And a temper on him like nobody would believe. Well, no way Glennie could have known about that, he'd kept it well hidden. Even Lottie didn't know what a vicious son of a bun he was until the first time they were at the emergency ward with a kid with a broken arm. The story just didn't fit. Nothing a person could prove, but only a moron ignores that gut feeling. The kids had the most godawful kinds of accidents and always when Glennie was busy somewhere else in the house.

But all the plans, the gonna-save-up-and-get-started-on-dreams, had sounded like ambition, sounded like someone who was on his way in the world. Well, there you had it, sounded-like wasn't the same as for-sure.

No wonder the kids came off the school bus grinning and screeching. There were swats handed out here, cracks on the backside to get them moving or straighten them up, but nothing that left a mark, no bruises or welts or lumps, no sprains or strains or fractures. Mr. Tony, no kin to any of them, and he'd grab one of them up and set him on top of the tool shed roof, then stand, arms out, ready to catch when the kid jumped. And Mr. Al, never an easy person to figure out or be around, but he was good to them, steady and unchanging: just be good, behave yourself and don't step out of line, and everything's hunky-dory.

Make a body wonder, the whole thing of it. Except she was through wondering about anything. Maybe the drunks had the right idea: one day at a time.

🐀

Brady's favourite part of the new place was the living room. She figured it was so big you could probably fit a bungalow inside and still have room to swing the longest-tailed cat you could find.

The front wall was mostly windows, with a door opening to a wide, roofed porch. The other outside-facing wall was where the high efficiency gas fireplace was fitted. It was nice, in the evenings, to sit and watch the flickering of the slightly hissing blue flames. Sometimes, some precious times, she'd sit in the big chair with Jess sitting on the floor between her legs. Brady used a wooden-backed boar bristle brush and the hair style experiments both entertained and regaled them. Hair brushed to a sheen, it was fingernail time and, lately, paint-your-toenails time as well. They whispered secrets to each other, they teased each other, sometimes they both crammed into the chair and simply snuggled, watching TV. Brady often felt sorry for Maude, missing out on all of this with Jess and probably no chance of anything like it with Mavis, poor odd thing that she was. None of them wanted to compare that poor blighted little thing with Cat, but a person couldn't help it really, especially with them born on the same day. Cat was toddling around, babbling and chattering, busy busy busy, learning this, trying that, impatient to catch up to the older kids. Mavis could sit if propped by pillows and still took most of her nourishment from a bottle and nipple.

God, the awful stuff people do to their kids even before they're born! And the government raking in taxes hand over fist, leaving the debt to be paid by someone else, selling the future as if it didn't matter.

Sometimes Mavis would seem to be aware of what was happening around her. Often Jess either wore a particular red shirt or took it with her when she went for her once-a-month weekend with Maude.

"She watches it sometimes," Jess confided to Brady. "I think it's just the bright colour. I don't think she recognizes me or anything. I don't think she even really recognizes Mom and Brew. She liked her birthday sparklers, too, but not for long." Nothing seemed to get through to Mavis for very long. "It's like she's got some kind of, I don't know, TV programme or light show or something going on in her head, and it's more fun than what's really happening. Sometimes I look at her and I think it's not right how hard everyone is working to keep her alive. Like it's some kind of crusade for them, or a way they can prove something. She doesn't even know when she's hungry! Lots of times she won't even suck and they have to hook her up to that pump jigger that goes right into her stomach. I'm not saying anyone should *kill* her, but maybe they should stop fighting so hard to keep her alive. It's not like she's going to wake up tomorrow all fixed, you know!"

Brady knew it. She also knew Maude didn't want to believe what they had was all they were ever going to get. She clutched desperately for any hint of improvement and refused to see there wasn't any; in fact, if anything, Mavis was quite simply fading away.

Tom flat-out didn't care. He seemed quite uninterested in Mavis and Brew and barely interested in his mother. He was getting good grades in school, he and Jess spent hours together playing music and, at least most of the time, he was right there to lend a hand where another one was needed. He played soccer on the school team but shrugged off basketball and rugby, claiming they were what he called "no brainers." He knew things were developing between Al and Glenda but acted as if none of it had anything to do with him anymore than the Maude-Mavis-Brew arrangement did. He was so detached from the lives of his parents he had no answer when Colleen asked him how he felt about Al and Glennie. He could only shrug and look blank. Brady wondered if they should take him to a shrink, but Colleen shook her head. "He had to learn to live without Al when he got sent off to the clink, and Maude's hardly been in her own life let alone his for years. Tommy learned who his real family was: it's the rest'a the kids. No wonder he doesn't give a hoot what Al and Maude do with their lives! They been living with not much thought for the kids for a long time, and if they didn't give a toot then, why should he now?"

"Why that's not true! Al's crazy about his kids!" Brady argued.

"*Now*, maybe. Now. After he was kept away from them for so long, but before that? For a long time all he gave them was money, so they learned to find what they needed from each other."

"Well, how could Al know how to be a parent when we hardly had any our own selves?" Brady defended.

"Well, there you have it then," Colleen said, grinning easily. "Tommy'll be fine, you'll see."

Brady almost snapped at Colleen and asked her what she had in mind to do if it turned out she was wrong, but she didn't want to tangle with anyone, least of all Colleen. The only one more bloody-minded was the Colonel, and she, thank god for miracles, was busy standing on guard for thee, and thee, and even the rest of thee.

🛦

One good thing, though: The Colonel was able to pull a few strings, call in a few favours and find out where good old Whozit had got himself to when he fled the scene. Some people just *had* to turn life into a soap opera, they just *had* to complicate things. Bad enough to be an undercover narc, but to turn around and go so deep under-cover even the local cops knew nothing was a bit much. Destroying the garden while digging for possible bones and other remains! Couldn't just say well, haven't found a thing here, guess I'll go snoop somewheres else. Oh no, he had to pretend to get drunker 'n' a skunk, then pull a Houdini-whodunnit and vanish, car and all, leav-ing other people to worry and fret. And replant their gardens, don't forget that part of it. Wheels within wheels were one thing, but this other, this being so secretive even the guys you're supposed to be working with know nothing—well, that came close to fanatic or obsessive or something. As if the guy was a good spook! The ones he'd been supposed to fool hadn't been fooled and the ones he man-aged to fool had nothing to hide anyway. It didn't, as some said, bode well. They'd be picking up a paper one day and reading about a body being found, hands and feet bound, a bullet in the head. Bodies found like that were a message. If all they wanted was to get rid of someone, they either dropped them where they stood or made sure the bodies were never found. The "execution-style" corpses were how the ones not in uniform told the ones with uniforms that they were not in any way as smart as they thought they were.

Mind you, some of those in uniform were so good nobody would believe it if told. The Colonel, Doreen, for example. Fifteen years and not so much as a hint of what she was doing. For more than ten years, Brady thought Doreen simply worked as a clerk typist, or something. But then Doreen showed up, on holiday she said, to visit with her baby sister, and nobody who spent hours typing at a com-puter console could be in such excellent physical condition. She looked and moved like a dancer and, when Brady hugged her, felt like a middleweight boxer. Brady knew about middleweight boxers, she'd hung out with one for more than two years. And what a shame *that* was: the guy had been bopped on the head so often and so hard that from hip bones to knees he might as well have been a nun, couldn't even get it up let alone *do* anything with it. But he'd been champeen. Had the belts to prove it and everything.

Brady hadn't known Doreen was coming, and she was booked as

warm-up to the headline act so there was no way she could take any time off without as good as ending her career, such as it was and would be. You don't get booking like that often, and if you pull out for any reason at all you probably won't get it again, especially when you're not as young as you once were and getting older with each beat of your heart. But Doreen didn't mind one bit. She was in the club every night, dressed, if not to the nines at least to the sevens, and she fit in as if she'd grown up in the place. She smilingly avoided any kind of personal or sexual involvement with any of the guys so obviously willing to put the tap on her. What she did, instead, was get very friendly with one of the honeys the boss kept on the side. If Boomer knew about it he didn't seem to care, although any man who had moved in on what the Boom saw as his property would have been turned to mush. That's how Boomer got his name. Whether it was a personal or professional hit his preferred method was to handcuff the soon-to-be-angel to the steering wheel, then blow the car, occupant included, sky-high.

The month-long vacation was great, so much so that Brady could hardly believe this was Doreen, the eldest sister and certified pain-in-the-arse who had, thanks be to god, left as soon as she was old enough to find the door to the recruiting office. Brady was so embarrassed by her sister's choice of job she had never mentioned to anyone that her sister had joined the air force. For a long time Brady had thought the only thing that could have been worse was if Dor had joined the Mounties!

Boomer disappeared. Just up and gone. Not a trace. His wife said he hadn't come home from work, and his several honeys each and all said he hadn't visited them. The security cameras showed him getting into his Jag and driving away; the Jag didn't show up, either. One by one the Boom's most trusted men found the same Bermuda Triangle. Even the out-of-town boys started to vanish. And then, nobody knew who or how, the casino was hit where it hurt. The security system didn't work, the cameras quit, the alarms were silent, the guards were found tied hand and foot with good old 3-M duct tape across their eyes, ears and mouths. And the money was gone. More mystery.

Then, in an obvious twist on the "execution style" body-in-the-street tradition, the Boom reappeared. His Jag was parked practically in the main doorway, and the Boom was lying on the front seat, handcuffed to the steering wheel. His fingertips had been flayed, no prints to compare. His teeth had been pulled, dental records useless even if available. But his face was unmarked, and printed on his chest in black magic marker was "Boom."

None of the others turned up, the money stayed gone, and even the upper echelons looked pasty-faced and worried. Brady didn't have to worry. She was a dancer, and she danced. She wasn't involved in any of the real stuff. Oh, there were bonuses and gifts, the occasional reward for keeping the old adage true—a fool and his money are soon parted—but even if she'd told every damned thing she knew it still wouldn't have been anything you couldn't find in the gossip columns. Still, like everyone else, she wondered who-what-how. The rumour mill turned out some fantastic stories about mob rivalry, tales of generational vendetta, even a movie made based on one of the theories. The new boss, Gino, rented the theatre for a special after-hours showing, and the employers and employees sat with tubs of buttered popcorn and howled with laughter. The dialogue was so bad, the delivery so terrible, that for days afterward they made jokes about it.

She had been lying beside the pool, comfortable on the long lawn chair, sipping a tall glass of cranberry juice over crushed ice, and—poof—just like that, she had a flash, like a photo, of Doreen, with a glass of the same, chatting companionably with Boomer as if he didn't know, as if she didn't know he had cameras recording every kiss, every dive, every joyous come.

And those tapes vanished when the Boom did, the only thing to go bye-bye except the Jag, and most people didn't even know they existed anyway. Brady knew about them because the Boom had invited her into his office and then shown her a few minutes' worth. "Just so's you know who and what your big sis really is," he said, smirking. "Hot stuff, huh?"

"Good god!" she gasped as she gaped.

"So what I was wondering was . . . do you play games like that, too?"

"Me? God, Boom, you know me. When we were a thing you told me I was vanilla ice cream."

"If you'd'a been as kinky as your sister, beauty, we'd *still* be a thing."

"Yeah, but . . . there's only *one* in every family, right? And it's not me."

Too cute. Everything about it, too cute. Well, you don't fink. You especially don't fink on family.

She took a week off, got a plane ticket to Ottawa, and once there made a phone call to the number Doreen had said was her pager number. Hey, sis, how ya doin'? I'm in town, gimme your address and I'll catch a cab.

The apartment looked lived in: there were some family photos in all the right places, food in the fridge and cupboards, clothes in the dressers and closets, probably it was where Dory slept and stayed. The reception Brady got was friendly, smiling, warm and welcoming. But leopards don't change their spots and Doreen really wasn't any of those things. Not really.

They went to a spaghetti house for supper, had a couple of beer, went back to Dory's place, and when Dory asked, "So how's things in fantasyland?" Brady told her. The facial expressions were right; it was what happened to the eyes told at least some part of the tale.

"And I think it's you," Brady finished.

"You think so? What are you going to do about it?"

"Nothing I can do." Brady smiled and knew it looked more like a grimace of pain. "I'm not a fink."

"I'm not either," Dory announced calmly. "But I'm good at my job and I do it."

"How do you sleep at night!"

"I sleep really well, Brade. I've never—not one single time— reported anything any member of the family's been involved in. And I won't. I'll quit, first. But anybody *not* family is"—her smile was wide and probably sincere—"up for grabs."

"You used me!"

"Nah, you know better."

They'd talked a bit more, not much, then went to bed. Brady intended to go back on the first possible flight, but somehow she put it off, then put it off again, and they'd actually had a not-bad week. It was thinking about it afterward, free of Dor's charm, that ticked Brady off all over again. Yeah, she'd been used. Maybe all she'd done was open a door, but even so it was a door she wouldn't have opened for anyone else.

Slick, some of those freaks in uniform. Real slick. Too slick for her to believe Old Greg had even the ghost of a chance of making it as one of them.

And no, she hadn't said a thing to any of the rest of the family. Not even them! You don't fink. You especially don't fink on family. And Dory was that, no doubt about it. No doubt as well that you could love a person and not like her one little bit.

She liked Jess, though. And liked the way Jess went her own way without pushing aside any of the other kids, without rejecting the person because of the behaviour. The kid even managed to be pleasant to bloody Norm! Had to have angel blood in her veins to pull that one off, Norm being who and how he insisted on being.

And his girlfriend; wasn't that a horse of a different garage? The same no matter what mood the owly spawn was in. You'd almost think she didn't have sense enough to know sulk from smile, but there wasn't much she didn't see. Sometimes she looked a bit like trailer trash, all that hair frizzed up and frowzed around, like a huge cotton candy fluff. The colour stayed the same so it probably wasn't out of a bottle, and she hadn't gone to the hair salon for recurling so that was probably hers, too. There was just so damn much of it. Now if she'd just do a few things, nothing drastic, that mop could look absolutely great. It wouldn't take much, and Brady could show her, but you can't just walk up to someone and say hey, gimme a chance to tame that mop, okay? That'd be a sure way to get your eyes clawed out and your nose ripped off your face.

✿

Lindy felt like the second-luckiest person in the world, and she couldn't have told you where to find the first luckiest. The house was the answer to most of her prayers of the past five years, and if Norm wasn't the easiest person to live with, well, so what? It wasn't always easy to live with a pack of kids, especially if only one of them was yours. She knew her kids were real going concerns, too much energy if the truth be known. And if they were, by and large, as good as could be expected, still in all, they were noisy. To some people, and no fault of theirs really, the shrill laughter and shrieks of glee were noise, same as any other. Norm was one of those people who needed peace and quiet. Well, small wonder, there he was eight hours a day in a noisy truck, stuck in traffic—and god, wasn't traffic a pain in the face almost any hour of the day, cars coming from the left, from the right, from behind and in front, horns honking, traffic rules fudged. And then one by one, from store to store, how many dozen, fill out the invoice and people yapping the whole time. No wonder he couldn't stand the noise of the kids in the living room. Well, at least there was room in the house; she could put the old TV in the downstairs activity room, and the kids could go there to watch their programmes. She'd rather have them in the living room, snuggling on the couch with her, like in the before-times, but Norm took up the entire sofa, and anyway, they were better off on their own rather than having him ride their butts to be quiet.

The new house was a wonder. Norm was still ticked off about no stained glass or cathedral entrance, but that was his trip, not hers. The big basement, built from the ground up, no excavation because of the rain and the groundwater and all, and built extra high, a good twelve feet, had room and to spare for kids on rainy days, even room for bouncing balls or nerf hockey pucks. They could go there and not rough-house in their bedrooms, so there was even a chance of keeping the bedrooms clean and tidy. Not much chance but a chance all the same.

And okay, so it wasn't *her* house. It was very clearly Griffon's house, but what a load was off her shoulders. Those grinning hill-billies with their carefully worded paper from the lawyer, handing it to her and talking about how Griff was the image of his grandma and thus like Jewen, who they said was so much like his mom they'd almost renamed him. Hearing that, even before she read the paper, which was really only a glorified lease, filled a part of the hole in her belly.

There was nobody to blame for the way things were. God knows, everyone around her had done their best. She'd had three foster families before she turned seven, but there are millions of reasons for that and nobody can blame people who, after five or ten or a dozen years, decide to cancel their contracts and have their home to themselves for a change. Just after her eighth birthday they moved her to Bonnie's place. The house was small and old, built by Bonnie's grandparents and left to her when they moved into an apartment next to the one where their daughter and son-in-law lived. It should have been like suddenly acquiring an entire family, but something in her refused to click. She wanted it to click, she even tried to make it click, but the feeling of *otherness* persisted and she continued to expect them to tell her to pack her stuff, to get moving again. She was twelve before she could refer to Bonnie as her mom and fifteen before she could say it without expecting someone to yell, "What a *lie*!"

Bonnie's grandparents were gone by then, first him, then her, and Bonnie's mother wanted her to sell the house and move into the apartment because she could see she was going to need help with her husband, who Bonnie called the old fart. Her mother said he had Alzheimer's. Bonnie said Alzheimer's was the *early* onset of senility and all that was wrong with him was he'd pickled his brain with vodka. "He'd still be sloshing it away by the quart if he could remember where he'd hidden the bottle," she said calmly. "Put him in extended care, he's too much for you. You've stuck by him better than he ever stuck by you. I don't know what you're trying to prove, but it's silly."

"You'd put your own father in one of *those* places?"

"We aren't talking about a leaky basement or a snake pit in Bedlam. The places are very nice, and he'll get full-time professional care. Best of all, when he goes into one of his terrible-two's temper tantrums they'll be able to restrain him before he gives you another black eye. Or worse."

Bonnie held firm. Her mother held just as firm until the old fart's slapping and swatting started to be a full-time behaviour pattern. He wound up in a four-man ward with some of his old poker-playing drinking buddies, and none of them knew an ace from a ten. They nattered and quarrelled with each other like pre-schoolers, and each one of them wept stormily and easily with each frustration.

Lindy told Bonnie she wanted a baby, and Bonnie suggested she wait a while: fifteen was a bit young, her body wasn't really ready. "Besides, you have to be able to support yourself and your kids, and you can't do that without an education and some kind of what they call employable skill."

Lindy waited until she finished grade twelve, graduated and had a job before she made her moves.

What she felt when she had her baby was so intense, so full, and warm and overwhelming, she knew she'd done the right thing. Finally, she had a full and real family. There was still that lump of—whatever—but it was reduced to something no bigger than a pigeon egg.

When she finally understood the legalese on the paper, the pigeon egg shrank. There was still a little hummingbird-egg-sized remnant, but maybe everyone felt that way. Bonnie had told her often enough that she wasn't really all that different from anyone else when it came to needing to belong. She couldn't have even begun to explain any part of it. All she knew was Griff's family had provided her and the other kids with a place and with people. When they so fully and happily enfolded Griffon in their family, they included the other kids. Even Norm suggested that, if she wanted, she could give all the kids the family name. Lindy thought she'd wait on that one. She had a name. She didn't know who had given it to her or what they were like or how they looked or if they had the same kind of hair she had, but it was a name and it would do. For all the difference it made, anyway.

She had her kids, and now they had a place. No way anyone was going to raise the rent or refuse to fix the leak in the roof or think because she was obviously unattached she'd be desperate enough for sex or companionship or rent reduction that she'd welcome or at least put up with their insistent advances. Odd, and more than odd, how they acted like informed judges at an animal show, grading beef, or ham or something—boy, she's a looker; hey, that one's an eight at least; look at the buns on her—and seemed convinced not only that they could hustle whoever they wanted but that somehow they had the god-given right to do so. And that right extended itself to sex, practically on demand. There they were, big beer belly by the time they were twenty-four, going bald by thirty, unacquainted with deodorant, teeth rapidly going the way of the hair, convinced they could pick and choose, dreaming of and fantasizing about getting it on with Miss Canada, as if they were Brad Pitt or Keefer Sutherland, attractive and desirable. Even Norm at times, although not as bad as most, and less all the time. Jewen, now, he wasn't the least little bit like that; he treated her the same as he treated Colly or Brady or even Glenda; friendly, funny, teasing, but never that undercurrent of sexual tension. When Jewen reached his hand toward you it was to take the cup of coffee and say, "Thank you very much." When he smiled it was because he meant it, not because he thought it would help get him some bounce-and-sweat.

She knew Norm had a wandering eye and a greased-lightning zipper, knew it even before she first lay down with him. But she'd seen Little Wil with her mom in the shoe store, and there was the hair, like her own at the same age except for the colour.

Jewen had that hair, too. Well, he was losing a bit at front, but he'd got his teeth fixed, and there wasn't even a hint of a beer gut. He wasn't as packed on as Singe, who would probably be buried flat-bellied and massed with muscles; and Jewen wasn't anywhere near built like Al, who had spent years doing time in the weight room, but there weren't many, regardless of age, who were as neatly put together.

When they'd handed her that piece of paper, she hadn't been able to say much more than thank you, and she would probably never be able to explain or describe the relief she felt. Being courted and wooed by Norm was exciting; he turned his full attention on her: he was attentive, listened to her, agreed with her and told her all the things anybody wanted to hear. When they'd moved into the new house, he had renewed his attentions; sometimes she wondered if he wasn't doing it just to show his brothers how much more he knew about women than they did. His sullenness toward her evaporated as soon as any of the others were around or even in sight. She knew there were a lot of men couldn't be comfortable around or easy with a pregnant woman, and the bigger she'd become the less interested and more surly he became, not only where sex was concerned either, but her opinions, feelings, emotions, her very presence seemed to put him off, and she figured if he'd been like that with Little Wil it was no wonder Big Wil had made sure she didn't get pregnant again. By the time Griff was actually, physically coming between her and the rest of the world, Norm could barely bring himself to talk at the meal table. If it hadn't been for "pass the salt" he might have gone mute. She was half-planning to pack up the kids and take a hike, and then Griff arrived and the family—almost hers, now—very quietly and unmistakably gave her their full and open support.

Norm was practically mesatchie about it at the time and was still madder than a wet hen. She could, those times she was feeling particularly mellow, almost understand his anger, but those soft and easy laid-back times were fewer and farther between the more Norm grumbled and bitched. She was pretty sure he had his eye on someone else—for all she knew he might already be stepping out—but she had no proof, wasn't sure, and didn't care enough one way or the other to go to the time and trouble of trying to find out for sure. He could nag and carp all he wanted, she wasn't going to get into it with him. Or with anyone. Life was too short for that. She had Griff, although he'd come without the hair she'd been hoping he'd have. Maybe the next one would have a wild frizz. Griff was so great in so many ways she'd be quite willing to have Norm be the father of the next one. She halfways doubted he'd be in the picture by then, though; he was past merely shirty, he was all the way to owly and aimed in the direction of rank. He was trying to pick fights, and when that didn't work he'd find some threadbare excuse to leave and not come back for hours. He, who only had to saunter to the nearby creek to catch good-sized, delicious trout, was suddenly moved by the urgent need to take entire weekends to head elsewhere in pursuit of fish he didn't catch.

Well, that was fine. No skin off her nose. She wasn't interested in sloppy seconds, thank you. And him taking off sure didn't leave her on her ownsome and lonesome, not with all these other people around, all of them willing to visit, chat, invite her and the kids along for this or that noisy entertainment, a game of scrub ball in the back clearing, a trip to the oyster plant for a half-dozen quarts of the best. Even Lottie was there: here I made pies, hope you like these, it's first rhubarb or it's last year's peaches we jarred up. Or here we go, we froze gallons of blackberries and might as well enjoy them before it's time to go picking more gallons. Here love, a couple of loaves of fresh bread, I know the kids love it.

When Bonnie came over to see Griff, the whole pack of them practically did handstands to ensure she had a good time. There they were, busy as one-armed paper hangers, cleaning up the mess from the big belch, construction going on all over the place, the new big house about halfways done, and didn't they just swing into gear and it was venison here, prawns there, and a huge oyster-extravaganza. They showed more sights than a person could absorb, and Jewen put an arm around Bonnie and squeezed gently. "When you got here I thought you were lucky to have a daughter like Lindy. Now I know she's lucky to have a mom like you. I'm real glad to have met you."

"Me, too," Singe agreed. "Anytime you want to move in, just say the word, we'll slap together a shack for you."

Bonnie wasn't ready to make the move, yet; she had her mother to think of and look after and she'd do that, willingly and happily, for however long it took. But Lindy knew there'd be visits, holidays, time together, lots of time together.

"You need new glasses, darling," Bonnie told her. "I know Norm is Griff's daddy, but instead of aiming for him you should have aimed at that good-looking brother of his. The nice one."

"I didn't see him until after it had started with Norm, and I didn't even get to really start to know him until we'd moved into the new house."

"Too bad. I can't understand how a man like that hasn't been snapped up long ago."

"Well, he's had some problems. He used to drink, from what I hear. Drink real bad. But I've never seen him take more than a few beer when everyone else is having a few. People, well, not all of them, but some people have some pretty harsh opinions about this family. They don't call them 'the Lancasters', they call them 'those Lancasters'. I guess they've been pretty wild and woolly."

"So? I don't see much wild wool now. Seem like a pretty much settled-down bunch."

Sometimes, when Norm was being sexy, Lindy wouldn't be able to stop herself from thinking of Jewen, wondering if he was an acrobat like Norm, or if with him things would be gentle and tender. Other nights, she awoke all warm and cuddly because of dreams she'd been having. God, wasn't life something? Seemed as if you just never knew what would be next.

Lottie knew she looked smug and she didn't care. That's fine, it's how she felt. No mother ever wants to see her daughter go through the pain and dislocation of a breakup. But when you've seen marks on skinny arms and legs and you know your grandchildren are being mistreated, when you've seen your own flesh and blood moving between a kid and a grown man and intervene almost desperately to ward off an explosion, when your daughter has a huge bruise on her arm and a leaky story about losing her balance and lurching into the door frame—she who was born with the grace and agility of a well-fed cat—you don't mind one little bit putting the boots to the situation.

Just a bit, at first: Mister Al, this is my daughter Glenda, come over to give a hand here with the cleanup. Glennie, could you take that platter of sammiches out to those men and tell them I'm on my way with the coffee pot? Next thing you know it's Mr. Al yelling, Hey, Glennie, can we sweet-talk you into a pot of tea out here? And Glennie, well, talk about a well-watered plant blossoming and wasn't it Al darlin' this and sweetheart that and the two of them walking hand in hand like moonstruck kids. Hey, tiger, Al called, go see if Tommy can give you a hand with them dangly shoelaces before you fall and break something. What's that, hon? Well, I don't know about that, you go run ask your mommy if you can deliver a load of crushrock with me.

She hadn't moved in, yet, but so what? If she felt odd about it, she felt odd about it, and whose business was that? "It's too much like inviting the whole lot of them in to watch us," she cried, red-faced and almost weeping. "I mean, well, you know what I mean."

"What about the moron?"

"That's another reason. He's *nuts*!"

"Well, we've known that for ages. It was you we were waiting on to wake up and smell the coffee."

"Now, Momma . . ."

"I mean it. Bruises on the kids. Especially little Fred. Why he picked on Freddie, I'm sure I don't know. On any of them, for that matter."

"I didn't know he'd be so totally berserk. He phones at all hours of the night, and then gives me these lectures, till death do us part, he says, and then he says *he* won't be the first to die. I come home and there's a note on the kitchen table with some dumb message like 'Don't work too hard, love . . .' I changed all the locks and it made no difference. Right in the middle of my *bed* I find a card, one of those To My Sweetheart ones with a big poem inside. Nuts, I mean it!"

"Call the cops."

"I can't. He'll go totally insane! The cops can't spend twenty-four hours a day sitting in front of my place and he can . . . and will."

Glenda and the kids got out of Lottie's car and stood waving as she drove away. "Come on." Glenda turned to the house. "Bath and bed."

"I'm too tired for a bath."

"Okay, but be sure to wash your feet. I don't want sand and dirt all over the sheets."

"My feet are clean."

"In a pig's eye they are, and don't forget your teeth."

"I rode the French bike." Caroline sighed contentedly. "Tommy rode with me until I was ready to try it myself."

"Tommy rode with you every time."

"He didn't do steering every time."

"He was on the rat trap the whole time."

"But I did the steering."

"I had rides, too," said Freddy, yawning. "Lots of rides."

"Four rides is all."

"Darryl, for crying out loud, you argue with everyone."

"They don't say it like it really is."

"You're even arguing with me!"

He shut up then. Every once in a while he could be reasonable. Well, actually he could be reasonable all the time, it was just that he wanted everyone to stick to the facts. If Tommy was on the rat trap, then Caroline didn't try it by herself. Period. She might have tried, but not by herself. She might have steered, but she still wasn't by herself. Oh well, there was good money to be made as a labour negotiator or mediator. Pick the nits clean, bare them bones.

The kids were in pyjamas with their teeth brushed and lined up for kisses and cuddles, and there was Fred, as if he'd come up through the floor or down the chimney like Santa.

"Where's my kids?" he said, grinning. They obediently went to him, kissed him, then hurried to bed, eyes wide with fear.

"The separation agreement says you'll only come here when it's mutually convenient."

"I come and go as I please," he said with a shrug. "I wanted to see them. And you."

She knew what he had in mind, knew and pretended she didn't. Casually, she moved to the sink, got a drink of cold water, picked up the dishcloth and pretended to wipe the countertop. When he lunged and grabbed her from behind, his hands finding her breasts and squeezing, she was close enough to yank open the drawer and grab the butcher knife. She flailed with it, he jumped back, shocked and wary.

"You'll be sorry," he warned.

"Leave me alone." She was crying but from a place of anger, not fear.

"I'll be back. You won't always have a knife. I'll get what I want."

She phoned the police then. He was still in the house when she dialled, but as soon as he heard who she was calling, he left. She was still holding the knife when the police arrived. They took her statement, toured the house and yard, and found the back door unlocked.

"But I *locked* it," she insisted.

"Well, the thing is, this is the kind you can jigger with a credit card. Get yourself some good deadbolts."

She was furious all night, unable to sleep for the adrenaline pumping

313

and the fantasies unrolling. She was Wonder Woman in disguise, and if he broke in again she'd do this or that and then the next, but she knew she would do none of those things and she knew she was scared. Scared spitless. The knife had worked only because he hadn't expected her to stand up for herself. Why should he expect that? She'd never done it before, not once. He'd be ready for anything next time, and there would be a next time, you could count on that.

She thought the police had done all they were going to do and was astounded when he was arrested and charged with break and enter and assault.

"We wouldn't do well with a charge of sexual assault," the crown council told her. "We have your word but . . . he says he just wanted to turn you around so he could talk face to face."

"Liar!"

"We wouldn't be able to prove it. If we go into court with a charge we can't win, we'll lose, and he'll see it as a victory for himself. And the last thing *you* need is for him to think he can barge in and then win in court."

Al was livid. She hadn't told him anything about it until she had to go see the prosecutor. She didn't feel right about keeping that to herself because she and Al had moved to a different place and to say nothing would have been like lying. He listened, and all he said when she finished was, "That bastard."

"I don't want you doing anything," she said, frightened again.

"You sure?"

"Sure as sure can be."

"I'd like to snap his neck."

"It isn't your business."

He gaped, opened his mouth to protest, then closed it again.

"This happened *before*," she said, moving closer. She put her head on his shoulder, ran her hand across his flat belly. "All those years I didn't stand up to him. And I have to. Not to convince *him* of anything, but *me*."

"Jesus, Glenda."

"Please."

"Talk to me about it. Tell me why you . . ." He swallowed, shook his head. "Christ, all I want to do is kill the bugger."

"I was afraid of him, years and years of being afraid. And I didn't *do* anything about the way he was. I'm still afraid of him. But *I'm* the one has to let him know that he has no right to . . . otherwise . . . otherwise I'm always going to be afraid. Of him, of everyone."

He nodded, but it stuck in his throat, and he was so enraged he felt as if he was going to start shaking. "When he came here . . . when he grabbed at me . . . you and I were . . . well, we were flirting and smooching, but you hadn't been in this bed . . . and I hadn't been in yours . . . if we were still smooching and flirting and wanting to eat each other but not doing it, I wouldn't say a word about any of it. But we're past the shy part, past the will-I-won't-I . . . and I can't start keeping secrets from you. I kept too many secrets for too many years and . . ."

"Hey." He pulled her to him, stroking her back, hoping he didn't start to weep like some kind of wimp in an encounter group or something. "I won't snap his neck. But even you can't get me not to *want* to snap it."

They talked until they both got sleepy. That was the first time Al spent the entire night at her place. The next morning he moved his shaving gear and some of his clothes to her place. He was convinced Glenda would move to the new big house soon, so he made no attempt to talk Tommy and Jess into going with him.

Of course, the fuss didn't stop. The phone calls continued until they simply unplugged the thing at bedtime. Rocks were tossed on the roof to roll noisily back down, scaring the kids, convincing them the boogers were on the loose. Glennie took out a peace bond that ordered Fred to stay at least one hundred metres away from her, the kids, the house or the property. The paper did not protect tires of her car: they were slashed. Another morning her aerial and wipers were snapped off. Someone dumped gooey raw pig manure on the front steps. Al's eyes narrowed, but he had promised Glenda to butt out, and he did.

The police caught Fred spray-painting the word "Slut" on the side of the house. He spent the rest of the night in jail and went up in front of the judge in the morning. He fully expected to be released, with a minimal fine. Instead, the judge ordered cash bail and he spent a week in the pokey before his family managed to dance the pavane required to take a second mortgage on his mother's house. His mother glared at him. "Pull some stunt that forfeits the bail and you'll be the sorriest puppy on the Coast," she promised.

"Maw!" he moaned. "Maw, she's shacked up with that Al Lancaster!"

"Freddy,"—the old woman looked at him and shook her head—"you and her split the sheets. If she wants to screw *Prince Charles* it's none of your business. She and Big Ears could get it on while riding one of his polo ponies in front of a crowd of ten thousand and it would *still* be none of your business."

"She's my *wife*!"

"No she's not. Give it up. You aren't proving anything, you're just making yourself look foolish. Spray-painting the goddamn house! That's what *kids* do! How'n hell you expect to sell the friggin' house if it's spray-painted with curses? Nobody's gonna buy a house that's been sprayed like that. Jesus christ, Freddy, grow up and join the world."

Al paid the Prince of Wales and his son to fix up Glenda's house, painting it inside and out, pruning the trees, making sure the grass was cut and the borders trimmed. The "for sale" sign was up for a month and then the "sold" sticker was slapped across it.

When all the commissions were paid, the outstanding bills cleared up and the lawyer satisfied, Glenda split the house money in five equal parts.

"Each of these kids is entitled," she said flatly. "Let's be blunt about it, half 'n' half would mean you spend your half and they get to share my half."

"Tilt your head sideways," Fred yelled. "That little bitty noise you hear is your pea-sized brain rattling. Half 'n' half!"

"She's right." His mother slapped him on the side of the head. "You haven't paid a dime of child support and we all know you won't. By rights the whole damn sum ought to be taken by the court and used to cover what those kids are entitled to have. Jesus, Fred, get a grip."

"Smarten up," his brothers told him. "You're makin' us all look bad."

"You're lucky she didn't take you to the cleaners," his sisters told him. "God knows she had reason enough. There wouldn't even be a house for you to fight over if Glenda hadn't taken care of things."

Eventually, Fred signed the papers. It was that or have his mother withdraw her bail and have him put back in the clinker.

"You'll be sorry," he promised. "You *and* that goddamn Lancaster stud of yours."

"That kind of talk isn't the least bit productive," his lawyer warned. "And the thing of it is, Fred, when you talk like that you leave yourself open to a charge of assault. You don't have to attack someone, all you have to do is threaten to attack them and . . ."

"And you're another!" Fred hissed.

Glenda didn't bother trying to talk to Fred about anything; he was at that point of rage where anything said to him was sure to send him into orbit. So she went to his mother.

"The furniture's in real good shape," she said shyly, "but, well, I . . . that is the kids and I don't really want . . ."

"I know what you're saying, Glenda. Clean slate. Start a new life with new stuff."

"And there's no use trying to talk to Fred, he'd just . . . well, you know. But maybe you can use some of it, or others in the family. I mean, I can ship it off to the Goodwill but if someone can make use of it, then . . ." Her voice trailed off. She blinked rapidly. "I'm sorry," she said. "I mean, I don't want to insult anyone or sound like I'm bragging or crowing or . . ."

"Oh, stop it," Fred's mother snapped. "You been apologizing for things ever since I first met you. You got nothing to apologize for! I'll send Ted and Pete over with the truck, and we can move your stuff over here. I can use a new bed, and I always did admire that one of yours. The matching dresser's nice, too. As for the rest, well, there's a lot of us, and nobody any richer 'n anybody else around here, so it'll get put to good use. Personally, I think you're outta your damn mind to get tangled up with those Lancasters, but it don't surprise me none that you off-loaded Fred. He's drinkin' bad and I think he's into some other stuff I'd as soon not even have to think about. Now let's us have a cup of tea. I made some of those lemon squares you like so much. Made enough you can take a bunch home for my grandchildren. Because they *are* my grandchildren, you know," she said, glaring defiantly. "I'll come see 'em any time I'm of a mind to see 'em and make no mistake about that! And no Lancaster is gonna stop me!"

"Nobody will try to stop you."

"Better not. Just better not."

Norm couldn't get Lindy to argue or fight with him but that didn't mean life was calm. He had a honey-on-the-side in town and several nights a week he visited her, usually meeting her at the bar and going home with her at closing time. "So if you've got your wife and me on the side, why can't I have you and a hunk on the side."

"You start in with someone else and so help me god . . ."

"God's got nothing to do with it. She couldn't care less. You're greedy, you bum. Just a spoiled little kid." And honey-on-the-side laughed. "You don't *own* me, Normie. Come out of the cave. Look, no dinosaurs, no sabre-toothed tigers . . . and don't bother frowning and glowering and looking grim because I don't give a shit. If it isn't a good time had by all, then forget it."

"Listen, woman . . ."

"Oh, wow. 'Listen, woman'. Hey, John Wayne died of cancer, didn't you hear?"

As if to deliberately insult him, Lindy insisted he use a condom. "I know you've been tomcatting," she told him quietly. "I don't want germs, bacteria or viruses either."

"Damned if I will!"

"Then you won't. I told you, I don't ask for a wedding ring, nor a ring through your nose either. But I will *not* catch crabs nor nothing else just because you're pole vaulting all over hell."

Finally, the excuse he'd been looking for. Norm stuffed his belongings into a plastic garbage bag and moved them to the new big house.

"Hell with her!" he yelled.

"Oh, now, you don't mean that," said Singe.

"See if I don't. Ever since you fools give her that hunk'a paper she's had the idea she's somebody she isn't!"

"It's got nothing to do with the piece of paper. She knows you're dinkin' around, is all. And of *course* she wants you to wear a rubber. Christ, Norm, used to be all a guy had to worry about was a dose, fix 'er up with penicillin. Now it's a death sentence waiting to happen."

"Hell if I will!"

"What about Griff?"

"What about him? Jesus, she's got a house, don't she?"

"Well, you know how it is, food for the baby is nice, too."

"She was on hoofare before I met her, she can go on it again."

"You want Griff on hoofare? Jeez, Norm, you got no pride!"

"I got too much pride to live with someone who's frigid! She's prob'ly a queer-dear anyway."

"Oh, don't be such a damn goof," Singe laughed.

"Talk about cut off your nose to spite your face." Jewen cackled with laughter. "Jesus, Norm, most of us'd wear raincoats and gumboots and weep with gratitude."

"Not me. Hell with her."

"I can't believe it. I honest to god can't believe it. That's the most woman I ever set eyes on. Hell, I'd wear a scuba suit if it would get me next to her!"

"You want her? You can have 'er. There's more and better fish in the sea than her."

"I never caught one. Hell, I never even caught sight of one!"

"Believe me. Lots better."

Jewen didn't think so. But there was no talking to Norm. He headed off every night, often without even eating the supper Lottie cooked. He had some short-term successes but didn't seem to find anyone who wanted to go steady. At first it didn't bother him, but after a while he began to wonder. He'd never had any trouble before. There'd always been any number of willing women. Finally, a thirty-year-old in a tank top and jeans gave him the word. "You're okay for a few hours, Norm, but once or twice is plenty for me. I got no time for moods and shitty temper and grumpiness. I mean it ain't as if you got a full head'a hair and an irresistible smile. And you sure as hell don't have what they call a winning personality."

He almost backhanded her, but knew the barkeep would flatten him if he did, so he laughed and told her she didn't know when she had it good. In return, she laughed, but not at what he was trying to pretend was a joke. That night, still smarting, still wishing he'd drifted her a good one, he stood in front of the mirror for several minutes, looking at his hairline and frowning. He bared his teeth and vowed he'd make an appointment with a dentist first thing in the morning. He sucked in his gut, then pinched his love handles and the roll around his waist. It wasn't fair! Some people could eat their faces off and still be slim. Well, dammit, did they think everyone was the same?

He lay in bed nattering to himself and fell asleep with the taste of bile in his mouth. In the morning he phoned the dentist and got an appointment, but was choked because there would be a three-week wait. They only do that to make you think you're lucky to get in to see them at all! He stopped eating chips and cheezies while driving his truck and made sure he had a big salad for lunch instead of a few donuts. He replaced his cans of pop with bottled water, and three times a week he went to the gym after work and pulled at the machines until he was pouring sweat.

The dentist tsk-tsk'ed at the condition of his teeth, then froze his mouth and got to work. Norm's mouth was so sore the next day he had no trouble at all sticking to his diet; in fact, he could manage only soup. He had four more appointments before the teeth were fixed, and by then the roll around his middle had begun to shrink.

He almost got into a row with Jewen but had a talk with himself, instead. For one thing, Jewen would probably whip his arse, and anyway it was Norm himself who had told Jewen he was finished with Lindy. He'd even said if you want her you can have her. And obviously Jewen had believed him. Did Norm want her back? No, he did not! Not even if she'd agree to it, which he was pretty sure she wouldn't. And that meant he was going to have to pretend the bullshit from Jewen didn't bother him one little bit.

Lindy had hung out with guys for only two reasons. Either they looked like prime breeding material or they were fun. When the fun ended, fine, easy enough to move on. She'd never felt emotionally dependent on any of them and hadn't really felt much by way of butterflies in her stomach. Except with Jewen. All he had to do was start talking to her and her mouth went dry, her throat felt stiff, she became certain she was totally stupid, convinced she'd blurt out something so utterly ridiculous Jewen would walk away, turned off and disgusted by her ignorance.

"Need to talk to you, Al." Jewen put the cooler of ice cubes and beer cans on the big burl table in the living room.

"I'll go wash m'socks or something." Tony began to rise.

"No need." Jewen handed him a beer. "I need all the help I can get."

"Want me to leave? I mean, is it guy stuff?" Brady asked.

"You're fine. Dar, too. But I need for Jess and Tom to take a hike."

"Oh, I can take a gentle hint like that," Jess said, rising from the sofa. "I mean I don't need the roof to fall in on me like happened last time."

"Wanna play some tunes?" Tom wasn't too happy about being excluded, but he left without open protest.

"How old *is* that guy, now? Fifteen? Sixteen?" Tony popped the tab on a can of beer, sipped quietly.

"Going on sixteen. Jessie's going to be fifteen soon. Why?"

"You had the talk with him yet?"

"Guess it's time, eh? Jesus. I'm not looking forward to *that* one. And I got no idea at all how to go about talkin' to Jess."

"Don't bother," Brady laughed. "Number one, they do a fine job of teaching the biology part of it in school, and Colly 'n' I've talked to her about the other stuff."

"I didn't know the two of you needed to learn anything." Al kept a poker face and Brady grinned.

"I need someone to give me 'the talk'." Jewen sipped his beer. "I don't know if I should shit or go blind. I mean I don't want to dump a big deal on you's all but, well, no matter what I do it's apt to impact the whole family."

"Jesus," Al said, grinning, "you are the beatingest-around-the-bush person I've ever seen. Go for it. Crazy bugger Norm never did treat her right and now he's off bein' a pussy bandit and sleepin' upstairs here when he isn't doing the dirty thing with some barfly.

Lindy's a damn fine woman. You sit playin' with your toes much longer and someone else is going to move in on her."

"You know?"

"I don't know why you can't believe us when we tell you there's no way you could keep a secret if you locked it in a vault. Jesus, the skyrockets between the two of you can be seen at noon on a sunny day."

"It's like, well, I mean, he's my brother, you know, and well, there's supposed to be boundaries and limits and all."

"Hey, gimme a break, okay. He shit in his nest. Again. If the crazy lugan can't keep his pecker under control then he's the one fuckin' hisself outta the picture."

"You know what he's like."

"You serious about her or just horny?" Brady demanded.

"Sister, I am crazy nuts about her. If it was just bones bouncin', hell, I'd try for that and t'hell with Norm. But I want . . ." he said, shrugging, "greedy me, I want it all."

"Well, there's trouble." Al peered at the hole in his beer can, as if the treasure of all time was hidden in there and if he just watched long enough he'd get a glimpse.

"Go for it." Darlene patted Jewen's leg. "Man, you deserve some of the good stuff in life."

"Norm's gonna shit a brick."

"Do you care?"

"Not for me. But he's going to say some awful stuff about *her*. You know him as well as I do; in his eyes nothing is ever *his* doin'."

"You've made some real asshole choices in life, Jewen." Al drained his beer, dropped the empty into the cooler and took a full one. "You've drunk up enough money for three houses and a car, and god only knows what kind of pills you've took or stuff you've shoved up your nose or in your arm or up your ass for all's I know. You been sober, what, two 'n' a half years now? That's a long dry for you. You gonna use this as an excuse for a toot?"

"No."

"If Norm wasn't in the picture, if she'd been hooked up with, say, Brew, would you be sittin' on your arse lookin' miserable? No, I thought not. Gimme the damn beer, it's gone flat and hot by now.

Here, gimme. Now take your sad ass over to Lindy's house and talk to *her*. Hell, you don't need me to do that for you, too, do you?"

He went almost to her steps, then his courage failed. He walked back and forth, smoking cigarettes and trying to rehearse all the things he had to say. Finally, almost unwillingly, he went to her door and knocked.

Lindy opened the door and her expression told Jewen how surprised she was.

"Is something wrong?" she asked, sounding frightened.

"Would you marry me?" he blurted, all his rehearsed words vanished.

"I'd love to," she said, then looked as if she wished she'd bitten off her tongue.

"Right away?"

"I think there's a three-day waiting period."

"Go in with me tomorrow for the licence?"

"Love to." She was smiling from ear to ear.

"I want Singe for best man."

"Can I phone Bonnie to be bridesmaid?"

Jewen could only nod and grin. He wanted to hold her, he wanted to smell her hair and he wanted so much else, so much more, and he just stood, smiling.

"I want you to come inside and make the call with me."

He nodded and stepped inside. Neither of them was seen until supper the following night. By then they had everything arranged. The family waited for Norm to go into orbit.

"You lazy bugger," he said with a laugh, punching Jewen on the shoulder but not hard. "You're as lazy as you guys' dad. Too damn lazy to make your own kids, you got to call on someone else to do it for you. Listen, dork, I'll give you lessons if you need them. The first kid, well, he's a freebie, but if you want any others, you're on your own unless you pay me *big* money."

"Appreciate it, Norm," Jewen said, nodding. "Might be I could use a few lessons."

"I thought it was Norman Lancaster she was involved with," a townie said to Lottie. Lottie smiled and shook her head as if again amazed and amused by the misinformation some people were will-ing to believe.

"I don't know where you got that idea," she almost purred. People in front of her in the checkout line tried to pretend they weren't eavesdropping. "She's marrying Jewen. He's the tall good-looking one with the frizzy hair. Well, they're all pretty much tall and good-looking, but you'd know Jewen by the mop of hair of his. Norm's the short one, kinda brown-haired, stocky build, drives delivery truck."

"I could have sworn . . ." the woman began, puzzled.

"Well, don't believe anything you hear. You know how it is, more baloney being spread than what's in the deli."

Colleen kept her job but two hundred others didn't. First, the com-pany shut down the cedar mill, claiming it was no longer economi-cal for them to run it. The mill had made a three-million-dollar profit the previous year but usually it made twice that. Where peo-ple saw a three-million-dollar profit, the company saw a similar-sized loss.

With the cedar mill shut there was no need for cedar logs, and other jobs were gone. The loss of all those paycheques rippled across the entire community.

The next big layoff was at the pulp mill. The company claimed a glut of paper products on the world market and a consequent drop in prices. Saying it was temporary and only until the problems were solved, the highly paid suits cut production—and the work force—by twenty-five percent. That affected the workers in the bush and more of them were laid off. This time the community was staggered; the ripple became a wave, and the layoffs spread. Full-time wait-ressing jobs became half time or even part time; mechanics had their hours cut; store clerks wound up on pogey; and those still working cut their expenditures to the bone, trying to save something for that inevitable day when the other shoe fell for them as well.

"Haven't got me, yet," Singe said, rolling a smoke and handing the makings on to Jewen. "But I been thinking, maybe I won't wait for them to make the choice. They're going to offer a buy-out retirement scheme. Even if they don't, there's guys need the job a lot more than I do."

"You 'n' Luce got a pack'a kids to raise," Jewen reminded gently.

"Well, I got a fair bit put aside. Lucy's gotta have a streak'a Scot in her somewhere. Either that or her mom was scared by bagpipe music when she was pregnant, because she don't waste a cent."

"Getting miserable out there." Colleen took the makings from Jewen, nodded her thanks and began to roll a smoke. "All the old-timers're getting layoff slips. There's crews out there where the most experienced guy's got five years on the job. That's dangerous."

"Too many situations come up," Singe agreed. "Especially now, they got them highballin' to beat all hell. Someone's gonna get hurt."

"If it isn't boom time out here, it's bloody bust time," Al said, taking the makings from Colleen. "I'd go fishin' if there were any fish left."

"Ain't it the truth." They nodded, as fatalistic as any swami could ever be.

Colleen continued her job, knowing her careful work was just eye candy for the critics. She made her duplicate maps, sent the copy off to Greenpeace, and on her days off left the place and went to spend time with her chosen honey. Even Singe knew nothing at all about Colleen's love life. She'd been so private about it for so long the family assumed she didn't have one.

For years being private had been her choice. God knows, the rest of them paraded that part of their lives as if they were on Jerry Springer, each episode or uproar adding to the gossip about Those Lancasters. They didn't need to sit in their nice houses and presume to know about her! But the Jewen-Lindy thing had put a bug in her ear. In theory, Colleen was dead set against the match-up. You just do not move in on your sib's ex. But theory fell on its duff when it was Jewen. Especially when the other part of the picture was Norm. He was a user and had been easing his arse out of the picture even before Griff was born. Right now he thought it was funny, made dumb jokes about Jewie doing him a favour, but that could turn in a minute and pitch them all into the same kind of la-la bullshit as was coming down on Glennie.

The rest of the family acted as if there was nothing the least bit extraordinary about anything at all. Jewen and Lindy were so completely wrapped up in each other it was a wonder they remembered to feed Lindy's kids. The more she thought about it the more she felt as if it was time to start acting ordinary about her own life.

"So, can I bring a date?" Colleen asked.

"More the merrier." Lindy nodded, and smiled. She was trying to help Lottie with buffet preparations but was so dithered she was basically wandering in circles, sipping coffee and watching her hands tremble. If she hadn't been the bride the others would have told her she was getting in their way.

"What time is Bonnie getting here?"

"She and Grandma will get here the night before. Grandma is kind of, well, frail."

"Probably she's as tough as an old boot and the frail part is how she runs the show."

"She's pretty old."

"Wonder what we'll be like when we're pretty old. How old *is* she?"

"I thought this was going to be a *quiet* wedding!" Lindy was suddenly on the verge of panic. "Jesus, it looks like you're expecting a horde! Jewen told me just family!"

"Darlin', this family *is* a horde."

"I can't do this. We should'a just slipped off by ourselves. We can still . . ."

"Calm down." Lottie took the coffee cup and emptied it into the sink, led Lindy to a chair and got her into it. "You sit, I'll make you a cup of tea."

"It *is* just family," Darlene said as she sat beside Lindy, patting her on the knee. "You relax. You just told Colly the more the merrier. Well, this is going to be *real* merry."

"It's all Lucy's fault anyway," said Brady as she did a bump and grind, her toosh rapping against Lucy's hip. "When Lucy says family she means the entire reserve. That's, what, six hundred people?"

"Adults. Count the kids and there's no end to it. But it ain't *my* family crowdin' up this place, it's all them old boyfriends of yours showin' up, hopeful as puppies."

"Don't blame me." Brady shook her head. "Them's Darlene's old honeys, not mine."

"I got no old honeys," Darlene argued. "All my honeys were young ones."

"Then it's probably Lottie's fault."

"Keep me out of it. You're all talkin' crazy, anyhow."

"I'm terrified," Lindy admitted.

"I told you she'd chicken out as soon as she realized Jewen was one of us. She doesn't want to be known as part of the pack." Darlene took the cup of tea Lottie handed to her, sipped it, and nodded gratefully. "Damn but my ankles are swollen!"

"I *told* you to keep your face out of that damned popcorn bowl," Lottie snapped. "You don't listen to a soul, even when you know they're right; you just do whatever it is you want."

"But it was so good!" Darlene laughed.

"It was 'soooo goood' got you in this pickle in the first place," Lottie told her, and the others turned, gaping. "What? You thought I thought women got pregnant because they took the last cookie off the plate?" She grinned at Brady and Lucy. "And I suppose you're going to tsk-tsk and tell each other you didn't know Lottie could talk like that. Jeez-Louise, the lot of you, I knew where babies came from before any of you did!"

"Now, you see? *That*'s why my people make such a big deal out of listenin' to and respectin' our elders," Lucy teased. "It's how we acknowledge that we know they were fuckin' their brains out when we were still riding tricycles."

"There's still ten pounds of spuds need peeled," Darlene said as she started to get off her chair. Lottie gave her a gentle push. "Not you. Unless you're going to promise me you'll peel 'em sitting down. Sitting down and drinking some cranberry juice."

"Oh, great, Lottie, fill me with cranberry juice so's I can pee my way through the whole wingding. Some friend you are. I'll have to take a bucket with me."

"I'll put a ribbon on the handle, how's that?"

"Don't have to think we don't know what *you're* up to," Brady

327

pretended to argue. "You've decided you'll go in labour before the I Dos, steal the whole damn show, get all the attention."

"Jesus, you can have all the attention." Lindy laughed. "Just get the spud salad made before you go into bearing down pains, okay? While you're writhing and groaning and promising never again, god, I give you my word I'll be munchin' down on a mountain of food."

"You watch." Lucy started in on a sink full of potatoes. "She'll steal the show. Steal the silverware, too, if we got any. Best to use plastic knives and forks, you know what she's like."

Darlene didn't steal the show. The spotlight was firmly focussed on Jewen and Lindy. The room in which the commissioner married them was too small for the whole pack to fit so, since Lindy's kids were directly affected, they went in, and because Singe was best man Lucy and the kids went in, then because Dar was pregnant, she got a chair, with Dorrit standing beside her and Tony waiting in the hall with the others. Al stood against the back wall with Tom on one side of him and Jess on the other, and Grandma's wheelchair took up front and centre where she could see everything, even how trembly Lindy was.

"You calm down, darling," she said clearly. "He's a good man, he deserves a fine woman like you. This is going to work out, you'll see."

After all the logistics of getting at least part of the pack into the little room, the ceremony was over quickly. Colleen and her date, Deb, stood on the sidewalk with a bag of rice and tossed handfuls at the bridal party as it moved toward the rented limo that was to drive them first to the photographers, then to the new place for the reception.

"My *god*," Deb breathed, "you weren't kidding. There *are* a lot of you!"

"This is but a fraction, my dear. The cousins, second cousins, shirt-tail cousins and seldom mentioned bastard cousins ought to be showing up at the house about twenty minutes after we get there."

"Getting married looks like fun," Glennie's daughter Caroline shrilled. "Why don't *you* get married?"

"First I have to get divorced," Glenda said.

"Then will you get married?" Darryl looked hopeful.

"Hey, Bud," Al said as he picked Darryl up and sat him on his hip, "don't bug your momma about it. You 'n' me'll get married. How's that?"

"Will we have flowers?"

"Oh, you betcha."

"Roady-dodies?"

"Rhododendrons? Sure, why not."

"Then you can stop pretending to be a nice guy," Jess teased, "and go back to being your usual ugly self."

"You wait until I'm your stepmother." Glenda hugged Jess quickly, a one-armed around-the-shoulder-squeeze. "I'll civilize you."

"Oh, sure you will." Jess laughed again. "The wicked stepmother, nothing but bread and water."

"Who said you could have water? Did I say you could have water? I did not."

When the limo arrived at the new place, Dar had her cameras ready and Chuck had the video rolling. Tom had a camera, as did Lucy.

"I want all the shots I can get of Singe in a suit," she said. "It may be the only chance we get to see him in one."

"I told you, marry me and I'll buy a new suit every year and wear it at supper every Friday night," said Singe.

"I'm not marrying anyone," Lucy said, and she wasn't laughing. "I told you that the first time you asked me. I never did marry anyone, and I never will."

"Ah, but I'll keep asking, all the same."

"Crazy man."

There was enough food for the city of Hanoi, and people coming from both directions of the highway to wish the newlyweds well, grab a plate and help in the assault. But since everyone brought a platter or bowl of food, the pile merely got rearranged, not diminished. There was still plenty when the airport cab stopped and Doreen got out with her oversized pack.

"Well, I'll be go-to-hell," Brady said, gaping. "It's the Colonel!"

"And they said *I'd* steal the show," Dar said.

"There's still time," Brady muttered, watching as the rest of the family moved forward for hugs and smooches and Oh my just *look* at you.

"See," Colleen whispered to Deb, "I told you nobody'd notice you in the crowd."

"A Colonel?"

"Oh, I don't think she's really a Colonel. That's just what Brady calls her. Prob'ly just a general or something."

"What kind of a one? I mean . . . you know what I mean."

"I don't know, she's never been really clear about it. Something to do with the military police, checking security clearances or something. Going into bars, pulling out drunks, maybe. She'd be good at it, she was El Disciplinario here for a while. I mean, Singe and Jewen were hopeless at it, and Al, hell, he went all the way the other way, so Dor, she appointed herself Mother Superior. She and Norm, god but they'd get into it sometimes. He was a rangytang kind of kid, could look you in the eye, smile like an angel, and lie in his teeth."

"You don't talk about her very much."

"I'm the youngest in this pack, okay? Sometimes when they tease me they call me the afterthought, or the caboose or the cow's tail. So I had the full impact of her, like she was my mother or something. Or thought she was. Strict? Jesus! I used to think it was because she was mean clear to the bone. But maybe not. I mean, they knew the welfare was just waiting for an excuse to scoop us. Especially me. If I'd got in any kind of trouble, well, that would have been all they'd have needed. So I had to be *good*. Don't give them the excuse, she'd say. Do your damn homework or they'll be here to take you to some place where you *have* to do it. I think now that she was scared a lot of the time."

"Do you love her?"

"I don't think so. Not much about her to love. I mean first memories are kind of like tattoos: whatever else, you've got them. And then, poof, she was gone and it was letters and postcards. Hard to love someone in those circumstances."

"What about the others? Dar and Brady?"

"I love you, have done for years. Dar just pisses me off, always has. And Brady? Hey, she's years older 'n I am and she was cat-assing by the time she was thirteen, even before the old fart went nuts.

I was ashamed of her for years. I'm not ashamed anymore, but love her? She's a stranger."

"Your brothers?"

"Love Singe like crazy. Love Jewen the same way. I like Al. Prob'ly I love him, but he can be a real owly bugger. And Norm? Not a chance. Him and Dar used to gang up on me. She was the youngest girl until I came along, right, and she liked being the baby. He *was* the baby until I was born, and he wasn't about to give up his throne without a fight. They were like a pair'a weasels or something. I mean lookit today. Norm'll show up soon, probably half-tanked and with a barfly floozie hangin' onto his arm. But he'll be in jeans and a ripped tee-shirt or maybe his motorcycle leathers. Prob'ly won't have shaved. And for no reason but to show everyone that he doesn't consider this important. I mean, hell, it's his brother's wedding, eh? But Norm'll find a way to get up everyone's nose."

Several vehicles pulled off the highway and parked, the occupants watching, trying to figure out if it was a private or public celebration. One by one they drifted over, asked a few people what was going on, and then just sort of became part of the mob.

Doreen nipped into the house long enough to grab a shower and put on fresh clothes, then she rejoined the party and did her best to put a dent in the food. She didn't have a prayer of a chance, but she did hit it off with Tom and Jess, both of whom made it their chosen function to make sure Doreen was introduced to everyone at the party.

Jewen had planned a honeymoon trip to Hawaii. Lindy asked if it could wait until Christmas when they could use a sunny break from the winter rain and fog. He agreed. He'd have agreed to anything she asked. They were supposed to push off at six-thirty to drive to Victoria and take the ferry across the chuck to the States. But Doreen's unexpected arrival threw that plan out the back window. "Hey, Mr. Lancaster," Lindy whispered, holding his arm, pressing against him, feeling as if she could never get close enough to him, "what say we cancel this trip? I know a *real* comfortable bed where you can rest your weary self and you can visit with the exterminator or whatever it is you call her."

"Mrs. Lancaster, if I wasn't already head over heels in love with you, I'd fall in love right now."

"Do you love me? Really?"

"Lindy Lancaster, I love you."

At midnight the first revellers left, and by three, only the family remained. They sat with loaded plates, ranged on the steps and along the porch, eating and yawning. "Dear Lord," Doreen sighed, "there is *nothing* in the world tastes better than this turkey."

"Patsy Larson raises them. Wild turkey stock, and she closes them up at night, turns them loose in the morning to free-range," Singe said. "I tried 'em, and the buggers all headed out into the bush, by ones, by twos, by the flock. They're prob'ly still out there. I put out food and it's always gone, but if we were to depend on my turkeys for food we'd all starve."

"Did you raise the chickens?"

"Chickens I can raise. I guess they aren't as smart as turkeys."

"I forgot how early spring comes around here. There's still snow back east."

"You look kinda tired."

"Yeah. Man, I'm worn out."

"Coupl'a weeks rest should put you right."

"Coupl'a years more like it."

"Al," Singe called, raising his voice, "that boy of yours is about half-swacked. He's been drinkin' beer like it was pop."

"Uncle," Tom said reproachfully, "you finked."

"Maybe you had enough, boy," Al suggested.

"Yessir," Tom said. "Dr. Pepper, here I come."

"Boot in the arse to get you started if you want one."

"Yessir. Thank you, sir. Should I feel in the need I'll be sure to call on you. Sir."

"Smartass," Al muttered but he was trying not to grin himself, so nobody took him too seriously. "I guess," he said mildly, "you're too gibbled and lumga to be able to strum us a tune or two."

"No sir." Tom put his arm around Al's shoulders, and hugged him openly. "Uncle exaggerates, you know that. I've had two beer. Honest. I can play. What would you like to hear?"

"Something soft, something . . . what was that one you were playing with Jess last night? I liked that."

"Yessir. One word and it's a command." And Tom stood up, half-turned to go into the house and get his guitar. "Oh great," he said clearly, "here comes good old Stormin' Norman. I thought he'd never show up and ruin the party."

"Cheeky bugger, you," Al said softly. "Where's your respect?"

"Right. I think it's in the case with the guitar. Maybe I'll go get it, too."

Norm sauntered toward the family, grinning like a dog caught sucking eggs. He was neatly dressed in clean jeans and a white shirt, collar unbuttoned, shirt sleeves rolled back.

"Hey, there," he slurred, "I'd'a been here sooner but I was afraid to head out this way in case I got an impaired charge. There's roadblocks all over the place." He moved to the buffet, looked at the food, then turned away without taking so much as a piece of crisp-skinned chicken.

"Congratulations, and all that good stuff." He stuck out his hand and Jewen took it, shook and smiled, fully prepared to be friendly. Norm didn't smile back. He looked at Lindy, and one eyelid flickered in a tic. "Well, I'd kiss the bride but I don't think, under the circumstances, it'd be 'propriate. Wish ya's all the luck in the world." He pulled an envelope from his back jeans pocket. "Brung ya's somethin'." He handed the envelope to Jewen, but his eyes were busy checking out the rest of the family. "All's ya gotta do is sign 'er and get one of the others to witness it."

"What's this?" Jewen was puzzled.

"Well, it's an agreement paper. I'm signin' all parental rights and claim to Griff over to you." His sly grin reappeared. "I mean you got the house, you got the wife, you might's well get the kid, too. After all, he looks like you, not like me."

"He looks like our mother," Jewen said carefully, opening the envelope and starting to read the paper. Lindy's face went white, her eyes filled with tears of anger. She knew Norm intended to insult her, and she tried hard not to give him the satisfaction of knowing he had scored a direct hit in her most vulnerable place.

"Now, Norman," Singe said reasonably, "this here's a celebration. First real wedding in this family in more'n a generation."

"Right." Norm nodded, sounding almost as reasonable as Singeon. "And I spent a lot of time thinkin' about what I could give them for a bridal gift. And I figured, well, it's got to be something meaningful."

"It certainly is." Jewen stood and stuck out his hand again. "Shake on 'er Norm. Best present anybody ever gave me. And," he grinned but his eyes were cold, "as you said yourself, he sure does so look like me."

Norm's smirk wavered. Whatever he had expected, this wasn't it. "Fine, then," he blustered. "Great. Glad you understand."

"Oh," Lindy purred, "we both understand, Norman. Understand fully. Maybe while you're at it, you might think about signing the same kind of paper for Big Wil so she can find herself a good father for Little Willy, too."

"Never know." The smirk was gone, and Norm's bitterness was exposed for all to see. "You just never know." He moved back to the food table, took a plate and put some chicken and potato salad on it, then moved to sit next to Doreen. "When'd you get here?" he grumbled.

"Oh, I've been here since about halfways through," she said, smiling. "Tried to get here yesterday but the airport was shut down because of snow."

"Snow? Jesus christ, Dory, what in hell keeps you in that place? Snow? It's almost the end'a April, that's no time'a the year for snow!"

"I've been thinking about that, Norman. It's starting to feel like time to come back again."

"Yeah? Startin' to feel to me like it's time to go. I'm gettin' fed up, I'll tell you. Got my layoff notice. Come two weeks from now I'll be on pogey like the rest of the town."

"No work back east, Norm. You'd be better off here, doing firewood or something. Shake bolts maybe."

"Hell. I don't want to do work like *that*!"

"It's work. It pays."

"I'm a fully qualified driver! I'm not a damn woodcutter."

"No use holding out for driving if there's nothing to drive. And there's nothing back east except cities full of poor people lookin' for work."

"I thought there were heaps of factories lookin' for . . ."

"Nope. They got hit before the hammer fell here."

"Helluva thing."

Tom and Jess sat facing each other, playing music and smiling. Doreen watched them, imagined she could see a glow of light joining them, turning them into one person with two brains and four hands.

"They're good," she said softly.

"Them?" Norm glanced over, shrugged. "They're okay."

CHAPTER NINE

By the beginning of May the weather was blistering hot and the trips to the beach after supper had started. The kids didn't go swimming, not really, but they did race up and down in the shallows, water flying from their feet, the dogs ripping after them, mouths open, tongues hanging, too intent on keeping up to the kids to have time or breath for yapping.

"Dear god," the adults sighed, "if it's this hot in May, what's it going to be like by August."

"Sweet Pete, someone pass me something cold to drink."

"Someone dunk that little one or he'll be a barbecued baby. Soak him a bit and cool him off."

"Darlene, you stay in the shade. You get sunburn on that belly of yours and you'll be some sorry."

"If I get much bigger they're going to issue me a licence plate, thinking I'm a municipal bus," she said lazily, sipping cold cranberry juice and eating a banana, because Lottie said they kept up your potassium levels and warded off milk fever.

"Move you over here and we'll be safe in the shadow of your tub."

"Tub? *Tub?* That's no tub; that, my dear, is my daughter."

"You're not getting any daughter. It's too quiet. Girls roll around so much you'd think they were doing aerobics in there. Boys are quiet."

"I'm having a girl."

"You get one of those determinant things, ultrasound or whatever they're calling it this week?"

"No. They asked if I wanted to know and I said no, I'd take my chances and wait my turn. But I'm getting a daughter."

"Not this time."

"You'll see. I'll bet you a soft ice cream cone."

✸

But it wasn't, it was a son. Tony stood at the glass, looking in on Anthony Andrew Brandeis. "Would you just look at that," he breathed.

"Looks more like one of us," Lucy teased. "Lookit how dark that head'a hair is. Look at those black black eyebrows. You drive too close to the rez and you'll lose him."

"Oh, dear no, not that! Please say it ain't so! I'd have to set about makin' another! I'm too tired."

"Start taking vitamins," Darlene purred, "I didn't get my girl."

"Maybe you could borrow Cat," he teased. "You know I'm wore out."

"Right. Well, take the vitamins. You'll be wearin' it out again real soon."

"Feed him herring eggs." Lucy sounded totally serious. "Herring eggs on kelp leaves. That'll put some lead in his pencil. And quit eatin' white bread from the store, it fills you up but doesn't *give* you anything. Fry bread, that's what you need, fry bread and herring eggs."

✸

Tommy tilled the garden repeatedly, and the troupe picked rocks. Most of the original garden had vanished in The Burp and Colleen mourned the loss of the beautiful soil. What they got in return was years of work away from equalling what the rumble had taken. The rocks were tossed into the wheelbarrow and taken to the pile.

"Boy, in case of invasion we got all the ammunition we need to hold off an army," Al teased, opening a brown paper bag and bringing out an orange popsicle. The smallest of the troupe got the first one, Jess and Tom, as oldest and tallest, got the last ones.

"Thanks, Dad."

"You're welcome. Garden doesn't look like much compared to the other one, eh?"

"Auntie Colly wants a load of manure for it. And she says we're to dump the grass clippings between the rows when they're in, to mulch out the weeds and to build up the soil. But it's a mess."

"She wants manure? Okay, be glad to. About time someone gave her shit."

"You're awfully corny, old man."

"Corn? I'll show you corn? Old? I'll show you . . ." He grabbed Tom suddenly, pinned him with one arm and pretended he was going to gobble the popsicle. When he released the kid he kept his arm around him, an easy and casual hug. "You're a good boy, Tom."

"Thank you. I ever tell you you're okay?"

"For an old man."

"For a *very* old man. A codger, in fact."

"We used to call the old fart the gaffer."

"What was he like?"

"Oh, you take the worst of each of us and put 'em in one person and you've got about half the misery he was. Mother got angry with him one time and called him ten pounds of shit in a five-pound sack. The man was never happy for long. You could'a given him the winning ticket on the lottery and he'd gripe because now he had to feel grateful to you."

"Probably his serotonin levels were off," Jess said quietly. "It happens, you know. I kind of figured that's what's wrong with Uncle Norm. Congenital predisposition to depressed behaviour."

"What?" Al gaped at her; she smiled up at him.

"Born to be a miserable asshole," she translated. She handed him the last bit of melting popsicle. "Finish it off," she suggested. "It's real good."

"Thanks, Jess. Next time I'll get one for myself."

"Big kid, you."

"Big *old* kid," Tom said. "Very old."

Colleen's load of manure arrived and was dumped at the edge of the garden. The Prince of Wales looked at the new space and shook his head. His son nodded, agreeing with his dad. Then they both got back into their pickup truck and drove off, waving and smiling, and not talking. Al wasn't home at the time so he missed seeing the pickup and the well-composted, virtually de-scented black soil. He arrived an hour later with his gravel truck loaded to the top with a reeking mix of cow, pig and horse manure. He backed the gravel truck to the middle of the rotovated plot and dumped the sloppy wet mess, trailing a wide path of it behind him as he drove out again, leaving deep ruts in the tilled soil. Then he went for a second and third load.

"What in the name of god are you doing?" Lottie yelled. "Miss Colly's gonna *kill* you."

Al didn't hear her words over the rumble of the truck engine and at first he thought she was encouraging him, then he took another look at the expression on her face and reconsidered. He pulled the truck to the side of the driveway, turned off the engine and leaned out the window. "Say something?" he called, smiling proudly.

"I said Miss Colly's gonna *kill* you," Lottie answered.

"Me? Why me?"

"That's not what she had in mind, Mr. Al. That stuff's so hot it's gonna burn everything. Stuff's supposed to age at least a year, better yet two, before you put it on your garden."

"This is good stuff," he argued.

Every fly for miles caught a whiff. They hovered in mid-air, their little sniffers working overtime, wings fluttering, then they turned and headed into the ripe scent, flying toward the source, eager and buzzing excitedly. Small black ones, medium-sized bluish ones, big glistening green ones, even bullet-shaped hairy golden ones. Horse flies, deer flies, barn flies, botflies and bluetail flies descended on the festering heap and settled happily about fly-business. They copulated like crazy, the females laid eggs which immediately set about the serious work of becoming maggots, which, in turn, became flies which sucked the juices in the heaps of muck, grew strong and vital, copulated like crazy and laid more eggs.

"Jesus, Al," Jewen said, coming from around the side of the house, bare-chested and wearing cut-off jeans and sandals. "What is this: you testing a new secret weapon for the Yankee war machine?"

"Smells like downtown Ottawa on a hot day." Doreen pretended anger and glared fiercely. "For this I flew four and a half hours?"

"Gotta compliment you on that broom of yours, Doreen. Most of 'em's only good for a coupl'a hours."

"Broom? You are so retrograde, Albert. I don't ride an old-fashioned broom, I've got a top-of-the-line vacuum cleaner. Solar-powered so I don't need a cord."

"Lottie figures I goofed," Al admitted.

"Believe her," she said as she looked at the muck, then at Al. "You'll be lucky if she doesn't bury you in that stuff."

"How'm I gonna turn out a supper that people enjoy eating if they have to smell *that* reeking mess? You have to start thinking, Mr. Al, not just reacting."

"Boy, not only is there a big heap of it over there, I'm catching it from all sides," he grumbled, then went for the hose to wash out the bed of the truck before what was stuck there hardened.

Colleen smelled the muck before she got out of the new company four-by. She stood by the garden, staring in disbelief.

"I, uh, guess I, uh, got the wrong stuff," Al admitted, looking sheepish.

"And so much of it," she agreed mildly. "Anyone ever suggest to you that there was a possibility you were a creature of excesses?"

"Might'a been hinted at, but nobody said it out loud."

"I'm saying it. Out loud. Jesus, Al."

"Sorry, Colly. You'd said you wanted . . ."

"Thank you, Al. It's the thought that counts." But she shook her head. "God*damn*. but that stinks!"

"I thought I'd go in there with a blade and kinda spread it around? Maybe when the gooey part of it drains into the ground or dries up in the sun or something, maybe we could turn it under?"

"Well, we aren't going to be able to take the little garden tractor in there. It'll get stuck in the mess and probably sink out of sight. Smack dab in the middle. Jesus, Al."

"That's all they've been sayin' since I got the last load here. Jesus Al this and jesus Al that. I feel like a bloody fool."

"Well, to tell you the truth you . . ."

"Not the truth! Please, Colly, not that, anything but!" And he pretended to weep on her shoulder.

The blade machine rumbled until past nine that night, spreading the gooey mess over the garden, inches deep. The tracks of the machine squished the wet manure into the dirt, then churned the dirt until there was no hint this was supposed to be a garden, no sign Tom had worked so hard tilling the soil. When Al finally parked his machine and hosed the stink off the treads, what had been intended as a garden plot looked like a battlefield after the conflict. And smelled to high heaven.

The flies batted at the windows, collected on the screen doors, and zizzed constantly. Lindy got so sick and tired of them she began hanging up long sticky paper flytraps, impregnated with a mating scent. The flies swarmed to them, covered them, and she had to change them every few hours. For all the hundreds and thousands of flies trapped and killed on them, the hordes swarming at the stench in the garden seemed totally undiminished.

The next morning Al drove to the feed store and got thirty bags of dolomite lime, fifty pounds per sack. He spread that on the mess and the stink was lessened.

"I figure we've dumped a ton of the stuff," said Tony, coated in white powder, his weight-room muscles pumped and hard.

"At least it seems to have cut the stench, and with any luck at all most'a the flies got emphysema from the dust. I can see 'em out there now, coughin' and hackin', and gaspin' and wheezin'."

"Rinse it offa yourself before you're doing the same." Dar stepped back, shaking her head. "God, Tony, look at your shoes! How'n hell you gonna get them clean?"

"Thought I'd burn 'em."

"I'll help."

"Good god, Al," Glenda sighed. "One load, maybe. Two? A bit much. But *three*?"

"Colly told Tommy she wanted a load'a shit," he defended. But Glennie shook her head. He sighed, then shrugged and went back to his lime-spreading chore.

The little garden tractor didn't have a hope of tilling under the mess. Tommy shook his head, knowing all his work had been undone.

"Fine thing," he grumbled. "There's probably some huge big lesson in all of this but I bet we won't find out what it is until it doesn't matter anymore. What a damn mess, Dad! It'd be funny if it wasn't so . . ."

"You're right," Al agreed, "and it really is 'so' . . ." Al went into the house and phoned for Tiny McFarlane to come out with the full-sized tractor and rotovater.

Tiny arrived with her treasures on a flat-deck, then stood looking at the mess. "My god, Al," she said mildly, "when you make a mess you make a real mess!"

"Don't start, Tiny, for god's sake. They've all had go's at me. Days of it. If I felt any stupider I'd change my name."

"Whose idea was this?"

"Mine," he admitted.

"You should stop having ideas," she said, grinning widely. "But I don't mind, I get paid by the hour. And this might take a few hours."

Glennie came from the house and moved to stand near Al. She slid her arm around his waist, gave him a brief hug, and shook her head. "Not a word," she promised.

"Best you don't," he agreed. "I might do something drastic if you do. Like this!" And he grabbed her. Glennie put one foot behind his leg and pushed. They fell, laughing, to the grass and the harsh *crack* of a rifle shot shattered the air.

"Fuck!" yelled Tiny, falling from her tractor, her left shoulder pouring gore.

"Get to the house!" Al hauled Glennie to her feet, pushing her toward the back door. The rifle sounded again and Al stumbled, gasping.

Jewen came from Lindy's house with a shotgun and Norm fired his deer rifle from the second-floor bedroom window. Al made it to the back door, still pushing Glennie, but he didn't make it to the back-room, he fell across the doorway. Glennie took one arm, Lottie the other, and they pulled him inside, as if a mere wall was protection.

The shotgun roared, the deer rifle barked, and there was an answering shot from the bush that punched a hole in the wall not six inches from where Norm was standing. Norm yelled curses and began firing, emptying his clip in the direction of the shot.

Doreen arrived with the first aid kit and Brady grabbed the phone. The shots from upstairs sounded again, backed up by the deep roar of the shotgun.

"Jesus, jesus, Al," Glennie wept. "Oh, god, please, no. Al, baby . . ."

"Keep talkin' to him," Doreen said quietly. "Keep him tied to us by the sound of your voice. Oh, christ, fella, you're a non-smoker for sure, now. This looks like it's hit your lung. Lottie, you got any Saran wrap or such? He's got a hole drilled right through him; if we're going to keep him breathing we have to plug it."

"Ambulance and police on their way," Brady announced. She knelt by Al's head, stroking his face. "Hang on, Al. Come on, boy, stay with us. Glennie's here, and she's real upset, you got to hang in for her."

Air whistled from the hole in his chest, blood bubbled, his face an unhealthy grey colour, his lips blue-tinged. Doreen sealed the entry and exit wounds with Saran wrap, and Brady watched. "You do that like someone who's done it before," she said softly.

"Ah, the hidden talents that usually go unheralded." Doreen forced a smile but her eyes were wide with fear, not for herself, not because any one of them could be hit by the shots still coming from the bush, but fear for her younger brother, whose lifeblood stained them all.

The firing from the bush stopped. Jewen put down the shotgun and rushed to where Tiny lay, her shirt soaked with blood, her face pallid.

"I'm okay," she whispered. "Just leave me here a while. Let them move me when they get here with a full crew."

"G'wan, you know how pisspoor slow they are," he said. He hunkered down and put his arms under her.

"You'll hurt your foolish self," she whispered. "I weigh a ton."

"Naw, you only like to brag that you do." He lifted her, his muscles straining, his face going red. "On the other hand," he gasped, "it might be two tons."

Staggering under the load of her he headed for the back door. His back felt hot and itchy; he half expected the rifle in the bush to fire at any second and drill him. He thought he even knew where the bullet would hit: right between the shoulders.

But no shot sounded. Jewen made it to the back steps and into the house, then lay Tiny on the floor beside Al. Lottie moved to her, took a look at the shoulder and shook her head.

"Hope you weren't planning on playin' the violin no time soon." And she patted Tiny's face.

"Hurts," Tiny grunted. "If I get my hands on that sucker . . ."

"Hand. You only got one hand workin' right now."

"Squeeze his throat for him," Tiny sighed, and her eyelids fluttered.

"She's goin' out," Lottie warned.

"Where *are* those guys!" Brady flared, then sobbed.

"You start crying," Doreen said clearly, "and so help me god there'll be three instead'a two when they finally get here."

The police arrived before the ambulance. They confiscated every gun on the place but didn't lay charges against either Jewen or Norm.

"I thought you guys were supposed to be some kind of sharp-shooting whizzes," one of the cops laughed. "Not even a bloodstain out there, let alone any sign of a body."

"We were shooting to scare 'im not to kill 'im," Jewen said. "Killing's against the law, you know." Norm didn't say anything, he just glared, and if looks could have killed there wouldn't have been a live cop for miles.

Finally, the ambulance arrived. Al was loaded first and put on oxygen; then the ambulance attendants, helped by Jewen and Norm, got Tiny loaded, her shoulder packed with thick gauze.

"I'm goin'," Glennie said, her voice shrill.

"Don't you go getting hysterical," Lottie said coldly. "There's enough for us to worry about without you getting all nervy."

"I'm fine!" Glennie snapped.

"Stay that way, then. Come on, get a grip, come down off the ceiling. If you're going to follow the ambulance you'd better change your clothes because you're a damn sight right now, your stuff is all bloodied up." Nattering and seeming to scold, Lottie led Glenda from the mess of gore in the backroom, took her to the bathroom and started the shower. "You get cleaned up," she ordered. "I'll get some clothes for you. When they've got him fixed up and he opens his eyes, it won't do him any good to see you looking like the Witch of Endor. You take some time and do it up right, let him see you as you really are."

"Yes, Momma," Glennie replied, stripping off her blood-soaked blouse. She looked at it, shuddered and tossed it in the basin. "Jesus," she whispered.

Singe and Tony arrived a half-hour later. By then there was only Lottie left in the house. The backroom was freshly scrubbed, the blood-stained clothes were in the washing machine, for the second time, and Lottie was peeling hard-boiled eggs.

"Was it him?" she asked, her face hard.

"Nothing to worry about." Singe hugged her, even dared to kiss her on the cheek. "She's all took care of, darlin'."

"Cops said they didn't see . . ."

"Hell." Tony hardly even looked like the person she knew. "No need to make a big mess. You got anything stronger'n beer in here, Lottie. I'm not the man I used to be."

"None of us are," Singe agreed. "I know where there's some of the old fart's finest. And man, I owe you. I want you to know that, I owe you."

"Amazing the things a guy will do for a friend, eh? You hear anything about Al?"

"Doreen phoned. Still in surgery, she said. You should get yourselves cleaned up and go join the others. You're good boys." She patted Singe. "Thank you, Mr. Singeon."

"Okay, Ma. It's okay."

Doreen paced back and forth, back and forth, on the sidewalk outside the emergency entrance of the hospital. She lit a cigarette, her fourth since arriving, her fifth in the past eight years. Jesus, jesus. Plus three reliable witnesses. What's the use of going through the hoops to quit smoking when you could as easy be hit by something falling out of the sky, a piece of comet, a chunk of cooling meteor, someone else's insanity. It had to have been Glennie's ex; from what she'd heard he was a typical mook, somewhat confused on the difference between love and control, between marriage and owning. Mine mine mine mine and I can treat it as badly as I want 'cause it's mine mine mine. Tell it I love it, then give it a good right cross; tell it I'm crazy about you, baby, then a fast left hook, maybe an uppercut or two. Then ten bucks' worth of flowers from Grandma's Nursery. And take potshots at anyone who promises any sort of happiness; oh no you don't, mine mine mine.

She'd been safer, for crying out loud, in Cambodia, picking leeches off some of the most private portions of her anatomy. Well, she'd done just fine by herself, and everyone else and had come away with some unusual insights, a few of them political, a few more social, and, of course, the one that made absolute stone-cold practical sense: the bugs, whether creeping, crawling, swimming or flying, had bitten her to hamburger, and yet the guides were hardly bothered at all. Oh, their arms and legs were bug-bitten, but they weren't going insane with bugs in their ears, in their eyes, in their noses, and there they were hidden in undergrowth, and she was just about ready to jump up screaming and tear at her head to get rid of the damned things. One day the guide, pressed so close against her in the cramped area that she could smell him, turned his head slightly and she almost recoiled. She'd never seen such dirty damned ears in her life. The wax was visible. Her North American quasi-fastidiousness prompted a mental scolding: jesus, even if you can't find a place to buy soap you can at least keep your damn self clean; instead of sitting around smoking a mix of god-knows-what and stinking tar, you could do what we do and go to the stream and clean the damn sweat stink off you. It's been so long since you were clean, your damn skin has a greasy sheen to it and those ears, jesus buddy, don't talk to me about oriental culture. I'll never look at another statue or painting or embroidered silk without remembering the wax is almost clogging your ear. Amazing thing is you can still hear! A plug like that might make a person next-best thing to deaf.

Then something clicked. She had an actual physical sensation, a sort of tightening of the muscles followed by immediate relaxation. Of course. There she was, so clean and pristine, with biting bugs of all kinds gnawing on her ear lobes until they were swollen, bleeding and so sore they throbbed, but wasn't she clean clean clean, just another wholesome Canadian: when in doubt wash it with soap, and because you're going into a jungle, use unscented or the bees and wasps will feed on you . . . And there he was, greasy with body oil and sweat, and ears clogged, *but* there were no gnawers, nippers, biters or chewers feasting on his lobes or crawling up and down in his ear canal, itching and annoying, enraging and insane-making.

Ear wax. Damn! And what's the first thing we teach our kids? Wash your ears, dear, Oh be sure to wash your ears. And don't worry at all that the sewers drain into the rivers or the garbage landfills leach into the lakes, just get those little ears clean, and once a week Mommy or Daddy will wash out your ears with peroxide. Then we'll pay money to get some spray that will repel the mosquitoes and maybe even help deplete the ozone layer, not to mention taking up space in the landfill.

Absolute practical sense, and it got her looking at things from a different perspective. Like some kind of secret weapon, because bit by bit by bit she went from ear wax and mosquitoes to why am I doing this? Well, it sure isn't to protect democracy because there really isn't any, not when corporations have more rights than citizens, not when deals are made and sanctioned by the politicians without the people even knowing about them, let alone getting a say. No, we've realized democracy is a sham, so that's not why I'm going along with the double-0 silliness. The clean-eared toothbrushed deodorized shampooed and hair-conditioned sleek at home might have more to eat and might be wasting their wages and the earth's resources on consumer goods, but when push comes to absolute shove they have no more say than any villager in any other place on earth. The death squads aren't as obvious, but then they aren't needed; the cars and TVs, the cablevision and processed food have bought off whatever it is in the human spirit that comes together to form revolutions and plot the overthrow of the system. Let the pampered start fomenting change and they'll be as disappeared as any of the other missing agitators.

But why was she pacing around out here doing mental rants and raves about ear wax and placid non-voters when her brother was in there stubbornly clinging to the life so many people were trying to save?

Guns guns guns, the old man and his gun, and look what mess he'd left behind, and now Al, and she had seen the mess that was his chest. She knew only too well how badly he was hurt. She'd seen men with wounds like that, she'd even given them enough shots of morphine to help their dying along fast and actually comfortable. Hurt that bad there's no chance to get them out; in other times and other places people like her had been forced to shoot their companions in the head to end the pain and misery. But now we have little packages of morphine surettes: one for pain, five for heaven.

She hadn't told them yet but Brady, at least, had guessed. You go along doing the things you've been trained to do right up to the point where you just very quietly refuse to do it anymore. And when that time comes you clean up the loose ends, make an appointment to see your supervisor—for behold, we all have them in one form or another—and you calmly and succinctly tell him you're going home, thank you very much for your understanding in this matter, ta ta, farewell, good bye-ee.

Oh, yes, we'll go home to the peace and quiet of the old homestead and be sitting having coffee when *pow*! and your brother is falling in the back door, chest shattered, blood . . . my dear god the stink of it!

"You okay?" Brady asked, falling in step beside Doreen.

"Worried. Angry. But okay. You?"

"All of the above plus scared shitless. I guess it was Fred, eh?"

"I suppose so. Next suspect would be Maude-the-Sod, but I doubt she could be counted on to hit what she thought she was aiming at. For that matter I can't see her pulling her brains together long enough to plan it and find a gun."

"Maude? Why would she want to shoot Al?"

"Well, for that matter, why would Fred?"

"Jealous, I guess."

"And Maude isn't?"

"What's *she* got to be jealous about?"

"Al's got the kids."

"So? She didn't look after 'em when she had 'em. Besides, she's got that poor Mavis, that's a full-time job."

"I'd still put her on the suspect list."

"I wouldn't. If she shot Al the rest of us would be mad at her and she don't want us mad at her. She tries overtime to have us *like* her."

"Why does she bother?"

"Because *we've* got the kids. Even more than Al has 'em, *we* have 'em. And if she shot Al, we'd be mad, and so would the kids, so she'd lose them completely. Didn't they teach you anything at spook school?"

"They taught me how to rip out your throat with one hand."

"Hell, Dory, you knew how to do that before you even left home." And Brady hip-bumped, catching Doreen off guard. "Gotcha."

They were all sitting together on the steps leading up to the manicured lawn and flower beds when Singeon and Tony arrived together. Glenda had been weeping, her eyes red and swollen, her nose still working overtime. She sniffed often and dabbed repeatedly at her tears, ready to break down again at the hint of a wrong word or gesture.

"How's he doing?" Tony sat down next to Darlene, handed her a can of Orange Crush, the condensation beaded on the outside. She took it, then wiped her hand on his jeans leg.

"He's still in there. Christ, it's been almost two hours."

"Been *more* than two hours, Dar. Your watch must have stopped."

"What do you know about my watch, anyway?" she snapped, then blinked rapidly. "Oh hell, Jewen, I'm sorry. I open my mouth and . . ."

"Yeah, you gotta stop doin' that, Dar, it's like you're proud of it or something."

"Don't lecture me, Jewie, please, or I'm gonna start bawlin'."

"Well, don't bother bawlin'," Glenda said, "I'm doing enough of it for everybody."

"You always did hog things. The rest of us might like a chance, too, you know."

"Christ, here we are, saying all these dumb things, trying to make jokes, and for chrissakes . . ." Tony cried.

"Easy." Jewen reached out and patted Tony's shoulder. "Hang on, guy."

"I'm not sure you guys have any idea just what that guy means to me."

"Yeah? He's our brother, you think *we* don't hurt?"

"Oh, hell." Doreen sounded weary beyond words. "Why don't you just whip 'em out and we'll measure 'em."

"Not unless we get to measure *yours*," Tony countered.

"You stop that." Darlene jabbed him with her elbow. "Calm your damn self down."

"Where were you?" Jewen asked. "Could'a used you."

"Him 'n' me were working on the digger. Heard the shots. By the time we got over there . . ."

"Took hell's own time to get over there, then, because we waited something like two and a half weeks for the ambulance."

"Yeah, well, we came in by the back way. Didn't think it'd do anyone any good if we drove up front like a coupl'a tourists and got ourselves shot."

Jewen looked at Singe, who smiled slightly. Jewen looked at Tony, but he was staring at his hands, clasped between his knees. Jewen looked back at Singe who nodded once, very slightly. Jewen sighed deeply, then put his arm around Glennie's shoulder.

"Hang on, sis," he said quietly. "He's tough."

"I gotta go." Lindy stood suddenly, held out her hands for the keys. "Can't leave Lottie alone with all those kids. Besides, if I get

350

any fuller I'll burst and there's no way Griff is going to be happy about *that*, he hates the bottle."

"Takes after his old man," Norm laughed.

"You?" Jewen snorted. "Hell, man, you *live* in the bottle."

"Not with no rubber nipple, I don't."

"Stop this before it even gets started," Darlene snapped.

"Damn straight." Brady slapped Norm's knee. "You just clean up your damn act, you hear."

"Did god die and put you in charge?"

"Stop it," Singe said quietly.

Norm blinked, then pretended to be very interested in the design on his cigarette package. "I'm goin' out of my skin here," he admitted. "Maybe I should . . ."

"Just sit where you are and calm yourself down. You head off now you'll go to a bar. One drink will lead to four or five and then the next thing you know, on top of this we'll have you in the drunk tank, charged with assault or something because of some big fight you get yourself into."

"So help me god, Jewen," Norm glared. "I don't know where you got the idea you were my daddy, but . . ."

"He's right." Brady reached over, took one of Norm's cigarettes. "He's not picking on you, Norm, so don't get proddy. He's just lookin' out for you, is all."

"Do I look like someone who needs . . ."

"Yeah," they all interrupted.

"Act like it, too." Singeon grinned. "Maybe I better go find a pay phone and let Lucy know what's happening here."

"I should call Mom." Glenda stood up and turned toward the hospital. "Oh, god, I hate to go back inside that place. What if they tell me . . ."

Six hours later the surgeon, looking like he hadn't seen a bed for so long he no longer knew what they were for, found them, still outside, still on edge, smoking and waiting, smoking and praying.

Glenda heard the words and sat blinking. Darlene finally dared to cry, and Tony held her, his own eyes wet.

"But he's basically going to be okay?"

351

"He's basically going to be a very long time recuperating, and even after he's up and on his feet and moving around, he's going to be weak. He's never going to be the man he was before he got shot."

"You mean he's crippled or something?" Norm blurted.

"I mean he's got one lung. He's going to tire easily. He might need to keep oxygen on hand at home, particularly in the evenings. He's going to have to take particularly good care of himself, a cold can be a major illness for him now. But he's going to make it, and no, he's not going to be a cripple."

"I'll bet you," Tony said clearly, "that even with only one lung he's still going to be more of a man than a good eighty percent of the people he meets."

"I'm going home," Norm proclaimed. "Someone's gotta tell those kids their old man's gonna be fine. And don't none of you just phone, either, you'll scare them spitless if you phone now. They need to be told in person."

"Good thought, Norm," Singeon agreed. "Maybe I could catch a ride back with you? Leave the truck here for the others?"

They walked away, a tall slender man and a stubby thick one.

"Can we see him?" Glennie asked.

"You can see him, but he's not conscious. He won't be talking to anyone for several days, maybe more. But yes, you can see him. And you can talk to him; who knows what we hear and understand when we're asleep the way he is. It might well be the best medicine for him right now."

Colleen was in the living room with Lottie and Lindy and most of the kids. She looked up when Norm and Singeon walked in.

"He's gonna make it," Norm said. "You kids can come apart now. Uncle Norm's here, Uncle Singe is here, and I give you my word, he's made it through the operation and everything."

"But he could still die!" Colleen cried.

"Colly, darling, you could be hit by lightning on your way home tonight." Singe patted her shoulder. "Yeah, he could get infection or throw a big blood clot or something, or have a heart attack, or the freakin' sky could fall. But right now he's got as much chance as any of us of living to collect his old-age pension."

"Who shot him?" Tom demanded.

"Big Fred."

"How's Tiny?" Jessie asked.

"Oh shit!" Singeon blurted. "We out and out forgot to ask! Now isn't *that* a caution!"

"Tea's ready." Deb came in from the kitchen with a cookie sheet loaded with cups, cream, sugar and the big Brown Betty teapot. She set it on the coffee table and looked inquiringly at Lottie, who nodded. "You look worn out," Deb said and Lottie nodded again.

"Glennie's fine, Ma," Singe said, then turned toward the door. "Can't stay, I want to get home to Lucy."

"She's going to feel so guilty," Lottie mourned. "Glennie always did take things hard. She'll blame herself for this."

"Well, what she don't know won't hurt her. She'll be fine. Soon as he can talk and all, she'll be fine."

Jessie sat sipping tea, her eyes flooding over, tears slickering down her face. "Why," she grieved, "why is everything around here so *much*?"

"Just lucky, darling." Deb sat beside her, not hugging her but giving her something even more comforting, the respect she would give any adult. "One thing I've learned in the couple of years I've been hanging out with your aunt, there's never a dull moment if those Lancasters are around."

♣

Tiny worried herself half sick over her business. "Frenchy LaFrennierre just bought himself a bunch'a gear," she moaned, "and by the time I'm out of here and fit to work he'll have all my customers. Rotten little fart," she added. "He didn't know diddly-squat and I gave him a job. Only dirt he'd ever seen was under his damn fingernails. Now? Hear him tell it he's a landscaping expert."

"Not to worry," Singe soothed. "We'll figure out something."

They visited the telephone company and had all calls to Tiny's number rerouted to a new phone at the big house. Above it Doreen put a little typed card so whoever answered would know exactly what to say. "Tiny's Yardwork, how may I help you?"

"People will think you've gone up-scale, Tiny," Singeon teased. "Sounds like you've got yourself a receptionist, maybe even a secretary. It's gonna be a status symbol to have their work done by you."

Tom wasn't old enough to drive the flat-deck with the equipment on the back, or at least not old enough to dare drive it down the highway. Doreen did that part of it, then Tommy did the ploughing, the rotovating, the rock picking and disking. It meant his evenings were full and that made homework something he had to schedule, but he didn't seem to mind: he was filling in, he was helping out, he was keeping things together while his dad was on the sick list.

For those customers who absolutely insisted on daytime service, when Tom was in school, there were others on hand to fill in. Sometimes Tony, sometimes Singe, sometimes Chuck. Tiny's competition complained: it wasn't fair, they had plenty of people to call on for work, and no wages to pay; besides which there was the other equipment, their own, in case the job called for more than Tiny's company owned. They could, he yelled into the phone, work twenty-four hours a day seven days a week and still not be tired. He, on the other hand, was practically dragging his knuckles on the gravel; he was only one man. None of this was fair.

"Gee, mister," Jesse said to the handset, "all you had to do was ask and we'd'a helped you, too. Any time you've got too much work to do you just phone, we'll do it for you."

"And rob me blind," he roared, slamming down the phone.

"That guy's in a real bad mood," she told Lottie as she hung up. "People shouldn't let themselves get so bent out of shape."

Colleen quit her job. She just walked in one day, put the four-by keys on the desk, then put her letter of resignation beside it. She gave two weeks' notice, just to be fair, and on her last day drove home singing. That was the same day the other workers got their layoff notices. They were told it was because of the forest fire hazard, but none of them expected to be called back soon, not even if the rains came and stayed until the ground was sodden and the rivers high. The newspapers wrote about the softwood dispute, about the European market wanting eco-certified lumber and not old growth from a threatened rain forest, but the ones closest to the terrain knew the fast, easy, profitable creaming of the big ones was finished, the easy pickings were done, and the company was preparing to move its focus to other places where they could bring it in hand over fist and keep the shareholders smiling.

"It's like a repeat of what happened with the coal mines," Jewen sighed. "They hauled it out and made fortunes right up until it was too dangerous. The easy stuff close to the surface was gone, and they'd'a had to invest money in safety gear. So they effed off. Now? Same old same old, I guess."

"What you going to do with yourself now?" Darlene asked, holding Andy on her shoulder, patting his back to encourage him to burp.

"I don't have any idea at all," Colleen said, laughing. "I've got some money saved up; if push comes to shove I can go work in the Bucket of Blood serving beer, I guess. Maybe I'll just pull my own back-to-the-land trip. I mean, hell, the old fart lived for years on next to bugger-nothing. Maybe I will, too."

"You going to set up a still and make hooch, too?"

"Hey, stranger things have been done around here." And they both laughed. Deb smiled, watching them—so alike, so different, able to be close and loving one minute and ready to kill the next.

Later, much later, after supper, after dishes and kitchen cleanup, after a warm bath together, with candles flickering and the scent of Algemarin in the air, after they dried each other with soft towels and went to bed early, with more on their minds than reading the evening paper, Deb asked the same question Darlene had asked.

"Oh, I might go back to school." Colleen yawned, cuddled close in bed, her body slack and lazy with loving. "I kinda like the idea of learning something next-best to totally useless. Something like, oh, I don't know, psychology or something."

"Well, hell, one thing about it, you've got a textbook full of case studies right here underfoot," Deb teased.

"Yeah. How's Al? I mean really."

"At the risk of violating hospital confidentiality and all that other good stuff . . . he must be made of stainless steel. He's going to be okay, Colly, you should stop worrying about it so much."

"I wouldn't worry so much if he was *your* brother," Colly teased. "It's just because he's mine that I fuss."

"Shut up and go to sleep."

"Yes, ma'am. You set your alarm clock?"

"Yes, ma'am. Just like always."

"We're a fine pair." Colly stroked Deb's belly. "I worry and fuss over you, and you worry and fuss over me . . . Of course you set your alarm clock. My christ, you've looked after yourself for years. Why would you stop just because you've moved in here?"

"I like it here. It's not what I expected, though. I thought . . . you know . . . miles from town, hundreds of acres of bush . . . birdsong, maybe and oh, like, look out the window and see a deer in the back-yard. Instead it's like shift-change at the mental hospital, and you can't tell the patients from the staff."

"At least we're on *this* side of the ravine. Think what it's like over there on the other side."

Colleen was up and drinking her second cup of coffee on the back porch before Deb's alarm sounded. Minutes later Deb appeared, freshly showered, her hair combed and dripping onto the shoulders of her bathrobe.

"You make a good cup of coffee." She smiled, bending forward and kissing Colleen's forehead. "It amazes me I didn't have to fight my way through a crowd of coffee-drinking ever-loving women just to get to talk to you."

"Oh, I was waiting for you," Colleen answered easily. "That's why I walked up to you so bold and brassy at the dance."

"You think so, eh? I'd been working on you, sending psychic messages: look for the tall blond one . . . and it worked."

"You're not so tall." Colleen slid her hand up the inside of Deb's leg, stroking gently, firmly. "You've just got loooooooong legs."

"What you got in mind for today? Anything?"

"Well, I think, all things considered, pressing as my schedule is, I should make some time to actually *do* something to that goddamn garden. I mean, all the fuss it caused . . ."

Tony hitched the new double leaf plough to Tiny's big tractor and turned the hot muck under, setting the plough to dig deep, bringing up dirt and rolling it in easy strips on top of the festering crap. Four times lengthwise and three times crossways and the stink faded rapidly. When Colleen went out on the garden tractor to rototill, she imagined scores and hordes of flies sitting puzzled, their noses twitching, trying in vain to find even a hint of the glorious reek that had brought them here.

Back and forth, round and round, and when the soil was fine and almost fluffy, she began to spread the well-composted black soil she'd bought from the Prince of Wales. And when that was turned under, she parked the garden tractor and measured and marked her rows. The potato trenches were ready when Lottie called her in for lunch, and by the time Deb got home from day shift, the spuds were planted, and so was the corn.

"My dear woman," Deb laughed, "this so-called garden is the size of a football field, at least!"

"Do you have any idea how much corn we'll have to grow? Count the number of kids, figure in that each and every one of them can gnaw through two cobs per meal, easy . . ."

"Lettuce . . . a few tomato plants . . . that's what I had in mind. A few green onions, maybe . . . this is serious business."

"Yeah. I'm looking forward to it. I'm worried about the spuds, though. All that muck, and then they spread all that lime. It's sure to make them scabbyskinned."

"So why plant them?"

"How could you call it a garden without spuds? How could you call it spring without baby spuds and mint sauce?"

When Al came home from hospital the garden was well established. Soaker hoses ran along the rows, while between them, the mulch was thick, a mix of alder sawdust and lawn clippings, smothering the weeds and helping keep the earth from drying out in the increasing heat. The corn was waist-high, the chard was ready, the beet tops had been harvested several times, and the green tomatoes hung heavy and full of promise.

"Hey," he said, "you sure you'll have enough stuff? Christ, Colly, it looks like one of those commercial produce gardens."

"You mean truck gardens?" She fed him the line.

"Trucks don't grow in gardens." He winked. "You know better'n that."

He was pale, he'd lost a scary amount of weight, and any kind of exertion tired him, but he was home and stronger every day. Lottie fussed over him, cooking his favourite meals, keeping soup hot and ready for his mug.

"Jeez, you got no coffee, Lot?" he complained. "Every time I turn around you're pushin' soup at me."

"I'll make you coffee, Mr. Al," she agreed, "as soon as you finish that soup."

"What's in my mug or what's in the pot?"

"Mug for now. Pot later."

He sipped his coffee and looked blissful. "Now if I just had a smoke," he mourned. "Nothing's the same without 'em."

"If you promise not to tell a soul," Lottie bargained.

"Not a word. Not one god-forsaken word."

She sat next to him, pulled out her cigarettes and lit one. She handed it to Al who took a hungry puff.

"Oh, god," he almost groaned. "There's some things a fellow just can't give up easy. I try, but so help me god, I can't even imagine myself not smoking."

"You've only got one lung," she warned.

"Right. But I've got it!" He coughed, then grinned. "Fuck, listen to me. Hacking and gasping here like an old codger. But"—he lifted his coffee mug in a toast to her—"at least I'm a very happy old codger."

Still, she noticed, he really only took a half-dozen puffs and didn't inhale all of them. He stubbed out the long butt, and nodded. "Appreciate it, Lottie."

"Well, don't expect more 'n one a day from me," she said, nudging him gently. "One from me and one from Singe, one from Tony and one from Chuck, one from Darlene and another from Doreen . . . you're prob'ly smoking as much now as you did before you got winged."

"And here I thought I was being real sneaky."

"Yeah, and leaving a trail behind you like a cow who's been stuffing herself on new green grass."

"Garden looks good."

"Don't try to change the subject. You don't fool me."

He didn't fool anybody. They all knew they weren't the only one giving him bootleg smokes. Only Colleen stood firm and refused to light one up for him.

"When you're up and moving around and can prove that one lung can do the work of two, maybe," she scolded. "But as long as you're sitting there looking like a sick man, forget it."

"Sick man? I'm not sick. Nothing wrong with me."

"Right. So prove it."

Bit by bit he expanded his world. At first he had all he could do to walk from the new big house to the garden plot to admire the crop. Without making any open comment about it Norm made sure there was a comfortable chair just inside the gate, where Al could sit and catch up to himself before making the trek back to the house, to the recliner set up on the porch. He sat there, pale and sweaty, and sipped the soup Lottie brought him. Sometimes waves of depression would wash over him and he'd have all he could do not to bust out bawlin' like a little kid. He wasn't at all sure he was going to be able to cope. What if this was as good as he was going to get? What if, for the rest of his life, he had to carry a little oxygen bottle with him, hanging from its harness like a huge wart riding on his hip. Worst of all, he had to use it: a few quick sucks at it in the garden chair so he could get back to the porch, a few quick sucks in the recliner so he could hold the mug of soup without his hand shaking so badly he spilled beef 'n' barley on himself.

The oxygen that came from the bottle tasted stale and metallic, it was cold and dried his throat and the lining of his nose. But within two weeks he could go to the garden and back before he needed to put the mask to his mouth.

Three weeks after he got out of hospital he made it all the way down to Singe's place. Lucy saw him coming and had fresh coffee made. He sat on the porch sucking his oxygen and listening to the rapid pounding of his own heart. But he'd made it.

"Here you go," she said and handed him the mug of coffee, and he took it, nodding his thanks. "Soon's you're finished with that canned air I'll take the riggin's somewhere else and we'll have us a smoke."

He nodded again, sucking deeply. It tasted like shit, but he was glad he had it.

He and Lucy were sitting on the porch drinking coffee when Singe and Tony came back in the truck. They were dusty and sweaty but grinning widely.

"You look like someone who just won a million dollars," Al greeted them.

"Nah, but we got to see Tiny back on her tractor, all ready-set-go for work," Tony answered. "Shoulder's stiff, but as she says, that's why god invented equipment."

"How you making out?" Singe sat beside Al and reached behind him to stroke Lucy's back.

"Bored out of my fuckin' skull if the truth be known," Al grumbled.

"Yeah? Well, why not head off on the boat, do some serious fishing? Tony'll go with you, won't you, guy?"

"Day or two," Tony offered. "Don't want to be gone off for weeks on end."

"Day or two'll probably do me fine," Al said. "Remind me to bring lots of canned air. You never know, I might find out I'm as addicted to the stuff as I am to coffee."

"Here, have a smoke and shut up." Lucy lit one and handed it to him.

"Colly sees you doing that she'll have a fit."

"The day I worry about Colly's fits is the day I'll sign myself into the loony bin," Lucy replied easily. "You know damn well if the rest'a you's were saying no no no and refusin' to give him smokes, it'd be Colly sneakin' them to him. As long as she's the contrary one, she's happy."

"I thought you liked her." Tony was surprised.

"I like her. I like her real well. She's family. That doesn't mean I can't see how she operates or who she really is."

The fishing trip lasted four days and they brought back a load of fish, quick frozen in the boat freezer. Lucy and Lottie got out the canning jars and Colleen rescued four of them for the supper barbecue. Lindy had her own recipe for potato salad and so did Lottie. With Deb's that made three kinds, and Darlene made her macaroni salad, which everyone ate but only she really liked. However, it was easier to swallow a half cup of it than deal with her hurt feelings. There were other salads: three-bean and five-bean, sliced tomato in garlic vinaigrette, and more devilled eggs than enough. Even Norm was in a good mood, and his new squeezie smiled, smiled and smiled, trying to remember everyone's name, knowing she was months and miles from figuring out who was with whom.

Brew and Maude set Mavis up in her padded recliner, where she lay, eyes roving, obviously not even trying to bring anything or anyone in focus. She was thin and pale, and just looking at her made the other children feel uneasy. Dorrit was drawn to her, stood beside her, stroking her arm, trying to get some sort of response from her. "What's that tube?" he asked.

"It goes into her stomach," Brew told him. "See?" He lifted the pretty pink tee-shirt, then moved the edge of the bandage, exposing the artificial dimple where the feeder tube was sutured in place. "The other end," he said as he replaced the gauze, smoothed the child's shirt gently, then showed Dorrit what looked like a travel valise. There was a groove where the lid met the bottom, a place just big enough for the tube to fit snugly. Brew opened the valise. The other kids were crowded around, trying to see, their faces bright with interest. Jessie lifted little Fred to her hip, and he gripped her with his skinny legs and stared, both fascinated and worried.

"The stuff in this bag is special food." Brew cleared his throat and swallowed several times, blinking his eyes. "You might hear a ding sound, that's the timer and it means the machine thing in here has turned on and is pumping food along the tube and into Mavis's stomach. Everything happens automatically, just to be sure we don't forget or sleep too hard at night and not wake up when it's time to do this."

"You mean she isn't going to get any salmon?" Dorrit asked. "No salad, no cake?"

"She used to be able to swallow, but she's forgotten how, I guess. Sometimes she remembers how to suck, and if we hear her sucking at her thumb, or her fist, or sometimes her lip, well, we can hurry up and maybe get her a popsicle or something. She doesn't really swallow it, mostly it dribbles back out of her mouth, but she at least gets to taste it, and she likes the orange ones best."

"I like blue," Freddy stated.

"I'll try her with blue some time," Brew said. He looked at the gnomish little boy and then quite openly wiped his eyes. "Thanks, kids," he coughed, and Dorrit patted Brew's arm.

"I'm real sorry." Dorrit looked at Brew. "You must be real sad."

"Yeah. I am real sad about it."

"I guess she's not going to live very long, eh?"

"No. The doctor says we'll probably go in one morning and she'll just be gone in her sleep."

Maude turned abruptly and headed into the house. Colleen waited for someone to go to her, to comfort her, and when nobody else moved, she did, less than willingly.

Maude was at the kitchen table with a can of beer and a cigarette, just sitting, fingers trembling, looking like someone with a private view of hell. Colleen got a beer and sat at the table, but couldn't think of a thing to say.

"Bummer, eh?" Maude managed.

"Bummer for sure."

"Sometimes"—Maude looked defiant—"I think we'd all be better off if I just put a pilla over her face and got it over with now and fast. Who else has a better right? I'd go to jail and be happy if I knew there was something . . . more . . . waiting for her. But I don't know that and so I don't just . . ."

"Nobody knows what goes on with her. For all we know she can hear and even understand, she might be lying there enjoying all kinds of stuff today: the kids laughing, the excitement. We don't know."

"Or," Maude whispered, "she might be there like a lump of unfinished flesh with no more thought or idea or awareness than a . . . oh, I don't know, a slug or something."

"We don't know that."

"I pick her up, I cuddle her, I talk to her, and there's no change I can see. You could leave her alone for days on end, I doubt she'd care."

"But you *don't* leave her alone for days on end because *you* care."

"Know what I really feel bad about? I mean really? Sometimes, when I'm cleaning her up and trying to make her comfortable . . . if she ever is . . . I remember when Jessie was a baby. Squirm, wriggle, kick . . . and all's I wanted to do was get it over with. I never took the time with the others that I take with Mavis . . . it was plop 'em down, wash 'em off, dry 'em and get a diaper on lickety-split, then into the playpen or the jolly jumper or something, because I was busy . . . or bored . . . or just fed up with the damn same old same old all the time. How many times were they laughing and hollering and trying to shout words and I said Here, you, be quiet . . . or stuffed a cookie in their mouths to shut 'em up . . . or turned the radio up so's I didn't have to listen to the babbling . . . and . . . well, hell, listen to me, morbid molly for sure. Think I'll have me another." She drained her beer and took the empty to the counter on her way to the fridge for a refill. "I gave it up for a long time," she laughed bitterly, "like I was making a deal, you know, dear god please fix her and I'll be a sober woman for life. Instead'a fixing her, well, she's gone downhill. I figure that means god likes me better half-tanked."

The kids were only briefly interested in Mavis. Even Dorrit gave up trying to get a reaction of some kind. They got out the softball and the bats, and moved to the smoothed-out place behind the houses where the dads and uncles had used the machinery to level a play area. First base was a loaf-sized rock, second base was a gunny sack half-filled with sawdust and third base was a piece of old plank. The pitcher stood more-or-less wherever was a comfortable distance, the only rule being that the mound had to be the same from one pitch to the other. Home plate was the fraying flap from a beer box, brand name side up so the red printing could be clearly seen.

Jessie was catching, Tom pitching and little Fred was at bat. He stood with the lightest bat balanced on his shoulder, face intent, waiting for the ideal pitch. When an old blue pickup turned from the highway, Fred's expression changed, became at once guarded and worried.

"Hey, Freddy, you playing?" Tom teased.

"It's Gramma," Freddy whispered.

"It's okay, Fred, he's not with her."

"You sure?"

"Sure, I'm sure." Tom dropped the softball to the ground and held out his hand. "C'mon, Freddy, I'll go over with you. It's okay."

Marian Webster moved to where Al was sitting in a lawn chair, nursing a can of beer. Glenda saw her coming and stood up, moving toward her, smiling.

"You're just in time for dinner." She leaned over and kissed her once mother-in-law on the cheek.

"You're looking good," Marian said. "You look ten years younger. Which one of these is Albert Lancaster?"

"I'm Al," he stood slowly, not smiling, half expecting trouble.

"I'm Marian Webster," she said flatly. "I came to see if we can cut us a polite deal so's I can see my grandchildren. I'm sorry about what happened to you. I'd do anything I could to make it up although I guess there's no way to make up a lung, but . . ."

"You're welcome here any time you feel like coming," Al said. "You're their grandma. That means you come and go here as you want to. There's just one thing, and I'm sorry I have to bring it up, but please, don't ever bring that mesatchie bastard with you. I don't want him on the place."

She gave him a slit-eyed look, as if she either couldn't believe what he'd just said, or couldn't be the least bit sure he meant it. "I doubt very much if he's going to be seen around here ever again," she said. "He's vanished. A person might think the very earth swallowed him."

They just looked at each other, each of them guarded and ill at ease, then Tom arrived with Freddy. Marian looked at him and her face softened.

"Hello there, my own dear Freddy-boy," she said, her voice soft. He stared at her, then moved forward stiffly, still gripping Tom's hand.

"And you're . . . ?" Marian tried to pretend she didn't recognize Freddy's fear.

"I'm Tom Lancaster, ma'am," he said, but did not smile. "I'm Freddy's big brother now."

"So you're going to take care of him . . . protect him?"

"If he needs it, I guess."

"Oh, we all need it, Tom Lancaster. Some of us more than others."

Caroline and Darryl ran up, Caroline hugging her grandmother around the waist, Darryl jostling for a place beside her. "Grandma, Grandma," they said, fussing over her, patting her arm, wanting closer, wanting more touch, more giving and receiving of affection.

"We'd be pleased if you'd stay and take a meal with us." Al moved back to his chair, sat comfortably. "We've got plenty, and it's a family get-together so you'll fit right in. I won't try to introduce you to everyone, you'll never remember them all, anyway. Besides, they all answer to 'you'. Except for the ones who are more used to 'you fool'."

"You're a charming man, Mr. Lancaster." Marian made it sound as if she was scolding him. He grinned, totally unbothered.

"Would you?" Glenda asked. "Stay, I mean."

"Yes," Marian said. "I have some things for the children in the truck. Maybe you could go get them, Tom Lancaster? There's two boxes on the seat, if you could bring them here, please."

"Yes, ma'am." He released Freddy's hand but Freddy hung on, squeezing. "Hey, guy, you're okay," Tom said. "That's your grandma, not the ogre."

"Freddy, you can relax," Marian said sadly. "I don't have anybody else hidden in the truck. I came by myself. Maybe you'd like to go with Tom and, while he's getting the boxes, you could see for yourself that Grandma's on her own."

Freddy trudged off still gripping Tom's hand. Marian watched them go, then shook her head sadly.

"That poor child," she mourned. "I can't even begin to imagine what must have happened to make him so fraidy. Funny thing, though, he hid it more before he moved here." She looked questioningly at Glennie. "Don't you think so?"

"He doesn't even try to hide it here," Glennie admitted. "He glommed onto Tommy from the very start, in ways he never glommed onto Darryl. I mean Freddy and Darryl hardly even bothered with each other! But Freddy even moved his pillow into Tommy's room. He'd go to bed in his own room with Darryl, but no more would Tom go to bed than Freddy'd come in with his pillow and quilt, and at first he was sleeping on the floor. So one day Tommy moved Freddy's bed in, too. Darryl doesn't care, it gives him a whole room to himself, and if Tom cares, he hasn't said anything. And Freddy, well, it's as if he thinks he's somehow been given permission to just . . . let it all hang out, I guess."

"I never did feel good about the way Fred was with the children," Marian admitted. "But . . . I didn't say anything. I guess I should have. No need to be that strict with them."

"Well, I didn't stand up to him much, either," Glenda said. "He has that way about him. It's easier to just back off and let him ramble than it is to try to stop something or change things."

Later, with the salmon devoured and the salads noticeably diminished, Marion turned to Al, and even tried to smile. "I haven't seen him," she said suddenly, "since the day you got hurt."

"I didn't get 'hurt', Mrs. Webster. I got shot. In the back."

She nodded, and repeated, "I haven't seen him since."

"I didn't even see him then." Al's short laugh was more like a bark. "All's I know is Tiny got knocked off her tractor. I figure if we hadn't been jack-assing around, and if Glennie hadn't tripped me and sent us both to the turf, that shot would have ripped her head off, then and there."

"Oh god," she mourned, forced by his words to take a long cold look at what she had been trying to avoid seeing clearly.

"He didn't come here to 'hurt' anyone," Al continued, "He came here to kill."

"God was holding you in the palm of his hand," she declared.

"Oh sheepshit," Al snorted. "If god gave the first part of a good damn, ma'am, she'd see to it nobody wound up so bent out of shape."

Anything she might have said was cut off short by a sudden uproar over near the barbecue. Norm was red in the face, practically coming out of his sneakers, yelling at his squeezie, yelling at Chuck, yelling at Big Wil, even yelling at Jewen.

"Shut up, Norm," Al called, coughing with the exertion. "Jesus," he managed, "can't even give a good hoot and holler anymore."

"Just get yourself on the goddamn bike is all. And don't bother to sass back at me. I told you and I told you, and now I'm tellin' you!"

"Well, *gee whiz*!" she yelled. "Will you just listen to your god-damn self? Who do you think you are, anyhow?"

"Stupid goddamn thing to say." He laughed suddenly. "Honest to god sometimes you come out with the stupidest damn things."

"I do? *Me*? If you'd listen to yourself once in a while you'd find out fast enough that *I'm* not saying stupid stuff."

They nattered and nagged their way to the bike, climbed on, and fitted their helmets to their heads. Everyone expected Norm to take off in a spray of grass and gravel. Instead, he moved sedately to the highway, checked in both directions, and drove off at a reasonable speed.

"What was that all about?" Doreen asked.

"I have no idea," Big Wilma said. "Does it matter?"

The next morning Deb awoke alone in the bed. She yawned, stretched, and checked her alarm clock. Plenty of time. Time enough for something a lot more interesting than an extra-long shower. She got out of bed and walked barefoot, wearing only an oversized tee-shirt, looking for Colleen.

Deb was on the porch, mug of coffee in hand, before she caught sight of Colleen, who had an ice cream pail and a stick with a nail in the end. Slug patrol. Even with the early morning promise of a hot day the little bastards were busy! You just had to get up a bit earlier to catch them. Given even half a chance they could gnaw off an iris stem in just about no time flat. What they did to begonias ought to be classed as a crime against humanity.

Colleen had tried all the supposed answers to the slug question. She'd put out little saucers of beer, supposed to attract them and then poison them. They'd been attracted, all right, but seemed to thrive on the beer, flat or not. She'd tried slug bait, but it disintegrated in the heavy night dew. She tried little collars of plastic, other collars of paper, of cardboard, of plexiglass. She'd even tried a coppery ribbon supposed to kill them by electrocuting them with their own bodily static, and still the effective cure was the old slug patrol.

"Hey, pretty lady," Deb called. "You really *really* dedicated to wiping out slugs or could I tempt you . . .?"

"Tempt me? Me? No way to tempt *me*. I'm incorruptible." Colleen moved quickly, emptied her ice cream bucket into what they called the death bucket: a bigger plastic pail in which waited a generous layer of triple-30 fertilizer. Within seconds the slugs began to disintegrate, turning into a sickening slimy mess. For years, Colleen had used salt to dissolve the marauders, but Tom had pointed out it wasn't efficient; they could use fertilizer just as effectively, then bury the mess in the ground where it might even be of some benefit.

Across the ravine Tom and Freddy were on slug patrol, too. Freddy had a stick, Tom carried the bucket. They patrolled first the garden, then around the fence line, Freddy keeping count; at a penny a slug they'd already made a dollar fifty. He didn't know how much each that was supposed to be, but he did know Tom would shrug and say Freddy could have it all.

"I gotta go, soon, Fred," Tom warned. "Tiny's supposed to pick me up at seven."

"Can I go with you?"

"No. It's my job, not *our* job."

"But I *want* to go."

"How many people do you think give a shit what you want?" Tom teased. "You ask the same thing every day, and you get the same answer each time. A person would think you'd learn."

"One day you might say yes." Fred speared a big fat juicy one.

"Yuck." His face twisted. "These things are *gross*. Why does Auntie Colly want them, anyway?"

"She uses them to make soup, you jerk."

"Does not!"

"Does so."

"Does *not*, Tom Lancaster!"

"Does *so*, Fred Webster."

The day the schools spit the kids out for summer holiday they put the phone on the answering machine and loaded food, kids, towels, beach blankets and lawn chairs, and headed to Lancaster Lake. They arrived to find a dozen families already installed, their kids racing in and out of the water, their barbecues filling the air with the smell of scorched fat and singed meat.

"Good god almighty," Doreen muttered, "at five bucks a family we're already out money."

"I don't mind 'em using the lake," Singe said, "but I do object to the way they've parked just any old which-a-way, hogging space and acting as if the whole damn thing belonged to them."

"Someone's got a tent trailer set up. And someone else has one of those little teardrop camping trailers."

"Better be room for *us*, I'll tell the world." Al was lifting kids from the pickup, giving each of them something to carry. "Here, Fredsters, you could maybe take these towels for us."

"My name's not Fredsters."

"Sorry. Fred."

"I'm not Fred, either. I'm Tommy."

"No, you're not, Tom's over there, and he's twice your size."

"He's Tom. I'm Tommy."

"You better talk to your mommy about this, guy; she might not want you to change your name."

"It's *my* name."

"Well, still and all, think you could carry these towels over to where Tom is spreading out the blankets?"

The little guy nodded and trotted off, dragging one end of a towel in the glittering shale and coal bits. "You hear that?" Al asked Glennie.

"I heard."

"What do you think?"

"Well, I guess we've got Big Wil and Little Wil so we can get used to Big Tom and Little Tommy. I mean, I can understand why he doesn't want to be Fred . . . can you?"

"Yep," he said easily, putting his arm around her waist. "Long as you don't mind it's fine with me."

They settled themselves and joined the kids in the water. Cars arrived and people got out, moved to find a spot and set up their spaces. By the time the first energetic swimming was over and the kids were gravitating back to the blanket in search of food, Lancaster Lake was becoming crowded.

"How much money you figure we're losing at this point?" Singeon teased Doreen.

"You're out a couple of day's wages for a caretaker."

"Gonna go broke at this rate."

"Gonna go *real* broke if someone decides to sue because their kid cut its foot or skinned its knee or cracked its head. I think it's what the insurance companies call an alluring risk, or something like that. Like when you've got a swimming pool in your backyard, you have to put an extra fence around it because it's such a temptation to neighbour kids."

"Have to fence the place off, I suppose. Of course, then they'll just fuck the fence, we'll be forever fixing it."

"Not if you put in a gate and charge 'em to use the place. Like I said, five bucks a family. Ten bucks a night if they think they're going to camp here. Which, if you notice, quite a few of them are getting ready to do. Put up a few biffies so they stop shitting in the bush, maybe put in a shower room, put up a big sign, 'No extra charge,' make 'em think they're really getting something for their money."

"A pop stand," Jessie contributed. "Maybe even a chip wagon or hot dogs or something. And you know where they're putting the new highway through? Well, there are two motels have to come down to make way for it. Bet we could buy the cabins real cheap;

370

set 'em up on the other side of the lake, put in lots of outdoor tables, the kind with the umberella's coming out of the middle . . . could charge probably fifty bucks a night."

"The part I don't understand is how we managed to wind up with so many capitalist pigs in the family," Colleen said.

"Enlarge your garden," Singe was teasing her, but she knew there were others listening who were serious. "You could have a vegetable stand here."

"If you were smart," Jessie continued, "you'd make up a big vat of Greek salad and give people a dixie cup full for free; your Greek salad is so good they'd all want more. Then you sell them the vegetables to make it, maybe sell 'em bottles of Greek Salad Dressing."

"Get a couple of lifeguards," Doreen warned, "or you'll be in doo-doo up to your eyebrows."

"Be easier and cheaper to just chase 'em off with a shotgun loaded with rock salt," Al grunted.

"Oh, I don't know," Singeon wasn't teasing. "I mean, think of it. Really, think. We got a motel that's full all the time and it doesn't even have a *view* of a lake let alone immediate access to it. Instead of tiddly-winkin' around with some second- or third-hand motel units we could put in a *real* one. Year-round. Dining room and everything. Get a liquor licence. Maybe a kind of cutesy-pootsy dock, and boats to rent or canoes or something. One side of the lake for the motel and the washed, this side for the campsite and unwashed."

"You people make me tired just listening to you," Lucy snapped. "Can't we just *enjoy* this place?"

"With all them strangers cluttering it up? If anybody understood that I'd'a thought it would be you," Al teased.

"*If* any of you were thinking," Lucy said clearly, "you'd build your hotel thing so's it looked like a traditional longhouse. Them canoes 'n' such? Get Louie Harry to make up some dugouts. Billy Moses would make you some totem poles for the place, you could have your waiters and waitresses in traditional regalia, you could even put little thingamajigs in the rooms telling how this used to be a deer pasture before it was stolen."

"Now *that's* an idea I could get behind!" Singe exclaimed.

"That'd be more fun than work. Maybe get like a museum happening, or a cultural centre."

"How did we wind up with a motel?" Colleen asked clearly, her eyes boring holes into Singeon's head. "I distinctly heard you say . . ."

"Well, yeah," he said, smiling, "I'm sure I told you about it, Colly."

"You didn't say word one!" she snapped.

"Oh, I can't believe that. Sometimes you must move in a dream world: a person can speak to you, get an answer, and not ten minutes later you've forgotten all about it."

"Singeon . . ." She was getting angry and they all knew it.

"I know for a fact," Al reached for the coffee thermos. "Singe talked to you about the family investment. I can clearly remember that. We were all sitting on the porch, except you. And you were in the living room on the sofa. It was in the old house, before The Burp. And you just kept saying uh huh, uh huh, like you agreed with him."

"I was probably nine-tenths asleep."

"How were we to know that? We talked about it. Talked about taking the family investment out of the mutual fund thing and moving it to them ethical investments you told us about."

"I remember talking about ethical investments," she admitted. "But I don't remember anything at all about any motel."

"Well, there you have it." He winked at her. "You snooze, you lose."

"And we own a motel? Where?"

"You know the place we stayed after The Burp? Well, that's where."

"*That* place? It's *huge*."

"Not as huge as this is going to be. You think the people would mind if we did that native theme thing?" he asked Lucy.

"Not if it meant jobs. Good jobs with good pay."

"A dining room, you think? Traditional foods?"

"Oh, sure," she said, laughing, "with French wine and German beer."

"What then?"

"A really good dining room with one or two traditional special-ties . . . barbecued salmon, baked cod . . . give them the chance to try sea urchin. But no more 'n four per person because otherwise they'll all be sound asleep and they don't spend their money when they're sleeping. The family would go for it."

"So," Colleen asked, "are you going to be the manager?"

"Me?" Lucy cried, almost choking on the new idea.

"You," Colleen agreed. "Your idea, your plan."

"Right," Al said. "And she'd know if it was authentic or Hollywood. I *hate* those damned neon-coloured feathers."

"Where are we going to get the money for something like this?" Colleen had to pull the idea apart, examine each paper-thin slice of it.

"Oh, hell, I don't know. I guess maybe I'll just have to haul out one of them boxes of money I got stashed under the house," Al said. "Might's well spend it, it'll go mouldy if it stays there too long."

"Right." Colleen lay down, put her forearm over her eyes. "Boxes of money. Sure. Picked them off the money tree, right?"

"Hauled them up out of the old mine," he corrected. "Just took myself down there with a flashlight and a shovel and . . . no sweat."

"Right." She was laughing softly. "Boy, you should stop driving truck and start writing science fiction stories. I'd probably be will-ing to pay, oh, a dollar ninety-nine for a story like that one."

When they got back home the sky was brilliant with sunset: streaks of salmon pink, shades of lavender and bands of brilliant gold layered the western sky. The chickens were in their pen, the gate closed, the sprinkler was going in the back garden, and Maude was sitting on the back steps with a mug of coffee and eyes like holes burned into a wool blanket.

"Hey, Maude," Al said politely. "What brings you here?"

"Hi, Mom," Tom said quietly.

"How are you, Mom?" Jessie asked, just as quietly. "You don't look so good."

"Brew's dead," Maude said, as conversationally as if she were telling them she was the one had closed up the hen yard. "And Mavis."

"Both?" Jewen gaped.

"He took every pill in the house. Even my birth control pills. Everything. Washed it down with booze. He was parked on the hospital parking lot at the time. When they found him, he was gone. Babe was on the seat beside him; he'd put a plastic bag over her head and she just . . . snuffed out. They said it wouldn't hurt her, but . . ." She looked at Glennie as if they had grown up in the same house, sharing a bedroom, possibly even a bed. "I'd kill myself but I don't got the energy," she said quietly. "Nor pills, either. Doctor would only give me two." Her bleary eyes blinked several times, and she shook her head. "I don't know what to do," she admitted.

"Well, get up off the steps, Maudie, you'll get yourself piles if you sit there too long. Come on, up on your feet, that's it. Into the house. Tom, you take your mother's arm, help her to the big chair in front'a the TV. Jessie, if you would, a pot of tea and another of coffee would be nice." Al patted Jessie's arm as if she, not Maude, was the bereaved.

✺

"We'll just put the horde to bed and be over later," Jewen said. "No need for all of us to get in the way."

"Whatever," Al agreed.

"Little Wilma, you come with us," Wilma coaxed.

"No, I'm sleeping here tonight," Little Wil answered, "with Dorry."

"You said she could," Dorrit dared. "We're puttin' up a tent, 'member?"

"Maybe the tent should wait until . . ."

"You said we could," she insisted, and walked into the new big house behind Dorrit. Wilma looked at Chuck, they both shrugged, then followed Little Wil.

✺

Maude sat in the big chair where Colleen usually sat so Colleen and Deb sat on one of the big couches. By the time the entire family was jammed into the living room it began to look like the ratepayers' association was holding a meeting.

"You can almost see the walls swelling out each time everyone exhales," Deb whispered. "You guys sure do add up after a while. It's like watching something on a petri dish in the lab."

"You saying we're like staph infection?" Colleen whispered back, pretending she was going to pinch Deb's hip.

"Only golden, darling, only golden."

"I don't know if that's a compliment or an insult, so I think I'll take it as the first and stuff the second in my gunny sack so I can haul it out the first time we have us a big argument."

Tom and Jessie brought in a cookie sheet loaded with cups and mugs, and Dorrit and Freddy-recently-self-named-Tommy brought in the cream and sugar and a handful of spoons. Dorrit went back to the kitchen and he and Little Wil brought a salad bowl of cookies and irregularly cut portions of lemon square and put them on the coffee table. The other kids trooped in with neatly torn-off pieces of paper towel, with an uncut loaf of spice cake, and several huge boxes of potato chips.

"We couldn't find any dip," one of them apologized. "Want me to go to the store for some?"

"We'll be okay like this, darling, thank you," Lindy soothed. "No need to fret."

"Do we sit in here to eat?" Simon asked. "Or would you guys rather we went outside and pretended to play."

"What do you want to do?" Lucy did not laugh.

"I don't feel much like playing," Simon answered. "I'm feeling kinda . . . you know . . . because of Mavis and Uncle Brew."

"Me, too," Peter agreed. He looked at Singeon. "I don't know what to do, Dad. I don't feel like cryin', but . . . almost."

"Well, you could come over here, sit on the floor in front of me, and let me pick the nits out of your hair," Singe said. "I haven't had a good feed of nits since the last time I got you to sit still."

Peter moved quickly, dropped gracefully to the floor, his back against the stuffed chair, his head between Singe's knees. When Singe put his big work-scarred hand on Peter's head the boy leaned sideways, his face against his stepfather's leg. Singe stroked the blue-black hair gently, his hand straying often to the side of the boy's face. Cat watched, her huge dark eyes blinking with concentration. She moved to Al, patted his leg, and he picked her up, sat her on his knee and handed her a cookie. She took it, leaned back against him and began to chew. Al patted her knee softly, and bit by bit the pats became strokes and Cat began to sag into sleep. Glennie watched, a faint smile on her face.

"This is real kind of you." Maude sounded as if she'd taken both the pills the doctor had given her. "I didn't want to be alone. I feel like I'm gonna pull out my hair or something. Feels like I have long, skinny worms under my skin."

"If you want to howl like a gutshot dog, this is the place to do it. You won't freak us out," Brady answered.

"It was the p'lice came to tell me." Maude sipped her coffee as if it was something she could taste and enjoy. "I guess I must'a got upset . . . I don't know. I don't seem to be able to remember how I got to the hospital. But I was there and they had me in one of those little sleeveless vests. You know the kind that cross on your chest and the ties go through little slits on the side and they do 'em up to the sides of the bed, underneath, where you can't get at them to undo them so you're stuck in place?" She looked over at Deb and half-smiled. "You must know the ones I mean."

"I do," Deb said.

"So then, later on, the doctor came in. Gave me a needle. Told me all over again what had happened. I remember each word, same as if he'd just said it to me here and now. And I told him I wanted to leave. Wanted to go home. So after a while he said I could. The house was empty. That's what made it seem real, instead of some kind of nightmare. I could hear all these sounds I'd never noticed before . . . the fridge . . . the freezer . . . and there was no way I could stay there. Just no way. And I didn't have the car because the cops impounded it because it was, they said, a crime scene. So I took a cab out here. Didn't feel any better once I got here but . . . This is good coffee, thank you."

After a while Singeon and Lucy took their kids and went home, Cat sound asleep with her face still smeared with peanut butter cookie. Jewen and Lindy took most of their gang, and Dorrit and

Little Wil went out to put up their tent. Of course, that meant Jared, Jeremy, Jason and Jasmine wanted to sleep in a tent, too, so Jewen went down into the basement and got the big one, and Tony went outside to help put it up. Al tried to help, too, but they told him to take his one lung back into the house.

"I'll help, you go look after Mom," Tom said quietly. "I'm no good around her. I get mad." He looked miserable. "Not because she effed off and left us, but because of what happened to Mavis, you know? I mean . . . no need at all for stuff like that. Mavis didn't do anything wrong to deserve *that*!"

"It's okay, son. What you feel and why, it's okay." Al wanted to grab his son and hug him tight, but knew Tom didn't want that. Maude wasn't the only one who had wound up leaving Tom and Jesse in a pickle, and just because Al had served his time and come home didn't mean he hadn't left in the first place. "I'm sorry about . . . all the shit stuff, Tom. I really am."

"Yeah." Tom nodded, then moved to help with the big tent.

The big tent was in fact big. Very big. With it erected there was really no need for the purple and white dome tent Dorrit and Little Wil had erected by themselves.

"It's like a 'brella," Dorrit bragged. "You just gotta get out of the way or it'll hit you when it pops open. It's all spring-things. Like a 'brella."

"*Umb*erella, Dorrit. Don't talk baby," Jessie corrected gently. "*Umb*erella."

"Umberella," he agreed. "I'll try to 'member."

"*Remember*." She reached out suddenly, grabbed a double handful of his dandelion fluff curls and pretended to shake him furiously. "Okay?"

He giggled and chortled and grabbed onto her, burying his face against her belly and making soft growling noises.

"Gobble you up," he threatened. "Munch munch munch." But he was hyper now and nothing could keep him still for long. He broke loose and ran toward the hen yard, little Wil right behind him, screeching. It was all the invitation the others needed, and they took off, yodelling and hollering for no reason except it was twilight and the mosquito hawks were in the sky, swooping and calling.

The men sat on the back steps with cigarettes, and laughed together. Jessie came out of the house with a cardboard case of chilled bottles of beer and put it where her uncles could reach in and help themselves. For a moment she considered racing off after the younger ones; there was always one or the other falling down, skinning a knee or an elbow, needing tears wiped and quick consoling hugs. But the thought passed, and she sat on a round of wood, staring across the gully at the place they had built for Colleen. It would be nice, one day, to have her own place. Just room enough for her. No spare bedroom for stayovers, no space waiting to be filled by people. Just room for her.

"Jess." Tom spoke quietly. She looked up. He was standing next to her, holding out her guitar.

"Thanks, guy." She took it, tested the tuning, adjusted a string by a mere fraction, tested again, nodded.

Tom sat on another round and waited for Jessie to take the lead. She began to pluck, slowly, searching out a tune. She looked at him. He nodded, and led off. If Jessie didn't have a song in mind right away maybe he could find one.

Jewen shook his head slightly. What a pair, they didn't even need words. They did it with looks and glances. He turned his head, and Tony nodded, handed him a beer, and Jewen twisted off the cap. He put the cap in the breast pocket of his not-work blue cotton shirt, sipped the cold beer and licked his lips.

Singeon and Lucy had Cat in bed and were just moving to their own back porch when Simon, Peter and Carol came racing out of the house, heading for the bulldozed and levelled back area which had once been a bike track, before the face of the place was altered. Singeon almost asked them where the hell they thought they were going at that time of night, but then he heard the sound of the others as the great chase-and-holler moved their way.

"I guess from upstairs they could hear it better," Lucy said.

"Makes you wonder if they even need ears. It's like ESP or something."

"I feel kinda bad about Maude," Lucy admitted. She uncapped a beer, handed it to Singeon, then uncapped her own. She put the caps in his shirt-front pocket. "I don't like the woman one little bit, if the truth be known. I don't like the way she, I don't know, just . . ."

"Yeah," he said, nodding. "It's like the only time she thinks of anybody but herself is when there's something in it for her. Girls used to call her Maude-the-Sod. Like, she never once got herself out to the house to see her kids; there was always some reason of her own that got her ass in gear. Then she'd come. And if the kids were there, fine. Give 'em a quarter and send 'em to the store. But sit in the goddamn pub for hours on end maundering into her draft about how much she missed 'em. Poor bitch, eh?"

"So what is this love thing, anyway?" Lucy rubbed her thumb around the lip of her beer bottle. "I mean, we've got 'em too, I'm not doin' a red power trip on you or laying the old superior culture routine. I'm askin' because it has always kind of puzzled me. I know what I mean when I say 'love'. I love you, old man. I love you like . . ." She used a word he didn't understand. He raised his eyebrows, and she smiled. "It's when a fire has stopped flaming and is a bed of coals that are hotter than the flames ever were," she explained. "That's when a fire is really dangerous. You can get burned in no time flat, nothing left of you but maybe a bit of bone. Flame-fire will scorch you black, maybe melt some of your meat but"—the word sounded again, deep in her throat, with a "click" in the middle of the sound—"that will finish you."

"Dangerous stuff."

"And that's how I love you. It's how I love my kids, too. Our kids. I don't understand this other thing. Dar's a bit that way, too. Not so much now as before but . . ."

"She's smoothed out, for sure," Singeon said. "Maybe she's just a late bloomer."

"I worry, though. I mean it's like stuff wears out for her. And if it starts to wear out with Tony . . . You know?"

"Well, one thing about it, old Tony, he seems part wood tick. Hang on until the last drop is drunk. Drank?"

"Would I know? It's not *my* language. Ticks fall off when they're full," she reminded him.

379

"Well, that's a true thing. With Dorrit, when he was first new and small and totally helpless, she was there with him every minute. You weren't around to see her with him back then. It was when he started, like, crawlin' around and gettin' into stuff, when he started fussing up if she, like, took something away from him or . . . that's when she weaned herself, I guess. Just, like, less and less *into* it, somehow."

"See? That's what I don't understand. That's like topsy-turvy for me. When they're real little, well, you could just as easy have, say, a meatloaf wrapped in a blanket."

Singeon burst out laughing and Lucy grinned. "Think about it. What do they do? Sleep." She sipped thirstily, licked her lips, then again. "I had a whole pile of emotion and stuff when each one was born. With Simon I felt a lot of scaredy-stuff. I mean, by then I knew his poppa wasn't going to be any help at all, and I knew he was two steps away from the back door all the time, so I knew I was as good as on my ownsome already. And that scared me. I'd thought I'd have help, you know? Even just, like, maybe a cup of tea once in a while or someone to say, It's okay, Luce, you're doin' just fine. I was terrified, I guess. By the time Peter came, well, I was used to doing for myself. For ourselves. I never did live with his poppa. By the time Peter came I think I'd'a lay down in a ditch so's Simon could cross over with his feet dry. It just grew, with each one. And Carol, well, I went out of my way to get her. Not *her*-her, maybe, but her poppa was one hunk of a man. Traditional man. And I wanted a kid that might look like that."

"She sure is one good lookin' little kid," Singeon agreed.

"And maybe because I set out to get her, you know, instead of just getting lucky, like with the others. But I was all primed to be nuts about her before she even arrived. And Cat, well . . ." Lucy smiled and leaned sideways slightly, just enough that she was touching Singeon's shoulder, the bulk of his heavily muscled side. "I felt like I'd split open with it all. And so, these people who say love love love and then hit the pike or just pile crap deeper and deeper on the kid's head, well, I don't understand any part of that. Now Colly, she's something different. She did more for Dorry than his momma did. Tom and Jess, too. And she didn't *have* to."

"Sure she did." Singeon put his beer in his left hand, put his right arm around Lucy's shoulders. "She's their auntie. You ought to know what that means."

"She didn't *have* to."

Whatever game the kids were playing involved a lot of screeching and laughing. Singeon grinned at the sound, and Lucy chortled agreement.

"Crows," she said.

"Or those black-headed blue Steller's jays," he said. "Noise for its own sake."

"I guess Big Wil is a bit like me," Lucy continued. "She wasn't always there with Little Wil, but it was because she was busy working."

"She had to, Norm bein' what Norm is."

"Well, there you have it. Him and Dar, see, it's like water on a saucer."

Colleen picked up the empty mugs and cups and took them into the kitchen, washed them and put them on the drain rack to dry. Deb came in and got the coffee pot, took it back into the living room for the ones who wanted refills. Brady brought her mug into the kitchen with the empty cookie bowl and untouched spice loaf, sipped coffee, wrapped the loaf in waxed paper and put it in the cake tin. It was hard to say what had originally been in the tin; it was square, it had once had some kind of design and advertising painted on it but that had worn away with years of use. Now it was just a shiny tin, squarish, dented a bit on one side. Colleen couldn't remember a time when "the cake tin" had meant anything other than this one.

Doreen brought the empty chip wrappers and boxes into the kitchen, put the plasticized wrappers in the garbage bag, then unfolded the boxes and took them into the backroom to add to the recycling pile of cardboard and box-board. Colleen finished the sink and counters and checked the kitchen to make sure it was clean and tidy; Lottie never said a word, but sometimes the look on her face was louder than a shout, and she was so prideful about the kitchen. Everybody called it hers, anyway. Lottie's kitchen.

381

Maude was lying on the couch now, with a cushion under her head and the three-shades-of-blue afghan spread over her. She was out like the proverbial light, her mouth partways open. Colleen checked her from the doorway, then went to the linen closet and got a face cloth, took it in and tucked it under Maudie's cheek so the fine strand of drool wouldn't stain the cushion. Colleen had a real thing about the liquid evidence of life: drooling, spitting, stained pillows, stained mattress covers. It bothered her. It seemed so intimate, so personal and so embarrassing to her. She wondered sometimes if other people felt shy when they saw some of the things that made her feel shy. But she had never asked anyone.

She left Maude alone in the living room, gave a quick check-over that all the mess was cleaned up. There were chip crumbs on the rug but they would have to wait; she wasn't plugging in a vacuum cleaner and waking Maude. She'd had as much of Maude as she could take for one night. She looked at the woman who had been and might legally still be her sister-in-law, and her main emotion was a strong desire to either spit or slap.

"She looks a wreck, doesn't she," Doreen said softly.

"She *is* a wreck," Colleen answered, and went back to the kitchen. Doreen followed, her coffee mug gone, a cold beer in her hand.

"I remember her as being one of those women who look like they've been given more than their fair share of everything."

"Yeah. Well, she traded that look in for the seedy and bloated one."

"You're a hard woman, Colly."

"Me? What do you want me to do, Doreen? Pretend?"

"Sometimes it helps."

"You've spent your whole goddamn life pretending," Colleen snapped. "What did it get you?"

"Well, there is that," Doreen said. "You still mad at me?"

"Mad?" Colleen looked surprised. "No. I'm not mad. Should I be?"

"I hope not. Brady is."

"Oh, well, if you're going to lose sleep over *that*," Colleen said. "Brade's always got something up her nose about something."

"Dar's mad, too."

"Ditto." Colleen went to the fridge, got two cold beer, then looked around for Deb. She saw her outside, sitting at the picnic table, watching Tom and Jess with their guitars, listening to the music. Colleen went outside, sat beside Deb, handed her a beer. Deb took it, smiled her thanks and nodded. Colleen leaned over and kissed Deb on the cheek. Deb's surprise showed clearly. Colleen wasn't a demonstrative person even in private, and about the last thing Deb had ever expected was that Colleen would let it all show, especially in front of her family. They knew, of course, but knowing and seeing aren't the same.

"Wow," she whispered. "Thank you."

"Any time, dear heart," Colleen answered. Her tone sounded easy, joking, almost dismissive, but her expression was intent.

Jessie saw the look and her playing stopped briefly. Tom chorded down, did a quick riff, then nodded and Jessie took the solo. None of the notes and phrases she played had been put on paper at any time, it wasn't something she had heard, liked, practised and learned to play. It was music that came from inside her, music that went from the tips of her fingers to the instrument, then out again, for others to share and enjoy. Tom wished he had a tape recorder going and sent a brief prayer to the great I AM that Jessie not forget all of this. He wanted to work on it, build on it, arrange accompaniment for parts of it.

"Mmmm-*mmm*," he grunted approvingly. Jess smiled at him, and repeated the notes. He nodded and began to find counter-point.

Al sat in the chair Jewen had placed outside for him. He watched his kids and nodded. Glennie sat on the grass beside him, watching him as he watched Tom and Jess with their guitars. She could hear the whooping and hollering out back and wondered how long it was going to take them all to wind down. Little Freddy, newly named Tommy, moved to sit on Al's knee.

"Hey, guy," Al whispered, "how's things?"

"Can I have one of those things?"

"One of what things?"

"Like Big Tom has."

"A guitar? Look how small your hands are. You think you could *do* anything with one?"

"Don't they make small ones?"

"As small as your hand?"

"Don't they?"

"Well, we could go into town tomorrow, just you and me together, and go to the music store and see. Maybe you'd have to get a chin-tucker."

"What's that?"

"You tuck 'er under your chin, move your fingers on 'er, like this, then drag a bow across the strings . . . they make them in flea-sized." .

"Flea-sized. I'm not no flea."

"No, you're a bug is what you are."

"I don't wanna be called Fred no more."

"Okay, Tommy, fine by me."

"Tom said it was okay with him."

"Tom Lancaster and Tommy Webster?"

"Tom Lancaster and Tommy Lancaster. I'm sorry you got hurt."

"Yeah, well, small price to pay. Everything has a price, you know. Everything has to be paid for, one way or the other."

"Gramma said that, too. Said we hadda pay our way. Do I pay my way?"

"You betcha you do. Look at Tom, he's watching you. See him smiling? That's because just looking at you makes him feel good. You making him feel good is a way to pay your way."

"I could get you a smoke if you want."

"Could you? Who would you get it from?"

"Auntie Dory."

"Maybe later. Your momma gets upset if she sees me smokin'."

"Maybe later I'll be asleep."

"If you are I'll tuck you in. You want to sleep in the tent?"

"No. Tom won't want to sleep in there. Not with all those little kids." And Tommy snuggled against Al, his eyes watching hungrily as Tom's fingers moved on the strings.

They were still sitting in the gathering dark, listening to music, when Lottie drove in and parked, home again after one of her evening visits with one or another of her other kids and their families. She closed her car door quietly, moved to sit at the picnic table with Colleen and Deb. Brady went back into the house briefly, returned with two beer, gave one to Lottie and kept the other for herself. Her coffee mug sat on the grass beside her, two-thirds full of cold coffee.

The kids straggled back in from the bush. They were red-faced and sweaty, all their hyper energy run out of them. They would gladly have sat and listened, but some hard looks, a finger pointed first at the house, then at the tent, told them all they needed to know.

The kids were asleep quickly, and so missed the unpleasant interlude when Maude woke from her sleep and came out to join the rest of them. Tom and Jess were still playing softly, and the big citronella candles were burning to discourage the nippers, biters, suckers and chewers. The flames flickered in the soft night air, and the dogs were not quite asleep, their eyes half open but glazed. They stirred and lifted their heads, suddenly alert, staring at the screen door. Without needing words, the ones sitting on the steps stood and moved aside to allow the door to open. It did, and Maude came out, looking like the Hesperus after a very bad night, carrying a pint jar of the old man's aged rocket fuel.

"Excuse me," she said as the screen door swung shut. She plunked herself on the steps. Those who had been sitting there looked at each other, then looked at the pint of rocket fuel and drifted to the picnic table with their beer and cigarettes. Maude ignored them. She watched the kids playing their guitars and sipped her rocket fuel. "Do either of you's sing?" she asked.

"Not much," Tom answered. "I only got two notes, one of 'em's flat and the other's sharp."

"Sometimes," Jess was more honest. "If I know the words."

"Do you know 'I Fall To Pieces'? I've always been partial to that song."

"I know it, but I haven't done it much. I'll probably make some mistakes."

"If the only ones you make in your life are when you sing that song tonight, you're gonna look like Mother Theresa." Maude licked her lips and with no change of tone at all asked, "Anybody got a smoke?"

"I do." Doreen handed over the near-new package. "Keep 'em, I got some others. And there's always the tobacco can."

"Just to let me know, eh?" Maude looked at Doreen, and it was the kind of look a puzzled child gives to a never-before-seen bug. "I thank you," she said, and the words were right, the tone seemed correct, but something . . . something . . . else was there, and it set Al's experienced radar to pulsing. He looked at Tom and Jess, and Tom nodded.

"What else?" he asked. "After Patsy Cline, I mean."

"Oh, something cheerful," Maude said, smiling, and for a moment Tom got to see the woman his mother had been when he was a toddler. "You're a good boy, Tom."

"Almost a man," Colleen said.

"That's right, Colleen, thank you for the correction." Again the smile flashed, and again Al's radar blipped.

Jess short-circuited the growing tension and potential explosion by starting to sing and play Maude's request. Maude listened, then laughed softly and took a good gulp of rocket fuel.

"Don't give up your day job, kid," she teased. Tom shot her a look and she ignored it. "Someone should dig deep and pay for some voice lessons for her," she said to nobody in particular. "It's not as if you're all on your uppers."

"You like something to eat?" Al asked. "We could get you something. Bacon and eggs. Warmed-up leftovers from supper?"

"Warmed-up leftovers, eh?" She didn't even look at him.

"Or we could haul out a couple of mowitch steaks and do 'em up the way you like 'em."

"You remember how I like 'em? See, you got nothing to worry about: you still got your mind, such as it ever was." She smiled widely, and Lindy wondered which signal a person should believe. It was like being confronted by a dog who was snarling and growling at one end while wagging its tail at the other.

Jess looked at Tom and he tried to patch over the incipient rift. He began to play "Malaguena," his eyes begging Jess to join him. She did, and they played loudly, drowning out the sound of Maude's next comment. But you can't sit outside playing even the most beautiful music forever. The song ended and Maude nodded. That nod as good as gave Jess permission to get up off the round of wood, and as she stood, Maude did, too, and opened the screen door. Jess and Tom took their musical instruments into the house.

"We were kind of enjoying that," Al said.

"I'm sure," she agreed. "They're very good. But sometimes enough of a good thing is just about too much if you get my drift."

"I think I do, Maude. I think I do."

Lindy decided she'd seen and heard about as much as was healthy for an outsider. Still, she wasn't going to go to her house and leave her kids in the tent, so close to what promised to become ground zero. Her baby was in that tent, snuggled in with his siblings, and however closely related he was to the Lancasters, he was, when all was said and done, her baby, and she wasn't leaving him behind. She could get him and take him to the house, but that would leave the others, no relations at all to the clanjamfree gathered here tonight, but hers as much as the baby was. She stood, prepared to go to the tent and crawl in with her kids.

"Why'n't you just set yourself?" Maudie purred. She raised her voice slightly, "Tom, bring some cold beers for the family."

"Yes, Mom," Tom answered, his voice betraying his anxiety.

"And settle yourself down, there's nothing coming down on you."

"Yes, Mom."

"Maudie . . ." Al began.

"Shut up, Al. Don't get started."

"I think I hear the sound of Brahms's 'Lullaby'." Deb stood and stroked Colleen's hair. "I'm going home to bed."

"Home, huh?" Maude looked at Deb and got set to strike. "Snuggled in all cozy and all? Nice house. Good for you for getting yourself set up so good."

"Why thank you, Maude," Deb said. "Please believe me when I tell you I'm very sorry for your troubles. I know it's been a heartache for you. I'm sorry."

"Yep." Maude nodded, lifted her pint mayonnaise jar. It might have been a toast or it might have been an up-yours gesture. "I know you are. Real sorry."

"Maude, don't get going," Colleen said. "There's no need for that."

"No need for anything, Colleen. When all's said and done there's no need for anything at all. Not even for you to ride that high horse, that big, fancy, white-as-snow high horse you been on for so many years."

"I think I'll just head off home, too." Colleen rose.

"Sit down," Maude ordered.

"No thank you, Maude," Colleen replied. "Appreciate the invitation and all but it's been a long day."

"Why run off now? Things might get way lots better real soon."

"Night all." Colleen walked from the picnic table, and when she caught up with Deb she put her arm around her waist, bent to say something private and quiet.

"Jesus." Maude sipped thirstily. "Not sure I want my kids growin' up thinkin' kinky shit like that is normal. They say all them queers are out to convert the kids. They can't have their own, you know."

"Oh, I'm sure all the necessary mechanical bits and pieces are there in both of them." Lindy was sitting at the picnic table again, her hair looking as if Nashville should take lessons. Jewen reached for her hand, she reached for his, and they linked fingers. Jewen looked exactly like a kid who has the champion snowball hidden behind his back, the one with the rock in the middle and a half inch of ice on the outside. "It doesn't take much to wind up pregnant."

"Well, you'd know, wouldn't you?" Maude laughed softly. "You been pregnant often enough. I didn't know none of 'em was nothing much, but if you say so, I'll believe you."

"Why wouldn't you believe me?" Lindy was smiling, too. "What with us being almost sisters-in-law and all."

"How do you figure almost?"

"Well, you know how it is, the divorce and all, and by the time I came into the picture you were Jewen's ex-sister-in-law so when I married him . . . but we did come close, Maude."

"Story of my life, close but no cookie. Tommy, where's them beer?"

"Coming, Mom."

"Leave the boy alone, Maude. I'll get the beer." Al started to rise; Maude pinned him with an open glare.

"You keep your crippled self in the chair. His legs are longer, stronger and younger 'n yours."

Tom nudged the screen door with his toe, it swung gently open, and before it could touch Maude's shoulder she hitched herself to her left, allowing the screen door to open enough to allow Tom to come out with a case of cold cans.

"Just leave 'em on the picnic table," she said. "And give your old mom a kiss."

Tom leaned over and kissed Maude on the cheek. "Take it easy, Mom," he said softly. "You've had an awful day. Try to get some rest. Jess 'n' me, we'll take care of . . . like, you know, the arrangements? We can get on the phone in the morning and . . ."

"Off to bed my Tommy-boy," Maude crooned. "Send your gorgeous sister out here for a good-night sleepy-smooch. Don't you worry yourself, Momma's okay and everything's gonna work out fine. I always did love you, as big as the whole wide world. Just polish them pearlies'a yours and off to bed."

As Tom started up the steps the screen door opened again and Jess came out with an empty glass and a full cup of coffee.

"Here, Mom." She put both of them on the steps beside Maude. "The rim of that jar doesn't look too good. Looks like the lid nearly rusted off it. Don't want to pick up salmonella or something."

"You get salmon-ella from eatin' fish. This stuff, well, don't you worry about my health, darlin'. This stuff wouldn't let a bacteria, virus, bug or germ survive. But thanks for the worry. And I'll use the glass, too. Gotta look re-feened, right?"

"You got 'er, Mom."

"You heard what I said to Tom?"

"Big as the whole wide world. Big as the moon."

"But not reciprocated, more's the pity."

"Reciprocity's a big word." Jess leaned over, kissed Maude's cheek. "But I'll send 'er right back to you all the same."

"You tell a real convincing lie." Maude smiled and put down the rocket fuel, grabbed Jess in a one-armed hug. "I really did enjoy your singing, Jessie. And I meant it, take some lessons. They can teach you how to get that, like . . . I don't even know the word for it, but it makes your voice sound fatter."

"Resonance?"

"Mushroom soup. Wastepaper basket. Filing cabinet. I know a *lot* of big words, okay?"

"Reciprocate," Jess agreed. She and Tom headed into the house, each of them looking as calm as placid toads in a dark cool place. Maude watched them leave, then poured rocket fuel into the glass and drank.

"Tastes a lot better," she decided.

"You think that stuff'll sit easy with the pills the doctor gave you?" Doreen tried.

"Why would you ask?" Maude looked at her. "You don't give a shit if I live or die."

"Just as soon you didn't do it here in the backyard. We've got a tent full'a little kids who might get upset at the sight of a corpse. And then there's all the hoorah and yahoo of calling the ambulance, getting the coroner out here, probably a few cops as well. At my age I enjoy peace and quiet."

"At your age you should know better than to butt your nose in where nobody asked you to put it."

"Well, there's always that," Doreen agreed. She reached over and took a package of cigarettes from Jewen's shirt pocket.

"There's always the tobacco can," Maude reminded.

"That's a true thing, too." Doreen lit a cigarette, then headed for the back steps. "Excuse me?" She opened the screen door enough to squeeze through. Maude didn't shift her weight. Doreen went into the house. Nobody said anything. After a while, Doreen came around the side of the house, tobacco can in her hand. Maude grinned.

"If you'd'a said something I'd'a shifted for you."

"Well, the can was in the living room, front door was closer." Doreen went back to the picnic table and slid to the bench. She put the tobacco can in the middle of the table, then took a package of cigarettes from her shirt pocket and removed the cellophane. She held the package to Lottie who took it, opened it, and took a cigarette.

"So the hired help sits and visits with the bosses now, huh?"

"My mother-in-law," Al said firmly, "can sit and visit any god-damn place she chooses."

"You 'n' me, we sure mucked it up, didn't we?" Maude took another of Doreen's cigarettes, lit it with a disposable lighter with a beer advertisement printed on the side. She looked at Glennie. "Watch out he don't leave you," she said clearly. "We'd'a been fine, except he was always leavin'. Second week we were together he was gone up a back road somewheres with a tent, his fishin' gear, and enough whiskey to float a canoe. All's he said was I'm goin fishin'. I thought he meant for the afternoon. People do that. They go fishin' for a day, maybe. But Al Lancaster? Gone two weeks. Fishin', he said."

"No need, Maude," Al said.

"No, you're right," she said but kept talking to Glennie. "Sometimes it was huntin'. We'd be up to our arses in deer meat, and that goddamn Colly'd be Dora Domestic herself, putting it in jars, putting it in the freezer, jesus, no end to it. But he'd go huntin'. Never knew when he'd be back. Or if. You watch 'im, don't let 'im do it. Maybe with only one lung he'll settle down some. If he don't, nail one foot to the floor, let the perambulating bugger walk around and around in circles. And the more I tried to let 'im know how it bothered me, the less we was able to talk easy. Finally, he went off at the Queen's pleasure. Now wouldn't you think she'd have other things to worry about, other things to please her? Owns a big chunk'a the world, for chrissakes. That ripped it. Not much left to rip by then, a'course."

"Maude. There's no need to . . ."

"Oh, shut up, Al. Save your air. Shape you're in you might need it for breathin'." She grinned at him.

"I think I'll just call it a night." Darlene made the mistake of opening her mouth.

"Call it a night?" Maude laughed. "Tryin' to make it sound like you been a busy little bee all day? Exhausted from all your efforts to keep the dysfunctional family whirlin' in circles?"

"Lay off me," Darlene warned.

"Lay off you? I ain't even started on you," she said and looked at Tony. "She might be playin' the part'a the happy little wifey-poo right now, but she'll get bored with it. She gets bored real easy. Got bored with Dorry as soon as he learned there was a world beyond his crib. Always was bored with work. She'd go trolling, catch herself a hunk, then get bored with 'im and head off trolling again. Careful she don't toss you back into the lake. Got 'er a good deal right now, but she's fickle. And lazier 'n a person could believe. She steals stuff, too. No idea about what the magazines call personal boundaries. She's like a fuckin' crow: she sees it, she wants it, she takes it. Supposed to be one of the sure signs of fetal alcohol. I'm an expert on fetal alcohol effect, y'know. I've taken courses and workshops and god knows what, and I'm tellin' ya right to your face, she's a classic case of it. Either that or she's just sociopathic, hard to tell in this family."

"You're out of line," Tony said coldly.

"Am I? Well, there you go. Now ask me if I care?"

"You should talk about lazy," Darlene snapped. "You of all people."

"Well, for sure, someone else did a damn fine job of raisin' my kids," Maude said agreeably. "I guess that was Colleen. Sure as hell wasn't you. You didn't even raise your own until the hunk came on the scene and started doing some of the bringing up hisself. Bloody Colly, whippin' around with her hair on fire, job in town and all. Growin' this, preservin' that, freezin' the next thing, jams 'n' jellies, and up to her ears in other peoples' kids. Enough to make a person feel inadequate. If a person gave a damn."

"Listen, you . . ."

"Ah, go to bed," Maude laughed. "Sulk yourself to sleep or somethin'." She peered over at the picnic table, seeking her next target. "Mother-in-law," she warned, "they'll work you into an old folks' home."

"Don't get started on me, Ms. Maude." Lottie stood up, leaned over, stubbed out her cigarette in the already full ashtray. "You have no right at all to get started in on me."

"You're right. You're nothing to me," she nodded. "On the other hand, there's the fan dancer. Off to take on the bright lights. Gonna be a big star. Anybody know the difference between a fan dancer and a hooker?" She waited while the silence deepened. "No, dam'f I do, either. And then," she smiled at Doreen, "there's the general there. Off she went, thought she was General Eisenhower or Montgomery or someone. Off to stand on guard for all of us. Type type type like hell, copies of this, copies of that, useless goddamn waste of time but oh my don't the uniform look good. And YOU," she glared at Jewen "aren't you just the . . ."

"Shut the fuck up," Jewen said calmly. "We've had enough of it. Okay, so you've had a kick in the teeth today. Fine. We made allowances. And that's it. Had enough of it, Maude. It's a damned shame about your kid, and it must'a been a shock when Brew checked 'em both out. Fine. Got some empathy for that. The rest of it? Had enough."

"Really?" She looked at him and laughed softly. "Have you really? There's nothing so firm and respectable as a reformed alkie loser, I guess."

"Well, we'll find out if you ever sober up and stay that way," he said.

"So why'n't you-all pack up your toys and just eff off and leave me here with what's left of this jug? Except for the little kids, I got no use for any of you's. And that includes the in-laws and outlaws."

"Reciprocal," Lindy drawled. Maude laughed, got off the steps, and walked from the house, past the new garden area, past the dogs' run, headed toward the new hen coop. Nobody made a move to stop her, nobody made a move to catch up to her and keep her company. Without a word they got up, began collecting empty bottles and cans, emptying the ashtrays into the outside garbage can, each one of them, at least one time, sighing, and each one of them, at least once, shaking her or his head.

In the morning Colleen's sports car was gone. The lock on the garage door was intact, everyone knew it had been locked when Colleen went to bed. But it was now unlocked, not a scratch on it, not a mark, not a hint of how it might have come to be unlocked, and the pop can was gone without a trace.

As was Maude. The cigarette package Doreen had given her was on the picnic table, empty except for a five-dollar bill, the package held safe from the breeze by the empty moonshine pint. Beside it, the rusted lid of the pint was nestled inside an equally rusted lid from a quart mayonnaise jar. When Tony went into the freezer for a new pack of smokes from his carton he found another five-dollar bill. He supposed that meant Maude had taken a pack of his smokes, too.

Doreen went into town and made the arrangements for Brew and Mavis. She saw no reason to pretend any particular kind of sentimentality and ordered the most basic, least expensive cremation. What the funeral parlour referred to as the "cremains" were placed in the same plastic bag which was stored inside an ordinary cardboard container on which was a regular peel 'n' stick label with both Brew's name and Mavis's name hand-printed in ballpoint.

They didn't bother with any kind of ceremony. Al took the box into the back bush with him and returned a half hour later with an empty plastic bag and the cardboard carton. He tossed the carton into the burning barrel, looked for a moment at the plastic bag, then shrugged and tossed it in as well. He went into the hen coop and came out with a couple of empty feed bags which he ripped into several pieces and dropped into the barrel. The final piece he lit with his old flip-top lighter, and when it was blazing, he let it drop from his fingers into the rusted barrel. He didn't wait to see the fire consume the contents of the trash barrel. He walked slowly back to the house.

Colleen sat on the back porch and watched Al walking to the back steps. He stopped at the picnic table and looked at the place where the cigarette package and empty pint jar had been. They were gone and he didn't know who had taken them. Not that it mattered.

"You going to report your car stolen?" Deb asked quietly.

"Oh, I don't think so," Colleen answered. "Either she'll show up and give 'er back or she won't."

"You really think she'll just drive up and hand you the keys?"

"I don't think she's driving anymore, and I don't think the keys will be found anymore than any other part of the sardine can."

"Where do you think . . .?"

"Oh, I don't know. There's no way she went out the front drive, the pickup's parked there and so is your car. That means she used the back way. It's too rough and too bumpy for the little pisspot, but I don't suppose Maude cared about that, and I don't suppose it matters now. There's miles and miles of miles and miles out back, some of it reforested, some of it trashed, and there's more lakes and swamps and rivers and gullies than any place else I know about."

"You think she . . .?"

"You gonna feel better if I put it into words?"

"Feel better?" Deb leaned over the back of Colleen's chair and kissed her on the cheek. "Darlin', it's no skin off my nose one way or the other."

"Me, neither," Colleen said.

The kids came from Jewen and Lindy's place carrying brooms and a bright blue dustpan. They disappeared into the big army surplus tent, then the sound of their voices, quarrelling like jays and starlings, carried on the afternoon air. The sides of the tent billowed and flapped, then Dorrit came out with the dustpan and walked to the driveway, emptied the accumulated gravel, dirt and detritus. He saw Colleen on her porch and waved. She waved back, grinning. He headed back into the tent with the dustpan. Moments later the whole pack came tumbling out, laughing, pushing, shoving and teasing. They lined themselves up, shoulder to shoulder, arms around each other's waists and began to bounce and kick in their version of a chorus line. Deb cracked up, and then Brady was running to join them. Her short light brown hair fit her head like a smooth cap, her long shapely legs were already lightly tanned, her light blue summer shorts and blue-striped white tee-shirt looked better on her than any of her elaborate costumes ever had. She was heading for the end of the line, but then Jason and Carol separated, making a place for her in the middle. Brady moved to the space, and the kids cheered and the chorus line picked up again. This time the kicks were more uniform and nowhere near as straggly.

"Look at her," Colleen said with a laugh. "She's counting time for them. She'll have her own routine rehearsed and perfected soon. We'll see 'em all on TV."

"Hey, Colly!" Jewen yelled. "Hey, Deb! Comin'?" And he moved to the end of the line.

Colleen and Deb stopped at the freezer to pick up an entire packet of freezies, then ran from the side door to the rope-and-picket access bridge that crossed the gully at the narrow place near where the big old drum had once ruled.

The chorus line came apart when the kids saw the packet of freezies. They swarmed forward, laughing. Jewen put his arm around Brady's waist and they cackled like loons.

"I guess if we got some help," Deb suggested, "we might be able to throw some kind of food together, head for the swimming hole or someplace."

"Not the lake," the kids chorused. "It's too crowded."

"There's a real good place," Jasmine suggested. "It's sort of under the big bridge? There's, like, a gravel beach? It sticks out and then it slopes off so the little kids won't . . ." She let it trail off, suddenly shy.

"Then let's us check it out." Colleen smiled at Jasmine. "It's a real good idea, honey," she said softly.

"Food run!" Jewen hollered. "Haul 'er together!"

"I'll phone Singe and Lucy." Brady ran for the house.

"Okay, get to it." Deb might well have grown up on the place she was so easy with the herd. "You know what we need."

Lottie wasn't caught off guard. She had been expecting someone to give birth to the idea. She went to the new freezer, brought out several plastic containers, longish ones with tight-fitting sealable lids. In each was a loaf-and-a-half worth of bread made into sandwiches. She also had two large bowls of potato salad in the fridge. She had intended it for supper, but she was, if nothing else, adaptable, and spaghetti would do just as well. In preparation for the altered menu she hauled out two large packages of frozen venison hamburger and put them on the drainboard to thaw.

"Tommy, could you take the meat out of the plastic bags, please," she ordered. "Put it on a plate and then cover it with a clean tea towel. A *clean* one," she repeated firmly.

The gravel spit was a good place for the portable barbecue, and Singeon set it up while Lucy and Cat debated whether or not Cat would keep her rubber sandals on her feet. Lucy won, and Cat trooped into the water wearing them. She was mollified by the fact Tommy was wearing his, too, and she soon forgot she was supposed to be angry.

The kingfisher screeched in total disgust. No matter *what* she did, they came back time and again. Even with the river running in a new place, even with an entire new lake, no matter *what* she did, or arranged or rearranged, there they were, and while they were there the fishing would be wretched. She hovered, her wings a blur, and gave them all the sharp side of her tongue, then, still enraged, flew off up-river, putting as much distance as possible between herself and the ever-growing noisy pack.

"Look at that little guy," Tony said proudly. Anthony Andrew Brandeis crawled for the water. The gravel bothered his bare legs so he sat on his well-diapered backside and pulled himself forward by digging his sneakered feet into the ground. "He's one of the crowd, and he knows it."

"Be another of those Lancaster brats heading for the water next year," Al said quietly. He smiled at Glennie. "Or the year after, I guess."

"I thought you were next best thing to a dead man," Singe teased. "I thought you were the one kept runnin' outta puff."

"Puff, maybe," Glennie said, laughing. "But otherwise he does just fine."

"Told ya," Lucy said quietly. "Herring eggs on kelp, right, Al?"

"You got 'er, Luce. Nothing like 'em."